Richard Chenevix Trench

Sacred Latin Poetry, Chiefly Lyrical

Richard Chenevix Trench

Sacred Latin Poetry, Chiefly Lyrical

ISBN/EAN: 9783744792301

Printed in Europe, USA, Canada, Australia, Japan

Cover: Foto ©Andreas Hilbeck / pixelio.de

More available books at **www.hansebooks.com**

SACRED LATIN POETRY,

CHIEFLY LYRICAL,

SELECTED AND ARRANGED FOR USE;

With Notes and Introduction:

BY

RICHARD CHENEVIX TRENCH, D.D.

ARCHBISHOP OF DUBLIN

AND CHANCELLOR OF THE ORDER OF ST. PATRICK.

SECOND EDITION, CORRECTED AND IMPROVED.

London and Cambridge:

MACMILLAN AND CO.

1864.

PREFACE

THE FIRST EDITION.

THE AIM of the present volume is to offer to members of our English Church a collection of the best sacred Latin poetry, such as they shall be able entirely and heartily to accept and approve— a collection, that is, in which they shall not be evermore liable to be offended, and to have the current of their sympathies checked, by coming upon that, which, however beautiful as poetry, out of higher respects they must reject and condemn—in which, too, they shall not fear that snares are being laid for them, to entangle them unawares in admiration for ought which is inconsistent with their faith and fealty to their own spiritual mother. Such being the idea of the volume, it is needless to say that all hymns which in any way imply the Romish doctrine of transubstantiation are excluded. In like manner all are excluded, which involve any creature-worship, or which speak of the Mother of our Lord in any other language than that which Scripture has sanctioned, and our Church adopted.

So too all asking of the suffrages of the saints, all addresses to the Cross calculated to encourage superstition, that is, in which any value is attributed to the material wood, in which it is used otherwise than in the Epistles of St Paul, namely, as a figure of speech by which we ever and only understand Him that hung upon it; all these have been equally refused a place.

Nor is it only poems containing positive error which I have counted inadmissible; but I have not willingly given room to any which breathe a spirit foreign to that tone of piety which the English Church desires to cherish in her children; for I have always felt that compositions of this character may be far more hurtful, may do far more to rob her of the affections, and ultimately of the allegiance, of her children, than those in which error and opposition to her teaching take a more definite and tangible shape. Nor surely can there be a more serious mistake, than to suppose that we have really "adapted" such works to the use of her members, when we have lopped off here and there a few offensive excrescences, while that far more potent, because far subtler and more impalpable, element of a life which is not her life remains interfused through the whole.

Having thus in a manner become responsible for all which appears in this volume, I may be permitted to observe, that I do not thereby imply that there may not be in it, here and there, though very rarely indeed, a phrase which will claim the interpretation of charity. The reader will in such a case remember how unfair it is to try the theological language of the middle ages by the greater strictness and accuracy which the struggles of the Reformation rendered necessary. Thus, for us at this day to talk of any " merits " save those of Christ, after all that the Reformation has won for us, would involve a conscious and a deliberate falling away from a sole and exclusive reliance upon his work. But it was a different thing once, and such language might quite be used by one who had *implicitly* an entire affiance on the work of Christ *for* him as the ultimate ground of his hope ; and who only waited to have the truth, which with some confusion he held and lived by, put before him in accurate form, to embrace it henceforth and for ever, not only with heart, as he had done already, but with the understanding as well.

Nor yet do I mean to affirm that there may not have found admission here one or two poems which some, whom I should greatly have desired altogether to have carried with me in my selection, may not wish had been away. It is indeed one of the mischiefs which Rome has entailed upon the whole Western Church, even upon those portions of it now delivered from her tyranny, that she has rendered suspicious so much, which, but for her, none could have thought other than profitable and edifying. She has compelled those, who before everything else would be true to God's word, oftentimes to act in the spirit of Hezekiah, when he said " Nehushtan " to the very " sign of salvation"*—to the brazen serpent itself. Yet granting that the superstitious, and therefore profane, hands which she has laid on so much, must oftentimes make it our wisdom, and indeed our duty, that we abridge ourselves of our rightful liberty in many things which otherwise and but for her we might have freely and profitably used, there is still a limit to these self-denials: and unless we are determined to set such a limit, there is no point of bareness and nakedness in all of imaginative and symbolic in worship and service, which we might not reach; even as some Reformed Churches, which have not shewn the mingled moderation and firmness, that have in these matters so wonderfully characterized our own, have undoubtedly made themselves much poorer than was need.

Of course, those who consider that the whole medieval theology is to be ignored and placed under ban— that nothing is to be learned from it, or nothing but harm—those I must expect to disapprove, not merely

* Σύμβολον σωτηρίας, Wisd. xvi.

of a small matter or two in the volume, but of it altogether; for the very idea of the book rests on the assumption that it *is* worth our while to know what the feelings of these ages were—what the Church was doing during a thousand years of her existence;—on the assumption also that the voices in which men uttered then the deepest things of their hearts, will be voices in which we may also utter and embody the deepest things of our own. For myself, I cannot but feel that we are untrue to our position as a Church, that is, as an *historic* body, and above all to our position as members of a Protestant Church, when we thus wish to dissever, as far as we may, the links of our historic connexion with the past. We should better realize that position, if we looked at those Middle Ages with the expectation (which the facts would abundantly justify), of finding the two Churches, which at the Reformation disengaged themselves from one another, in the bosom of the Church which was then—if we looked at those ages, not seeking (as sometimes is done, I cannot but feel most unfairly, in regard to earlier times) to claim them as Protestant, but as little conceding that they were Romanist. It were truer to say that in Romanism we have the residuum of the middle age Church and theology, the lees, after all, or well nigh all, the wine was drained away. But in the medieval Church we have the wine and the lees together—the truth and the error—the false observance, and yet at the same time the divine truth which should one day be fatal to it, side by side. Good were it for us to look at those ages, tracing gladly, as Luther so loved to do, the footsteps of the Reformers before the Reformation; and feeling that it is our duty, that it is the duty of each successive age of the Church, as not to accept the past in the gross, so neither in the gross to reject it; since rather by our position as the present representatives of that eternal body, we are bound to recognize ourselves as the rightful inheritors of all which is good and true that ever has been done or said within it. Nor is this all: but if our position mean anything, we are bound also to believe that to us, having the Word and the Spirit, the power has been given to distinguish things which differ,—that the sharp sword of judgment has been placed in our hands, whereby to sunder between the holy and profane,—that such a breath of the Almighty is now and evermore breathing over his Church, as shall enable it, boldly and with entire trust that He will winnow for it, to exclaim, " What is the chaff to the wheat ? " Surely it is our duty to believe that to us, that to each generation which humbly and earnestly seeks, will be given that enlightening Spirit, by whose aid it shall be enabled to read aright the past realizations of God's divine idea in the visible and historic Church of successive ages, and to distinguish the human imperfections, blemishes, and errors, from the divine truth which they obscured and overlaid, but which they could not destroy, being one day rather to be destroyed by it; and, distinguishing these, as in part to take warning from and to shun, so also in part to live upon and to love, that which in word and deed the Church of the past has bequeathed us.

In this sense,—namely, that there is here that which we may live on and love, as well as that which we must shun and leave, I have brought together the poems of this present volume, gathering out the tares, which yet I could recognize but as the *accident* of this goodly field, and seeking to present to my brethren that only which I had confidence would prove wholesome nutriment for souls. Undoubtedly there are tares enough in the field out of which these sheaves have been gathered, if a man will seek them, if he should believe that it is his occupation to do so; which yet I have not believed to be mine. And I have published this volume, because, granting a collection made upon these principles to be desirable, it appears to me that it has not yet been made; that those which we possess still leave room for such a one as the present. What need is there, for example, that the *Veni, Redemptor*

Gentium, or the *Dies Iræ*, or any other of these immortal heritages of the universal Church, should be presented to us as part or parcel of the Roman or any other breviary? They were not written for these; their finding a place in these is their accident, and not their essence. Why then should they be offered, as coming through channels, and with associations linked to them, which can scarcely fail to make them distasteful to many? Not to say that, while pieces of sacred Latin verse drawn from such obvious sources have been published again and again—and not only the good, but very often with it much also of very slightest worth,—other noblest compositions, whether contemplated as works of art, or from a more solemn point of view, have been left unregarded and apparently unknown. If I may conclude, in regard of others, from a few friends to whom I have submitted portions of this volume, as it was gotten together, most of my readers will acknowledge that they here have met something which was new to them, yet with which they were glad to be made acquainted.

And even were this not the case, the poems here offered in a collected form, are many of them only to be found, as a reader familiar with the subject will perfectly know, one here, one there, in costly editions of the Fathers or medieval writers, or in collections of

very rarest occurrence. The extreme difficulty I have myself experienced in obtaining several of the books which I desired to use, and the necessity under which I have remained of altogether foregoing the use of many that I would most gladly have consulted, has sufficiently shewn me how little obvious they can be to most readers. Often too the poems one would care to possess are lost amid a quantity of verse of little or no value; or mixed up with much which, at least for purposes such as those which the present volume is intended to serve, the reader would much prefer to have away. They are to be met too, for the most part, without those helps for their profitable study which they so greatly require—with no attempt to bring them into relation with the theology of their own or of an earlier day, which at once they illustrate, and from which alone many of their allusions can be explained.

In respect of the notes with which I have sought to supply this last deficiency, I will say at once that had I followed my own inclinations, I should much have preferred to give merely the text, without adding any of these. At the same time, the longer I was engaged with these poems, the more I was struck with the extent to which they swarmed with Scriptural and patristic allusions, yet such as oftentimes one might miss at a first or second perusal, or, unless they were pointed out, might overlook altogether. I felt how many passages there were, which, without some such helps, would remain obscure to many readers; or at any rate would fail to yield up to them all the riches of meaning which they contained; and that an Editor had no right to presume that particular kind of knowledge upon their parts, which should render the explanation of these superfluous. Thus none, I trust, will take ill the space bestowed on the elucidation of these typical allusions with which many of these poems so much abound nor count that I have at too great a length explained these. Whatever the absolute worth of the medieval typology may be, its relative worth is considerable, giving us such insight as it does into the habits of men's thoughts in those ages, and the aspect under which they were wont to contemplate the Holy Scriptures and the facts of which Holy Scripture is the record. Nor may we forget that, however the Old Testament typology is now little better than a wreck, considered as a branch of scientific theology,—the capricious and oftentimes childish abuse which has been made of it having caused many to regard the whole matter with averseness and distaste, yet has it, as we are sure, a deep ground of truth; one unaffected by the fact that we have been at so little pains accurately to determine its limits, or the laws which are to guide its application, and have thus left it open to such infinite abuse.

And yet, with the fullest sense of the necessity of giving some notes, I cannot hope that this volume has escaped that which, with only the difference of more or less, must be the lot of all annotated books. Doubtless it has often a note where none was needed, and none where the reader might justly have looked for one. As in part an excuse for their inadequacy and imperfections, I must plead the very little that had hitherto been done in this regard; so that, although assistances from those who have gone before are not altogether wanting, yet these are only few and insufficient. Had my own notes been exclusively, or even mainly, critical, I should have felt myself bound to compose them in Latin, which has been so happily called " the algebraic notation of criticism ; " but being in the main theological, there would have been much loss with no compensating gain, in putting myself under the restraints of a language in which I certainly should not have moved as easily as in my own. At the same time I have endeavoured to avoid that which I have observed as the common evil of notes in English, namely, the " small talk " into which they are apt to degenerate.

In the arrangement of the different pieces which this

volume contains, two ways seemed open to me. I
might either follow the chronological order, which
would have had a most real value of its own; or else
dispose, as I have done, the several poems according to
an inner scheme, and thus combine them, as it were,
anew into one great poem. To the choice of this last
plan I was directed by the idea on which this volume
is constructed. Had I desired first and mainly to illustrate the theology of successive epochs by the aid of
their hymns, or to trace the rise and growth of Latin
ecclesiastical poetry, the other or chronological would
have been plainly the method to have adopted; in the
same way as, had I presented these poems as *documents*,
I should not have felt myself at liberty to make the
omissions which I have occasionally made in some, with
no loss I believe to the reader, and without which their
length, or even a more serious flaw, might have excluded them from the volume. But the personal and
the devotional being my primary objects, and all else
merely secondary, it was plain that the order to be
followed was that which should best assist and further
the end I had specially in view.

That occasional liberty of omission which I have
used—by which I mean, not so much presenting the
fragments of a poem, as *thinning* it—is not, let me

observe, so perilous an interference with the unity, and thus the life, of medieval, as it would be of many other, compositions. *Form* these writers thought of but little; and were little careful to satisfy its requirements. Oftentimes indeed the instincts of Art effectually wrought in them, and what they gave forth is as perfect in form as it is in spirit. But oftentimes also the stanzas, or other component parts of some long poem, jostle, and impair the effect of, one another. It is evident that the writer had not learned the painful duty of sacrificing parts to the interests of the whole; perhaps it had never dawned on him that, in all higher art, there is such a duty, and one needing continually to be exercised. And when this is done *for* him, which he would not do for himself, the effect is like that of thinning some crowded and overgrown forest. There is gain in every respect; gain in what is taken away, gain for what remains: so at least it has seemed to me, when on more than one occasion I have used the knife, or even the axe, of excision.

Great as is the length to which these prefatory words have run, I cannot conclude them without giving utterance to this as my earnest desire and prayer,—that there may be nothing found in these pages to minister to error, or with which wise and understanding children

of our own spiritual mother might be justly displeased.
If I have attained this, I shall abundantly be rewarded
for some anxious and laborious hours, which the preparation of this volume has cost me.

ITCHENSTOKE: *Jan.* 1849.

PREFACE

TO

THE SECOND EDITION.

THIS VOLUME has been for several years out of print. Since the former edition was published, now some fifteen years ago, several collections of Sacred Latin Poetry have appeared. The most important of these are as follows:—Mone, *Lateinische Hymnen des Mittelalters*, 1853; in the second and third volumes, 1854, 1855, the title is changed to *Hymni Latini Medii Ævi*. Daniel has added two supplementary volumes (a fourth and fifth) to his *Thesaurus Hymnologicus*, 1855, 1856. Dr. Neale has followed up his *Sequentiæ*, 1852, with a series of articles in the *Ecclesiologist;* while M. Gautier has given to the world *Les Œuvres Poétiques d'Adam de S. Victor*, 1858, 1859.

Mone's is on the whole a disappointing work. The notes seem at first sight full of promise; but on closer inspection they prove rather appendages to the text, than elucidations of it; still, his illustrations of the Latin hymns from the Greek liturgies are often novel and interesting. Daniel by his later volumes has increased the obligation under which all lovers of the old hymnology already lay to him; and for myself I must praise his magnanimity, that in reprinting a considerable body of my notes and prefaces, he has not excluded some in which I had spoken severely of certain small inaccuracies and errors in his earlier volumes. I rejoice to hear that a new edition of his *Thesaurus*, such as, it may be hoped, will fuse his five volumes into a harmonious whole, is preparing. Later in this volume I take occasion to speak of the happy discovery, by Gautier, of a large number of Adam of St Victor's hitherto unpublished hymns. The edition of Adam's poetical works, which in consequence of this discovery he has given to the world, is wanting in accurate scholarship, but has, notwithstanding, been gratefully welcomed by all to whom this poet is dear. The too favourable manner in which Dr. Neale has expressed himself in regard of any contributions of mine to the knowledge of the Latin hymnology makes it difficult for me to say merely the truth about his own. I will only, therefore, mention that by patient researches in almost all European lands, he has brought to light a multitude of hymns unknown before; in a treatise on *Sequences*, properly so called, has for the first time explained their essential character; while to him the English reader owes versions of some of the best hymns, such as often successfully overcome the almost insuperable difficulties which many among them present to the translator.

MARLAY: *Aug.* 8, 1864.

CONTENTS.

CONTENTS.

BIOGRAPHICAL NOTICES.

INTRODUCTION.

CHAPTER I.

ON THE SUBSTITUTION OF ACCENT FOR QUANTITY IN LATIN VERSE.

THE Latin poetry of the Christian Church presents a subject which might well deserve a treatise of its own; offering, as it does, so many sides upon which it is most worthy of regard. It is not, however, my intention to consider it except upon one side, or to prefix to this volume more than some necessary remarks on the relation in which the *forms* of that poetry stand to the *forms* of the classic poetry of Rome; tracing, if I may, the most characteristic differences between those of the earlier and heathen, and the later and Christian, Art. Yet shall I not herein be dealing so merely with externals, as might at first sight appear. For since the form of ought which has any real significance is indeed the manifestation and utterance of its innermost life—is the making visible, so far as that is possible, of its most essential spirit—I shall, if I rightly seize and explain the difference of the forms, be implicitly saying something, indeed much, concerning the differences between the spirit of this poetry, and that of the elder or classical poetry of Rome. A few considerations on this matter may help to remove offences which otherwise the reader, nourished exclusively upon classical lore, might easily take at many things which in this volume he will find; and may otherwise assist to put him in a fairer position for appreciating the compositions which it contains.

When, then, we attempt to trace the rise and growth of the Latin poetry of the Christian Church, and the manner in which, making use, in part and for a season, of what it found ready to its hand, it did yet detach itself more and more from the classical poetry of Rome, we take note of the going forward at the same time of two distinct processes. But these, distinct as they are, we observe also combining for the formation of the new, together giving to it its peculiar character, and constituting it something more than such a continuation of the old classical poetry, as should only differ from it in the subjects which supplied to it its theme, while in all things else it remained unchanged. These processes, as I have said, are entirely distinct from one another, have no absolutely necessary connexion, closely related as undoubtedly they were; the first being the disintegration of the old prosodical system of Latin verse, under the gradual substitution of accent for quantity; and the second, the employment of rhyme, within, or at the close of, the verse, as a means for marking rhythm, and a resource for the producing of melody. They have no absolutely necessary connexion. There might have been the first without the second—accent without rhyme—as in our own blank heroic verse, and occasional blank lyrics; nor are there wanting various and successful examples, in this very later Latin poetry, of the same kind. There was the second, rhyme without the displacing of quantity by accent, in the rhymed hexameters, pentameters, and sapphics wherein the monkish poets of the middle ages indulged, still preserving as far as they knew, and often altogether, the laws of metrical quantity, but adding rhyme as a further ornament to the verse.

Thus the results of the two processes, namely, an accentuated, and a rhymed, poetry, might have existed separately, as indeed occasionally they do; and growing up independently of one another, they ought to be traced independently also. Yet still, since only in the union of the two could results have been produced so satisfying, so perfect in their kind, as those which the Latin sacred poetry offers to us; since they did in fact essentially promote and sustain one another; the manner in which they mutually re-acted one on the other, in which the one change rendered almost imperative the other, the common spirit out of which both the transformations proceeded, should not be allowed to pass unobserved—being rather a principal matter to which he who would explain and trace the change should direct his own and his reader's attention.

I propose to say something first on the substitution of accent for quantity, an accented for a prosodic verse; which, however, is a subject that will demand one or two preliminary remarks.

There is one very noticeable difference between the Christian literature of the Greek and Roman world on the one side, and all other and later Christian literatures on the other—namely, that those Greek and Latin are, so to speak, a new budding and blossoming out of an old stock; and this a stock which, when the Church was founded, had already put forth, or was in the act of putting forth, all that in the natural order of things, and but for the quickening breath of a new and unexpected life, it could ever have unfolded. They are as a second and a later spring, coming in the rear of the timelier and the first. For that task which the word of the Gospel had to accomplish in all other regions of man's life, it had also to accomplish in this. It was not granted to it at first entirely to make or mould a society of its own. A harder task was assigned it— being, as it was, superinduced on a society that had come into existence, and had gradually assumed the shape which now it wore, under very different conditions, and in obedience to very different influences from its own. Of this it had to make the best which it could; only to reject and to put under ban that which was absolutely incurable therein, and directly contradicted its own fundamental idea; but of the rest to assimilate to itself what was capable of assimilation; to transmute what was willing to be transmuted; to consecrate what was prepared to receive from it a higher consecration; and altogether to adjust, not always with perfect success, but as best it might, and often at the cost of much forbearance and self-sacrifice, its relations to the old, that had grown up under heathen auspices, and was therefore very different from what it would have been, had the leaven of the word of life mingled with and wrought in it from the first, instead of coming in, a later addition to it, at the end of time.

Thus was it in almost every sphere of man's life and of his moral and intellectual activity; yet we have here to speak only of one—that, namely, of literature and language. All the modern literatures and languages of Europe Christianity has mainly made what they are; to it they owe all that characterizes them the most strongly. For although, as it needs not to say, the languages themselves reach back in their elemental rudiments to a time far anterior to the earliest in which the Gospel came, or could have come, in contact with them, or indeed had been proclaimed at all; yet it did thus mingle with them early enough to find them still in that wondrous and mysterious process of their first evolution. They were yet plastic and fluent, as all languages are at a certain period of their existence, though a period generally just out of the ken of the history. And the languages rose to a level with the claims which the new religion of the Spirit made upon them. Formed and fashioned under its influence, they dilated till they were equal to its needs, and adequate exponents, as far as language ever can become so, of the deepest things which it possessed.*

But it was otherwise in regard of the Latin language. That, when the Church arose, requiring of it to be the organ of her Divine Word, to tell out all the new, and as yet undreamt of, which was stirring in her bosom; demanding of it that it should reach her needs, needs which had hardly or not at all existed, while the language was in process of formation—that was already full formed; it had reached its climacteric, and was

---

* See some beautiful remarks on the Christianizing of the German language in the *Theol. Stud. und Krit.*, vol. xxii. p. 308, sqq.; and again in Rudolf von Raumer's *Einwirkung d. Christenthums auf die Althochdeutsche Sprache*, p. 168, sqq.

indeed verging, though as yet imperceptibly, toward decay, with all the stiffness of commencing age already upon it.   Such the Church found it—something to which a new life might perhaps be imparted, but the first life of which it was well nigh overlived.   She found it a garment narrower than she could wrap herself withal, and yet the only one within reach.   But she did not forego the expectation of one day obtaining all which she wanted, nor even for the present did she sit down entirely contented with the inadequate and insufficient.   Herself young and having the spirit of life, she knew that the future was her own—that she was set in the world for this very purpose of making all things new—that what she needed and did not find, there must lie in her the power of educing from herself —that, though it might not be all at once, yet little by little, she could weave whatever vestments were required by her for comeliness and beauty.   And we do observe the language under the new influence, as at the breath of a second spring, putting itself forth anew, budding and blossoming afresh, the meaning of words enlarging and dilating, old words coming to be used in new and higher significations, obsolete words reviving, new words being coined*—with much in all this to offend the classical taste, which yet, being inevitable, ought not to offend, and of which the gains far more than compensated the losses.   There was a new thing, and that being so, it was of necessity that there should be a new utterance as well.   To be offended with this is, in

----

* See Funccius, *De Vegetâ Latinæ Linguæ Senectute*, p. 1139, seq.

truth, to be offended with Christianity, which made this to be inevitable.

We may make application of all which has been just said to the metrical forms of the classical poetry of Rome. These the Church found ready made to her hand, and in their kind having reached a very high perfection. A true instinct must have told her at once, or after a very few trials, that these were not the metrical forms which she required. Yet it was not to be supposed that she should have the courage immediately to cast them aside, and to begin the world, as it were, afresh; or that she should have been enabled at once to foresee the more adequate forms to be one day developed out of her own bosom. But these which she thus inherited, while she was content of necessity to use, yet could not satisfy her.* The Gospel had brought

* Dans le monde grec d'abord, puis, dans le monde romain, les chrétiens éprouvèrent le besoin de se servir des formes de la poésie antique et de les appliquer aux idées nouvelles. Les IVe et Ve siècles virent naître un assez grand nombre d'efforts en ce genre, surtout en Italie et en Espagne. Evidemment, ces tentatives souvent renouvelées étaient sans portée, sans avenir; les sentiments chrétiens les traditions chrétiennes ne pouvaient s'accommoder des formes créées pour un autre emploi, vieillies au service d'une autre Muse; évidemment, la littérature chrétienne devait produire sa propre forme, et c'est ce qu'elle a fait plus tard. Ce n'est pas quand elle a cherché à traduire ses inspirations dans le langage de Virgile, qu'elle a enfanté des ouvrages de quelque valeur; c'est quand elle a inventé son épopée, avec Dante et Milton, et son drame dans les mystères du moyen âge, ou les actes sacramentaux de Calderon, qui ne sont qu'une résurrection et un raffinement des mystères; c'est quand elle a inspiré ces beaux chants qui, depuis Luther, n'ont cessé de retentir sous les voûtes des églises d'Allemagne. Alors la poésie chrétienne a fait son œuvre; jusque là elle n'était qu'un calque pâle

into men's hearts longings after the infinite and the eternal, which were strange to it, at least in their present intensity, until now. Beauty of outline, beauty of form—and what a flood of light does that one word *forma*, as equivalent to beauty, pour on the difference between the heathen and the Christian ideal of beauty ! —this was all which the old poetry yearned after and strove to embody ; this was all which its metrical frameworks were perfectly fitted for embodying.

But now heaven had been opened, and henceforward the mystical element of modern poetry demanded its rights; vaguer but vaster thoughts were craving to find the harmonies to which they might be married for ever. The boundless could not be content to find its organ in that, of which the very perfection lay in its limitations and its bounds. The Christian poets were in holy earnest ; a versification therefore could no longer be endured, attached, as in their case at least it was, by no living bonds to the thoughts, in which sense and sound had no real correspondence with one another. The versification henceforth must have an intellectual value, which should associate it with the onward movement of the thoughts and feelings, whereof it professed to be, and thus indeed should be, the expression.   A struggle therefore commenced from the first, between

et un écho affaibli de la poésie païenne (Ampère, *Hist. Litt. de la France*, vol. ii. p. 196). And again : Il faut que le chant chrétien dépouille entièrement ces lambeaux de métrique ancienne, qu'il se fasse complètement moderne par la rime comme par le sentiment; alors, on aura *cette prose rimée* empreinte d'une sombre harmonie, qui par la tristesse des sons et des images et le retour menaçant de la terminaison lugubre fait pressentir le Dante, on aura le *Dies Iræ* (vol. ii. p. 412).

the form and spirit, between the old heathen form and
the new Christian spirit—the latter seeking to release
itself from the shackles and restraints which the former
imposed upon it; and which were to it, not a help and
a support, as the form should be, but a hindrance and a
weakness—not liberty, but now rather a most galling
bondage.*   The new wine went on fermenting in the

---

* We see already in Prudentius the process of emancipation
effectually at work, the disintegration of the old prosodic system
already beginning. He still affects to write, and in the main
does write, prosodically ; yet with largest licences. No one will
suppose him more ignorant than most schoolboys of fourteen
would be now, of the quantitative value which the old classical
poets of Italy, with whose writings he was evidently familiar,
had attributed to words ; yet we continually find him attributing
another value, postponing quantity to accent, or rather allowing
accent to determine quantity, as in cyāneus, Sardīnia, ĕnigma.
As his latest editor has observed : Metrum haud rarò negligitur,
quia poeta in arsi vv. majorem vim accentui quàm quantitati tribuit (*Obbarii Prudentius*, p. 19). The whole scheme of Latin
prosody must have greatly loosened its hold, before he could have
used the freedom which he does use, in the shifting and altering
the value of syllables. We mark in him especially a determination not to be deprived altogether of serviceable words through a
metrical notation excluding them *in toto* from a place in the
hexameter. Thus he writes tĕmulentus, delībutus, idŏlolatrix,
calceămentum, margāritum ; though as regards this last word,
in an iambic verse, where there was no motive, but the contrary,
for producing the antepenultima, he restores to that syllable its
true quantity, and writes margărita. In the same way not
ignorance nor caprice, but the feeling that they must have the
word ecclesia at command, while yet, if they left it with the
antepenultima long, it could never find place in the pentameter,
and only in one of its cases in the hexameter, induced the almost
universal shortening of that syllable among the metrical writers
of the Church. Amid the many motives which prompted the

old bottles, till it burst them asunder, though not itself to be spilt and lost in the process, but so to be gathered into nobler chalices, vessels more fitted to contain it—

Christian poets to strive after emancipation from the classical rules of quantity, first to slight, and then to cast them off, this had its weight: true, the opposition to the metrical scheme lay deeper than this, which was but one moment of it: yet the fact, that the chief metres excluded a vast number of the noblest and even most necessary words, and though not absolutely excluding, rendered many more inadmissible in most of their inflexions,— this must have been peculiarly intolerable to them.   Craving the whole domain of words for their own, finding it only too narrow for the uttering of all they were struggling to express, desiring, too, as must all whose thoughts and feelings are real, that their words should fit close to their sense, they could ill endure to be shut out from that which often was the best and fittest, by arbitrary, artificial, and to them unmeaning restrictions.   Thus Augustine distinctly tells us that he composed his curious *Psalmus contra partem Donati* in the rhythm which he did, that so he might not be hampered or confined in his choice of words by the necessities of metre: Ideo autem non aliquo *carminis* genere id fieri volui, ne me necessitas metrica ad aliqua verba quæ vulgo minus sunt usitata compelleret.   *Carmen* signifies here a poem composed after the old classical models ; his own, as being popularly and not metrically written, he counts only a *canticum.*   The distinctive and statelier diction of the *carmen* is indicated by Terentianus Maurus, 298 :

Verba si non obvia
Carminis servant honorem, non jacentis *cantici.*

One has but to turn to the lyrical poems of Horace, to become at once aware of the wealth of words, which for the writer of the hexameter and pentameter may be said not to exist. What a world, for example, of noble epithets—tumultuosus, luctuosus, formidolosus, fraudulentus, contumax, pervicax, insolens, intaminatus, fastidiosus, periculosus—with many more among the most poetical words in the language, are under the ban of a perpetual exclusion.

new, even as that which was poured into them was new.

We can trace step by step the struggle between the two principles of heathen and Christian life, which were here opposed to one another. As the classical or old Roman element grew daily weaker in the new Christian world which now had been founded; as the novel element of Christian life strengthened and gained ground; as poetry became popular again, not the cultivated entertainment of the polite and lettered few, a graceful amusement of the scholar and the gentleman, but that in which all men desired to express, or to find expressed for them, their hopes and fears, their joys and their sorrows, and all the immortal longings of their common humanity;—a confinement became less and less endurable within the old and stereotyped forms, which, having had for their own ends their fitness and beauty, were yet constituted for the expressing of far other thoughts, sentiments, and hopes than those which now stirred at far deeper depths the spirits and the hearts of men. The whole scheme on which the Latin prosodical poetry was formed, was felt to be capricious, imposed from without; and the poetry which now arose demanded—not, indeed, to be without law; for, demanding this, it would have demanded its own destruction, and not to be poetry at all; but it demanded that its laws and restraints should be such as its own necessities, and not those of quite a different condition, required.*

---

* The *Instructiones* of Commodianus, a poem quite valueless in a literary point of view, is yet curious in this respect; and the more curious now that it is placed by scholars in the latter

It is something more than mere association, more
than the fact that these metres, in all of most illustrious
half of the third century rather than in the fourth, where it used
to be set. Very singular is it to find, more than a hundred
years before the last notes of the classical muse had expired in
Claudian, a poem of considerable length composed on the system
of a total abandonment of quantity, and substitution of accent in
its room—maintaining the apparent framework of the old classical hexameter, but filling it up on a principle entirely new.
Nor can we suppose that a poem so long, and in its fashion so
elaborate, is the first specimen of its kind, however it is the
first which has come down to our days. It is of so little value
as to be in few hands; three or four lines may therefore be
quoted as a specimen. These are part of a remonstrance
against the pomp of female dress, § 60:

> Obruitis collum monilibus, gemmis, et auro,
> Necnon et inaures gravissimo pondere pendent :
> Quid memorem vestes et totam Zabuli pompam ?
> Respuitis legem, cùm vultis mundo placere.

Utterly prosaic if regarded as poetry, this work still bears the
marks of a strong moral earnestness, is the utterance of one who
had something to say to his brethren, and was longing to say
it : and no doubt here lay that which tempted the writer to
forsake a system of versification which had become intolerably
artificial in his time and for him ; and to develop for himself, or
finding developed to use, one in which he should in great part
be released from its arbitrary obligations. In the following
lines, forming part of a hymn first published by Niebuhr (*Rhein.
Museum*, 1829, p. 7), lines plainly intended to consist of four
dactyles each. dactyles, that is, in sound, which with a little
favouring of one or two syllables, they may be made to appear,
there is the same intention of satisfying the ear with accentuated
and not prosodic feet. The lines relate to St Paul, and are
themselves worthy to be quoted :

> Factus œconomus in domo regiâ,
> Divini muneris appone fercula;
> Ut quæ repleverit te sapientia,
> Ipsa nos repleat tua per dogmata.

This hymn also, though considerably later than the poem of

and most memorable which had been composed in them, had been either servants of the heathen worship, or at least appropriated to heathen themes, which induced the Church little by little to forsake them: which even at this day causes them at once to translate us into, and to make us feel that we are moving in, the element of heathen life. The bond is not thus merely historic and external, but spiritual and inward. And yet, at the same time, the influence of these associations must not be overlooked, when we are estimating the causes which wrought together to alienate the poets and hymnologists of the Christian Church ever more and more from the classical, and especially from the lyrical, metres of antiquity, and which urged them to seek more appropriate forms of their own. In those the heathen gods had been celebrated and sung, the whole impure mythology had been arrayed and tricked out. Were they not profaned for ever by these unholy uses to which they had been first turned? How could the praises of the true and living God be fitly sung in the same? A like feeling to that which induced the abandonment of the heathen temples, and the seeking rather to develop the existing basilicas into Christian churches, or where new churches were built, to build them after the fashion of the civil, and not the religious, edifices already existing, must have been here also at work. The faithful would have often shrunk from the involuntary associations which these metres suggested, as we should shrink from hearing a psalm or spiritual

---

Commodianus, is certainly of a very early date. Niebuhr thinks he finds evidence in the MS. from which it is taken, that it cannot be later than the seventh century.

song fitted to some tune which had been desecrated to lewd or otherwise profane abuse. And truly there is, and we find it even now, a clinging atmosphere of heathen life shed round many of these metres, which it is almost impossible to dissipate; so that, reading some sacred thoughts which have arrayed themselves in sapphics,* or alcaics, or hendecasyllables, we are more or less conscious of a certain contradiction between the form and the subject, as though they were awkwardly and unfitly matched, and one or other ought to have been different from what it is.

The wonderful and abiding success of the hymns of St Ambrose, and of those so-called Ambrosian which were formed upon the model of his, lay doubtless in great part in the wise instinct of choice, which led him to select a metre by far the least markedly metrical, and the most nearly rhythmical, of all the ancient metres out of which it was free to him to choose;—I mean the iambic dimeter. The time was not yet come when it was possible altogether to substitute rhythm for metre: the old had still too much vitality to be cast aside, the new had not yet clearly shaped itself forth; but choosing thus, he escaped (as far as it was possible, using these forms at all, to escape,) the disturbing reminiscences and associations of heathen art.†
While in a later day hardly anything so strongly

---

* Take, for instance, this from a sapphic ode in honour of the Baptist :

> Oh nimis felix, meritique celsi,
> Nescius labem nivei pudoris,
> Præpotens martyr, eremique cultor
> Maxime vatum.

† See Bähr, *Die Christl. Dichter Roms*, p. 7.

revealed the extent to which Roman Catholic Italy had fallen back under pagan influences, was penetrated through and through at the revival of learning with the spirit of heathen, and not of Christian, life, as the offence which was then everywhere taken by Italian churchmen, Leo the Tenth at their head, at the un-metrical hymns of the Church, and the determination manifested to reduce them by force, and at the cost of any wrong to their beauty and perfection, to metre ;— their very exemption from which was their glory, and that which made them to be Christian hymns in the highest sense.*

This movement, then, which began early to manifest itself, for an enfranchisement from the old classical forms, this impatience of their restraints, was essentially a Christian one. Still we cannot doubt that it was

* The history of the successive revisions which the non-metrical hymns sustained, is given by Arevalus, an enthusiastic admirer of the process, in his *Hymnodia Hispanica*, Romæ, 1786, pp. 121—144, with this ominous heading: Romanorum Pontificum in reformandâ Hymnodiâ Diligentia. Daniel (*Thesaurus Hymnologicus*, Halis, 1841; Lipsiæ, 1844—6) has frequently given in parallel columns the hymn as it existed in earlier times, probably as it came from the author, and as it was recast in the Roman breviary. The comparison is very instructive, as shewing how well-nigh the whole grace and beauty, and even vigour, of the composition had disappeared in the process. With Scripture upon our side, it would not much trouble us, if Rome had for the present that æsthetical superiority, that keener sense of artistic beauty, which she claims: this would not trouble us, since, ultimately, where truth is, there highest beauty must be as well. But such facts as these, or as the hideous Italian Churches of the last three hundred years, need to be explained and accounted for, before she can make good her claim.

assisted and made easier by the fact that the metrical system, against which the Church protested, and from . which it sought to be delivered, had been itself brought in from without. Itself of foreign growth, it could oppose no such stubborn resistance as it would have done, had it been native to the soil, had its roots been entwined strongly with the deepest foundations of the Latin tongue. But this they were not. It is abundantly known to all who take any interest in the early poetry of Rome, that it was composed on principles of versification altogether different from those which were introduced with the introduction of the Greek models in the sixth century of the City—that Latin hexameters, or 'long' verses, were in all probability first composed by Ennius*, while the chief lyric metres belong to a much later day, having been introduced, some of the simpler kinds, as the sapphic by Catullus, and the more elaborate not till the time, and only through the successful example, of Horace.† It is known too that while the hexameter took comparatively a firm root in the soil, and on the whole could not be said to be alien to the genius of the Latin tongue, the lyric metres remained exotics to the end, were never truly acclimated,—nothing worth reading or being preserved having been produced in them, except by those who first transplanted them from Greek to Italian ground.‡ It was not that the Latin language should

---

* Cicero, *De Legg.* ii. 27. .

† Horace, *Epistt.* i. 19, 21—34.

‡ Quintilian's judgment of his countrymen's achievements in lyric poetry is familiar to most (*Instit. Orat.* x. 1, 96): Lyricorum Horatius ferè solus legi dignus.

be without its great lyric utterances, and such as should
be truly its own ; but it was first to find these in the
Christian hymns of the middle ages.

The poetry of home growth,—the old Italian poetry
which was thrust out by this new,—was composed, as
we learn from the fragments which survive, and from
notices lying up and down, on altogether a different
basis of versification. There is no reason to believe
that quantity, except as represented by and identical
with accent, was recognized in it at all. For while
accent belongs to every language and to every age of
the language,—that is, in pronouncing any word longer
than a monosyllable, an *ictus* or stress must fall on one
syllable more than on others,—quantity is an invention
more or less arbitrary. At how late a period, and how
arbitrarily, and as from without, it was imposed on the
Latin, the innumerable anomalies, inconsistencies, and
contradictions in the prosodical system of the language
sufficiently testify.

. I know, indeed, that some have denied the early Latin
verse to have rested on a merely accentual foundation.
I certainly would not have gone out of my way to
meddle with a controversy upon which such high names
are ranged upon either side. But lying as it does so
directly in my path as not to be avoided, I cannot forbear
saying, that, having read and sought to make myself
master of what has come within my reach upon the question, and judging by the analogy of all other popular
poetry, I am convinced that Ferdinand Wolf*, Bähr †,

* *Ueber die Lais*, p. 159.
† *Gesch. d. Römischer Litteratur*, vol. i. p. 89; Edélestand du
Méril, *Poésies populaires Latines*, Paris, 1843, p. 45.

and those others are in the right, who, admitting indeed the existence of Saturnian, that is old Italian, verses, deny that there was properly any such thing as a Saturnian metre—that is, any fixed scheme or frame-work of long and short feet, after the Greek fashion, according to which these verses were composed; these consisting rather, as all ballad-poetry does, of a loosely defined number of syllables, not metrically disposed, but with places sufficiently marked, upon which a stress of the voice fell, to vindicate for them the character of verse.*

Into what these numbers would have unfolded themselves, as the nation advanced in culture, and as the ear, gradually growing nicer and more exacting in its requirements, claimed a finer melody, it is not easy to say; but Latin poetry at all events, as it would have had a character, so would it have rested on a basis of versification, which was its own. And knowing this, we can scarcely sympathize without reserve in the satisfaction which Horace expresses at the change which presently came over it; however we may admit that, with the exception of his one greater predecessor, he accomplished more than any other, to excuse and justify, and even to reconcile us to, the change. That change came, as is familiar to all, when, instead of being allowed such a process of natural developement from

* It is characteristic of this, that *numeri* should be the proper Latin word for verses rather than any word which should correspond to the Greek *metre*. The Romans, in fact, counted their syllables and did not measure them, a certain *number* of these constituting a rhythm. *Numeri* is only abusively applied to verses which rest on music and time, and not on the number of the syllables (Niebuhr, *Lectures on Early Roman History*, p. 11).

within, it was drawn out of its own orbit by the too prevailing attractions of the Greek literature, within the sphere and full influence of which the conquests of the sixth century brought it,—though indeed, that influence had commenced nearly a century before.*

It is, indeed, a perilous moment for a youthful literature,—so youthful as not yet to have acquired confidence in itself,—and, though full of latent possibilities of greatness, having hitherto actually accomplished little,—to be brought within the sphere of an elder, which is now ending a glorious course, and which offers to the younger for its imitation finished forms of highest beauty and perfection. Most perilous of all is it, if these forms are not so strange, but that with some little skill they may be transplanted to the fresher soil, with a fair promise of growing and flourishing there. For the younger to adhere to its own forms and fashions, rude and rugged, and as yet only most imperfectly worked out—to believe that in them, and in cleaving to them, its true future is laid up, and not in appropriating the more elaborate models which are now offered ready to its hands—for it thus to refuse to be dazzled by the prospect of immediate results, and of overleaping a stage or two of slow and painful progress, this is indeed most hard ; the temptation has proved oftentimes too strong to be resisted.

It was so in the case which we are considering now. The Roman spirit could not, of course, utterly disappear, or be entirely supprest. Quite sufficient of that

* See the limitations upon Horace's well-known words, Græcia *capta* ferum victorem cepit (*Epp.* ii. 1, 156), which Orelli (in loc.) puts, and in like manner Niebuhr.

spirit has remained to vindicate for Roman literature
an independent character, and to free it from the charge
of being merely the echo and imitation of something
else; but the Roman forms did nearly altogether disappear, and even the Roman spirit was very considerably
depressed and affected by the alien influence to which
it was submitted.

The process, in truth, was wonderfully like that
which found place, when, in the first half of the sixteenth century, the national poetry of Spain yielded to
the influence of Italian models, and Castillejo was obliged
to give place to Boscan and Garcilasso. The points of
resemblance in these parallel cases are many. Thus in
either case, the conquered, and at that time, morally,
and so far as strength went, intellectually, far inferior
people,—the people, therefore, with much less of latent
productivity for the future, whatever may have been
the marvels it had accomplished in the past,—imposed
its literary yoke on the conquering and the nobler
nation; caused it in a measure to be ashamed of that
which hitherto it had effected, or of all which, continuing
in its own line, it was likely to bring to pass. Nor was
this the only point in which the processes were similar.
There were other points of resemblance—as this, that
it is impossible to deny but that here, as there, poetry
of a very high order was composed upon the new
models. Great results came of the change, and of the
new direction in which the national taste was turned.
Every thing, in short, came of it but the one thing, for
the absence of which all else is but an insufficient compensation; namely, a thoroughly popular literature,
which should truly smack of the soil from which it

sprung, which should be the utterance of a nation's own life; and not merely accents, which, however sweet or musical, were yet caught from the lips of another, and only artificially fitted to its own.

But with the fading and growing weak of every thing else in the classical literature of Rome, this foreign usurpation faded and grew weak also. It is more than possible, for indeed we have satisfactory evidence to the fact, that traditions of the old rhythms were preserved in the popular poetry throughout the whole period during which the metrical forms borrowed from the Greek were alone in vogue at the capital, and among those who laid claim to a learned education, that Saturnian or old Italian verses lived upon the lips of the people during all this interval.* We have continual allusion to such rustic melodies: and even were we

---

* Muratori (*Antiqq. Ital. Diss.* 40): Itaque duplex Poëseos genus olim exsurrexit, alterum antiquius, sed ignobile ac plebeium; alterum nobile et a doctis tantummodo viris excultum. Illud *rhythmicum*, illud *metricum* appellatum est. Sed quod potissimum est animadvertendum, quamquam Metrica Poësis primas arripuerit, omniumque meliorum suffragio et usu probata laudibus ubique ornaretur: attamen Rhythmica Poësis nou propterea defecit apud Græcos atque Latinos. Quum enim vulgus indoctum et rustica gens Poëtam interdum agere vellet, nec legibus metri addiscendis par erat; quales poterat, versus efformare perrexit: hoc est, Rhythmo contenta, Metrum coutemsit: Metrum, inquam, hoc est, rigidas prosodiæ leges, quas perfecta Poësis sequitur. So Santen, in his *Notes on Terentianus Maurus*, p. 177: Nec tamen post Græciæ numeros, ab Andronico agresti Latio introductos, vetus Saturniorum modorum rusticitas cessavit, immo vero non solum ejus vestigia, sed ipsa etiam res in omne ævum superstes mansit. Yet he has certainly committed an oversight in adducing among his proofs the well-known lines of Horace, *Epp.* ii. 1. 156—

without any such, we might confidently affirm that a people could never have been without a poetry, which existed under circumstances so favourable for its production as the Italian peasantry; and, if possessing a poetry, that it would be such as should find its expression in the old Italian numbers, and not in the Greek exotic metres. It is true that verses composed in these old and native numbers, on rhythmic, and not on metrical, principles, do not openly re-appear, that is, with any claims to be considered as literature, until the foreign domination began to relax its hold; but that no sooner was this the case, than at once they witness for their presence, putting themselves forth anew.*

160, in which, having spoken of the ruder verses of an earlier day he goes on to say :

> . . . sed in longum tamen ævum
> Manserunt, hodieque manent vestigia ruris.

All that he is here affirming is, that there were yet marks of rusticity (vestigia ruris) which had not been quite got rid of, cleaving to the cultivated poetry of his country, to that which in the main was formed upon Greek models. Muratori falls into the same error, who explains the words of Horace in this way: Hoc est, quamvis a Græcis didicerimus metri regulas, et pro rudibus rusticorum rhythmis castigatos nunc politosque versus conficiamus, attamen rhythmica poësis perduravit semper et adhuc apud vulgus viget.

* There is much instructive on this subject in a little article by Niebuhr, in the *Rhein. Museum*, 1829, p. 1—8. On the re-appearance of the supprest popular poetry of Italy, he says: Es ist auch wohl sehr begreiflich wie damals, als das eigentliche Latein, und die Formen der Litteratur nur mühselig durch die Schulen erhalten wurden, manches, volksmässige sich frey machte, wieder empor kam, und einen Platz unter dem einnahm, was die verblödete Schule seit Jahrhunderten geweiht hatte. Der neugriechische politische Vers, welcher dem Tact des Tanzes ent-

As something of an analogous case, we know that many words which Attius and Nævius used, and which during the Augustan period seemed to have been entirely lost, do begin to emerge and present themselves afresh in Appuleius, Prudentius, and Tertullian. The number of words which are thus not Augustan, and yet are at once *ante-* and *post-*Augustan, must have struck every attentive observer of the growth and progress of the Latin tongue. The reappearance of these in writers of the silver age, is often explained as an affected seek-ing of archaisms on their parts; yet much more probably, the words were under literary ban for a time, but had lived on in popular speech, and when that ban was removed, or was unable any more to give effect to its decrees, shewed themselves anew in books, as they had always continued alive in the common language of the people.

By thus going back toward the origins of the Latin literature, we can better understand how it came to pass, that when there arose up in the Christian Church a desire to escape from the confinement of the classical metres, and to exchange metrical for rhythmical laws, the genius of the language lent, instead of opposing, itself to the change. It was instinctively conscious, that this new which was aimed at was also the old, indeed, the oldest of all; the recovering of a natural position from an unnatural and strained one:—to which there-fore it reverted the more easily.

spricht, ist ja der nämliche wonach König Philippus siegstrunken tanzte:

Δημοσθένης Δημοσθένους Παιανιεὺς τάδ᾽ εἶπε—

nur dass Accent, nicht Sylbenmaass, dabey beachtet wird.

And other motives,—having their origin no less in the same fact, that quantity was not indigenous to the Latin soil, and therefore had struck no deep root, and obtained no wide recognition, in the universal sense of the people,—were not wanting to induce the poet of these later times to abandon the ancient metres, and expatiate in the freer region of accented verse. Such a consummation was helped on and hastened by that gradual ignorance of the quantity of words, which, with the waning and fading away of classical learning under the barbarian invasions, became every day wider spread. Even where the poet himself was sufficiently acquainted with the quantitative value of words, the number of readers or hearers who still kept this knowledge was every day growing less in the Roman world; the majority being incapable of appreciating his skill, or finding any satisfying melody in his versification, the principles of which they did not understand; while the accentual value of words, as something self-evident, would be recognized by every ear.

And this fact that it was so, wrought effectually in another way. For perhaps the most important step of all, for the freeing of verse from the fetters of prosody, and that which was most fatal to the maintenance of the old metrical system, was the introduction of liturgic chanting into the services of the Church—although this indeed was only the working out, in a particular direction, of that new spirit which was animating it in every part. The Christian hymns were composed to be sung, and to be sung at first by the whole congregation of the faithful, who were only little by little thrust out from their share in this part of the service. But the classical or prosodical valuation of words would have been clearly inappreciable by the greater number of those whom it was desired thus to draw in to take part in the worship. If the voices of the assembled multitudes were indeed claimed for this, it could only be upon some scheme which should commend itself to all by its simplicity—which should appeal to some principle intelligible to every man, whether he had received an education of the schools, or not. Quantity, with its values so often merely fictitious, and so often inconsistent one with another, could no longer be maintained as the basis of harmony. The Church naturally fell back on accent, which is essentially popular, appealing to the common sense of every ear, and in its broader features, in its simple rise and fall, appreciable by all;—which had also in its union with music this advantage, that it allowed to those, who were much more concerned about what they said, than how they said it, and could ill brook to be crossed and turned out of their way by rules and restraints, the necessity of which they did not acknowledge, far greater liberty than quantity would have allowed them; inasmuch as the music, in its choral harmonies, was ever ready to throw its broad mantle over the verse, to conceal its weakness, and, where needful, to cover its multitude of sins.*

* See F. Wolf, *Ueber die Lais*, p. 82—84.

CHAPTER II.

ON RHYME IN LATIN VERSE.

THIS much on the substitution of accent for quantity. But hand in hand with the process of exchanging metre for a merely accentuated rhythm went another movement, I mean the tendency to rhyme. Of this it might doubtless be affirmed no less than of the other, that it was only a recovery of the lost; having its first origin, or at all events its very clear anticipation, in the early national poetry of Rome. This too, except for that event which gave to the Latin language a second lease of life, and evoked from it capacities which had been dormant in it hitherto, might not and probably would not now have ever unfolded itself there, the first and apparently more natural opportunity having long since past away. Such an opportunity it had once enjoyed. There is quite enough in the remains of early Latin poetry which we possess, to shew that rhyme was not a new element, altogether alien to the language, which was forced upon it by the Christian poets in the days of its decline. There were early preludings of that which should indeed only fully and systematically unfold itself at the last. The tendencies of the Saturnian, and of such other fragments of ancient Latin verse as have reached us, to terminations of a like sound, have been often noticed*, as this from the *Andromache* of Ennius:

---

* Lange however goes much too far, when he affirms (see Jahn, *Jahrbuch der Philologie*, 1830, p. 256) that it systema-

> Hæc omnia vidi inflammari,
> Priamo vi vitam evitari,
> Jovis aram sanguine turpari.

The following, of more uncertain authorship, is quoted by Cicero (*Tusc.* 1, 28):

> Cœlum nitescere, arbores frondescere,
> Vites lætificæ pampinis pubescere,
> Rami bacarum ubertate incurvescere.

Of that poetry rhyme may be considered a legitimate ornament. And even after a system had been introduced resting on altogether different principles of versification, that, I mean, of the Greek metres, yet was it so inborn in the language and inherent to it, that it continually made its appearance; being no doubt only with difficulty avoided by those writers, whose stricter sense of beauty taught them not to catch at ornaments which were not properly theirs; and easily attained by those, who with a more questionable taste were well pleased to sew it as a purple patch on a garment of altogether a different material.*   Thus we cannot doubt

tically found place in the old popular poetry of Rome; which was Casaubon's opinion as well (*ad Pers. Sat.* i. 93, 94). Näke (*Rhein. Museum*, 1829, p. 388-392) takes a more reasonable view.

* See Bähr, *Gesch. d. Röm. Literatur*, vol. ii. p. 681. It is evident that the Latin prose writers, even the best, and the comic writers whose verse was so like to prose, were quite willing sometimes to avail themselves of the satisfaction which the near recurrence of words of a similar sound affords to the ear.   Thus Cicero himself (*Brut.* 87): Volvendi sunt libri Catonis: intelliges nihil illius lineamentis, nisi eorum pigmentorum, quæ inventa nondum erant, *florem* et *colorem* defuisse.   So Pliny the younger: Illam *veram* et *meram* Græciam. And Plautus (*Cistell.* i. 1, 70): Amor et *melle* et *felle* est fecundissimus.   And Caracalla of the

that these coincidences of sound were sedulously avoided by so great a master of the proprieties as Virgil—in whose works therefore rhyming verses rarely appear: while it is difficult not to suspect that they were sometimes sought, or, if not sought, yet not diligently shunned, but rather welcomed when they offered themselves, by Ovid, in whom they occur far more frequently, and whose less severe taste might not have been unwilling to appropriate this as well as the more legitimate adornments which belonged to the verse that he was using.

They occur indeed, verses with middle and with final rhymes, in every one of the Latin poets. Thus, as examples of the middle rhyme, we have in Ennius:

> Non cauponantes bellum, sed belligerantes;

and in Virgil:

> Limus ut hic durescit, et hæc ut cera liquescit;

so too in Ovid:

> Quem mare carpentem, substrictaque crura gerentem;

---

brother whom he murdered: Sit licet *divus*, dummodo non *vivus*. In the Christian prose-writers they are more frequent still, especially in Augustine. All readers of his will remember how often such chimes as this (having reference to Stephen's sharp chiding of the Jews) recur: Lingua *clamat*, cor *amat*; or this, on the two Testaments: In Novo *patent*, quæ in Vetere *latent*; or, on the Christian's 'hope of glory': Præcedat *spes*, ut sequatur *res*; or, on faith: Quid est enim *fides*, nisi credere quod non *vides?* or, interpreting John xxi. 9: Piscis *assus*, Christus est *passus*; or, on obedience and reward: Hoc agamus *bene*, ut illud habeamus *plene*; or, once more, of the Heavenly City: Ibi nullus *oritur*, quia nullus *moritur*. Näke (*Rhein. Museum*, 1829, pp. 392–401) has accumulated examples in like kind from almost all the Latin prose writers.

and again :

> Quot cœlum stellas, tot habet tua Roma puellas ;

and in a pentameter :

> Quærebant flavos per nemus omne favos ;

and in Martial :

> Sic leve flavorum valeat genus Usipiorum ;

thus also in Claudian :

> Flava cruentarum prætenditur umbra jubarum.

These examples might easily be multiplied. As we descend lower, leonine verses become still more frequent. They abound in the *Mosella* of Ausonius.

Nor less have we final rhymes even in Virgil, as the following :

> Nec non Tarquinium ejectum Porsena jubebat
> Accipere, ingentique urbem obsidione premebat.

and again :

> omnis campis diffugit arator,
> Omnis et agricola, et tutâ latet arce viator.*

and in Horace, as in his well-known precept :

> Non satis est pulcra esse poëmata ; dulcia sunto,
> Et quocumque volent, animum auditoris agunto.

once more :

> Multa recedentes adimunt. Ne forte seniles
> Mandentur juveni partes, pueroque viriles.

As we reach the silver age, they are more frequent : they abound in Lucan, though one example may suffice :

> Crimen erit Superis et me fecisse nocentem,
> Sidera quis mundumque velit spectare cadentem ? †

---

* Other examples of this in Virgil, *Æn.* i. 319, 320 ; iii. 656, 657 ; iv. 256, 257 (where see Forbiger) ; v. 385, 386 ; viii. 620, 621.

† I have not seen any collection of ὁμοιοτέλευτα out of Greek

When therefore at a later day rhyme began to enter as a permanent element into poetical composition, and to be accounted almost its necessary condition, this was not the coming in of something wholly strange or new. Rhyme, though new to Latin verse in the extent to which it was now adopted, yet had already made itself an occasional place even in the later or prosodic poetry of Rome; as no doubt it was, and would have continued to be, of far more frequent recurrence in that earlier national poetry, which, as we have seen, was supprest without having ever reached its full and natural development.

This much may be said in proof that the germs, so to speak, of rhyme were laid in the versification already existing, that it had that ' early anticipation' which one has urged as among the sure marks of a true development. Here indeed it would be a serious mistake, and one which all the documents that have reached us would refute, to regard the hexameter or pentameter as the earliest sphere in which rhyme displayed itself, the attempt having been first made to reconcile the old and the new, and to preserve the advantages of both; while

poetry, in which, indeed, they would be scarcely of so frequent occurrence as in Latin. The author of the treatise *De Vitâ et Poësi Homeri*, sometimes ascribed to Plutarch, adduces (c. 35) the ὁμοιοτέλευτον as one among the σχήματα of the Homeric poetry, and very distinctly recognizes the charm which rhyme has for the ear; for, having instanced as an example,

> 'Ηΰτ' ἔθνεα εἶσι μελισσάων ἀδινάων
> Πέτρης ἐκ γλαφυρῆς ἀεὶ νέον ἐρχομενάων.

he goes on to say: Τὰ δὲ εἰρημένα καὶ τὰ τοιαῦτα μάλιστα προστίθησι τῷ λόγῳ χάριν καὶ ἡδονήν.

only at a later day it was discovered that the two were incompatible, and that nothing of abiding value could result from this attempt to superinduce rhyme upon a system of versification resting wholly on a different basis, and to which it served but as a new patch upon an old garment. The regular addition of rhyme to the old Greek and Latin metres, with all the artificial and laborious refinements into which this ran, was of much later date than the birth of rhyme itself in the Latin poetry of the Church, the first leonine verses, or hexameters with internal rhyme, not certainly dating higher than the sixth, and any large employment of them than the eighth or ninth, centuries; other more elaborate arrangements of rhyme being later still. Rhyme itself, on the contrary, belongs to the third and fourth centuries: and that poetry in which it first appears was far too genial and true a birth of something altogether different from literary idleness, to have fallen into any tricks or merely artificial devices, such as were afterwards abundantly born of the combined indolence and ingenuity of the cloister.* Rather it displayed itself first in lines, which, having a little relaxed the strict-

* See the wonderfully curious and complex rules about rhyme, and directions for an infinite variety of its possible arrangements, in Eberhard's *Labyrinthus*, a sort of *Ars Poëtica* of the middle ages, published in Leyser's *Hist. Poëtt. Med. Ævi*, p. 832–837. Something may be fitly said here on the leonine, and other kinds of verses, more or less nearly related to the leonine, which figure so prominently in the literary productions of those ages. The name leonine, which is sometimes, although wrongly, extended to lines with final as well as with sectional or internal rhymes, has been variously derived from various persons of the name of

ness of metrical observance, sought to find a compensation for this in similar closes to the verse—being at

Leo, who were presumed first to have written them. Thus Eberhard:

Sunt inventoris de nomine dicta Leonis.

Oftener still they have been derived from one Leonius or Leoninus, a canon of Notre Dame and Latin versifier of the twelfth century. We have a curious example here of the manner in which literary opinions once started are repeated again and again, no one taking the trouble to enquire into their truth. For, in the first place, it is certain that leonine verses existed long before his time. Muratori (*Antt. Ital. Diss.* 40) has abundantly proved this, adducing perfect leonine verses which belong to the eighth, ninth, and tenth centuries; as the following, which do not date later than the ninth:

Arbor sacra Crucis fit mundo semita lucis ;
Quam qui portavit, nos Christus in astra levavit.

And thus too J. Grimm (*Lat.in. Ged. d.* x. *u.* xi. *JH.* p. xxiv): In Deutschland erscheinen leoninische Verse gleich mit dem Beginn der lateinischen Dichtkunst, und sind die Lieblingsform der Mönche vom neunten bis zum funfzehnten Jahrhundert. Some, still wishing to trace up the leonines to this Leonius, have urged, that though not the first to compose, he was the first to bring these verses to any perfection (*Muratori*, vol. iii. p. 687). But this is only propping up error with error; for Edélestand du Méril asserts (*Poésies populaires Latines,* p. 78) from actual inspection, that in his poetry, which is considerable in bulk, there does not occur a single leonine verse (except, I suppose, such accidental ones as will escape from almost every metrical writer in Latin). His chief poem, on the history of the Old Testament, is in the ordinary heroic metre. There is indeed one epistle written with final or tail rhymes, but no other portion of his poetry with rhyme at all. Du Méril himself falls in with the other derivation, namely, that this metre was so called, because as the lion is king of beasts, so is this the king of metres ; or as one has said : Leonini dicuntur a leone, quia sicut leo inter alias feras majus habet dominium, ita hæc species

this time very far from that elaborate and perfect instrument which it afterwards became. We may trace

versuum. Slow as one may be to admit this kingly superiority of the leonine verse, it must be acknowledged that sometimes it is no infelicitous form for an epigram or a maxim, uttering it both with point and conciseness. We may take the following in proof:

> Permutant mores homines, cum dantur honores:
> Corde stat inflato pauper honore dato.

Or this, expressing an important truth in the spiritual life:

> Cum bene pugnabis, cum cuncta subacta putabis,
> Quæ mox infestat, vincenda superbia restat.

or this, on the different ways in which wise and foolish accept reproof:

> Argue consultum, te diliget; argue stultum,
> Avertet vultum, nec te dimittet inultum.

or on hid talents:

> In mundo duo sunt, quæ nil, abscondita, prosunt;
> Fossus humi census, latitans in pectore sensus.

or this, on the permanence of early impressions:

> Quæ nova testa capit, inveterata sapit.

or this, on the venality of Rome:

> Curia Romana non quærit ovem sine lanâ;
> Dantes exaudit, non dantibus ostia claudit.

or once more, on the need of elementary teaching:

> Parvis imbutus, tentabis grandia tutus.

Not a few proverbs clothe themselves in this form; as the following:

> Est avis in dextrâ melior quam quattuor extra.
> Non habet anguillam, per caudam qui tenet illam.
> Sepes calcatur quâ pronior esse putatur.
> Amphora sub veste raro portatur honeste.
> Quo minime reris de gurgite pisce frueris.

And here is a brief epigram in praise of Clairvaux

> Clara vale Vallis, plus claris clara metallis;
> Tu, nisi me fallis, es rectus ad æthera callis.

They were sometimes used in more festive verse, which also they did not misbecome:

> Cervisiæ sperno potum, præscute Falerno,
> Sed tamen hanc quæro, deficiente mero.

it step by step from its rude, timid, and uncertain
beginnings, till, in the later hymnologists of the twelfth

> Est pluris bellus sonipes quam parvus asellus,
>   Hoc equitabo pecus, si mihi desit equus.

And here is a bitter epigram on the *villein* of the middle ages,
one of the many sayings which bridge over the space between
the word's original and present meaning:

> Quando mulcetur villanus, pejor habetur:
> Ungentem pungit, pungentem rusticus ungit.

And the writer of this one expresses without reserve his
opinion of lawyers:

> Dirue Juristas, Deus, ut Satanæ citharistas;
> O Deus, extingues hos pingues atque bilingues.

So too the story of Boniface the Eighth's pontificate is summed
up in another couplet:

> Vulpes intravit, tanquam leo pontificavit;
> Exiit utque canis, de divite factus inanis.

Easily recollected, they were much in use to assist keeping in
remembrance the arrangement of the Church Calendar, and the
order of the Festivals. Durandus in his *Rationale* often quotes
them. Jacob Grimm observes well: In ihnen ergebt sich die
Kloster-poesie am behaglichsten, und ihre Feierlichheit fordert
sie: daher Inscriften für Gräber und Glocken, kleinere Sprüche
und Memorabilien fast nur in ihnen verfasst wurden: sie tönen
auch nicht selten klangvoll und prachtig. Thus on the fillet of
a church-bell it was common to have these lines:

> Festa sonans mando, cum funere prælia pando;
> Mcque fugit quando resono cum fulmine grando.

The Frankish monarchs, as claiming to be Roman emperors, had
a leonine verse on their seals:

> Roma caput mundi regit orbis fræna rotundi.

In most of these lines there is a certain strength and energy.
Here is a somewhat longer specimen, drawn from a poem by
Reginald, an English Benedictine monk, cotemporary and friend
of Anselm and Hildebert:

> Sæpe jacet ventus, dormit sopita juventus:
> Aura vehit lenis, natat undis cymba serenis;

and thirteenth century, an Aquinas, or an Adam of
St Victor, it displayed all its latent capabilities, and

> Æquore sed multo Nereus, custode sepulto,
> Torquet et invertit navem dum navita stertit :
> Mergitur et navis, quamvis vehat aura suävis :
> Res tandem blandæ sunt mortis causa nefaudæ.

A brief analysis of this poem, and further quotations not without
an elegance of their own, may be found in Sir A. Crooke's *Essay
on the History of Rhyming Latin Verse*, pp. 63–75. These too
of Hildebert on the Crucifixion are good :

> Vita subit letum, dulcedo potat acetum :
> Non homo sed vermis, armatum vincit inermis,
> Agnus prædonem, vitulus moriendo leonem.

It is curious to observe how, during the middle ages, rhyme
sought to penetrate and make a place for itself everywhere.
Thus we have leonine sapphics as well as leonine hexameters and
pentameters. The following may belong to the twelfth or thirteenth century (Hommey, *Supplementum Patrum*, p. 179), and,
like the poem of Commodianus, see p. 11, must be scanned by
accent only, and not by prosody :

> Virtutum chori, summo qui Rectori
> Semper astatis atque jubilatis,
> Ovis remotæ memores estote,
>   Nosque juvate.
> Felices estis, patriæ cœlestis
> Cives, cunctorum nescii malorum,
> Quæ nos infestant, miseramque præstant
>   Undique vitam.

Hexameters and pentameters with final rhymes, and these
following close upon one another, as in our heroic verse, not
artificially interlaced (*interlaqueati*), as in our sonnet or Spen-
serian stanza, were called *caudati*, as having tails (*caudas*).
They were not, I think, quite as much cultivated as the leonine,
although of them also immense numbers were written; nor do
they very often reach the strength and precision which the
leonine sometimes attain ; yet they too are capable of a certain
terseness and even elegance, of the same character as we have
seen the leonine verses to display. Thus Hildebert describes

attained its final glory and perfection, satiating the ear
with a richness of melody scarcely anywhere to be sur-

how the legal shadows are outlines of the truth, which as such
disappear and flee away, Christ the substance being come:

> Agnus enim legis carnales diluit actus,
> Agnum præsignans, qui nos lavat hostia factus:
> Quis locus auroræ, postquam sol venit ad ortum?
> Quisve locus votis, teneat quum navita portum?

He sums up in two lines the moral of Luke xiv. 16–24:

> Villa, boves, uxor, cœnam clausere vocatis:
> Mundus, cura, caro, cœlum clausere renatis.

A passing and repassing from one of these arrangements of rhyme
to the other is not uncommon. Thus to quote Hildebert again
(*Opp.* p. 1260), and here, as everywhere, I seek to make citations
which, besides illustrating the matter directly in hand, have
more or less an independent merit of their own:

> Crux non clara parum spoliis spoliavit avarum;
> Crux lætæ sortis victi tenet atria fortis;
> Crux indulcavit laticem, potumque paravit;
> Crux silicem fregit, et aquas exire coëgit.
> Crux per serpentem Crucifixi signa gerentem
> Læsos sanavit, lædentes mortificavit;
> Crux crucis opprobrium, Crux ligni crimen ademit;
> Crux de peccato, Crux nos de morte redemit;
> Crux miseros homines in cœlica jura reduxit;
> Omne bonum nobis cum sanguine de Cruce fluxit.

Or take another example from the *Carmen Parœneticum* ascribed
to St Bernard (*Opp.*, vol. ii. p. 909):

> Amplius in rebus noli sperare caducis,
> Sed tua mens cupiat æternæ gaudia lucis:
> Fallitur insipiens vitæ præsentis amore,
> Sed sapiens noscit quanto sit plena dolore.
> Quidquid formosum mundus gerit et pretiosum
> Floris habet morem, cui dat natura colorem
> Mox ut siccatur, totus color annihilatur;
> Postea nec florem monstrat, nec spirat odorem.

He presently passes back from the leonine to the tail rhymes,
intermingling besides with these a third form, springing from a
combination of the two. The *caudati tripertiti* are divided, as
their name indicates, into three sections, each containing two

passed.   At first the rhymes were often merely vowel
or assonant ones, the consonants not being required to
agree; or the rhyme was adhered to, when this was
convenient, but disregarded, when the needful word was
not readily at hand; or the stress of the rhyme was
suffered to fall on an unaccented syllable, thus scarcely
striking the ear; or it was limited to the similar termination of a single letter; while sometimes, on the
strength of this like ending, as sufficiently sustaining
the melody, the whole other construction of the verse,
and arrangement of the syllables, was neglected.*

feet; the first and second sections in every line rhyme with one
another, and so far they resemble the Leonine; but they are also
tailed, in that the close of one line rhymes with the close of the
succeeding.   I know none of this kind which are not almost too
bad to quote.   Here however is a specimen:

Est data sævam causa per Evam perditionis,
Dum meliores sperat honores voce draconis.

They are curious, however, inasmuch as in these triparted distichs
we trace the rudiments, as F. Wolf has clearly shown (*Ueber die
Lais*, p. 200), of that much employed six-line strophe of our
modern poetry, in which the rhymes are disposed thus, *a a b c c b*,
the stanza which has attained its final glory in Wordsworth's
Ruth; each of the Latin lines falling into three sections, and
thus the couplet expanding into the strophe of six lines.
Besides Wolf's admirable treatise just referred to, there are two
treatises on the rhymed poetry of the middle ages in *Gebaveri
Anthologia Dissertationum*, Lips., 1733; one, p. 265, *Pro
Rhythmis, seu Omoioteleutis Poeticis*; another by Elias Major,
p. 299, *De Versibus Leoninis*.   Sir A. Crooke. in his *Essay on
Rhyming Latin Verse*, has drawn freely on these, but has also
information of his own.

* It may be that they who first used it, were oftentimes
scarcely or not at all conscious of what they were doing.   Thus

The first in whose hymns there are distinct traces of
the adoption of rhyme is Hilary, who died bishop of
Poitiers in 368.   His hymn on the Epiphany,

> **Jesus refulsit omnium**
> **Pius redemptor gentium,**

consists of eight quatrains, the four lines composing
each of which have a like termination, while otherwise
they observe the ordinary laws of the iambic dimeter.
In the hymn of Pope Damasus (who died a very few
years later) on St Agatha, the four lines of the quatrain
do not rhyme all together, but two and two; and the
verses consist, or are intended to consist, of three
dactyls with a terminal rhyming syllable, as thus :

> **Stirpe decens, elegans specie,**
> **Sed magis actibus atque fide,**
> **Terrea prospera nil reputans,**
> **Jussa Dei sibi corde ligans.**

It is true that earlier than either of these is the poem of
Commodianus, referred to already, and that in one
section all the words end in *o*.   This could not be
accidental; yet at the same time, as nothing similar
occurs in other parts of the poem, it must be counted,

Ampère says very beautifully upon the hymns of St Ambrose,
in which he traces such unconscious preludings to the later
rhymed poetry of Christendom: Ces hymnes sont versifiés
d'après la règle de la métrique ancienne, mais il est curieux de
voir une tendance à la rime se produire évidemment dans ces
strophes analogues à celles d'Horace.   Ce qui sera le fondement
de la prosodie des temps modernes, la rime, n'est pas encore une
loi de la versification, et déjà un besoin mystérieux de l'oreille
l'introduit dans les vers pour ainsi dire à l'insu de l'oreille elle
même (*Hist. Litt. de la France*, vol. i. p. 411).

where it does appear, rather as an arbitrary ornament than an essential element, of the rhythm.

Seeing, then, that it thus lies in our power to trace distinctly, and as it were step by step, the rise and growth of the Latin rhymed poetry, to preside at its very birth and cradle,—one cannot but wonder at a very common assertion, namely, that it borrowed rhyme from languages, which assuredly do not now preserve any examples in this kind that are not of far later origin than much which we possess in the Latin tongue. "I know of no poem," says Dr. Guest,* "written in a Gothic dialect with final rhyme, before Otfrid's Evangely. This was written in Frankish, about the year 870." He, it is true, supposes the Latin rhymers to have gotten rhyme from the Celtic races,—among some of whom undoubtedly it existed very early, as among the Welch in the sixth century—and then in their turn to have imparted it to the Gothic nations. But a necessity for this unlikely hypothesis rests only on the assumption, that "the Romans were confessedly ignorant of rhyme." Certainly, if we found it in the Latin poetry suddenly starting up in its final perfection, complete and lacking nothing,—as we do find some of the Greek lyric metres, the complex alcaic, for example, in the pages of Horace, —we could then hardly come to any other conclusion, but that it had been imported *ab extra*, even though we might not be able to say with certainty from what quarter it had been obtained. But everything about its introduction serves rather to mark it as autochthonic.†

---

* *History of English Rhythms*, vol. i. p. 119.

† Ampère has expressed the same conviction. Of the Latin poetry of the eleventh century he says: La tendance à la rime,

We see it in its weak and indistinct beginnings, not yet knowing itself or its own importance; we mark its irregular application at first; the lack of skill in its use, the poor assonances instead of the full consonances; with an only gradual discovery of all which it would effect;—the chimes having been at first, probably, but happy chances, found, like the pointed arch, without having been sought; but which yet, being once lighted on, the instinct of genius did not let go, but adopted and improved, as that very thing which it needed, and unconsciously had been feeling after; and now at length had attained.

But when we thus refuse to admit that the Latin rhyming poetry borrowed its rhyme from the Romance or Gothic languages, we are not therefore obliged to accept the converse, and with Tyrwhitt* and others to assume that *they* obtained it from the Latin, however that might be of the two the more tolerable supposition. For, after the investigations of later years, no one ought any longer to affirm rhyme to have been the exclusive invention of any one people, and from them to have past over into other languages and literatures; which Warton and Sismondi have done, who derive it originally from the Arabs. Rhyme can as little be considered the exclusive discovery of any one people as of any

qui nous avait déjà frappés chez Saint Ambroise, a toujours été, de siècle en siècle, s'accusant plus nettement. Au temps où nous sommes parvenus, elle a fini par triompher. Ce qui n'était d'abord qu'une fantaisie de l'oreille a fini par devenir un besoin impérieux et par se transformer en loi. Il n'est donc pas nécessaire de chercher d'autre origine à la rime; elle est née du sein de la poésie latine dégénerée.

* *Essay on the Language and Versification of Chaucer*, p. 51.

single age. It is rather, like poetry, like music, like dramatic representation, the natural result of a deep craving of the human mind; as it is the well-nigh inevitable adjunct of a poetry not quantitative, being almost certain to make a home for itself therein. This last point has been well expressed, and the causes of it rightly stated by a writer already quoted, and whose words must always carry weight :* "When the same modification of sound recurs at definite intervals, the coincidence very readily strikes the ear, and when it is found in accented syllabies, such syllables fix the attention more strongly than if they merely received the accent. Hence we may perceive the importance of rhyme in accentual verse. It is not, as it is sometimes asserted, a mere ornament: it marks and defines the accent, and thereby strengthens and supports the rhythm. Its advantages have been felt so strongly, that no people have ever adopted an accentual rhythm, without also adopting rhyme."

In this the universality of rhyme, as in the further fact that it is peculiar neither to the rudeness of an early and barbarous age, nor to the over-refined ingenuity of a late and artificial one, but runs through whole literatures from their beginning to their end, we find its best defence ;—or, more accurately, that which exempts it from needing any defence against charges like that brought by Milton against it †; for there is

---

* Guest, *History of English Rhythms*, vol. i. p. 116.

† It will be remembered what he calls it in the few words which he has prefixed to *Paradise Lost*—"the invention of a barbarous age, to set off wretched matter and lame metre; . . . . a thing of itself to all judicious ears trivial and of no true musical delight"—with much more in the same strain.

here the evidence that it lies deep in our human nature, and satisfies an universal need, since otherwise so many people would not have lighted upon it, or having lighted, so inflexibly maintained it. For we do encounter it everywhere—in the extreme West, in the earliest Celtic poems, Welsh and Irish—in the further East, among the Chinese, in the Sanscrit,—and no less in the Persian and Arabic poetry,—in the Gothic and Scandinavian;—no formal discovery, as no borrowed skill, in any case; but in all the well-nigh instinctive result of that craving after periodic recurrence, proportion, limitation,—of that sense out of which all rhythm and all metre springs, namely, that the streams of passion must have banks within which to flow, if they are not to waste and lose themselves altogether,—with the desire to mark and to make distinctly noticeable to the ear these limits and restraints, which the verse, for its own ultimate good, imposes upon itself.* We may

Over against this we might set what I much esteem the wiser words of Daniel in his *Defence of Rhyme*, or indeed more honourably confute him out of his own mouth, and by the fact that the noblest lyrics which English literature possesses, being his own, are rhymed.

* Ewald (*On the Poetic Books of the Old Testament*, vol. i. p. 57) has expressed himself very profoundly on this matter: "A stream of words and images, an overflowing and impetuous diction, a movement which in its first violence seems to know no bounds nor control—such is the earliest manifestation of poetic diction! But a diction which should only continue in this its earliest movement, and hurry onward, without bounds and without measure, would soon destroy its own beauty, even its very life. Yea rather, the more living and overflowing this onward movement is, by so much the more needful the restraint and the limitation, the counteraction and tranquillization, of this becomes.

observe that the prosodic poetry of Greece and Rome was equally obliged to mark this, though it did it in another way. Thus, had dactyles and spondees been allowed to be promiscuously used throughout the hexameter line, no satisfying token would have reached the ear to indicate the close of the verse; and if the hearer had once missed the termination of the line, it would have been almost impossible for him to recover it. But the fixed dactyle and spondee at the end of the line answer the same purpose of strongly marking the close, as does the rhyme in the accentuated verse : and in other metres, in like manner, licenses permitted in the beginning of the line are excluded at its close, the motives for this greater strictness being the same.

The non-recognition of this, man's craving after, and deep delight in, the rhythmic and periodic—a craving which nature everywhere meets and gratifies, and which all truest art seeks to gratify as well,—a seeing nothing in all this but a trick and artifice applied from without,— lies at the root of that singular theory concerning the unfitness of poetry to be the vehicle for our highest addresses to God and most reverent utterances about Him, which the accomplished author of the *Day in the Sanctuary* has put forth in the preface to that volume. Any one who, with at all the skill in versification and command over language which he himself has manifested elsewhere, undertakes to comply with the requirements

This mighty inspiration and exspiration ; this rise with its commensurate fall ; this advance in symmetrical diction, which shall combine rest and motion with one another, and mutually reconcile them ; this is rhythm, or regulated beautiful movement."

which verse imposes, knows that the obligations which he thus assumes are very far from being felt as a bondage, but rather that here, as everywhere else, to move according to law is felt to be the freest movement of all.* Every one, too, who without this peculiar experience has watched the effect on his own mind of the orderly marching of a regiment, or of the successive breaking of waves upon the shore, or of ought else which is thus *rhythmic and periodic*, knows that in this, inspiring as it does the sense of order, and proportion, and purpose, there is ever an elevating and solemnizing power—a truth to which language, the best, because the most unconscious, witness, sets its seal, having in the Latin but one and the same word, for the solemn and the recurring.

I have said above, that we are not bound to assume that the poetrics of modern Europe derived rhyme from the Latin; because we reject the converse proposition, that the Latin derived it from them. At the same time the medieval Latin poetry, without standing in so close a technical relation as this to the modern poetry of Europe, without having been thus the source from which the latter obtained its most characteristic ornament, does yet stand in most true and living relation to it; has exerted upon it an influence which probably

---

* Goethe's noble words, uttered with a larger intention, have yet their application here:

> Vergebens werden ungebundne Geister
> Nach der Vollendung reiner Höhe streben:
> *In der Beschränkung zeigt sich erst der Meister,*
> *Und das Gesetz nur kann uns Freiheit geben.*

has been scarcely estimated as highly as it deserves. To how great an extent must it have acted as a conductor of the thoughts and images of the old world to the new, making the stores of that old world to be again the heritage of the popular mind—stores which would else have been locked up till the more formal revival of learning, then perhaps to become not the possession of the many, but only of the few. How important was the part which it played, filling up spaces that were in a great measure unoccupied by any other works of imagination at all; lending to men an organ and instrument by which to utter their thoughts, when as yet the modern languages of Europe were in the first process of their formation, and quite unfit to be the adequate clothing for these.

Thus the earliest form in which the *Reineke Fuchs,* the great fable-epic of the middle ages, appeared,—the significance of which in European literature, no one capable of forming a judgment on the matter will lightly esteem,—is now acknowledged to have been Latin. A poem in four books, in elegiac metre, whose author is unknown, supplied mediately or immediately the ground-plan to all the subsequent dispositions of the matter. Of course it is not meant hereby to deny the essentially popular character of the poem, or to affirm that the Latin poet invented that, which, no doubt, already lived upon the lips of the people; but only that in this Latin the fable-lore of the German world first took shape, and found a distinct utterance for itself.*

* The existence of such an original was long unsuspected, even after an earnest interest had been awakened in the *Reineke*

And thus, too, out of that dreariest tenth century, that wastest place, as it is rightly esteemed, of European literature and of the human mind, James Grimm has published a brief Latin epic of very high merit;* while Fulbert, bishop of Chartres, who died early in the eleventh (1027), could celebrate the song of the nightingale in strains such as these :

Cum telluris, vere novo, producuntur germina,
Nemorosa circumcirca frondescunt et brachia;
Fragrat odor cum suävis florida per gramina,
Hilarescit Philomela, dulcis sonûs† conscia,
Et extendens modulando gutturis spiramina,
Reddit veris et æstivi temporis præconia.
Instat nocti et diei voce sub dulcisonâ,
Soporatis dans quietem cantûs per discrimina,
Necnon pulcra viatori laboris solatia.
Vocis ejus pulcritudo clarior quàm cithara;
Vincitur omnis cantando volucrum catervula;
Implet sylvas atque cuncta modulis arbustula,
Gloriosa valde facta veris præ lætitiâ.
Volitando scandit alta arborum cacumina,
Ac festiva satis gliscit sibilare carmina.
Cedit auceps ad frondosa resonans umbracula,
Cedit olor et suävis ipsius melodia;
Cedit tibi tympanistra et sonora tibia;
Quamvis enim videaris corpore permodica,
Tamen cuncti capiuntur hác tuâ melodiâ :

Fuchs itself. It was first published by Mone, *Reinhardus Vulpes,* Stuttgart, 1832.

* *Waltharius.* It had been published indeed before; and has since been so by Du Méril, *Poésies popul. Lat.* 1843, p. 313–377.

† *Sonus* re-appears here as of the fourth declension (see Freund's *Lat. Wörterbuch,* s. v.).

Nemo dedit voci tuæ hæc dulcia carmina,
Nisi solus Rex cœlestis qui gubernat omnia.*

Surely with all its rudeness and deficiencies this poem has the true passion of nature, and contains in it the prophecy and pledge of much more than it actually accomplishes.   In that

Gloriosa valde facta veris præ lætitiâ,

we have no weak prelude of that rapturous enthusiasm and inspiration, which at a later day have given us such immortal hymns as the *Ode to the Skylark*, by Shelley.

Or consider these lines of Marbod, bishop of Rheims in the twelfth century; which, stiffly and awkwardly versified as they may be, have yet a deep interest, as touching on those *healing* influences of nature, the sense of which is almost, if not entirely, confined to modern, that is to Christian, art.   They belong to a poem on the coming of the spring; and, as the reader will observe, are in leonine hexameters :

Moribus esse feris prohibet me gratia veris,
Et formam mentis mihi mutuor ex elementis.

----

* *D. Fulberti Opera Varia*, Paris, 1608, p. 181.   I believe we owe to Dr. Neale the following very graceful translation :

" When the earth, with spring returning, vests herself in fresher sheen,
And the glades and leafy thickets are arrayed in living green ;
When a sweeter fragrance breatheth flowery fields and vales along,
Then, triumphant in her gladness, Philomel begins her song :
And with thick delicious warble far and wide her notes she flings,
Telling of the happy spring tide and the joys that summer brings.
In the pauses of men's slumber deep and full she pours her voice,
In the labour of his travel bids the wayfarer rejoice.
Night and day, from bush and greenwood, sweeter than an earthly lyre,
She, unwearied songstress, carols, distancing the feathered choir,
Fills the hillside, fills the valley, bids the groves and thickets ring,
Made indeed exceeding glorious through the joyousness of spring.
None could teach such heavenly music, none implant such tuneful skill,
Save the King of realms celestial, who doth all things as He will."

Ipsi naturæ congratulor, ut puto, jure :
Distinguunt flores diversi mille colores,
Gramineum vellus superinduxit sibi tellus.
Fronde virere nemus et fructificare videmus :
Egrediente rosâ viridaria sunt speciosa.
Qui tot pulcra videt, nisi flectitur et nisi ridet,
Intractabilis est, et in ejus pectore lis est ;
Qui speciem terræ non vult cum laude referre,
Invidet Auctori, cujus subservit honori
Bruma rigens, æstas, auctumnus, veris honestas.*

May we not say that the old monkish poet is anticipating here—and however faintly, yet distinctly—such strains as the great poets of nature in our own day have made to be heard—the conversion of the witch Maimuna in Thalaba, Peter Bell, or those loveliest lines in Coleridge's *Remorse?*

With other ministrations thou, O Nature,
Healest thy wandering and distempered child ;
Thou pourest on him thy soft influences,
Thy sunny hues, fair forms, and breathing sweets,
Thy melodies of woods, and winds, and waters !
Till he relent, and can no more endure
To be a jarring and a dissonant thing
Amid this general dance and minstrelsy :
But bursting into tears wins back his way,
His angry spirit healed and harmonized
By the benignant touch of love and beauty.

Hard measure is for the most part dealt to this poetry.†

* *Hildeberti et Marbodi Opera*, ed. Beaugendre, Paris, 1708, p. 1617.

† Few are so just to it as Bähr (*Die Christl. Dichter Rom's*, p. 10): Wenn wir daher auch nicht unbedingt die Ansicht derjenigen theilen können, welche die Einführung dieser Christlichen Dichter statt der heidnischen in Schulen zum Zwecke des Sprachunterrichts wie zur Bildung eines ächt christlichen Gemüths vorschlagen, aus Gründen, die zu offen da liegen, um weiterer

Men come to it with a taste formed on quite other models, trying it by laws which were not its laws, by the approximation which it makes to a standard which is so far from being its standard, that the nearer it reaches that, the further removed from any true value it is. They come trying the Gothic cathedral by the laws of the Greek temple, and because they do not find in it that which, in its very faithfulness to its own idea, it cannot have, they treat it as worthy only of scorn and contempt. Nor less have they forgotten, in estimating the worth of this poetry, that much which appears trite and commonplace to us was yet very far from being so at its first utterance.* When the Gothic nations which divided the Roman empire began to crave intellectual and spiritual food, in the healthy hunger of their youth there lay the capacity of deriving truest nourishment from that which to us, partly from our far wider range

Ausführung zu bedürfen, die auch nie, selbst in Mittelalter, verkannt worden sind, so glauben wir doch dass es zweckmässig und von wesentlichem Nutzen seyn dürfte den Erzeugnissen christlicher Poesie auch auf unseren höheren Bildungsanstalten eine grössere Aufmerksamkeit zuzuwenden, als diess bisher der Fall war, die Jugend demnach in den obern Classen der Gymnasien und Lyceen mit den vorzüglicheren Erscheinungen dieser Poesie, die ihnen jetzt so ganz fremd ist und bleibt, bekannt zu machen, ja selbst einzelne Stücke solcher Dichtungen in die Chrestomathien Lateinischer Dichter, in denen sie wahrlich, auch von anderen Standpunkten aus betrachtet, eine Stelle neben manchen Productionen der heidnischen Zeit verdienen, aufzunehmen, um so zugleich den lebendigen Gegensatz der heidnischen und christlichen Welt und Poesie erkennen zu lassen, und jugendlichen Gemüthern frühe einzuprägen.

* Ampère (vol. iii. p. 213) says with truth, and on this very matter: Ce qui est peu important pour l'histoire de l'art peut l'être beaucoup pour l'histoire de l'esprit humain.

of choice, and partly also from a satiated appetite, seems little calculated to yield it.*

But considerations of this kind would lead me too far, and lie too wide of the immediate scope of this

* Ferdinand Wolf, in his instructive work, *Ueber die Lais*, p. 281, and James Grimm, have both observed, that a history of this medieval Latin poetry is a book still waiting to be written, and which, when it is written will fill up a huge gap in the literary history of Europe. We have nothing in the kind but Leyser's compendium, *Historia Poëtarum et Poëmatum Medii Ævi*, Halæ, 1721, which would have its use for the future labourer in this field, and which he would find especially serviceable in its copious literary notices; but for a book making, as by its title it does, some claim to completeness, absurdly fragmentary and imperfect — and this, even when is added to it another essay, which Leyser published two years earlier, *Diss. de fictâ Medii Ævi Barbarie, imprimis circa Poësin Latinam*, Helmstadt, 1719. Less complete than even in his own day he might have made it, it is far more deficient now, when so much bearing on the subject has been brought to light, which was then unknown. The volume, too, is as much at fault in what it has, as what it has not — including as it does vast poems of very slightest merits; and from which an extract or two would have sufficed. Edélestand du Méril's two volumes, *Poésies populaires Latines antérieures au douzième Siècle*, Paris, 1843, and *Poésies populaires Latines du Moyen Age*, Paris, 1847, contain many valuable notices, and poems which had not previously, or had only partially or incorrectly, been printed. But, as the titles indicate, they have only to do with the *popular* Latin poetry of the middle ages.—Whoever undertakes such a work, must be one who esteems as the glory of this poetry, and not the shame, that it seeks to emancipate itself, if not always from the forms, yet always from the spirit, of the classical poetry of the old world — desires to stand on its own ground, to grow out of its own root. Indeed no one else would have sufficient love to the subject to induce him to face the labours and wearinesses which it would involve. The later Latin poetry, that which has flourished since

volume, to allow me to follow them further. Already what I thought to put into a few paragraphs has insensibly grown almost into an essay, having from its length some of the pretensions of an essay, with at the same time little that should justify those pretensions. I may not further encroach upon the room which I would reserve for other men's words, rather than pre-

the revival of learning, and which has drawn its inspiration not from the Church, but from ancient classical literature, has found a very careful and enthusiastic historian; but one who, according to my convictions, has begun his work just where all or nearly all of any true value has ended, leaving untouched the whole period which really offers much of any deep or abiding interest. I mean Budik, in his work, *Leben und Wirken der vorzüglichsten Latein. Dichter des XV.—XVIII. Jahrhunderts*, Vienna, 1828. Such, however, was not *his* mind, who could express himself about the Christian middle ages with a fanaticism of contempt, possible some thirty years ago, but hardly so now, when we are in danger rather of exaggerations in the other extreme. He says: " Since the ages of Pericles and Augustus, the perfect creations of which enjoy an everlasting youth, until the middle of the fifteenth century, one sees nothing but a waste, whose dreary and barren uniformity is only broken by some scattered brushwood, and whose most vigorous productions awaken rather astonishment than admiration." For myself, I never so felt the inanity of modern Latin poetry as, when looking over the entire three volumes of Budik (and I have repeated the experiment with much larger collections), I could find no single poem or fragment of a poem which I cared to use, save, indeed, a few lines from Casimir, which I already possessed. It was from no affected preference of the old that my extracts from modern Latin poetry are so few; but three or four is all. If Vida, or Saunazar, or Buchanan, or any other of the moderns, would have offered anything of value, I would gladly have adopted it; but repeatedly seeking for something, I always sought in vain.

occupy with my own : and whatever else might have
been said upon the subject,

spatiis exclusus iniquis

Prætereo.

Nor do I unwillingly conclude with a word from him,
the chiefest in Latin art, for whom our admiration need
not in the least be diminished by our ability to admire
Latin verse, composed on very different principles
from his; and, if possessing, yet needing also, large
compensations, for all which *it* has not, but which he
with his illustrious fellows has; and which must leave,
in so many aspects, the great masterpieces of Greece
and Rome for ever without competitor or peer.

POEMS.

ADAM OF ST VICTOR.

OF the life of Adam of St Victor, the most fertile, and, as I am inclined to believe, the greatest of the Latin hymnologists of the middle ages, very little is known. He was probably a native of Brittany, although the terms *breton*, *brito*, which in the early writers indicate his country, leave in some doubt whether England might not have had the honour of giving him birth. The authors of the *Histoire Littéraire de la France*, vol. xv. p. 40—45, account this not altogether unlikely; and it is certain that this illustrious foundation drew together its scholars from all parts of Europe; thus, of its other two chiefest ornaments, Hugh was a Saxon, and Richard a Scot. Yet the fact that France was the great seat of Latin poetry in the twelfth century, and that all the chief composers in this kind, as Hildebert, the two Bernards, Abelard, Marbod, Peter the Venerable, were Frenchmen, leaves it more likely that he, the chiefest of all, was such as well. At all events he made his studies at Paris, where he entered the religious foundation of St Victor, then in the suburbs, but at a later day included within the walls, of Paris, in which he continued to his death. The year of his death is unknown; the *Gallia Christiana* places it somewhere between 1172 and 1192. Gautier, of whose edition of Adam's hymns I shall have presently to speak, thinks the latter year to be itself the most probable date (vol. i. p. lxxxviii). His epitaph, graven on a plate of copper in the cloister of St Victor, near the door of the choir, remained till the general destruction of the first Revolution. The ten first verses of it, as Gautier has shown, are his own, and constituted an independent poem, which, with the title *De Miseriâ Hominis*, is still to be found among his works. The four last were added by a later hand, so to fit them for an epitaph on their author. His own lines possess a grand moral flow, and are very well worthy to be quoted.

> Hæres peccati, naturâ filius iræ,
>   Exiliique reus nascitur omnis homo.
> Unde superbit homo, cujus conceptio culpa,
>   Nasci pœna, labor vita, necesse mori?
> Vana salus hominis, vanus decor, omnia vana;
>   Inter vana nihil vanius est homine.
> Dum magis alludit præsentis gloria vitæ,
>   Præterit, immo fugit; non fugit, immo perit.
> Post hominem vermis, post vermem fit cinis, heu, heu!
>   Sic redit ad cinerem gloria nostra simul.
>
> Hic ego qui jaceo miser et miserabilis Adam,
>   Unam pro summo munere posco precem:
> Peccavi, fateor, veniam peto, parce fatenti,
>   Parce pater, fratres parcite, parce Deus.

We may certainly conclude that Adam of St Victor shared to the full in the theological culture of the school to which he belonged. This, indeed, is evident from his hymns, which, like the poetry of Dante, have oftentimes as great a theological, as poetical or even devotional interest, the first indeed sometimes predominating to the injury of the last. The aim of that illustrious school of theology, especially in its two foremost representatives, Hugh, and his scholar Richard, of St Victor, the first called in his own day *Lingua Augustini, Alter Augustinus*, and both of them cotemporaries of Adam, though Hugh belonged to an elder generation, was to unite and harmoniously to reconcile the scholastic and mystic tendencies, the light and the warmth, which had appeared more in opposition in Abelard and Bernard: and to this its noble purpose and aim it long remained true: nor would it be easy to exaggerate the influence for good which went forth from this institution during the twelfth and thirteenth centuries upon the whole Church. (See Liebner, *Hugo von St Victor*, p. 9—16.) It long remained faithful to the cultivation of sacred song: for, in later times, Santeuil, a poet, it is true, of a very different rank indeed from him with whom we now have to do, was a Victorine as well.

Very different estimates have been formed of the merits of Adam of St Victor's hymns. His most zealous admirers will hardly deny that he pushes too far, and plays overmuch with, his skill in the typical application of the Old Testament.* So too they must own that sometimes he is unable to fuse with a perfect success his manifold learned allusion into the passion of

---

* Calderon is often, consciously or unconsciously, an imitator of Adam of St Victor's manner—knitting together, as he does, a succession of allusions to Old Testament types, and weaving them

his poetry.　How full of this learned allusion they are,
I have had evidence while preparing this volume, in the
amount of explanatory notes which they required,—so
far larger than almost any other equal quantity of verse
which it contains.　Nor less must it be allowed that he
is sometimes guilty of *concetti*, of plays upon words, not
altogether worthy of the solemnity of his theme.　Thus
of one martyr he says:

> Sub securi stat securus;

of another, St Lawrence namely:

> Dum torretur, non terretur;

———

with more or less success into the woof of a single poem.　This
hymn, drawn from an *Auto* of his, on the Holy Eucharist, will
illustrate what I mean:

> Honey in the lion's mouth,
> Emblem mystical, divine,
> How the sweet and strong combine;
> Cloven rock for Israel's drouth;
> Treasure-house of golden grain,
> By our Joseph laid in store,
> In his brethren's famine sore
> Freely to dispense again;
> Dew on Gideon's snowy fleece;
> Well from bitter changed to sweet;
> Shew-bread laid in order meet,
> Bread whose cost doth ne'er increase
> Though no rain in April fall;
> Horeb's manna, freely given,
> Showered in white dew from heaven,
> Marvellous, angelical;
> Weightiest bunch of Canaan's vine;
> Cake to strengthen and sustain
> Through long days of desert pain:
> Salem's monarch's bread and wine;—
> Thou the antidote shalt be
> Of my sickness and my sin,
> Consolation, medicine,
> Life and Sacrament to me.

of the blessed Virgin, (for he did not escape, as it was
not to be expected that he should, the exaggerations of
his time) :

O dulcis vena veniæ;

of heaven :

O quam beata *curia,*
Quæ *curæ* prorsus nescia.

Sometimes too he is overfond of displaying feats of
skill in versification, of prodigally accumulating, or
curiously interlacing, his rhymes, that he may shew his
perfect mastery of the forms which he is using, and how
little he is confined or trammelled by them.*

These faults it will be seen are indeed most of them
but merits pushed into excess. And even accepting
them as defects, his profound acquaintance with the
whole circle of the theology of his time, and eminently
with its exposition of Scripture,—the abundant and
admirable use, with indeed the drawback already men-
tioned, which he makes of it, delivering as he thus does
his poems from the merely *subjective* cast of those,
beautiful as they are, of St. Bernard—the exquisite
art and variety with which for the most part his verse
is managed and his rhymes disposed—their rich melody
multiplying and ever deepening at the close—the
strength which often he concentrates into a single line†

* Augustine had already shewn him the way to this play of
words. Addressing the sinner as the barren fig-tree of Luke
xiii. 9, he says: " Dilata est securis, noli esse secura;" and
again: "Distulit securim, non dedit securitatem."

† Thus of a Roman governor, who, alternating flatteries with
threats, is seeking to bribe one of the early martyrs from her

—his skill in conducting a story*—and most of all, the evident nearness of the things which he celebrates to his own heart of hearts—all these, and other excellencies, render him, as far as my judgment goes, the foremost among the sacred Latin poets of the middle ages. He may not have any single poem to vie with the austere grandeur of the *Dies Iræ*, nor yet with the tearful passion of the *Stabat Mater*, although concerning the last point there might well be a question ; but then it must not be forgotten that these stand wellnigh alone, in the names of their respective authors, while from his ample treasure-house I shall enrich this volume with a multitude of hymns, all of them of considerable, some of the very highest, merit.   Indeed were I disposed to name any one who might dispute the palm of sacred

---

allegiance to Christ, by the offer of worldly dignities and honours :

Offert multa, spondet plura,
Periturus peritura.

* Thus with what graceful ease his hymn on the martyrdom of St Catharine commences :

Vox sonora nostri chori	Nam perlegit disciplinas
Nostro sonet Conditori,	Sæculares et divinas
Qui disponit omnia ;	In adolescentiâ.
Per quem dimicat imbellis,	
Per quem datur et puellis	Vas electum, vas virtutum,
De viris victoria :	Reputavit sicut lutum
	Bona transitoria :
Per quem plebs Alexandrina	Et reduxit in contemptum
Fœminæ non fœminina	Patris opes, et parentum
Stupuit ingenia ;	Larga patrimonia.
Cum beata Catharina	
Doctos vinceret doctrinâ,	Vasis oleum includens,
Ferrum patientiâ.	Virgo sapiens et prudens,
	Sponso pergit obvia ;
Florem teneri decoris	Ut adventûs ejus horâ
Lectionis et laboris	Præparata sine morâ
Attrivere studia :	Intret ad convivia.

Latin poetry with him it would not be one of these, but
rather Hildebert, Archbishop of Tours.

There are readers who may possibly consider that I
have set the merits of Adam of St Victor too high;
yet fresh from the perusal of his hymn on St Stephen,
or his longer one on the Resurrection, or those on
Pentecost, they will certainly wonder at the taste and
judgment of his countrymen, who could apportion him
no higher praise than the following: A l'égard du
mérite de ses pièces, ce serait outrer l'admiration que
d'adopter sans réserve les éloges qu'on leur a donnés.
Elles étaient bonnes pour le temps, et même les meil-
leurs qu'on eût vues jusqu'alors. Mais il a paru depuis
des modèles en ce genre, qui les ont fait totalement
oublier, et avec lesquelles elles ne peuvent réellement
entrer en comparaison. (*Hist. Litt. de la France*, vol.
xv. p. 41.) Over against this I will set another and a
fairer estimate of the merit of his hymns, the writer,
probably John of Toulouse, (he died in 1659, and was
himself Prior of St Victor,) seizing, as it seems to me,
very happily the character at once learned and ornate,
the "decorated" style, which is so characteristic of
many of them : Valde multas prosas fecit … quæ suc-
cincte et clausulatim progredientes, venusto verborum
matrimonio subtiliter decoratæ, sententiarum flosculis
mirabiliter picturatæ, schemate congruentissimo com-
ponuntur, in quibus et cum interserat prophetias et
figuras, quæ in sensu quem prætendunt videantur
obscurissimæ, tamen sic eas adaptat ad suum proposi-
tum manifeste, ut magis videantur historiam texere
quam figuram (Martene, *Thes. Anecdot.* vol. vi. p. 222).
Rambach calls him, I know not whether very felici-

tously, " the Schiller of the middle ages," Dom Guéranger, le plus grand poète du moyen âge.

Several of the hymns of Adam of St Victor had got
abroad, and were in use at a very early date, probably
during the author's life : but till very lately we were
mainly indebted to the care of Clichtoveus, a theologian
of the first half of the sixteenth century for what larger
acquaintance with them we could obtain.   Among
numerous other works which he composed was the
Elucidatorium Ecclesiasticum, Paris, 1515; Basle, 1517,
1519; Paris, 1540, 1556 (the best edition); Cologne,
1732, and in an abridged form, Venice, 1555: written
for the instruction of the parochial clergy in the meaning of the various offices of the Church.   The book,
which is rather scarce, was till very lately of absolute
necessity for the student of the Christian hymnology,
above all for the student of Adam of St Victor's hymns.
Besides containing grains of gold to be washed from the
sands of a diffuse exposition, it was long a principal
source of the text, and had highest authority therein ;
Clichtoveus having drawn it, as he himself assures us,
from copies of the hymns preserved in the archives of
St Victor itself.   Recent discoveries, however, have
much diminished the importance of this work.   Almost
until the other day it had been taken for granted that
Clichtoveus had published all the hymns of Adam which
were in existence in his time, all therefore which could
be in existence in ours.   No one thought it worth
while to call in question his statement to this effect;
nor, though it was well known that such of the manuscript treasures of the Abbey of St Victor as had
escaped the Revolution were deposited in the Imperial

Library in Paris, to make researches there, and prove whether this was indeed the case. At length, however, the suspicions of the M. Gautier were aroused, mainly by observing that while we possessed hymns of his in honour of some of the obscurest saints, some of the mightiest events of the Christian Year, Christmas for example, were altogether uncelebrated in them; and he resolved to prove whether other hymns, which he was sure must once have existed, might not still be discovered. The search which he instituted was abundantly rewarded; and he has been able to publish an edition of the poetical works of Adam of St Victor (*Œuvres Poétiques d'Adam de S. Victor*, Paris, 1858, 1859), containing one hundred and six hymns, or sixty-nine more than were hitherto ascribed to him. It is true indeed that *all* of these were not unknown before; some were going about the world, but without attribution to their author. Far the larger portion, however, were thus for the first time drawn from their hiding-place of centuries, and not a few of these worthy to take rank with the noblest compositions of Adam himself, or any other among the foremost hymnologists of the mediæval Church. I have enriched this second edition of my book with several of these, the beauty and grandeur of which will, I feel sure, be acknowledged by all competent judges.

I. DE SS. EVANGELISTIS.

JUCUNDARE, plebs fidelis,
  Cujus Pater est in cœlis,
Recolens Ezechielis
Prophetæ præconia :
Est Joannes testis ipsi,   5
Dicens in Apocalypsi,
Vere vidi, vere scripsi
Vera testimonia.

Circa thronum majestatis,
Cum spiritibus beatis,   10
Quatuor diversitatis
Astant animalia.
Formam primum aquilinam,
Et secundum leoninam,
Sed humanam et bovinam   15
Duo gerunt alia.

I. Clichtoveus, *Elucidat. Eccles.* vol. ii. p. 218 ; *Sequentiæ de Tempore,* Argentinæ, 1516, p. 21 ; Corner, *Promptuarium Devotionis,* Viennæ, 1672, p. 346 ; Daniel, *Thes. Hymnol.* vol. ii. p. 84 ; Gautier, *Adam de S. Victor,* vol. ii. p. 425.

5. *testis ipsi*] Cf. Rev. iv. 6—8 with Ezek. i. 4—28; x. 9—22.

6—8. Cf. Rev. xxi. 5 ; xxii. 6.

12. *animalia*] The ζῶα of Rev. iv. 6, &c., are in our Version "beasts ;"—"living creatures" it should have been, as *animalia* in the Vulgate ; and "beast" should have been reserved for the θηρίον of the 13th and later chapters. The distribution made in

Formæ formant figurarum
Formas Evangelistarum,
Quorum imber doctrinarum
Stillat in Ecclesiâ :   20
Hi sunt Marcus et Matthæus,
Lucas, et quem Zebedæus
Pater tibi misit, Deus,
Dum laxaret retia.

---

this hymn of these four to the four Evangelists is St Jerome's, (*Comm. in Ezek* c. 1 ; *Prol. in Matt.* ; *Ep.* 50), is that of St Ambrose (*Prol. in Luc.*), of Gregory the Great (*Hom.* 4 *in Ezek.*; *Mor.* xxxi. 47), and through his influence became the prevailing though not the exclusive one (for Bede has another), during the middle ages. In earlier times there was much fluctuation in the application of the four to the four; and, strangely enough, even the eagle was not by universal consent attributed to St John : Irenæus, the first who makes the application at all, giving the lion to him, and the eagle to St Mark (*Con. Hær.* iii. 2. 8) ; his other two are as in this hymn ; and so Juvencus. Athanasius (*Opp.* vol. ii. p. 155), shifts them in another fashion. Leaving St Matthew untouched, he gives the calf to St Mark, the lion to St Luke, and the eagle to St John. Augustine (*De Cons. Evang.* 1. 7), whom Bede follows, makes yet another transposition. With him the lion belongs to St Matthew, the man to St Mark, the calf and eagle respectively to St Luke and St John. One might be tempted by these variations to dismiss the whole matter as an idle play of the fancy ; and yet there was more than this, and indeed a deep insight into the nature of the Gospels, in the desire which thus manifested itself of claiming for them to be at once four and one, an εὐαγγέλιον τετράμορφον (Irenæus), τετράγωνον (Origen), setting forth in four cardinal aspects, the inexhaustible fulness of the life of Christ. The subject in its artistic aspect is fully treated by Mrs. Jameson, *Poetry of Sacred and Legendary Art*, vol. i. pp. 98—110.

Formam viri dant Matthæo,   25
Quia scripsit sic de Deo,
Sicut descendit ab eo,
Quem plasmavit, homine.
Lucas bos est in figurâ,
Ut præmonstrat in Scripturâ,   30
Hostiarum tangens jura
Legis sub velamine.

Marcus, leo per desertum
Clamans, rugit in apertum,
Iter fiat Deo certum,   35
Mundum cor a crimine.
Sed Joannes, alâ binâ
Caritatis, aquilinâ
Formâ fertur in divina
Puriori lumine.   40

Quatuor describunt isti
Quadriformes actus Christi,
Et figurant, ut audîsti,
Quisque suâ formulâ.
Natus homo declaratur,   45
Vitulus sacrificatur,

25—28. Mat. i. 1—16.

29—32. For explanation of these lines see ver. 37—42 in the next hymn.

37. *alâ binâ*] The love of God, and of our neighbour. Thus H. de S. Victore (*Serm.* 97): Columba sancta Ecclesia est: quæ duas alas habet per dilectionem Dei et proximi, a dextris dilectionem Dei. a sinistris dilectionem proximi.

41, 42. Clichtoveus: Scilicet Matthæus Nativitatem, Lucas Passionem, Marcus Resurrectionem, et Johannes Ascensionem Christi.

Leo mortem deplædatur,
Et ascendit aquila.

Ecce forma bestialis,
Quam scriptura prophetalis   50
Notat; sed materialis
Hæc est impositio.
Currunt rotis, volant alis;
Inest sensus spiritalis;
Rota gressus est æqualis,   55
Ala contemplatio.

Paradisus his rigatur,
Viret, floret, fœcundatur,
His abundat, his lætatur
Quatuor fluminibus: 60
Fons est Christus, hi sunt rivi,
Fons est altus, hi proclivi,
Ut saporem fontis vivi
Ministrent fidelibus.

53—56. *currunt...volant*] Wheels *run on earth*, wings *soar to heaven*. In these symbolic representations of the Evangelists we hear of both; for they now tell of the *earthly* life of the Saviour (*currunt rotis*); they now ascend to the contemplation of the *heavenly* world (*volant alis*). The *gressus æqualis* is the mutual consent of the four; they keep step. But the allusions to the medieval typology in this and the next following hymns are so infinite and complex, that I should exhaust my room long before I had exhausted them. I must be content but to touch on a few, only observing that the key to a multitude of them lies in Gregory the Great's homilies on Ezekiel (*Opp.* vol. i. p. 1183, sqq. Bened. ed.).

57—64. Irenæus, in his famous passage (iii. 11. 8), the foundation of so much which has followed in the same line, does not refer to the four streams of Paradise, as prefiguring the four

Horum rivo debriatis   65
Sitis crescat caritatis,
Ut de fonte pietatis
Satiemur plenius.
Horum trahat nos doctrina
Vitiorum de sentinâ,   70
Sicque ducat ad divina
Ab imo superius.

Evangelists, near as such an application lay to him, and likening as he does the four to the four principal winds, πανταχόθεν πνέοντας τὴν ἀφθαρσίαν, καὶ ἀναζωπυροῦντας τοὺς ἀνθρώπους. Nor does St. Ambrose (*De Paradiso*, c. 3), though finding a mystical meaning in the four streams, find this one. We meet it in Jerome (*Ep. ad Euseb.*): Quemadmodum unus fluvius erat Paradisi, qui in quatuor capita dividitur; ita unica Christi evangelica doctrina per quatuor ministros ad irrigandum et fœcundandum ecclesiæ hortum est distributa; cf. *Prol. in Matt.*; Augustine, *De Civ. Dei*, xiii. 21, and Durandus, *Rational.* vii. 46. The image has passed into the region of Christian Art (Aringhi, vol. i. pp. 181, 183, 195), where we often find in the early mosaics a hill surmounted by a cross, or by a lamb holding a cross, and four streams flowing out in several ways from its sides; in the words of Paulinus of Nola:

Petram superstat Ipse, petra ecclesiæ,
De quâ sonori quatuor fontes meant,
Evangelistæ, viva Christi flumina :

or, as we may express the thought in an English quatrain:

As those four streams that had in Eden birth,
And did the whole world water, four ways going,—
With spiritual freshness fill our thirsty earth
Four streams of grace from one cleft mountain flowing.

Sometimes, as in the magnificent mosaic filling the cupola of St. Mark's, at Venice, the Evangelists appear as four aged men, each with his urn, from which a stream of water flows.

65. *debriatis*] In some editions *ebrietatis*; but thus, plainly in ignorance of there being such a word as *debrio*. It is a mediæval form of *inebrio* (see Du Cange, s. v.); I find it as early as Gregory the Great (*Hom.* 6. *in Ezek.*).

ADAM OF ST VICTOR.

II. DE SS. EVANGELISTIS.

PSALLAT chorus corde mundo,
  Hos attollat, per quos mundo
Sonant Evangelia;
Voce quorum salus fluxit,
Nox recessit, et illuxit   5
Sol illustrans omnia.

Curam agens sui gregis
Pastor bonus, auctor legis,
Quatuor instituit,
Quadri orbis ad medelam;   10
Formam juris et cautelam
Per quos scribi voluit.

II. Clichtoveus, *Elucidat Eccles.* vol. ii. p. 221 ; Daniel, *Ths.
Hymnol.* vol. ii. p. 88 ; Mone, *Hymn. Lat. Med. Ævi*, vol. iii.
p. 130 ; Gautier, *Adam de S. Victor*, vol. ii. p. 417.

1. This first line Gautier reads :
        Plausu chorus lætabundo.

9, 10. Augustine (*De Cons. Evang.* i. 2) : Quatuor Evangelistæ,...ob hoc fortasse quatuor, quoniam quatuor sunt partes
orbis terræ, per cujus universitatem Christi Ecclesiam dilatari
ipso sui numeri sacramento quodammodo declararunt.

11. *cautelam*] A juristic word. Ducange explains it perfectly: *Cautelæ* sunt instrumenta et chartæ, quibus privilegia,
jura, possessiones, etc., asseruntur ; hinc *cautelæ* dicta, quod sint
veluti *cautio* (ἀσφάλισμα) res illas ita se habere.

Circa thema generale
Habet quisque speciale
Stili privilegium ;   15
Quod præsignat in prophetâ
Formâ pictus sub discretâ
Vultus animalium.

Supra cœlos dum conscendit,
Summi Patris comprehendit   20
Natum ante secula ;
Pellens nubem nostræ molis,
Intuetur jubar solis
Joannes in aquilâ.

Est leonis rugientis   25
Marco vultus, resurgentis
Quo claret potentia :
Voce Patris excitatus
Surgit Christus, laureatus
Immortali gloriâ.   30

Os humanum est Matthæi,
In humanâ formâ Dei
Dictantis prosapiam :
Cujus genus sic contexit,
Quod a stirpe David exit   35
Per carnis materiam.

-----

25. *rugientis*] The legend, frequent in the middle ages, and indeed already alluded to by Origen (*Hom.* xvii. *in Gen.* xlix. 9), that the lion's whelps were born dead, and first roused to life on the third day by the roar of their sire, was often contemplated as a natural type of the resurrection : so is it here. The subject will recur in a note on Adam of St Victor's Resurrection hymn, *Zyma vetus expurgatur,* later in this volume.

Ritus bovis Lucæ datur,
In quâ formâ figuratur
Nova Christus hostia :
Arâ crucis mansuëtus   40
Hic mactatur, sicque vetus
Transit observantia.

Paradisi hæc fluenta
Nova pluunt sacramenta,
Quæ descendunt cœlitus.   45
His quadrigis deportatur

---

37. *Ritus*] So Clichtoveus, and this reading has manuscript authority (see Mone); but Daniel, Mone, and Gautier read *rictus*; in favour of which may be urged that it is the rarer word, less likely therefore to find its way into a text to which it did not belong : yet *ritus* seems preferable after all.

40. *Arâ crucis*] Elsewhere he has a beautiful stanza on the cross *as the altar* on which Christ was offered :

Oh, quam felix, quam præclara	Agni sine maculâ,
Fuit hæc salutis ara,	Qui mundavit sæcula
Rubens Agni sanguine,	Ab antiquo crimine !

46. *His quadrigis*] Clichtoveus sees here, but wrongly, an allusion to Zech. vi. : Zacharias vidisse ipse dicit in spiritu quatuor quadrigas egredientes de medio duorum montium, et equos in eis varios, quibus jussum est ut totam terram perambularent : Hæ autem quadrigæ figura sunt SS. quatuor Evangelistarum, quibus Dei cognitio per universum orbem defertur et promulgatur. The traces are very slight among the Fathers of any such application of Zechariah's vision of the four chariots : St Jerome (in loc.) giving a whole series of mystical interpretations of these, does not give this; while elsewhere he makes abundantly plain that the poet is still drawing his imagery from that grand vision of Ezekiel (*Ep.* 50): Matthæus, Marcus, Lucas, et Johannes, *quadriga Domini* et verum Cherubim, per totum corpus oculati sunt, scintillæ emicant, discurrunt fulgura, pedes habent rectos et in sublime tendentes, terga pennata et ubique

Mundo Deus, sublimatur
Istis arca vectibus.

Non est domus ruitura
Hâc subnixa quadraturâ,   50
Hæc est domus Domini :
Gloriemur in hâc domo,
Quâ beate vivit homo
Deo junctus Homini.

---

volitantia.   Tenent se mutuo, sibique perplexi sunt, et quasi rota
in rotâ volvuntur, et pergunt quoquumque eos flatus S. Spiritûs
perduxerit.   Cf. Augustine, *De Cons. Evang.* i. 7 ; and Durandus,
Rationale, vii. 46, who indeed suggests quite another allusion,
namely to Cant. v. 11.

48. *vectibus*] Cf. Exod. xxv. 13—15. The *vectes*, of shittim-
wood overlaid with gold, were the staves which lifted the ark
from the ground.   They passed through the four golden rings at
the four corners of the ark ; and, though being only in fact *two*,
had *four* extremities.   Sometimes these, but oftener the four
golden rings through which they pass, are made symbolic of the
four Evangelists.   Thus Hugh of St Victor: Quatuor annuli, qui
arcæ inhærent, quatuor sunt Evangeliorum libri.   Clichtoveus
unites both : Per hos autem quatuor circulos et vectes illis in-
sertos, quibus deferebatur arca, intelliguntur Evangelistæ,
quorum narratione Christus, arca mystica et spiritualis, in
omnem mundi partem, quantum ad sui notitiam, est delatus.

50. *quadraturâ*] The allusion is to Rev. xxi. 16. The house
stands firm which stands on a foursquare foundation: in this
shape is the greatest strength and stability of all. See the symbolic use of the λίθος τετράγωνος in the *Tabula* of Cebes, c. 18.
Even so the fourfold history of the Lord's life, the εὐαγγέλιον
τετράγωνον, is the strong foundation on which the faith of the
Church reposes.   Thus Durandus (*Rational.* vii. 46): Sicut enim
inter cæteras formas quadratum, sic inter cæteras doctrinas Evangelium solidius et stabilius perseverat ; nam illud undique
stat, et ideo legitur (Apocal. c. 21) quod civitas in quadro posita
est.

ADAM OF ST VICTOR.

III. DE S. JOANNE EVANGELISTA.

VERBI vere substantivi,
    Caro cum sit in declivi
Temporis angustiâ,
In æternis verbum annis
Permanere nos Johannis   5
Docet theologia.

Dum Magistri super pectus
Fontem haurit intellectûs,
Et doctrinæ flumina,
Fiunt, ipso situ loci,   · 10

III. Gautier, *Adam de S. Victor*, vol. i. p. 241. This grand
poem, a noble addition to our Latin hymnal, was by him published for the first time.

1—6. I cannot but think that Dr Neale, to whom we are indebted for a translation of this hymn (*Mediæval Hymns.* 1863,
p. 125), has failed to seize the true meaning of this first stanza.
He renders it thus :

> That substantive Word, united
> To the flesh, and therein plighted
> To a life of misery sore,
> Him to be the Co-eternal,
> John's theology supernal
> Testifieth evermore.

By *caro* he understands that flesh which the Word assumed at
the Incarnation, and the contrast which the poet, so understood,
would find taught in the theology of St John is that between

Verbo fides, auris voci,
Mens Deo contermina.

Unde mentis per excessus,
Carnis, sensûs super gressus,
Errorumque nubila,   15
Contra veri solis lumen
Visum cordis et acumen
Figit velut aquila.

Verbum quod non potest dici,
Quod virtute creatrici   20
Cuncta fecit valde bona,
Iste dicit ab æterni
Patris nexu non secerni
Nisi tantum in personâ.

Quem Matthæus de intactæ   25
Matris alit casto lacte

Christ's human nature and his divine. But what then is made of
the *verbum Verbi* of the original, not to speak of other objections?
I take the passage altogether differently, and find a key to its
meaning at 1 John ii. 16, 17 ; John xii. 48 ; cf. 1 Pet. i.
24, 25; understanding the poet to say as follows : The theology of John teaches us that while the flesh (that is, all which
is in the world and of the world), declines, wastes, and decays, the
word of the Word (*verbum Verbi*), all which Christ utters, en-
dures for everlasting years, shall never pass away.

12. *Mentis per excessus*]. Cf. Rev. i. 10, 19—48. The poet
urges that the *theology*, properly so called, belongs to St John.
The other Evangelists set forth Christ's earthly ministry of labour
and toil and passion ; St John rather the relation of Him, the
creative Word, to the Father (John i. 3 ; Gen. i. 1), and his return, at
the end of time, *cum ultrici framed* (ver. 48)—these last words
containing an allusion to that sublimest of all visions, Rev. xix.
11—16.

Cum labore et ærumnâ,
Quem exaltat super cruce
Cornu bovis, penna Lucæ,
Ut serpentem in columnâ ;   30

Quem de mortis mausoleo
Vitæ reddit Marci leo,
Scissis petris, terrâ motâ,
Hunc de Deo Deum verum,
Alpha et Ω, patrem rerum   35
Solers scribit idiota.

Cujus lumen visuale
Vultus anceps, leves alæ,
Rotæ stantes in quadrigâ,
Sunt in cœlo visa, prius   40
Quam hic esset vel illius
Forma capax, vel auriga.

---

36. *idiota*]. A reference to Acts iv. 15, where Peter and John are described as homines sine litteris et *idiotæ* (Vulg.).

37—42. A difficult stanza. Gautier, who is prodigal of unneeded help, gives not a word of assistance here. The first three lines contain no serious difficulty, or at any rate none which an accurate study of Ezekiel, chap. i. and x. will not remove. Thus we can explain *lumen visuale* by aid of Ezek. i. 18 ; x. 12 (Macarius calling the living creatures of the prophet ὀλοφθάλμα ζᾶα); the *vultus anceps* by Ezek. i. 6, 10; the *leves alæ* by i. 6, 9 : and the *rotæ stantes* by i. 21. But what is exactly the force of the last three lines is harder to say. I take however Adam to mean that St John's eagle glance (*lumen visuale*), with all else ascribed to him here, was seen in heaven, anticipated in Ezekiel's vision, before John himself, or his Lord, the charioteer (*auriga*) of that wondrous chariot which John, with the other "living creatures," upbore, took form and shape on earth.

Illi scribunt Christum pati
Dolum, inde vim Pilati,
Cum coronâ spineâ.   45
Hic sublimis tractu pennæ
Tractat Christi jus perenne
Cum ultrici frameâ.

Pennis hujus idiotæ
Elevantur regis rotæ,   50
Secus animalia ;
Et cœlestes citharœdi
Se prosternunt Patris sedi
Canentes, Alleluia.

49, 50. Cf. Ezek. i. 19 : Cumque ambularent animalia,
ambulabant pariter et rotæ juxta ea, et cum elevarentur animalia de terrâ, elevabantur simul et rotæ (Vulg.).

IV. DE S. JOANNE EVANGELISTA.

VERBUM Dei, Deo natum,
  Quod nec factum, nec creatum,
Venit de cœlestibus,
Hoc vidit, hoc attrectavit,
Hoc de cœlo reseravit   5
Joannes hominibus.

Inter illos primitivos
Veros veri fontis rivos

IV. *Sequentiæ de Tempore,* Argentinæ, 1516, p. 2 ; Clichtoveus, *Elucidat. Eccles.* Paris, 1556, p. 213 (not in the earlier
editions); Rambach, *Anthol. Christl. Gesänge,* Altona u. Leip-
zig, 1817, p. 340; Daniel, *Thes. Hymn.* vol. ii. p. 166; Mone,
Hymni Lat. Med. Ævi, vol. iii. p. 118.—This sublime hymn,
though not Adam of St Victor's, proceeds from one formed in
his school, and on his model, and is altogether worthy of him.
It is, indeed, to my mind grander than his own, which has just
preceded it.   Daniel ascribes it to the thirteenth or fourteenth
century, but has nothing certain to say about its authorship.

4—6. Cf. 1 Joh. i. 1.

6. It is seldom that we meet in Christian sapphics so fine a
stanza as this, which occurs in a hymn of Damiani's to St John :
and which may here be brought into comparison :

> Fonte prorumpens fluvius perenni
> Curris, arentis satiator orbis ;
> Hausit ex pleno modo quod propinat
> Pectore pectus.

7—9. See note on no. I. 57—64.

Joannes exsiliit;
Toti mundo propinare   10
Nectar illud salutare,
Quod de throno prodiit.

Cœlum transit, veri rotam
Solis vidit, ibi totam
Mentis figens aciem ;   15
Speculator spiritalis
Quasi Seraphim sub alis
Dei vidit faciem.

12. *de throno*] Cf. Rev. xxii. 1.

13. *Cœlum transit*] Ambrose (*Prol. in Exp. in Luc.* c. 3):
Nemo enim, audeo dicere, tantâ sublimitate sapientiæ majestatem
Dei vidit, et nobis proprio sermone reseravit. Transcendit nubes,
transcendit virtutes cœlorum, transcendit angelos, et *Verbum in
principio* reperit, et *Verbum apud Deum* vidit.

15. *figens aciem*] Augustine (*In Joh., Tract.* 36): Aquila
ipse est Johannes, sublimium prædicator, et lucis internæ atque
æternæ fixis oculis contemplator. Dicuntur enim et pulli aqui-
larum a parentibus sic probari, patris scilicet ungue suspendi,
et radiis solis opponi ; qui firme contemplatus fuerit, filius agno-
scitur; si acie palpitaverit, tanquam adulterinus ab ungue di-
mittitur.

17, 18. These verses can only be fully understood by reference
to Isai. vi. 2 (Vulg.), where "with twain he covered his face,"
i. e. the seraphim with two wings covered their (own) face, (faciem
suam, as it should have been), is given: Duabus velabant faciem
ejus, i.e. Domini. This was referred to the obscure vision of
God vouchsafed under the Old Covenant, so that even prophets
saw but δι' ἐσόπτρου, ἐν αἰνίγματι: the wings of the seraphim
being as a veil between God and them. Thus H. de S. Victore
(*De Arcû Mor.* i. 3): Quod autem in Esaiâ scriptum est, Velabant faciem ejus, eo modo intelligi debet, quo dictum est ad
Moysem: Non poteris videre faciem meam: non enim videbit
me homo, et vivet. But St John, the poet would say, looking

Audiit in gyro sedis
Quid psallant cum citharœdis 20
Quater seni proceres:
De sigillo Trinitatis
Nostræ nummo civitatis
Impressit characteres.

Volat avis sine metâ 25
Quo nec vates nec propheta
Evolavit altius:
Tam implenda, quam impleta,
Nunquam vidit tot secreta
Purus homo purius. 30

Sponsus rubrâ veste tectus,
Visus, sed non intellectus,

---

beneath these covering wings (*seraphim sub alis*) saw the unveiled glory of God. A passage in St Bernard (*Opp.* 1, 955.
Bened. ed.) shews that even in the middle ages they were aware
suam would have been a more accurate translation.

19—21. Cf. Rev. iv. 4; xiv. 2.—22—24. I said in the first
edition, that by the "money of our city" we must understand
the mind of man. This, as I am now convinced, was a mistake.
Language is the money by aid of which the moral and intellectual business of the world is carried on between man and man.
On this St John set his stamp. Thus the Greek Logos, our
English "Word," since they have past under his hands, mean
something quite else, and something far higher and deeper.
than they ever did, before he put a heavenly stamp, the *sigillum*
Trinitatis, upon them.

25—30. *Volat avis*] Olshausen has taken this stanza, than
which sacred Latin poetry does not possess a grander, as the
motto of his *Commentary on St John*. The *implenda* are the
Apocalypse, the *impleta* the Gospel.

31. Cf. Isai. lxiii. 1—3; Rev. xix. 11.

32. *non intellectus*] Cf. Isai. liii. 2—4.

> Redit ad palatium :
> Aquilam Ezechielis
> Sponsæ misit, quæ de cœlis   35
> Referret mysterium.
>
> Dic, dilecte, de Dilecto,
> Qualis adsit, et de lecto
> Sponsi sponsæ nuncia :
> Dic quis cibus angelorum,   40

---

34. *Aquilam Ezechielis*] Cf. Ezek. i. 10 ; Rev. iv. 7.

38, 39. So Clichtoveus ; but Daniel and Mone :

> Qualis sit, et ex dilecto
> Sponsus sponsæ nuncia :

But, not to say that, so read, the lines yield no tolerable sense, the reading violates the laws of rhyme which the Latin medieval poets observe. They allow themselves, it is true, greater freedom than we do : with us a syllable may not rhyme with itself, even when in the second line it belongs to an entirely different word from that to which it belonged in the first. Thus *vine* and *divine* are faulty as rhymes, though many—Spenser in particular— frequently admit them. But the medieval Latin poets, permitting rhymes such as these, so that a word may even rhyme with itself, if different senses be attached to it, as *mundus* the world, with *mundus* clean ; yet would not rhyme *mundus* to itself, the word in both places signifying the world. And rightly : such rhymes contradicting the fundamental idea of rhyme, which is that of likeness *with difference*—difference, if possible, in the sound, since that is the region in which rhyme moves ; but if not there, at least in the sense. Moreover the mystics had much to say of the *lectus Domini*, the deep rest and joy of perfected souls in innermost communion with their Lord ; deriving, as is needless to observe, the image from the Canticles.

40. *cibus angelorum*] Allusion to the Incarnation was often found in the words of the Psalmist (lxxviii. 25), "Man did eat angels' food." The Eternal Word, from the beginning the food of angels, in the Incarnation became also the food of men. Thus Augustine (*In Ep. Joh. Tract.* 1): Erat enim [Vita] ab initio;

Quæ sint festa superorum
De Sponsi præsentiâ.

Veri panem intellectûs,
Cœnam Christi super pectus
Christi sumptam resera: 45
Ut cantemus de Patrono,
Coram Agno, coram throno,
Laudes super æthera.

---

sed non erat manifestata hominibus; manifestata autem erat angelis videntibus, et tanquam pane suo cibantibus. Sed quid ait Scriptura? Panem angelorum manducavit homo. Ergo manifestata est ipsa Vita in carne. So too Hildebert:

> Quam felix Panis, caro felix, hostia dives,
> In terris homines, qui pascit in æthere cives.

And Damiani yields a fine stanza here:

> En illa felix aquila   Quæ cœli cives vegetat,
> Ad escam volat avida,   Et nos in viâ recreat.

44, 45. That he who was named ἐπιστήθιος, drew, from his greater nearness to that bosom (John xiii. 23), the deeper depths of his wisdom, has been often urged. Thus, to rescue the best lines from a poem otherwise of no eminent merit:

> Hic, cujus alæ virtutum scalæ,   Præminens scientiæ,
> Horâ cœnæ hausit plene   Figens visum non elisum
> Meæ fontem gratiæ;   In me, Solem gloriæ.
> Ales alis spiritalis

46. *Patrono*] Led away by this word, Clichtoveus will have it, that the end to which the enraptured poet aspires is, that he may sing the praises of St John before the throne and the Lamb! A reference to Rev. v. 9 should have taught him better. That *Patronus* may be used of a divine Person the following quotation makes abundantly plain (*Hymn. de Temp.* Argent. p. 25):

> Præsta, Pater et Patrone,
> Præsta Fili, Pastor bone,
> Præsta, Spiritus amborum,
> Medicinam peccatorum.

V. LAUS S. SCRIPTURÆ.

STRINGERE pauca libet bona carminis hujus, et ipsum

    Laude vel exili magnificare libet.

Hic ea triticea est pannisque allata farina

    Hebræo populo de Pharaonis humo.

Hic illud missum de cœlo manna saporum.   5

    Omnem gustanti qui sapit ore cibum:

Ut brevius curram per singula; præminet auro

    In pretio; soli luce; sapore favo.

Hic facit humano generi quod sol facit orbi;

    Sol terræ lucet; luce cor ipse replet.   10

Fons est hortorum, puteus vel abyssus aquarum,

    Quarum potus alit pectora, corda rigat.

V. Leyser, *Hist. Poett. Med. Ævi*, p. 748.—It is the *Aurora*, a *metrical* version of the larger part of Holy Scripture, which, as Leyser informs us, the anonymous author of this poem has immediately in his eye. This is the explanation of the *carminis* in the first line, which would not otherwise be intelligible. He passes, however, at once from it to the praise of Scripture itself.

3, 4. Cf. Exod. xii. 34.

5, 6. The Jewish legend, that the manna tasted to every man like that which he liked the best, is well known (Wisd. xvi. 21). Even such heavenly manna, meeting every man's desires, is Scripture. Gregory the Great (*Mor.* xxxi. 15): Manna quippe est verbum Dei, et quidquid bene voluntas suscipientis appetit, hoc profecto in ore comedentis sapit.

11. *Fons . . . puteus*] The words of Cant. iv. 15 (Vulg.): Fons hortorum; puteus aquarum viventium, quæ fluunt impetu

Pascua cœlestis, cellaria regia, cœlum
   Tot signis fulgens quot sacramenta tegens.
Hic calamus Scribæ subito scribentis; hic arcus, 15
   Qui curativo vulnere corda ferit.
Hic rota sive rotæ, quarum ut mare visio mira,
   In medioque rotæ fertur inesse rota.

---

de Libano; were applied to Scripture, a fountain for its abundance, a well for its depth. Thus a mystical expositor of the Canticles (*Bernardi Opp.* vol. ii. p. 125): Accipiamus in fonte sufficientiam doctrinæ, in puteo secretum: in illo abundantiam, in isto alta mysteria.

13. *cellaria regia*] Cf. Cant. i. 3 (Vulg.): Introduxit me rex in cellaria sua. For the sense in which Scripture is thus the king's cellar, see St Bernard, *In Cant. Serm.* 23.

15. The old exposition of Ps. xlv. 2, namely, that the Holy Spirit was "the ready writer," and that the Psalmist would say his tongue did but utter, and his hand set down, that which was suggested by that Spirit, must explain this line. The poet transfers to all Scripture what had been spoken of a single Psalm.

Ibid. *arcus*] Gregory the Great, speaking of the different uses of the word "bow" in Scripture, observes (*Mor.* xix. 30): Aliquando autem per arcum etiam Sacra Scriptura signatur. Ipsa quippe arcus est Ecclesiæ, ipsa arcus est Domini, de qua ad corda hominum, sicut ferientes sagittæ, sic terrentes sententiæ veniunt.

17. *Hic rota sive rotæ*] Cf. Ezek. i. 15, 16. At ver. 15, the prophet sees "*one* wheel;" apparuit *rota una* (Vulg.), while immediately in the next verse it is said, Et aspectus *rotarum* quasi visio maris. The wheel or wheels is Holy Scripture; and the wheel within wheel, of which the same verse presently speaks (quasi sit rota in medio rotæ), is the New Testament; which is contained and shut up in the Old. Gregory the Great (*Hom.* 6 *in Ezek.*): Rota ergo in medio rotæ est; quia inest Testamento Veteri Testamentum Novum. Quod Testamentum Vetus promisit, hoc Novum exhibuit; et quod

Quatuor his facies, species est una : levantur,
    Stant, vel eunt, prout has Spiritus intro regit.   20
Hic liber in dextrâ regnantis scriptus et intus
    Et foris; intus habens mystica, plana foris.
Hic Moysi facies, quæ velo tecta, videri
    Non valet; at Christi luce retecta patet.
Per Moysen typico, per Christum sanguine vero   25
    Hic liber aspersus, remque typumque gerit.
Lex nova, res; antiqua, typus: diffusior illa,
    Hæc brevior: retegit ista, quod illa tegit.

---

illud occulte annunciat, hoc istud exhibitum aperte clamat.
Prophetia ergo Testamenti Novi, Testamentum Vetus est; et
expositio Testamenti Veteris, Testamentum Novum. Cf. Anselm,
Dial. Christ. et Jud. iii. p. 539.—*Quarum ut mare visio mira*]
Et aspectus rotarum et opus earum, quasi visio maris; (Ezek.
i. 16, Vulg.) on which Gregory the Great (*ibid.*): Recte sacra
eloquia visioni maris similia narrantur, quia in eis magna sunt
volumina sententiarum, cumuli sensuum. These words have
nothing answering to them in our text, or in the Hebrew.

19. *Quatuor . . . una*] Gregory the Great (*ibid.*): Rota
quatuor facies habere describitur [Ezek. i. 15], quia Scriptura
Sacra per utraque Testamenta in quatuor partibus est distincta.
Vetus enim Testamentum in Lege et Prophetis, Novum vero in
Evangeliis atque Apostolorum Actibus et Dictis. Una similitudo
ipsarum est quatuor (Ezek. i. 16), quia divina eloquia, etsi
temporibus distincta, sunt tamen sensibus unita.

21, 22. *intus et foris*]   Richard of St Victor (*In Apoc.* v. 1):
Liber qui in dexterâ Dei tenetur, est Sacra Scriptura. Intus
scriptus est per spiritualem intelligentiam, foris per literam. Cf.
Gregory the Great, *Hom. 9 in Ezek.* § 30.

23, 24. Cf. Exod. xxxiv. 33; 2 Cor. iii. 13–16.

25, 26. Cf. Exod. xxiv. 8; Heb. ix. 19. There is no mention,
as is well known, in the former passage, of a sprinkling *of the
book* with blood.

28. *retegit*] The lengthening of the last syllable of *retegit*

Dumque rei testis typus exstat, abyssus abyssum
    Invocat. Utraque lex nomen abyssus habet. 30
Sic brevitate libri geminæ clauduntur abyssi;
    Utraque magna nimis, nullus utramque capit.
Jugiter hic legem meditari, inquirere, nosse,
    Quid nisi cœlesti luce ciboque frui?
Nil homini melius, quam si divina legendo 35
    Figat ibi vitam, quo sibi vita venit.
Felix qui sitit hæc, et eodem fonte saporem
    Attrahit, ut vitam condiat inde suam.
Nam nisi sic sapiat, sapientem non puto, quando
    Nil sibi, quod didicit codice, corde sapit. 40
Qui studet his, vel propter opes vel propter honores,
    Non sapit; it prorsus a sapiente procul.
Non nisi propter se vult se Sapientia quæri;
    Qui colit hanc, audi, quæ metit inde bona.
Purior affectus, sensus fit clarior, et mens 45
    Liberior mundo, carneque pressa minus.
Lectio jugis alit virtutes, lucida reddit
    Intima, declinat noxia, vana fugat.

---

here, by the force of the arsis and on the strength of the two
moræ which must here be made, is not without its parallels
among the best writers of elegiac verse. It was another sign of
the way in which accent was penetrating into the domain of
quantity, that the later Latin poets, most of all the medieval,
assumed the entirest liberty of making short a long syllable—
even a short vowel—at this place, whenever it was convenient
to them. They used the same freedom with the hexameter,
where, when the cæsura occurred immediately after the arsis in
the third foot, the syllable on which the pause thus fell, was
always, and on this ground alone, considered long. The reader
will find examples of both kinds in this volume, and should not
regard them as neglects or ignorances, but as parts of a system.

ST AMBROSE.

ST AMBROSE, born about 340, and probably at Treves, was intended by his father, who was prefect of Gaul, for a secular career. He practised as an advocate at Milan; and was already far advanced on the way to the highest honours and offices of the state, having been appointed about 370 Consular Prefect of Liguria, when it became plain that for him other and more lasting honours were in store. For, having won the affections alike of Catholics and Arians by the mildness and justice of his rule, on the death of Auxentius, bishop of Milan, A.D. 374, he was chosen as by a sudden inspiration, and under circumstances which are too well known to need being repeated, his successor, being as yet only a layman and unbaptized. He died in 397.

The hymns which are current under the name of *Ambrosian* are very numerous, yet are not all his; the name having been freely given to as many as were formed after the model and pattern of those which he composed, and to some in every way unworthy of him. The Benedictine editors do not admit more than twelve as with any certainty of his composition: and even these some in later times have affirmed to be " ascribed to him upon doubtful authority; " so the *Dictionary of Greek and Roman Biography;* although no evidence can well be stronger than that which in regard of some of them we possess.*

After being accustomed to the softer and richer strains of the later Christian poets, to the more ornamented style of a Bernard or an Adam of St Victor—to the passionate sinking of himself in the great objects which he contemplates, that marks the first of these great poets of the Cross—to the melodies long drawn out and the abundant theological lore of the second,—it is some little while before one returns with a hearty consent and liking to the almost austere simplicity which characterizes the hymns of St Ambrose. It is felt as though there were a certain coldness in them, an *aloofness* of the author from his subject, a refusal to blend and fuse himself with it. The absence too of rhyme, for which the almost uniform use of a metre, very far from the richest among the Latin lyric forms, and with singularly few resources for producing variety of pause or cadence, seems a very insufficient compensation, adds to this feeling of disappointment. The ear and

---

* This evidence is well brought together by Cardinal Thomasius in a preliminary discourse, *Ad Lectorem* (unpaged), prefixed to the *Hymnarium*, in the second volume of his *Works* (*J. M. Thomasii, S. R. E., Cardinalis, Opera Omnia*, Romæ, 1747, vol. ii. p. 351—434). This book, of rare occurrence in England, is important in fixing the text, especially of the earlier hymns. The Cardinal's position gave him access to the oldest Vatican and other Italian MSS., of all which he made diligent and careful use. Ex illo libro, says Daniel, tanquam fonte primario hauriendum est. For an estimate of St Ambrose's merits in promoting the new Christian psalmody, see Rambach, *Anthol. Christl. Gesänge*, vol. i. p. 58—60.

the heart seem alike to be without their due satisfaction.

Only after a while does one learn to feel the grandeur
of this unadorned metre, and the profound, though it
may have been more instinctive than conscious, wisdom
of the poet in choosing it; or to appreciate that confidence in the surpassing interest of his theme, which has
rendered him indifferent to any but its simplest setting
forth. It is as though, building an altar to the living
God, he would observe the Levitical precept, and rear
it of unhewn stones, upon which no tool had been lifted.
The great objects of faith in their simplest expression
are felt by him so sufficient to stir all the deepest affections of the heart, that any attempt to dress them up, to
array them in moving language, were merely superfluous. The passion is there, but it is latent and
represt, a fire burning inwardly, the glow of an austere
enthusiasm, which reveals itself indeed, but not to every
careless beholder. Nor.do we fail presently to observe
how truly these poems belonged to their time and to
the circumstances under which they were produced—
how suitably the faith which was in actual conflict
with, and was just triumphing over, the powers of this
world, found its utterance in hymns such as these,
wherein is no softness, perhaps little tenderness; but
in place of these a rock-like firmness, the old Roman
stoicism transmuted and glorified into that nobler Christian courage, which encountered and at length overcame
the world.

VI. DE ADVENTU DOMINI.

VENI, Redemptor gentium,
   Ostende partum Virginis;
Miretur omne sæculum :
Talis decet partus Deum.

Non ex virili semine,   5
Sed mystico spiramine,
Verbum Dei factum est caro,
Fructusque ventris floruit.

Alvus tumescit Virginis,
Claustrum pudoris permanet,   10
Vexilla virtutum micant,
Versatur in templo Deus.

VI. *S. Ambrosii Opp.* Paris, 1836, vol. iv. p. 201 ; *Card. Thomasii Opp.* Romæ, 1747, vol. ii. p. 351 ; Mone, *Hymn. Lat. Med. Ævi*, vol. i. p. 42. The German hymn-book is indebted to this immortal hymn of St Ambrose for one of its choicest treasures—I mean John Frank's Advent hymn, commencing:

> Komm, Heidenheiland, Lösegeld,
> Komm, schönste Sonne dieser Welt,
> Lass abwärts flammen deinen Schein,
> Denn so will Gott geboren sein.

It is not a translation, but a free recomposition of the original, beside which it is wellnigh worthy to stand, even though we may not count it, as Bunsen does, noch tiefer und lieblicher als das Lateinische.

> Procedit e thalamo suo,
> Pudoris aulâ regiâ,
> Geminæ Gigas substantiæ,　　　15
> Alacris ut currat viam.

---

13. So Thomasius, on good MS. authority. The line is oftener read, *Procedens de thalamo suo*, which is quite inadmissible, no single instance in the genuine hymns of St Ambrose occurring of a line beginning with two spondees; invariably the second foot is an iambic. *Talis partus decet Deum*, which Daniel prints as the fourth line of this present hymn, is a transposition of words of which the older MSS. know nothing.

15. *Gigas*] The "giants" of Gen. vi. 4, were, according to the interpretation of the early Church, *geminæ substantiæ;* the "sons of God" who begot them (ver. 2) being angels, who formed unions with the "daughters of men." This scripture, so understood, must be brought into connexion with Ps. xviii. 6, (Vulg.), xix. 5 (E. V.), before we can enter into the full meaning of this line. In the "double substance" of the giants, thus born of heaven and of earth, Ambrose sees a resemblance .to Him who in like manner was of twofold nature, divine and human. He might hardly have dared trace an analogy, but for the words of the Psalmist, referred to above, in which he saw an undoubted reference to the earthly course of the Lord. Elsewhere (*De Incarn. Dom.* c. 5) he unfolds his meaning at full: Quem [Christum] quasi gigantem Sanctus David propheta describit, eo quod biformis geminæque naturæ unus sit consors divinitatis et corporis: qui tanquam sponsus procedens de thalamo suo exsultavit tanquam gigas ad currendam viam. Sponsus animæ secundum Verbum: gigas terræ, quia usûs nostri officia percurrens, cum Deus semper esset æternus, Incarnationis sacramenta suscepit. Thus too in another hymn he sings:

> Processit aulâ Virginis,
> Suæ Gigas Ecclesiæ.

And Adam of St Victor, in a Christmas hymn:

> Gigas velox, gigas fortis,　　　Ad currendam venit viam,
> Gigas nostræ victor mortis,　　Complens in se prophetiam
> Accinctus potentiâ,　　　　　　Et legis mysteria.

Egressus ejus a Patre,
Regressus ejus ad Patrem,
Excursus usque ad inferos,
Recursus ad sedem Dei.   20

Æqualis æterno Patri,
Carnis tropæo cingere,
Infirma nostri corporis
Virtute firmans perpeti.

17—20. He still draws his imagery from the 18th Psalm
(19th, E. V.). It is written there of the sun: A summo cœlo
egressio ejus: et occursus ejus usque ad summum ejus (Vulg.).
This he adapts to Him who said concerning Himself: Exivi a
Patre, et veni in mundum: iterum relinquo mundum et vado ad
Patrem (John xvi. 28); who was acquainted with the deepest
depths of humiliation, and afterwards with the highest heights
of glory. In one of Augustine's *Sermons* (372, 3) he quotes this
stanza as having just been sung in the Church: Hunc nostri
Gigantis excursum brevissime ac pulcherrime cecinit beatus
Ambrosius in hymno quem paulo ante cantâstis.

22. *tropæo*] I preferred *stropheo* (*strophium* or *stropheum*
=στρόφιον) in the first edition; and defended the reading, though
supported by inferior MS. authority, at some length; but erro-
neously, I am now convinced, and from insufficient acquaintance
with the language of the Fathers. For them the risen flesh of
Christ is constantly a *tropæum* which He erected in witness of
his completed victory over death, and him that had the power of
death; a τρόπαιον κατὰ δαιμόνων, with reference to the heathen
custom of claiming and celebrating a victory by the erection of
a τρόπαιον κατ' ἐχθρῶν. Thus Clichtoveus: Christus per carnem
assumptam debellato diabolo victor evasit, ipsamque glorificatam
carnem tandem cœlo intulit.

Ibid. *cingere*] This is commonly read *accingere*; but Mone,
after Thomasius and the best MSS., as in the text. What, however, Mone means, when he remarks here, Ambrosius braucht

> Præsepe jam fulget tuum,   25
> Lumenque nox spirat novum,
> Quod nulla nox interpolet,
> Fideque jugi luceat.

----

mauchmal *den Infinitiv* mit dem Particip wie die Griechen den Aorist, nämlich als historischen Aorist, it is difficult to guess. He cau hardly take *cingere* as the infinitive active. What I understand St Ambrose to say is this: "Equal to the Eternal Father, Thou clothest Thyself with the trophy of redeemed flesh, so strengthening with everlastiug strength the infirmities of our body."

25. *fulget*] Thus in the *Evangel. Infant.* ch. 3, some enter the cave where the new-born child is laid,—et ecce repleta erat illa luminibus, lucernarum et candelarum fulgoribus excedentibus, et solari luce majoribus.

27. *nox interpolet*] Gregory the Great (*Moral.* iv. 6): Antiquus hostis dies est, per naturam bene conditus; sed nox est, per meritum ad tenebras delapsus.

PISTOR.

THE only notice which I have of the probable author of the following hymn is drawn from Clichtoveus, p. 198 : Auctor ejus fuisse traditur eximius pater Henricus Pistor, doctor theologus Parisiensis, et in religiosâ domo Sti Victoris juxta Parisios monasticam vitam professus, qui etiam Concilio Constantinensi [1414—1418] interfuit, eâque tempestate, doctrinâ et virtute mirifice floruit. Referring to the histories of the Council of Constance, I can find no notice of his having taken any prominent share in its deliberations. Yet the internal evidence of the poem itself, as far as it reaches, is all in favour of this statement. That the writer was an accomplished theologian is plain ; and no less so that he was trained in the school, and formed upon the model, of Adam of St Victor, as indeed we have just been told that he was himself a Victorine as well.

VII. DE S. JOHANNE BAPTISTA.

PRÆCURSORIS et Baptistæ
  Diem istum chorus iste
Veneretur laudibus.
Vero die jam diescat,
Ut in nostris elucescat   5
Verus dies mentibus.

Præcursore nondum nato,
Nondum partu reserato,
Reserantur mystica.
Nostro sole tunc exclusus,   10·
Verioris est perfusus
Solis luce typicâ.

Prius novit diem verum,
Quam nostrorum sit dierum
Usus beneficio.   15
Hic renascens nondum natus
Nondum nascens est renatus
Cœlesti mysterio.

Clausa pandit, ventre clausus;
Gestu plaudens, fit applausus   20
Messiæ præsentiæ.

VII. Clichtoveus, *Elucidat. Eccles.* p. 198; Rambach, *Anthol.
Christl. Gesänge,* p. 364; Daniel, *Thes. Hymnol.* vol. ii. p.
169.
    20, 21. Cf. Luke i. 41.

Linguæ gestus obsequuntur;
Dum pro linguâ sic loquuntur,
Serviunt infantiæ.

Tori fructus matri dantur, 25
Et jam matris excusantur
Sterilis opprobria.
Ortus tanti præcursoris
Multus terret, sed terroris
Comes est lætitia. 30

Se a mundo servans mundum,
Munde vivit intra mundum
In ætate tenerâ.
Ne formentur a convictu
Mores, loco, veste, victu 35
Mundi fugit prospera.

Quem dum replet lux superna,
Veræ lucis fit lucerna,
Veri solis lucifer;
Novus præco novæ legis, 40
Immo novus novi regis
Pugnaturi signifer.

---

27. Cf. Luke i. 25.

29. *terret*] Luke i. 69. Daniel has *tenet*; one of the serious misprints with which his book, in many respects so carefully and conscientiously prepared. too much abounds.

36. Cf. Luke i. 60; Matt. iii. 4.

38. *lucerna*] In the words of the Psalmist, Paravi lucernam Christo meo (Ps. cxxxi. 7, Vulg.), it was very common to find an express prophecy of the Baptist. The application was helped on by the reappearance of *lucerna* in the Lord's words about him: Ille erat lucerna ardens, et lucens (John v. 35, Vulg.). Cf. Augustine, *Serm.* 293, 4; Tertullian, *Adv. Jud.* 9.

39. *lucifer*] This title of the light-bringer, the morning

Singulari prophetiâ
Prophetarum monarchiâ
Sublimatur omnium.   45
Hi futurum, hic præsentem,
Hi venturum, venientem
Monstrat iste Filium.

Dum baptizat Christum foris,
Hic a Christo melioris   50
Aquæ tactu tingitur:
Duos duplex lavat flumen,
Isti nomen, illi numen
Baptistæ conceditur.

Dum baptizat, baptizatur,   55
Dumque lavat, hic lavatur
Vi lavantis omnia.

---

star, was a nomen proprium applied to the Baptist: ἡ φωνὴ τοῦ
Λόγου, ὁ λύχνος τοῦ φωτός, ὁ ἐωσφόρος ὁ τοῦ ἡλίου πρόδρομος, as
he was called in the Greek Church. Durandus: Ideo autem
Joannes dictus est Lucifer, quia obtulit novum tempus. To
remember this, explains St Bernard's comparison of him and
that other 'son of the morning,' or *Lucifer* (Isai. xiv. 12, 13,
Vulg.), who sought not to go before the true Sun, but to usurp
his place: Lucet ergo Johannes, tanto verius quanto minus
appetit lucere. Fidelis Lucifer, qui Solis justitiæ non usurpare
venerit, sed prænuntiare splendorem.

43—45. *sublimatur*] Clichtoveus sees here allusion to
Christ's word concerning John, that he was a prophet, 'and
more than a prophet' (Matt. xi. 9); compare Gregory the
Great (*Hom.* 6 *in Evang.*). But it was often urged as a prero-
gative of the Baptist, that he was the only prophet who was
himself prophesied of before his birth; thus by Augustine
(*Serm.* 288, 3): Hic propheta, immo amplius quam propheta,
prænuntiari meruit per prophetam. De illo namque dixit Isaias,

Aquæ lavant et lavantur,
His lavandi vires dantur
Baptizati gratiâ. 60

O lucerna Verbi Dei,
Ad cœlestis nos diei
Ducat luminaria,
Nos ad portum ex hoc fluctu,
Nos ad risum ex hoc luctu 65
Christi trahat gratia.

Vox clamantis in deserto; and this is possibly the *singularis prophetia*, which the poet would say lifted him above all his fellows.

58—60. *lavantur*] So Marbod, in a leonine couplet:

> Non eguit tergi, voluit qui flumine mergi :
> Lotus aquas lavit, baptismaque sanctificavit.

66. Other hymns upon John the Baptist, though inferior to this, have much merit. Thus in Daniel's *Thes. Hymnol.* vol. ii. p. 217, an anonymous one beginning thus, but not at all maintaining the merits of its opening :

In occursum præcursoris
Concurrenti cordis, oris,
Curramus obsequio ;
In lucernâ Lux laudetur,
In præcone veneretur
Judex, Sol in radio.

Solem solet repentinum,
Vel quid grande vel divinum
Vulgus ægre capere :

Quare nobis hebetatis
Sol supernæ veritatis
Præluxit in sidere.

Hic præcursor et propheta,
Immo prophetarum meta,
Legi ponens terminum,
Mire cœpit, per applausum
Ventre matris clausus clausum
Revelando Dominum.

Another by Adam of St Victor (Gautier, vol. ii. p. 28), yield these stanzas :

Ad honorem tuum, Christe,
Recolat Ecclesia
Præcursoris et Baptistæ
Tui natalitia.

Laus est Regis in præconis
Ipsius præconio,
Quem virtutum ditat donis,
Sublimat officio.

Agnum monstrat in aperto	Multa docet millia.
Vox clamantis in deserto,	Non lux iste, sed lucerna,
Vox Verbi prænuncia.	Christus vere lux æterna,
Ardens fide, verbo lucens,	Lux illustrans omnia.
Et ad veram lucem ducens,	

These stanzas swarm with patristic and Scriptural allusion.
And first, the poet brings out the exceptional circumstance, that,
while for all other saints it is the day of their death, it is that of
his birth, his *natalitia*, which the Church celebrates—the
Nativity of the Baptist. Augustine gives the reason (*Serm.*
290, c. 2): Denique quia in magno Sacramento natus est Johannes, ipsius solius justi natalem diem celebrat Ecclesia. Et
natalis Domini celebratur, sed tanquam Domini. Date mihi
alium servum, præter Johannem, inter Patriarchas, inter Prophetas, inter Apostolos, cujus natalem diem celebret Ecclesia
Christi. Passionum diem servis plurimis celebramus ; nativitatis
diem nemini nisi Johanni. The reasons thus touched on by
Augustine, Durandus (*Rationale*, vii. 14) gives at full. They are
found in the words of the angel, that many should rejoice *at his
birth* (Luke i. 14); that he should be filled with the Holy Ghost
from his mother's womb (i. 15) ; and in his relation to his Lord
as the morning star, whose appearing heralded the rising of the
true Sun ; Cant. ii. 12 being in like manner applied to him ; and
his the voice of the turtle, which, being heard in the land, told
that winter was past, and the rain was over and gone. Nor
should the reader miss, in the second stanza, the play with the
words *Vox* and *Verbum*, which is indeed much more than a
play—John a *sound*, a startling cry in that old world to which
he himself belonged, a *voice* crying in the wilderness ; but Christ
a new utterance out of the bosom of the Eternal, an articulate
Word. Compare Origen (*In Joan.* ii. 26) ; and Augustine (*Serm.*
288, 3). The next line, *Ardens fide, verbo lucens*, is a commentary on the Saviour's words : Ille erat lucerna *ardens* et
lucens.

VIII. DE NATIVITATE DOMINI.

PUER natus in Bethlehem,
   Unde gaudet Jerusalem.

Hic jacet in præsepio,
Qui regnat sine termino.

Cognovit bos et asinus   5
Quod puer erat Dominus.

VIII. Corner, *Prompt. Devot.* p. 278; Daniel, *Thes. Hymnol.*
vol. i. p. 334.—This hymn, of a beautiful simplicity, and absorb-
ing easily so much theology in its poetry, continued long a great
favourite in the Lutheran Churches of Germany; surviving
among them till wellnigh the present day.

5. *bos et asinus*] Two passages in the Old Testament supplied the groundwork to that wide-spread legend which painters
have so often made their own, and to which here the poet alludes, viz. that the ox and the ass recognized and worshipped
that Lord whom the Jews ignored and rejected. The first, Isai.
i. 3: Cognovit bos possessorem suum, et asinus præsepe domini
sui: Israel autem me non cognovit, et populus meus non intel-
lexit (Vulg.); in which was seen a prophetic reference to the
manger at Bethlehem; and no less at Hab. iii. 2, where the
Septuagint has strangely enough, ἐν μέσῳ δύο ζώων γνωσθήσῃ: and
the old Italic: In medio duorum animalium innotesceris. The
bos and *asinus* were further mystically applied to the Jew and
Gentile, who severally, in the persons of the shepherds and the
wise men, were worshippers at the cradle of the new-born
King.

6. There is some merit in these lines from the *Musæ Angli-*

Reges de Sabâ veniunt,
Aurum, tus, myrrham offerunt.

Intrantes domum invicem
Novum salutant Principem.   10

De matre natus Virgine
Sine virili semine;

Sine serpentis vulnere
De nostro venit sanguine;

In carne nobis similis,   15
Peccato sed dissimilis;

Ut redderet nos homines
Deo et sibi similes.

In hoc natali gaudio
Benedicamus Domino: 20

Laudetur sancta Trinitas,
Deo dicamus gratias.

---

canæ, vol. i. p. 115. Christian alcaics, which are not wholly
profane, are so rare, that on this score they are worth quoting:

> Doloris expers, Mater amabilem
> Enixa prolem gramineo in toro
> Deponit immortale pignus,
> Arma timens pecorumque vultus.
>
> Ast ille cunas fortiter occupat,
> Fassusque numen, et jubare aureo
> Perfusus, absterret paventes
> Quadrupedes animosus infans.

7. *Reges*] The old Church legend—the Roman Church
makes it almost a matter of faith—that the wise men from the
East were kings, rests on Isai. lx. 3; Ps. lxxii. 10, 15. To this
last passage also we owe *Saba*, as the interpretation of the
ἀνατολαί of Matt. ii. 1.

PETER THE VENERABLE.

PETER the Venerable, born 1092 or 1094, of a noble family of Auvergne, was elected in 1122 abbot of Clugny—being constituted thereby the chief of that reformed branch of the Benedictine order, the head-quarters of which were at Clugny in Burgundy. This admirable man, one of that wonderful galaxy of illus-trious men who adorned France in the first half of the twelfth century, was probably only second, although second by a very long interval, to St Bernard in the influence which, by his talents and virtues, and position at the head of a great and important congregation, he was able to exercise upon his time. His history is in more ways than one bound up with that of his greater cotemporary. He is indeed now chiefly known for his keen though friendly controversy with St Bernard, on the respective merits of the " black " and " white " monks, the Clugnian, and the yet later Cistercian, who now in their fervent youth were carrying the world before them. The correspondence is as characteristic in its way as that with which it naturally suggests a comparison, between St Augustine and St Jerome; casting nearly as much light on the characters of the men, and far more on that of their times. But besides this, it was with him that Abelard found shelter, after the condemnation of his errors, and to his good offices the reconciliation which was effected before Abelard's death, between him and St Bernard, was owing. Nor ought it to be forgotten, that to Peter the Venerable western Christendom was indebted for its first accurate acquaintance with the Koran. Travelling in Spain, he was convinced how important it was that the Church should be thoroughly acquainted with that system with which it was in hostile contact, and at a great cost he caused a translation of the Koran into Latin to be made. That he should have done this, is alone sufficient to mark him as no common man. He has also himself written a refutation of Mahometanism. He died in 1156.

The poems which bear his name are not considerable in bulk, nor can they be esteemed of any very high order of merit. Yet apart from their interest as productions of one who played so important a part in the history of his age, these lines which immediately follow, and another hymn occupying a later place in this volume, possess a sufficient worth of their own to justify their insertion.

IX.   DE NATIVITATE DOMINI.

CŒLUM gaude, terra plaude,
  Nemo mutus sit in laude:
Auctor rerum creaturam
Miseratus perituram,

IX. *Bibliotheca Cluniacensis*, Paris, 1614, p. 1349.

Præbet dextram libertatis   5
Jam ab hoste captivatis.
Cœlum terræ fundit rorem,
Terra gignit Salvatorem.
Chorus cantat angelorum,
Cum sit infans Rex eorum.   10
Venter ille virginalis,
Dei cella specialis,
   Fecundatur Spiritu.
Et ut virga parit florem,
Sic et Virgo Redemptorem,   15
   Carnis tectum habitu.
Matris alitur intactæ
Puer-Deus sacro lacte,
   Res stupenda sæculis !
Escâ vivit alienâ   20
Per quem cuncta manent plena ;
   Nullis par miraculis !
Pastu carnis enutritur
Vitam carni qui largitur :
Matris habet gremium,   25
Quem et Patris solium :
Virgo natum consolatur,
Et ut Deum veneratur.

ALANUS.

ALANUS de Insulis, or of Lille, in Flanders, called Doctor Universalis from the extent of his acquirements, was born in the first half of the twelfth century, and died at the beginning of the next. His life is as perplexed a skein for the biographer to disentangle as can well be imagined, abundantly justifying the axiom of Bacon : Citius emergit veritas ex errore quam ex confusione—the main perplexity arising here from the difficulty of determining whether he and Alanus, also de Insulis, the friend of St Bernard and bishop of Auxerre, be one and the same person. The *Biographie Universelle* corrected this as an error, although a generally received one ; Oudinus, it is true, having already shewn the way (*De Script. Eccles.* vol. ii. p. 1389—1404) ; but Guericke and Neander again identify the two. The question, however, does not belong to this volume. The Doctor Universalis is undoubtedly the poet, and it is only with the poet we are here concerned.

The only collected edition of his works was published by Charles de Visch, Antwerp, 1654 ; a volume so rare that only in the Imperial Library at Paris was I able to get sight of it, and to obtain a perfect copy of a very beautiful Ode, inserted later in this volume. His *Parables* were a favourite book before the revival of learning ; but the work of his which enjoyed the highest reputation was a long moral poem, entitled *Anti-*

Claudianus, it does not very clearly appear why. (See Leyser, p. 1017, who gives copious extracts from it.) I know not whether it will bear out the praises which have been bestowed upon it and on its author. One says of him (Leyser, p. 1020): Inter ævi sui poëtas facile familiam duxit; and Oudinus (vol. ii. p. 1405), characterizes the poem as singulari festivitate, lepore, et elegantiâ conscriptum; see also Rambach, *Anthol. Christl. Gesänge*, vol. i. p. 329. Certainly, in the following lines, the description of a natural Paradise, Ovidian both in their merits and defects, we must recognize the poet's hand.

> Est locus ex nostro secretus climate, tractu
> Longo, nostrorum ridens fermenta locorum :
> Iste potest solus quidquid loca cætera possunt.
> Quod minus in reliquis, melius suppletur in uno ;
> In quo pubescens tenerâ lanugine florum,
> Sideribus stellata suis, succensa rosarum
> Murice*, terra novum contendit pingere cœlum.
> Non ibi nascentis exspirat gratia floris,
> Nascendo moriens ; nec enim rosa, mane puella,
> Vespere languet anus, sed vultu semper eodem
> Gaudens interni juvenescit munere veris.
> Hunc florem non urit hyems, non decoquit æstas,
> Non ibi bacchantis Boreæ furit ira, nec illic
> Fulminat aura noti, nec spicula grandinis instant.
> Ambit silva locum, muri mentita figuram :
> Non florum prædatur opes, foliique capillum
> Tondet hyems, teneram florum depasta juventam.
> Sirenes nemorum, citharistæ veris, in illum
> Convenere locum, mellitaque carmina sparsim

---

* Elsewhere he has this couplet :

> Ver, quasi fullo novus, reparando pallia pratis
> Horum succendit muricis igne togas.

Commentantur aves, dum gutturis organa pulsant.
In medio lacrymatur humus, fletuque beato
Producens lacrymas, fontem sudore perenni
Parturit, et dulces potus singultat aquarum.
Exuit ingemitas (?) facies argenteus amnis ;
Ad puri remeans elementi jura, nitore
Fulgurat in proprio, peregrinâ fæce solutus.

The following lines form part, or, as Oudinus asserts, the whole, of the genuine epitaph of Alanus. The last of them is striking enough :

Alanum brevis hora brevi tumulo sepelivit,
Qui duo, qui septem, qui totum scibile scivit ;
Scire suum moriens dare vel retinere nequivit.

X. DE NATIVITATE DOMINI.

HIC est qui, carnis intrans ergastula nostræ,
  Se pœnæ vinxit, vinctos ut solveret; æger
Factus, ut ægrotos sanaret; pauper, ut ipsis
Pauperibus conferret opem; defunctus, ut ipsâ
Vitâ donaret defunctos: exsulis omen   5
Passus, ut exilio miseros subduceret exul.
Sic livore perit livor, sic vulnere vulnus,
Sic morbus damnat morbum, mors morte fugatur :
Sic moritur vivens, ut vivat mortuus ; hæres
Exulat, ut servos hæredes reddat; egenus   10
Fit dives, pauperque potens, ut ditet egenos.
Sic liber servit, ut servos liberet ; imum
Summa petunt, ut sic ascendant infima summum ;

X. *Alani Opera*, ed. C. de Visch, Antwerp, 1654, p. 377.

Ut nox splendescat, splendor tenebrescit; eclipsi
Sol verus languescit, ut astra reducat ad ortum.   15
Ægrotat medicus, ut sanet morbidus ægrum.
Se cœlum terræ conformat, cedrus hysopo,
Ipse gigas nano, fumo lux, dives egeno,
Ægroto sanus, servo rex, purpura sacco.
Hic est, qui nostram sortem miseratus, ab aulâ   20
Æterni Patris egrediens, fastidia nostræ
Sustinuit sortis; sine crimine, criminis in se
Defigens pœnas, et nostri damna reatûs.

HILDEBERT.

HILDEBERT, born in 1057, shared as the scholar of Berengarius, in all the highest culture of his age; and having himself taught theology for a while at Mans, was in 1097 consecrated bishop of that see, and in 1125 became archbishop of Tours. A wise and gentle prelate, although not wanting in courage to dare, and fortitude to endure, when the cause of truth required it, he must ever be esteemed one of the fairest ornaments of the French Church. In his *Letters* he more than once seeks earnestly to check some of the superstitions of his time, as, for instance, the exaggerated value attributed to pilgrimages made to the Holy Land, and to the shrines of saints. He died in 1134. There is an interesting sketch of his character and of his work in Neander's *Life of St Bernard*, pp. 447—458.

His verses amount, as the Benedictine editors calculate, to ten thousand or more. The enforced leisure of imprisonments and exiles may have given him opportunity for composing so many. Of these a great number consist of versifications of scriptural history, or of the legends of saints, in heroic or elegiac verse, sometimes rhyming and sometimes not, and possess a very slight value. More curious than these is a legendary life of Mahomet, whereof Ampère (vol. iii. p. 440) has given a brief analysis; and his lines on the death of his master Berengarius display true feeling, and a very deep affection: however hard we may find it to go along, in every particular, with praise such as this:

> Cujus cura sequi naturam, legibus uti,
> Et mentem vitiis, *ora negare dolis;*
> Virtutes opibus, verum præponere falso,
> Nil vacuum sensu dicere, nil facere.

Two or three further specimens of his poetry will shew that he could versify with considerable elegance and ease, as the following lines from a poem in praise of England:

> Anglia, terra ferax, tibi pax diuturna quietem,
> Multiplicem luxum merx opulenta dedit.
> Tu nimio nec stricta gelu, nec sidere fervens,
> Clementi cœlo temperieque places.
> Cum pareret Natura parens, varioque favore
> Divideret dotes omnibus una locis,
> Elegit potiora tibi, matremque professa,
> Insula sis locuples, plenaque pacis, ait,
> Quidquid luxus amat, quidquid desiderat usus,
> Ex te proveniet, aut aliunde tibi.
> Te siquidem, licet occiduo sub sole latentem,
> Quæret et inveniet merce beata ratis: &c.

And the following have a real energy. They make part of the soul's complaint against the tyranny of the flesh:

> Angustæ fragilisque domûs jam jamque ruentis
> Hospita, servili conditione premor.
> Triste jugum cervice gero, gravibusque catenis
> Proh dolor! ad mortem non moritura trahor.
> Hei mihi! quam docilis falli, quam prompta subire
> Turpia, quam velox ad mea damna fui.

But grander still are the lines which follow. I have not inserted them in the body of this collection, lest I

might seem to claim for them that entire sympathy
which I am very far from doing. Yet, believing as we
may, and, to give any meaning to a large period of
Church history, we must, that Papal Rome of the middle
ages had a work of God to accomplish for the taming
of a violent and brutal world, in the midst of which she
often lifted up the only voice which was anywhere heard
in behalf of righteousness and truth—all which we may
believe, with the fullest sense that her dominion was an
unrighteous usurpation, however overruled for good to
Christendom, which could then take no higher blessing,
—believing this, we may freely admire these lines, so
nobly telling of that true strength of spiritual power,
which may be perfected in the utmost weakness of all
other power.　　It is the city of Rome which speaks:

> Dum simulacra mihi, dum numina vana placerent,
> 　Militiâ, populo, mœnibus alta fui:
> At simul effigies, arasque superstitiosas
> 　Dejiciens, uni sum famulata Deo ;
> Cesserunt arces, cecidere palatia divûm,
> 　Servivit populus, degeneravit eques.
> Vix scio quæ fuerim : vix Romæ Roma recordor ;
> 　Vix sinit occasus vel meminisse mei.
> Gratior hæc jactura mihi successibus illis,
> 　Major sum pauper divite, stante jacens.
> Plus aquilis vexilla crucis, plus Cæsare Petrus,
> 　Plus cinctis ducibus vulgus inerme dedit.
> Stans domui terras ; infernum diruta pulso ;
> 　Corpora stans, animas fracta jacensque rego.
> Tunc miseræ plebi, nunc principibus tenebrarum
> 　Impero ; tunc urbes, nunc mea regna polus :
> Quod ne Cæsaribus videar debere vel armis,
> 　Et species rerum meque meosque trahat,
> Armorum vis illa perit, ruit alta Senatûs
> 　Gloria, procumbunt templa, theatra jacent.

> Rostra vacant, edicta silent, sua præmia desunt
> Emeritis, populo jura, colonus agris.
> Ista jacent, ne forte meus spem ponat in illis
> Civis, et evacuet spemque bonumque crucis.

As modern Rome builds in here and there an antique frieze or pillar into her more recent structures, so the poet has used here, as will be observed, three or four lines that belong to the old Latin anthology.

XI.   DE NATIVITATE CHRISTI.

NECTAREUM rorem terris instillat Olympus,
  Totam respergunt flumina mellis humum,
Aurea sanctorum rosa de prato Paradisi
  Virginis in gremium lapsa, quievit ibi.
Intra virgineum decus, intra claustra pudoris,   5
  Colligit angelicam virginis aula rosam.
Flos roseus, flos angelicus, flos iste beatus
  Vertitur in fœnum, fit caro nostra Deus.

XI. *Hildeberti et Marbodi Opp.* p. 1313.—These very beautiful lines—for their violation of some ordinary rules of the classical hexameter and pentameter ought not to conceal their beauty from us—form part of a longer poem; but gain much through being disengaged from verses of an inferior quality.

7. *Flos roseus*] Elsewhere Hildebert has some lines on Christ, the rose of Paradise, of which in like manner the real grace is not affected by some metrical and other faults. After a long description of the loveliness of this world, he turns suddenly round:

> At quia flos mundi cito transit et aret, ad illam
> Quæ nunquam marcet currite, quæso, rosam :

Vertitur in carnem Verbum Patris, at sine damno,
   Vertitur in matrem virgo, sed absque viro.   10
Lumine plena suo manet in nascente potestas,
   Virgineum florens in pariente decus,
Sol tegitur nube, fœno flos, cortice granum,
   Mel cerâ, sacco purpura, carne Deus.
Ætheris ac terræ sunt hæc quasi fibula, sancto   15
   Fœderis amplexu dissona regna ligans.

Est rosa quæ dicit, Ego flos campi ; rosa certe
   Aurea, principii nescia, fine carens.
Floruit in cœlis, in mundo marcuit; illic
   Semper olens, istic pallida facta parum.
Hunc florem Paradisus habet, Seraphim videt, orbis
   Non capit, infernus nescit, adorat homo.

11. *Lumine*] Should we not read *Numine*?

ADAM OF ST VICTOR

XII. IN NATIVITATE DOMINI.

POTESTATE, non naturâ
Fit Creator creatura,
Reportetur ut factura
Factoris in gloriâ.
Prædicatus per prophetas,   5
Quem non capit locus, ætas,
Nostræ sortis intrat metas,
Non relinquens propria.

Cœlum terris inclinatur,
Homo-Deus adunatur,   10
Adunato famulatur
Cœlestis familia.
Rex sacerdos consecratur
Generalis, quod monstratur

XII. Mone, *Hymni Lat. Med. Ævi*, vol. ii. p. 85 (but without ascription to the author); Gautier, *Adam de S. Victor*, vol. i. p. 10.—Dr. Neale, who before Mone had printed this grand hymn from a MS. missal (*Sequentiæ*, p. 80), had rightly divined Adam of St Victor to be its author. It is certainly the richest and fullest of his Nativity hymns; although the *Jubilemus Salvatori*, first rescued by Gautier from oblivion (vol. i. p. 32), for which I have been unable to find room, does not fall very far behind it.

3. *Reportetur*] Mone reads *Reparetur*.

11, 12. Cf. Luke ii. 10, 13; Matt. iv. 11; Luke xxii. 43; Matt. xxviii. 2.

7. *metas*] So in the Greek theology, ὁ ἀχώρητος χωρεῖται.

Cum pax terris nuntiatur   15
Et in altis gloria.

Causam quæris, modum rei?
Causa prius omnes rei,
Modus justum velle Dei,
Sed conditum gratiâ.   20
O quam dulce condimentum,
Nobis mutans in pigmentum
Cum aceto fel cruentum,
Degustante Messiâ!

O salubre sacramentum,   25
Quod nos ponit in jumentum,
Plagis nostris dans unguentum,
Ille de Samariâ.
Ille alter Elisæus,
Reputatus homo reus,   30
Suscitavit homo-Deus
Sunamitis puerum.

23, 24. Cf. Matt. xxvii. 34; Ps. lxix. 21.

26—28. The poet claims here, as so many have done before him, the good Samaritan of the parable as the type of Christ. He does so more at length in a sequence on the Circumcision (Gautier, *Adam de S. Victor*, vol. i. p. 49):

> Dum cadit secus Jericho vir Hierosolomita,
> Samaritanus affuit, quo lapso datur vita.
> Perduxit hunc in stabulum clementia divina,
> Vinum permiscens oleo suävi medicinâ.
> Curantis ægri vulnera sunt dulcia fomenta,
> Dum cunctis pœnitentia fuit reis inventa.
> Bini dati denarii sunt duo Testamenta,
> Dum Christus, finis utriusque, complet sacramenta.

29—32. Cf. 2 Kin. iv. 7—37; and on Elisha as a type of Christ, Bernard, *In Cant. Serm.* 15, 16.

Hic est gigas currens fortis,
Qui, destructâ lege mortis,
Ad amœna primæ sortis   35
Ovem fert in humerum.
Vivit, regnat Deus-homo,
Trahens Orco lapsum pomo;
Cœlo tractus gaudet homo,
Denum complens numerum.   40

39, 40. An allusion to that interpretation of the parable of the ten pieces of silver (Luke xv. 8—10), which makes the nine pieces which were *not* lost to be the nine ranks of angels who stood in their first obedience, and the one lost to be the race of mankind.

MAUBURN.

JOHN Mauburn was born at Brussels in 1460, and died abbot of the Cloister of Livry, not far from Paris, in 1502. He was the author of several ascetic treatises, among others the *Rosetum Spirituale*, from which the following hymn is derived.

XIII. DE NATIVITATE DOMINI.

HEU ! quid jaces stabulo,
 Omnium Creator,
Vagiens cunabulo,
Mundi reparator ?

XIII. Mauburnus, *Rosetum Spirituale*, Duaci, 1620, p. 416; Corner, *Prompt. Devot.* p. 280; Daniel, *Thes. Hymnol.* vol. i. p. 335. —These three stanzas are taken from a longer poem, consisting of thirteen in all, which commences:

> Eja, mea anima,
> Bethlehem eamus.

I have not selected them, for they had long since been separated from the context, and constituted into a Christmas hymn—a great favourite in the early reformed Churches, so long as the practice of singing Latin compositions survived among them. It still occasionally retains a place in the German hymnals, but now in an old translation which commences thus:

> Warum liegt im Krippelein—

As this hymn sometimes appears with a text differing not a little

Si rex, ubi purpura,   5
Vel clientum murmura,
Ubi aula regis?
Hic omnis penuria,
Paupertatis curia,
Forma novæ legis.   10

Istuc amor generis
Me traxit humani,
Quod se noxâ sceleris
Occidit profani.
His meis inopiis   15
Gratiarum copiis
Te pergo ditare:
Hocce natalitio,
Vero sacrificio,
Te volens beare.   20

O te laudum millibus
Laudo, laudo, laudo;
Tantis mirabilibus
Plaudo, plaudo, plaudo:
Gloria, sit gloria,   25
Amanti memoria
Domino in altis:
Cuï testimonia
Dantur et præconia
Cœlicis a psaltis.   30

---

from that here presented, I may say that mine has been obtained, not from any secondary source, but from the *Rosetum* itself; not indeed from the original edition, Basle, 1491, which lay not within my reach, but from that referred to above, which has much appearance of having been carefully edited.

XIV. DE NATIVITATE DOMINI.

O TER fœcundas, o ter jucundas
   Beatæ noctis delicias,
Quæ suspiratas e cœlo datas
In terris paris delicias!

Gravem primævæ ob lapsum Evæ   5
Dum jamjam mundus emoritur,
In carne meus, ut vivat, Deus,
Sol vitæ, mundo suboritur.

Æternum Lumen, immensum Numen
Pannorum vinculis stringitur;   10
In vili caulâ, exclusus aulâ,
Rex cœli bestiis cingitur.

In cunis jacet, et infans tacet
Verbum, quod loquitur omnia;
Sol mundi friget, et flamma riget: 15
Quid sibi volunt hæc omnia?

XIV. [Walraff.] *Corolla Hymnorum*, Coloniæ, 1806, p. 8;
Daniel, *Thes. Hymnol.* vol. ii. p. 339.—This pretty poem, for it
can claim no higher praise, is certainly not old, can scarcely be
earlier than the fifteenth century; and thus belongs, if I am right
in my conjecture, to a period when the fountains of inspiration,
at least of that inspiration which has given us the great medieval
hymns, were very nearly exhausted.

XV.　SEQUENTIA DE TRIBUS REGIBUS.

MAJESTATI sacrosanctæ
Militans cum triumphante
Jubilet Ecclesia :
Sic versetur laus in ore,
Ne gravetur cor torpore,　　　　　5
Quod degustat gaudia.

Novum parit virga florem,
Novum monstrat stella solem ;
Currunt ad præsepia
Reges magi, qui non vagi,　　　　10
Sed præsagi, gaudent agi
Stellâ duce præviâ.

Trium regum trinum munus ;
Christus, Homo-Deus, unus
Cum carne et animâ ;　　　　　15
Deus trinus in personis
Adoratur tribus donis,
Unus in essentiâ.

XV. Corner, *Prompt. Devot.* p. 367 ; Daniel, *Thes. Hymnol.*
vol. v. p. 48.

14. Compare on these Eastern Magi the grand lines of Prudentius (*Cathemer.* xii. 1—76), which rank among the noblest
passages of his poetry.

Myrrham ferunt, tus, et aurum,
Plus pensantes, quam thesaurum, 20
Typum, sub quo veritas;
Trina dona, tres figuræ:
Rex in auro, Deus in ture,
In myrrhâ mortalitas.

Turis odor deitatem, 25
Auri splendor dignitatem
Regalis potentiæ:
Myrrha caro Verbo nupta,
Per quod manet incorrupta
Caro carens carie. 30

Tu nos, Christe, ab hâc valle
Duc ad vitam recto calle
Per regum vestigia;
Ubi Patris, ubi Tui,
Et Amoris Sacri, frui 35
Mereamur gloriâ. Amen.

---

36. The following lines, blending into a single stanza the twofold homage of the Jewish shepherds and the Gentile sages, were great favourites at and after the Reformation. They belong probably to the fourteenth century (Rambach, *Anthol. Christl. Gesänge*, p. 333).

Quem pastores laudavere,
Quibus angeli dixere,
'Absit vobis jam timere'
Natus est Rex gloriæ:
Ad quem reges ambulabant,
Aurum, tus, myrrham, portabant;
Hæc sincere immolabant
Leoni victoriæ.

PRUDENTIUS.

AURELIUS Clemens Prudentius was born, as there is good reason to suppose, in Spain. But the evidence from certain expressions which he uses, in favour of Saragossa as his birth-place, is equally good in favour of Tarragona, and of Calahorra; and therefore, since he could not have been born in more places than one, is worthless in regard of them all. All that we know with any certainty about him, is drawn from a short autobiography in verse, which he has prefixed to his poems, and which contains a catalogue of them. From this we gather that he was born A.D. 348: that, having enjoyed a liberal education, and for a while practised as a pleader, he had filled important judicial posts in two cities which he does not name, and had subsequently received a high military appointment at the Court; but that now, in his fifty-seventh year, in which this sketch of his life was given, he looked back with sorrow and shame to the sins and follies of his youth, to the worldliness of his middle age, and desired to dedicate what remained of his life to an earnest and devoted service of God. The year of his death is not known.

Barth, who in his *Adversaria* is always prodigal in his commendations of the Christian poets, is most prodigal of all in regard of Prudentius. Poëta eximius —eruditissimus et sanctissimus scriptor—nemo divinius de rebus Christianis unquam scripsit—such is the ordinary language which he uses about him : and even Bentley, who for the most is not at all so lavish of admiration, calls him "the Horace and Virgil of the Christians." Extravagant praises, compensated on the other side by as undue depreciation ! For, giving, as it must be owned he does, many and distinct tokens of belonging to an age of deeply sunken taste, yet was his gift of sacred poetry a most true one; and when it is charged against him in the *Dictionary of Greek and Roman Biography*, that "his Latinity is not formed, like that of Juvencus and Victorinus, upon the best ancient models. but is confessedly impure," this is really his praise,—namely, that, whether consciously or unconsciously, he did act on the principle, that the new life claimed new forms in which to manifest itself, —that he did not shrink from helping forward that great transformation of the Latin language, which it needed to undergo, now that it should be the vehicle of truths which were altogether novel to it, having not yet risen up above the horizon of men's minds, at the time when it was in its first growth and formation. Let any one compare his poems with those of Juvencus or Sedulius, and his vast superiority will be at once manifest—that superiority mainly consisting in this, that he does not attempt, as they did, to pour the new wine into old bottles ; but has felt and understood that the new thoughts and feelings which Christianity has brought into the world, must of necessity weave new garments for themselves.

The poems on which the reputation of Prudentius as a poet mainly rests. are his Cathemerinōn = Diurnorum. The tenth, Deus, ignee fons animarum, is confessedly

the grandest of them all. The first also, on Cockcrow,
and the twelfth, an Hymn for Epiphany, though they
attain not to the grandeur of this, may well share with
it in our admiration.

XVI. DE SS. INNOCENTIBUS.

SALVETE, flores martyrum,
  Quos lucis ipso in limine
Christi insecutor sustulit,
Ceu turbo nascentes rosas.

Vos, prima Christi victima,   5
Grex immolatorum tener,
Aram ante ipsam simplices
Palmâ et coronis luditis.

Audit tyrannus anxius
Adesse regum Principem,   10
Qui nomen Israel regat,
Teneatque David regiam.

XVI. *Prudentii Carmina*, ed. Obbarius, Tubingæ, 1845, p.
48; Daniel, *Thes. Hymnol.* vol. i. p. 124.—This hymn, as given
in the text above, is not exactly as Prudentius wrote it; rather is
it a piece of mosaic, constructed from his twelfth *Cathemerinōn*.
It has, however, been so long current in the form in which it
here appears, and is so skilfully put together, that I have neither
excluded it, nor attempted to restore it to the form in which it
appears in the text of the poet.

1. *flores martyrum*] Augustine, or rather one in the name of
Augustine, says, and with manifest reference to this hymn (*Serm.*

Exclamat amens nuncio :
Successor instat, pellimur;
Satelles, i, ferrum rape,   15
Perfunde cunas sanguine.

Mas omnis infans occidat,
Scrutare nutricum sinus,
Fraus nequa furtim subtrahat
Prolem virilis indolis.   20

Transfigit ergo carnifex,
Mucrone districto furens,
Effusa nuper corpora,
Animasque rimatur novas.

O barbarum spectaculum !   25
Vix interemptor invenit
Locum minutis artubus
Quo plaga descendat patens.

Quid proficit tantum nefas ?
Quid crimen Herodem juvat ?   30
Unus tot inter funera
Impune Christus tollitur.

Inter coævi sanguinis
Fluenta solus integer,
Ferrum, quod orbabat nurus,   35
Partus fefellit Virginis.

220, Appendix): Jure dicuntur *martyrum flores*, quos in medio frigore infidelitatis exortos, velut primas erumpentis Ecclesiæ gemmas, quædam persecutionis pruina decoxit.

ADAM OF ST VICTOR.

XVII. IN EPIPHANIA.

TRIA dona reges ferunt :
  Stellâ duce regem quærunt,
Per quam certi semper erunt
De superno lumine.
Auro regem venerantes,   5
Ture Deum designantes,
Myrrhâ mortem memorantes,
Sacro docti Flamine.

Dies iste jubileus
Dici debet, quo Sabæus,   10
Plene credens quod sit Deus,
Mentis gaudet requie ;
Plebs Hebræa jam tabescit ;
Multa sciens, Deum nescit;
Sed gentilis fide crescit,   15
Visâ Christi facie.

XVII. Gautier, *Adam de S. Victor*, vol. ii. p. 341.—It was by
him edited for the first time.   I regret to have no choice but to
omit the first stanza of this truly noble poem.

10. *Sabæus*] This is to be explained by Ps. lxxi. 10 (Vulg.) :
Reges Arabum *et Saba* dona adducent, which was always interpreted as having its fulfilment in the coming of the wise men
(kings they were often, therefore, assumed to be), from the East.
Thus, in a Nativity Hymn (see p. 98) we find this line :

Reges de Sabâ veniunt.

Synagoga pridem cara,
Fide fulgens et præclara,
Vilis jacet et ignara
Majestatis parvuli;   20
Seges Christi prius rara,
Mente rudis et amara,
Contemplatur luce clarâ
Salvatorem sæculi.

Synagoga cœca, doles,   25
Quia Saræ crescit proles,
Cum ancillæ prolem moles
Gravis premat criminum.
Tu tabescis et laboras;
Sarah ridet dum tu ploras,   30
Quia novit quem ignoras,
Redemptorem hominum.

Consecratus patris ore,
Jacob gaudet cum tremore :

25—32. The poet follows up the hint of St Paul (Gal. iv.
22—31), to the effect that in Isaac, the child of the free woman,
we have the type of the Church; that in Ishmael, the son of the
bondwoman, we have the type of the Synagogue, serving in the
oldness of the letter, not in the newness of the spirit. Every
line almost contains its own scriptural allusion; thus, 25—28 to
Gen. xxi. 8, 9; 29, to ver. 6, 16 of the same chapter.

33—39. He now shifts the types from Isaac and Ishmael to
Jacob and Esau; and again, as will be seen, is extraordinarily
rich in his allusions to Scripture.

33. *Consecratus*] Cf. Gen. xxvii. 27   29; xxviii. 1—4.

34. *cum tremore*] Cf. Gen. xxxii. 7.

Tu rigaris cœli rore   35
Ex terræ pinguedine;
Delectaris in terrenis
Rebus vanis et obscenis,
Jacob tractat de serenis,
Et Christi dulcedine.   40

Unguentorum in odore
Sancti currunt cum amore,
Quia novo fragrat flore
Nova Christi venia.
Ad peccatum prius prona   45
Jam percepit sponsa dona,
Sponsa recens, et coronâ
Decoratur aureâ.

---

35. *Tu rigaris*] This *tu* is addressed to Esau, as representing the Jewish Synagogue, and he is here reminded that he did but receive earthly promises from his father's mouth (in pinguedine terræ et in rore cœli desuper erit benedictio tua, Gen. xxvii. 39, 40, Vulg.), the heavenly having been all anticipated by his brother. Not to him, delighting in earthly things, but to his brother, it was given to behold the marvellous ladder reaching from earth to heaven, and with angels ascending and descending upon it (Gen. xxviii. 11—22); for, though it is not very clear, I must see an allusion to this at ver. 39.

41. *Unguentorum*] So the Bride in the Canticles (i. 3, Vulg.): Trahe me. Post te curremus in odorem unguentorum tuorum.

45. *Ad peccatum*] Cf. Hos. ii. 2—24; Ephes. v. 26, 27. This line is alone sufficient to refute Gautier's assertion that the Blessed Virgin, and not the Church, is contemplated as the Bride of these latter stanzas.

Adstat sponsa regi nato,
Cuï ritu servit grato   50
In vestitu deaurato,
Aureis in fimbriis:
Orta rosa est ex spinis,
Cujus ortus sive finis
Semper studet in divinis,   55
Et regis deliciis.

Hæc est sponsa spiritalis,
Vero Sponso specialis;
Sponsus iste nos a malis
Servet et eripiat;   60
Mores tollat hic ineptos,
Sibi reddat nos acceptos,
Et ab hoste sic ereptos
In cœlis recipiat.   Amen.

49—52. Cf. Ps. xliv. 10, 14 (Vulg.): Astitit regina a dextris
tuis in vestitu deaurato, ... in fimbriis aureis.

XVIII. IN EPIPHANIA.

TRIBUS signis Deo dignis
  Dies ista colitur;
Tria signa laude digna
Cœtus hic persequitur.

Stella magos duxit vagos   5
Ad præsepe Domini,
Congaudentes omnes gentes
Ejus psallunt nomini.

Novum mirum, aqua vinum
Factum est ad nuptias: 10
Mundus credit, Christus dedit
Signorum primitias.

XVIII. *Bibl. Max. Patrum*, Lugduni, 1677, vol. xxvii. p. 517.
—This little poem, sometimes ascribed to Hartmann, a monk of
St Gall, brings together well the three events of the Lord's life,
the three *manifestations* of His glory, which the Western Church
brought into connexion with the feast of Epiphany, and com-
memorated upon that day. Thus Maximus Taurinensis, at the
beginning of the fifth century (*Hom.* 23): In hâc celebritate
multiplici nobis est festivitate lætandum. Ferunt enim hodie
Christum Dominum nostrum vel stellâ duce a gentibus adora-
tum: invitatum ad nuptias aquas in vinum vertisse: vel suscepto
a Johanne baptismate consecrâsse fluenta Jordanis. Oportet
itaque nos ad honorem Salvatoris nostri, cujus nativitatem debitâ
nuper cum exultatione transegimus, etiam hunc virtutum ejus
celebrare natalem. Cf. Durandus, *Rational.* vi. 16.

A Johanne in Jordane
Christus baptizatus est:
Unde lotus mundus totus   15
Et purificatus est.

Lector, lege; a summo Rege
Tibi benedictio
Sit in cœlis: plebs fidelis
Psallat cum tripudio.   Amen.   20

FORTUNATUS.

VENANTIUS Fortunatus, an Italian by birth, whose life, however, was chiefly spent in Gaul, belongs to the latter half of the sixth century. He was born in the district of Treviso, in the year 530, but passed the Alps a little before the great invasion of the Lombards and the desolation of Northern Italy, and is memorable as one of the last, who, amid the advancing tide of barbarism, retained anything of the old classical culture. A master of *vers de société*, which he made with a negligent ease, yet not without elegance, he wandered, a highly favoured guest, from castle to cloister in Gaul, repaying the hospitalities which he everywhere received, with neatly-turned compliments in verse. Such was the manner of his life, until Queen Rhadegunda, now separated from her husband Clotaire, persuaded him to attach himself to her person, and, having received ordination, to settle at Poitiers, in the neighbourhood of which she was presiding over a monastic institution that had been founded by herself. Here he remained till his death, which some place in the year 609, having become, during the latter years of his life, bishop of Poitiers.

There is a chapter of singular liveliness in Thierry's *Récits des Temps Mérovingiens*, *Récit 5me*, on the character of Fortunatus, and on his relations, which, though intimate, even Thierry does not pretend to consider otherwise than perfectly innocent, and removed from all scandal, with the Queen. It is impossible to deny that there is some truth in the portraiture of the poet which he draws. Even Guizot (*Civilisation en France*, 18me Leçon) must be taken to allow it. Yet had Fortunatus been merely that clever, frivolous, self-indulgent and vain character, which Thierry describes, he would scarcely have risen to the height and elevation which, in two or three of his poems, he has certainly attained;—poems, it is true, which are inconceivably superior to the mass of those out of which they are taken. In Barth's *Adversaria* there is the same exaggerated estimate of Fortunatus which there is of Prudentius, and with far less in his poetry to justify or excuse it. It would indeed have been otherwise, had he often written as in the lines which follow.

XIX. DE CRUCE CHRISTI.

CRUX benedicta nitet, Dominus quâ carne pependit,
  Atque cruore suo vulnera nostra lavat;
Mitis amore pio pro nobis victima factus,
  Traxit ab ore lupi quâ sacer agnus oves;
Transfixis palmis ubi mundum a clade redemit,   5
  Atque suo clausit funere mortis iter.

XIX. Thomasius. *Hymnarium, Opp.* vol. ii. p. 433; Daniel, *Thes. Hymnol.* vol. i. p. 168.—These lines are only the portion of a far longer poem; yet have a completeness in themselves which has long caused them to be current in their present shape, till it is almost forgotten that they only form part of a larger whole.

Hic manus illa fuit clavis confixa cruentis,
  Quæ eripuit Paulum crimine, morte Petrum.
Fertilitate potens, o dulce et nobile lignum,
  Quando tuis ramis tam nova poma geris;   10
Cujus odore novo defuncta cadavera surgunt,
  Et redeunt vitæ qui caruere die;
Nullum uret æstus sub frondibus arboris hujus,
  Luna nec in nocte, sol neque meridie.
Tu plantata micas, secus est ubi cursus aquarum, 15
  Spargis et ornatas flore recente comas.
Appensa est vitis inter tua brachia, de quâ
  Dulcia sanguineo vina rubore fluunt.

---

8. *Paulum—Petrum*]   Cf. Acts ix. 5; xii. 7.

13, 14. Cf. Ps. cxx. 6.

14. The double false quantity of *meridie*, which it would be impossible to ascribe to ignorance, must be taken as a token of the breaking up of the metrical scheme of verse which had already begun, and the coming in of quite another in its room.

15. *secus*]   The use of *secus* as a preposition governing an accusative (here understand *loca*), and equivalent to *secundum*, though unknown to Augustan Latinity, belongs alike to the anterior and the subsequent periods of the language, at once to Cato and to Pliny.   And thus we have Ps. i. 3 (Vulg.), words which doubtless were in the poet's mind when he wrote this line: Et erit tanquam lignum, quod plantatum est secus decursus aquarum, quod fructum suum dabit in tempore suo.

17. *vitis*]   The cross as the tree to which the vine is clinging, and from which its tendrils and fruit depend, is a beautiful weaving in of the image of the true Vine with the fact of the Crucifixion.   The blending of one image and another comes perhaps yet more beautifully out, though not without a certain incoherence in the images, in that which sometimes appears in ancient works of Christian Art,—namely, Christ set forth as the Lamb round which the branches of a loaded vine are clustering and clinging.

XX. DE PASSIONE DOMINI.

QUISQUIS ades, mediique subis in limina templi,
  Siste parum, insontemque tuo pro crimine passum
Respice me, me conde animo, me in pectore serva.
Ille ego qui, casus hominum miseratus acerbos,
Huc veni, pacis promissæ interpres, et ampla   5
Communis culpæ venia : hic clarissima ab alto
Reddita lux terris, hic alma salutis imago;
Hic tibi sum requies, via recta, redemptio vera,
Vexillumque Dei, signum et memorabile fari.
Te propter vitamque tuam sum Virginis alvum   10
Ingressus, sum factus homo, atque horrentia passus
Funera, nec requiem terrarum in finibus usquam
Inveni, sed ubique minas, et ubique labores.

   *   *   *   *   *   *   *   *   *

XX. Fabricius, *Poëtt. Vett. Christ. Opp.* Basileæ, 1562, p.
759; *Lactantii Opp.* Antverpiæ, 1555, p. 589.—This poem, consisting of about eighty lines, of which I have here given something less than half, appears in Fabricius, with the title *De
Beneficiis suis Christus.* It is there ascribed to Lactantius, in
most editions of whose works it in like manner appears, with the
title *De Passione Domini.* Although Barth (*Advers.* xxxii. 2)
maintains the correctness of this its ascription to Lactantius,
there cannot be any doubt that it pertains to a somewhat later
age. But whosoever it may be, it does, in Bähr's words (*Die
Christl. Dichter Rom's*, p. 22), "belong to the more admirable
productions of Christian poetry, and in this respect would not
be unworthy of Lactantius," having something of the true flow
of the Latin hexameter, which so few of the Christian poets, or
indeed of any of the poets who belonged to the silver age, were
able to catch.

Nunc me, nunc vero desertum, extrema secutum
Supplicia, et dulci procul a genetrice levatum,   15
Vertice ad usque pedes me lustra; en aspice crines
Sanguine concretos, et sanguinolenta sub ipsis
Colla comis, spinisque caput crudelibus haustum,
Undique diva pluens vivum super ora cruorem;
Compressos speculare oculos et luce carentes,   20
Afflictasque genas, arentem suspice linguam
Felle venenatam, et pallentes funere vultus.
Cerne manus clavis fixas, tractosque lacertos,
Atque ingens lateris vulnus; cerne inde fluorem
Sanguineum, fossosque pedes, artusque cruentos.   25
Flecte genu, innocuo terramque cruore madentem
Ore petens humili, lacrymis perfunde subortis,
Et me nonnunquam devoto in corde, meosque
Fer monitus, sectare meæ vestigia vitæ,
Ipsaque supplicia inspiciens, mortemque severam,   30
Corporis innumeros memorans animique dolores,
Disce adversa pati, et propriæ invigilare saluti.
Hæc monumenta tibi si quando in mente juvabit
Volvere, si qua fides animo tibi ferre, meorum
Debita si pietas et gratia digna laborum   35
Surget, erunt veræ stimuli virtutis, eruntque
Hostis in insidias clypei, quibus acer in omni
Tutus eris victorque feres certamine palmam.

XXI. MEDITATIONES.

DESERE jam, anima, lectulum soporis,
Languor, torpor, vanitas excludatur foris,
Intus cor efferveat facibus amoris,
Recolens mirifica gesta Salvatoris.

Mens, affectus, ratio, simul convenite,　　5
Occupari frivolis ultra jam nolite;
Discursus, vagatio, cum curis abite,
Dum pertractat animus sacramenta vitæ.

XXI. *Bibl. Max. Patrum*, vol. xxvii. p. 444.—These stanzas
form part of a very long rhymed contemplation of our Lord's life
and death, sometimes ascribed to Anselm, bishop of Lucca, a
cotemporary of his more illustrious English namesake. He died
1086.—These trochaic lines of thirteen syllables long, disposed
in mono-rhymed quatrains, were great favourites in the middle
ages, and much used for narrative poems; and though, when too
long drawn out, wearying in their monotony, and in the necessity of the pause falling in every line at exactly the same place,
are capable both of strength and beauty. These *Meditations*
have both; and Du Méril has lately published, for the first time,
a long poem on the death of Thomas à Becket (*Poésies Popul.
Lat.* 1847, p. 81), which will further yield a stanza or two, if
such were wanted, in proof. They relate to the feigned reconciliation of Henry with the archbishop, by which he drew him
from his safer exile in France:

Ægras dat inducias latro viatori,
Sabulo vis turbinis, vis procellæ flori;
Lupi cum oriculâ ludus est dolori;
Vere lupus lusor est qui dat dolo mori.

Ut post syrtes mittitur in Charybdim navis,
Ut laxatis laqueis inescatur avis,
Sic remisit exulem male pax suävis,
Miscens crucis poculum sub verborum favis.

Jesu mi dulcissime, Domine cœlorum,
Conditor omnipotens, Rex universorum,   10
Quis jam actus sufficit mirari gestorum,
Quæ te ferre compulit salus miserorum ?

Te de cœlis caritas traxit animarum,
Pro quibus palatium deserens præclarum,
Miseram ingrediens vallem lacrymarum,   15
Opus durum suscipis, et iter amarum.

Tristatur lætitia, salus infirmatur,
Panis vivus esurit, virtus sustentatur ;
Sitit fons perpetuus, quo cœlum potatur ;
Et ista quis intuens mira, non miratur ?   20

Oh mira dignatio pii Salvatoris,
Oh vere mirifica pietas amoris ;
Expers culpæ nosceris, Jesu, flos decoris,
Ego tui, proh dolor ! causa sum doloris.

Ego heu ! superbio, tu humiliaris ;   25
Ego culpas perpetro, tu pœnâ mulctaris ;
Ego fruor dulcibus, tu felle potaris ;
Ego peto mollia, tu dure tractaris.

ST BERNARD.

ST BERNARD, born in 1091, of a noble family, at Fontaine in Burgundy, became in 1113 a monk of Citeaux, and in 1115 first abbot of Clairvaux. He died Aug. 20, 1153. There have been other men, Augustine and Luther for instance, who by their words and writings have ploughed deeper and more lasting furrows in the great field of the Church, but probably no man during his lifetime ever exercised a *personal* influence in Christendom equal to his; who was the stayer of popular commotions, the queller of heresies, the umpire between princes and kings, the counsellor of popes, the founder, for so he may be esteemed, of an important religious Order, the author of a crusade. Besides all deeper qualities which would not alone have sufficed to effect all this, he was gifted by nature and grace with rarest powers of persuasion, (Doctor mellifluus as he was rightly called, though the honey perhaps was sometimes a little too honied,) and seems to have exercised a wellnigh magical influence upon all those with whom he was brought into contact. The hymns which usually go by his name were judged away from him on very slight and insufficient grounds, by Mabillon, in his edition of St Bernard's works. But with the exception of the *Cur mundus militat*, there is no reason to doubt the correctness of their attribution to him. All internal evidence is in favour of him as their author. If he did not write, it is not easy to guess who could have written, them; and indeed they bear profoundly the stamp of his mind, being only inferior in beauty to his prose.

XXII. ORATIO RHYTHMICA AD CHRISTUM A CRUCE PENDENTEM.

1. Ad Pedes.

SALVE, mundi salutare,
  Salve salve, Jesu care!
Cruci tuæ me aptare
Vellem vere, tu scis quare,
Da mihi tui copiam.   5
Ac si præsens sis, accedo,
Immo te præsentem credo;
O quam mundum hic te cerno!
Ecce tibi me prosterno,
Sis facilis ad veniam.   10

Clavos pedum, plagas duras,
Et tam graves impressuras

XXII. *Bernardi Opp.* ed. Bened., Paris, 1719, vol. ii. pp. 916, 919; Mone, *Hymn. Lat. Med. Ævi,* vol. i. p. 162.—The full title of the poem from which two of its seven portions, each however complete in itself, are here drawn, is commonly as follows: Rhythmica oratio ad unum quodlibet membrorum Christi patientis, et a cruce pendentis. I have chosen these two, the first and the last, because in a composition of such length, extending to nearly four hundred lines, it was necessary to make some selection; yet its other divisions are of no inferior depth or beauty: quæ omnia, as Daniel says with merest truth, omnes divini amoris spirant æstus atque incendia, ut nil possit suavius dulciusque excogitari.

Circumplector cum affectu,
Tuo pavens in aspectu,
Meorum memor vulnerum.   15
Grates tantæ caritati
Nos agamus vulnerati :
O amator peccatorum,
Reparator constratorum,
O dulcis pater pauperum !   20

Quidquid est in me confractum,
Dissipatum aut distractum,
Dulcis Jesu, totum sana,
Tu restaura, tu complana,
Tam pio medicamine.   25
Te in tuâ cruce quæro,
Prout queo, corde mero ;
Me sanabis hic, ut spero,
Sana me et salvus ero,
In tuo lavans sanguine.   30

Plagas tuas rubicundas,
Et fixuras tam profundas,
Cordi meo fac inscribi,
Ut configar totus tibi,
Te modis amans omnibus.   35
Quisquis huc ad te accessit,

---

15. *Meorum*] So Mone, on good MS. authority. It is a
wonderful improvement on *tuorum*, the ordinary reading; and
at once carries conviction with it.

36—40. So Mone; but more commonly the latter half of
this strophe is read as follows:

> Dulcis Jesu, pie Deus,
> Ad te clamo, licet reus,

Et hos pedes corde pressit
Æger, sanus hinc abscessit,
Hic relinquens quidquid gessit,
Dans osculum vulneribus.   40

Coram cruce procumbentem,
Hosque pedes complectentem,
Jesu bone, me ne spernas,
Sed de cruce sanctâ cernas
Compassionis gratiâ.   45
In hâc cruce stans directe
Vide me, o mi dilecte,
Ad te totum me converte;
Esto sanus, dic aperte,
Dimitto tibi omnia.   50

2. Ad Faciem.

Salve, caput cruentatum,
Totum spinis coronatum,

Præbe mihi te benignum,
Ne repellas me indignum
De tuis sanctis pedibus.

51. *Salve, caput cruentatum*] I have observed already how
these great hymns of the early or medieval Church served
as the foundation of some of the noblest post-Reformation
hymns; the later poet, no slavish copyist nor mere translator,
yet rejoicing to find his inspiration in these earlier sources. It
has been so in the present instance. Paul Gerhard's Passion
Hymn—

O Haupt voll Blut und Wunden,
Voll Schmerz und voller Hohn!

is freely composed upon the model of what follows now.

Conquassatum, vulneratum,
Arundine verberatum,
Facie sputis illitâ.   55
Salve, cujus dulcis vultus,
Immutatus et incultus,
Immutavit suum florem,
Totus versus in pallorem,
Quem cœli tremit curia.   60

Omnis vigor atque viror
Hinc recessit, non admiror,
Mors apparet in adspectu,
Totus pendens in defectu,
Attritus ægrâ macie.   65
Sic affectus, sic despectus,
Propter me sic interfectus,
Peccatori tam indigno
Cum amoris intersigno
Appare clarâ facie.   70

In hâc tuâ passione
Me agnosce, Pastor bone,
Cujus sumpsi mel ex ore,
Haustum lactis cum dulcore,
Præ omnibus deliciis.   75
Non me reum asperneris,
Nec indignum dedigneris;
Morte tibi jam vicinâ
Tuum caput hic inclina,
In meis pausa brachiis.   80

-----

73. Cf. Judg. xiv. 8, 9.

Tuæ sanctæ passioni
Me gauderem interponi,
In hâc cruce tecum mori
Præsta crucis amatori,
Sub cruce tuâ moriar.　　　　85
Morti tuæ tam amaræ
Grates ago, Jesu care,
Qui es clemens pie Deus,
Fac quod petit tuus reus,
Ut absque te non finiar.　　　　90

Dum me mori est necesse,
Noli mihi tunc deesse;
In tremendâ mortis horâ
Veni, Jesu, absque morâ,
Tuere me et libera.　　　　95
Cum me jubes emigrare,
Jesu care, tunc appare;
O amator amplectende,
Temetipsum tunc ostende
In cruce salutiferâ.　　　　100

BONAVENTURA.

BONAVENTURA, a Tuscan by birth, was born in 1221, and educated at Paris, which was still the most illustrious school of theology in Europe. Upon entering the Franciscan Order, he changed his family name, John of Fidanza, to that by which he is known to the after world. In 1245 he became himself professor of theology at Paris, in 1256 General of his Order, and in 1273 cardinal-bishop of Alba. He died in 1274 at Lyons, during the Council which was held there, to which he had accompanied Pope Gregory the 10th. At once a master in the scholastic and mystical theology, though far greater in the last, he received from the Church of the middle ages the title Doctor Seraphicus, and his own Order set him against the yet greater Dominican, Thomas Aquinas. His *Biblia Pauperum* is an honourable testimony to his zeal for the spread of Scriptural knowledge through the ministry of the Word among the common people: nor can any one have even that partial knowledge of his writings, which is all that I myself would claim, without entirest conviction that he who could thus write, must have possessed a richest personal familiarity with all the deeper mysteries of that spiritual life whereof he speaks. Yet this ought not to tempt us to deny, but rather the more freely to declare, that he shared, and shared largely, in the error as well as in the truth of his age. At the same time, if we except the *Psaltery of the Virgin,* there is no work of his by which he could be so unfavourably known as his *Meditations on the Life of Jesus Christ*, of which some may remember a most offensive reproduction some years ago in England. If indeed that *Psaltery of the Virgin* be his, of which happily there are considerable doubts, it is too plain that he did not merely acquiesce in that amount of worship of the creature which he found, but was also its enthusiastic promoter to a yet higher and wilder pitch than before it had reached. His Latin poetry is good, but does not call for any especial criticism.

XXIII. IN PASSIONE DOMINI.

QUAM despectus, quam dejectus,
   Rex cœlorum est effectus,
Ut salvaret sæculum;
Esurivit et sitivit,
Pauper et egenus ivit   5
Usque ad patibulum.

Recordare paupertatis,
Et extremæ vilitatis,
Et gravis supplicii.
Si es compos rationis,   10
Esto memor passionis,
Fellis, et absinthii.

XXIII. *Bonaventuræ Opp.* Lugduni, 1668, vol. vi. p. 423.

Cum deductus est immensus,
Et in cruce tunc suspensus,
Fugerunt discipuli.   15
Manus, pedes perfoderunt,
Et aceto potaverunt
Summum Regem sæculi;

Cujus oculi beati
Sunt in cruce obscurati,   20
Et vultus expalluit:
Suo corpori tunc nudo
Non remansit pulcritudo,
Decor omnis aufugit.

Qui hæc audis, ingemisce,   25
Et in istis planctum misce,
Et cordis mœstitias:
Corpus ange, corde plange,
Mentem frange, manu tange
Christi mortis sævitias.   30

Virum respice dolorum,
Et novissimum virorum,
Fortem ad supplicia.
Tibi gratum sit et æquum
Jam in cruce mori secum,   35
Compati convicia.

---

35. *secum*] All are aware that there are, even in the Latin
of the best age, some slight anticipations of the breaking down
of the distinction between the demonstrative and the reflective
pronouns (Zumpt, *Lat. Gramm.* § 550). In medieval Latin they
are continually confounded, and the reflective put instead of the
demonstrative, as here, and again in the next stanza.

Bone frater, quicquid agas,
Crucifixi vide plagas,
Et sibi compatere ;
Omni tempore sint tibi 40
Quasi spiritales cibi ;
His gaudenter fruere.

Crucifixe, fac me fortem,
Ut libenter tuam mortem
Plangam, donec vixero. 45
Tecum volo vulnerari,
Te libenter amplexari
In cruce desidero.

BONAVENTURA.

XXIV. DE PASSIONE DOMINI.

QUANTUM hamum caritas tibi praesentavit,
  Mori cum pro homine te solicitavit;
Sed et escâ placidâ hamum occupavit,
Cum lucrari animas te per hoc monstravit.

Te quidem aculeus hami non latebat,   5
Sed illius punctio te non deterrebat,
Immo hunc impetere tibi complacebat,
Quia desiderium escae attrahebat.

Ergo pro me misero, quem tu dilexisti,
Mortis in aculeum sciens impegisti,   10
Cum te Patri victimam sanctam obtulisti,
Et in tuo sanguine sordidum lavisti.

Heu! cur beneficia Christi passionis
Penes te memoriter, homo, non reponis?
Per hanc enim rupti sunt laquei praedonis,   15
Per hanc Christus maximis te ditavit bonis.

Suo quippe corpore languidum te pavit,
Quem in suo sanguine gratis balneavit,
Demum suum dulce' cor tibi denudavit,
Ut sic innotesceret quantum te amavit.   20

XXIV. *Bonaventurae Opp.* vol. vi. p. 424; Corner, *Prompt.
Devot.* p. 117.

Oh! quam dulce balneum, esca quam suävis,
Quæ sumenti digne fit Paradisi clavis:
Est ei quem reficis nullus labor gravis,
Licet sis fastidio cordibus ignavis.

Cor ignavi siquidem minime perpendit   25
Ad quid Christus optimum suum cor ostendit,
Super alas positum crucis, nec attendit
Quod reclinatorii vices hoc prætendit.

Hoc reclinatorium quoties monstratur
Piæ menti, toties ei glutinatur,   30
Sicut et accipiter totus inescatur
Super carnem rubeam, per quam revocatur.

XXV. DE CORONA SPINEA.

S I vis vere gloriari,
  Et a Deo coronari
Honore et gloriâ,
Hanc Coronam contemplari
Studeas, atque sectari   5
Portantis vestigia.

Hanc cœlorum Rex portavit,
Honoravit et sacravit
Sacro suo capite;
In hâc galeâ pugnavit,   10
Cum antiquum hostem stravit,
Triumphans in stipite.

Hæc pugnantis galea,
Triumphantis laurea,
Tiara pontificis: 15

XXV. Clichtoveus, *Elucidat. Eccles.* Paris, 1556 (not in the
earlier editions).—Balde has a series of brief poems on the
several instruments of the passion.   This on the thorn-crown:

> Hoc quale vides pressit Regem
> Diadema tuum : fulget acutus
> Utrinque lapis.   Ferus in mediis
> Sentibus istas reperit gemmas
> Lictor, et alto vulnere fixit.
> En ut radiant! rhamnus iaspis,
> Paliurus onyx, spina smaragdus,
> Tanto posthac verius omnes,
> Homo, divitias regnaque mundi
> Opulenta potes dicere *Spinas.*

13—18. There appeared a very good translation of some of

Primum fuit spinea,
Postmodum fit aurea
Tactu sancti verticis.

Spinarum aculeos
Virtus fecit aureos   20
Christi passionis ;
Quæ peccatis spineos,
Mortis æternæ reos,
Adimplevit bonis.

De malis colligitur,   25
Et de spinis plectitur
Spinea perversis :
Sed in aurum vertitur,
Quando culpa tollitur,
Eisdem conversis.   30

Jesu pie, Jesu bone,
Nostro nobis in agone
Largire victoriam ;
Mores nostros sic compone,   .
Ut perpetuæ coronæ   35
Mereamur gloriam.

---

these stanzas in *Fraser's Magazine*, May, 1849, p. 530. This
stanza was rendered thus :

> Helm on soldier's forehead shining,
> Laurel, conqueror's brows entwining,
>   High Priest's mitre dread !
> 'Twas of thorns ; but now, behold,
> 'Tis become of purest gold.
>   Touched by that blest head.

XXVI. DE PASSIONE DOMINI.

ECQUIS binas columbinas
  Alas dabit animæ?
Ut in almam crucis palmam
Evolet citissime,
In quâ Jesus totus læsus,   5
Orbis desiderium,
Et immensus est suspensus,
Factus improperium !

Oh cor, scande; Jesu, pande
Caritatis viscera,   10
Et profunde me reconde
Intra sacra vulnera ;
In supernâ me cavernâ
Colloca maceriæ ;
Hic viventi, quiescenti   15
Finis est miseriæ !

XXVI. [Walraff,] *Corolla Hymnorum,* p. 16 ; Daniel, *Thes. Hymnol.* vol. ii. p. 345.—Of this graceful little poem, which, to judge from internal evidence, is of no great antiquity, I am not able to give any satisfactory account. I have only met it twice, as noted above, and in neither case with any indication of its source or age. It is certainly of a very rare perfection in its kind.

8. *improperium*] = *convicium, derisio,* and probably connected with *probrum,* is a word peculiar to Church Latin. It occurs several times in the Vulgate, as Rom. xv. 3 ; Heb. xi. 26. The verb *improperare* (= ὀνειδίζειν) is used by Petronius.

13, 14. *cavernâ...maceriæ*] He alludes to Cant. ii. 14 (Vulg.):

O mi Deus, amor meus !
Tunc pro me pateris ?
Proque indigno, crucis ligno,
Jesu mi, suffigeris ? 20
Pro latrone, Jesu bone,
Tu in crucem tolleris ?
Pro peccatis meis gratis,
Vita mea, moreris ?

Non sum tanti, Jesu, quanti 25
Amor tuus æstimat;
Heu ! cur ego vitam dego,
Si cor te non redamat ?
Benedictus sit invictus
Amor vincens omnia; 30
Amor fortis, tela mortis
Reputans ut somnia.

Iste fecit, et refecit
Amor, Jesu, perditum ;
O insignis, Amor, ignis, 35
Cor accende frigidum !
O fac vere cor ardere,
Fac me te diligere,
Da conjungi, da defungi
Tecum, Jesu, et vivere ! 40

Columba mea in foraminibus petræ, *in cavernâ macceriæ* : on
which words St Bernard writes (*In Cant. Serm.* 61) : Foramina
petræ, vulnera Christi. In his passer invenit sibi domum et
turtur nidum, ubi reponat pullos suos : in his se columba tutatur,
et circumvolitantem intuetur accipitrem.

FORTUNATUS.

XXVII. DE RESURRECTIONE DOMINI.

SALVE, festa dies, toto venerabilis ævo,
    Quâ Deus infernum vicit, et astra tenet.
Ecce renascentis testatur gratia mundi
    Omnia cum Domino dona redîsse suo.
Namque triumphanti post tristia Tartara Christo   5
    Undique froude nemus, gramina flore favent.
Legibus inferni oppressis super astra meantem
    Laudant rite Deum lux, polus, arva, fretum.
Qui crucifixus erat, Deus ecce per omnia regnat,
    Dantque Creatori cuncta creata precem.   10

XXVII. Creuzer, *Symbolik*, vol. iv. p. 742; Daniel, *Thes. Hymnol.* vol. i. p. 170.

ADAM OF ST VICTOR.

XXVIII. DE RESURRECTIONE DOMINI.

MUNDI renovatio
Nova parit gaudia,
Resurgente Domino
Conresurgunt omnia :
Elementa serviunt,   5
Et Auctoris sentiunt
Quanta sint sollemnia.

Ignis volat mobilis,
Et aër volubilis,
Fluit aqua labilis,   10
Terra manet stabilis,
Alta petunt levia,
Centrum tenent gravia,
Renovantur omnia.

XXVIII. Clichtoveus, *Elucidat. Eccles.* p. 168; Daniel, *Thes. Hymnol.* vol. ii. p. 68; Gautier, *Adam de S. Victor*, vol. i. p. 82. —The thought of the coincidence of the natural and spiritual spring, the falling in of the world's Easter and the Church's, and of the ἀπαρχαὶ of both, which is the underlying thought of this and the last poem, comes beautifully out in a noble Easter Sermon by Gregory of Nazianzum, in which he exclaims : Νῦν ἔαρ κοσμικὸν, ἔαρ πνευματικόν · ἔαρ ψυχαῖς, ἔαρ σώμασιν · ἔαρ ὁρώμενον, ἔαρ ἀόρατον.

Cœlum fit serenius,   15
Et mare tranquillius,
Spirat aura levius,
Vallis nostra floruit;
Revirescunt arida,
Recalescunt frigida,   20
Quia ver intepuit.

Gelu mortis solvitur,
Princeps mundi tollitur,
Et ejus destruitur
In nobis imperium;   25
Dum tenere voluit
In quo nihil habuit,
Jus amisit proprium.

Vita mortem superat;
Homo jam recuperat   30
Quod prius amiserat
Paradisi gaudium.
Viam præbet facilem
Cherubim, versatilem
Amovendo gladium.   35

---

23. *tollitur*] Some MSS. read *fallitur.*
34. *versatilem*] Cf. Gen. iii. 24 (Vulg.).

XXIX. DE RESURRECTIONE DOMINI.

HᴁꞏC est dies triumphalis,
  Mundo grata perdito,
Dans solamen nostris malis,
  Hoste jugo subdito.
Hæc est dies specialis,   5
  Tanto nitens merito,
Quod peccati fit finalis,
  Mali malo irrito.

Duce fraudis demolito
  Terris pax indicitur,   10
Et exhausto aconito
  Salus ægris redditur:
Morte mortis morsu trito
  Vitæ spes infunditur,
Claustro pestis inanito   15
  Nefas omne pellitur.

Cum nos Christus fecundare
  Tanto vellet fœdere,

XXIX. Flacius Illyricus, *Poëmm. de Corrupto Ecclesiæ Statu*,
Basle, 1556, p. 71.

8. *Mali malo*] The first *mali* is probably *mālum*, and a play
intended on the word; such it often provoked, as in Quarles'
Totus mundus jacet in *mali-ligno*.

17, 18. *fecundare···fœdere*] This at first sight seems a strange
mixture of metaphors; but by *fœdus* doubtless the poet means
the marriage-union betwixt the Church or single soul and its

Et se morti gratis dare
Pro reorum scelere,
Jure decet hunc laudare,
Et ei consurgere,
Pascha novum celebrare
Corde, voce, et opere.

Lord, whereby the former is made fruitful (fecundata), and enabled to bring forth spiritual children to him. Thus Hugh of St Victor: Quatuor sunt propter quæ anima dicitur sponsa ... and then among these four: proles virtutum, quibus fecundata est divini Verbi dogmate.

PETER THE VENERABLE.

XXX. DE RESURRECTIONE DOMINI.

MORTIS portis fractis, fortis
    Fortior vim sustulit;
Et per crucem regem trucem
Infernorum perculit.
Lumen clarum tenebrarum   5
Sedibus resplenduit;
Dum salvare, recreare,
Quod creavit, voluit.
Hinc Creator, ne peccator
Moreretur, moritur;   10
Cujus morte novâ sorte
Vita nobis oritur.
Inde Sathan victus gemit,
Unde victor nos redemit;
Illud illi fit letale,   15
Quod est homini vitale,
Qui, dum captat, capitur,
Et, dum mactat, moritur.
Sic decenter, sic potenter
Rex devincens inferos,   20
Linquens ima die primâ,
Rediit ad superos.

XXX. *Bibliotheca Cluniacensis*, Paris, 1614, p. 1349.

Resurrexit, et revexit
Secum Deus hominem,
Reparando quam creando   25
Dederat originem.
Per Auctoris passionem
Ad amissam regionem
Primus redit nunc colonus:
Unde lætus fit hic sonus.   30

XXXI. IN RESURRECTIONE DOMINI.

PONE luctum, Magdalena,
  Et serena lacrymas;
Non est jam Simonis cœna,
Non cur fletum exprimas;
Causæ mille sunt lætandi,   5
Causæ mille exultandi:
  Alleluia resonet.

Sume risum, Magdalena,
Frons nitescat lucida;
Demigravit omnis pœna,   10
Lux coruscat fulgida;

XXXI. [Walraff,] *Corolla Hymnorum*, p. 36; Daniel, *Thes. Hymnol.* vol. ii. p. 365.

3. *Simonis cœna*] This identification of Mary Magdalene and "the woman that was a sinner" (Luke vii. 37) runs through all the theology of the Middle Ages; constantly recurring in the hymns; thus in the *Dies Iræ;* and in another hymn, published, I believe, for the first time in the *Missale de Arbuthnott*, 1864, p. 176; where of Mary Magdalene it is said:

> Hæc est illa fœmina,
> Cujus cuncta crimina
> Ad Christi vestigia
> Ejus lavit gratia.
> Quæ dum plorat, et mens orat,
> Facto clamat quod cor amat
> Jesum super omnia;
> Non ignorat quem adorat,
> Quid precetur; sed deletur
> Quod mens timet conscia.

Christus mundum liberavit,
Et de morte triumphavit :
  Alleluia resonet.

Gaude, plaude, Magdalena,   15
Tumbâ Christus exiit,
Tristis est peracta scena,
Victor mortis rediit ;
Quem deflebas morientem,
Nunc arride resurgentem :   20
  Alleluia resonet.

Tolle vultum, Magdalena,
Redivivum obstupe ;
Vide frons quam sit amœna,
Quinque plagas aspice ;   25
Fulgent sicut margaritæ,
Ornamenta novæ vitæ :
  Alleluia resonet.

Vive, vive, Magdalena,
Tua lux reversa est,   30
Gaudiis turgescat vena,
Mortis vis abstersa est ;
Mœsti procul sunt dolores,
Læti redeant amores :
  Alleluia resonet.   35

ADAM OF ST VICTOR.

XXXII. DE RESURRECTIONE DOMINI.

ECCE dies celebris!
  Lux succedit tenebris,
Morti resurrectio.
Lætis cedant tristia,
Cum sit major gloria,   5
Quam prima confusio.
Umbram fugat veritas,
Vetustatem novitas,
Luctum consolatio.

Pascha novum colite;   10
Quod præit in capite,
Membra sperent singula;
Pascha novum Christus est,
Qui pro nobis passus est,
Agnus sine maculâ.   15

Hostis, qui nos circuit,
Prædam Christus eruit:

XXXII. Clichtoveus, *Elucidat. Eccles.* p. 173; Daniel, *Thes. Hymnol.* vol. v. p. 194; Gautier, *Adam de S. Victor*, vol. i. p. 54.

16. *qui nos circuit*] Cf. 1 Pet. v. 8 (Vulg.).

Quod Samson præcinuit,
Dum leonem lacerat.
David fortis viribus   20
A leonis unguibus,
Et ab ursi faucibus,
Gregem Patris liberat.

Qui in morte plures stravit,
Samson, Christum figuravit,   25
Cujus mors victoria :
Samson dictus *Sol eorum* ;
Christus lux est electorum,
Quos illustrat gratia.

Jam de crucis sacro vecte   30
Botrus fluit in dilectæ
Penetral Ecclesiæ.

18, 19. Cf. Judg. xiv. 6.

20—23. Cf. 1 Sam. xvii. 34—36.

24—26. *mors victoria*] Gregory the Great (*Mor.* xxix. 14):
Pauci enim ex plebe Israeliticâ ipso prædicante crediderunt:
innumeri vero gentium populi viam vitæ moriente illo secuti sunt.
Quod bene Samson in semetipso dudum figuraliter expressit, qui
paucos quidem, dum viveret, interemit ; destructo autem templo,
hostes innumeros, cum moreretur, occidit.

27. *Sol eorum*] This etymology of Samson's name is derived
from Jerome, who (*De Nom. Heb.*) explains Samson: *Sol eorum,
vel solis fortitudo—their* light, or, the light of them that are his.
So too Augustine (*Enarr. in Ps.* lxxx. 10): Unde Samson noster,
qui etiam interpretatur *Sol ipsorum,* eorum scilicet quibus lucet ;
non omnium, sicuti est oriens super bonos et malos, sed sol quo-
rundam, sol justitiæ, figuram enim habebat Christi. They may
have been right in seeing *shemesh,* or the sun, in Samson's name ;
but ' sol *eorum*' is of course a mistake.

31. *Botrus*] Among the Old Testament types of Christ and
his cross, that of Num. xiii. 23, 24, was ever counted as one:

Jam calcato torculari,
Musto gaudent ebriari
Gentium primitiæ.   35

Saccus scissus et pertusus
In regales transit usus ;
Saccus fit soccus gratiæ,
Caro victrix miseriæ.
Quia regem peremerunt,   40
Rei regnum perdiderunt :

---

thus Hugh of St Victor (*Inst. Mor.* i. 4): Christus est Botrus
de terrâ promissionis in desertum translatus ; the type of the
cross being the pole (vectis is the word of the Vulgate), on which
this bunch of grapes was suspended. Augustine (*Enarr. in Ps.*
viii. 1): Nam et Verbum divinum potest *Uva* intelligi. Dictus
est enim et Dominus botrus uvæ, quem ligno suspensum, de terrâ
promissionis, qui præmissi erant a populo Israel, tanquam cru-
cifixum, attulerunt. In Christ's passion this bunch of grapes
was trodden as in the winepress (Isai. lxiii. 3, 6), and his blood
as the wine flowed into the *penetral* or ὑπολήνιον of the Church.

In ligno botrus est pendens, in cruce Christus ;
   Profluit hinc vinum, profluit inde salus.
Ejicitur prælo de botro gratia vini ;
   Prælo pressa crucis sanguis et unda fluit.—*Pet. de Riga.*

36—38. *Saccus scissus*] The poet has in his eye Ps. xxix.
12 (Vulg.), xxx. 11 (E. V.): Conscidisti saccum meum, et cir-
cumdedisti me lætitiâ ; upon which words Augustine (*Serm.*
336, c. 4): Saccus ejus erat similitudo carnis peccati. In passione
conscissus est saccus. And then presently, with allusion to the
saccus as the purse or bag of money: Conscidit saccum lanceâ
persecutor, et fudit pretium nostrum Redemtor [John xix. 34].
—Clichtoveus ; *In regales transit usus*, quando per resurrectionem immortalitatis stolâ corpus est indutum, et incorruptibili-
tatis virtute præcinctum.

41. *Rei*] A far better reading, as it seems to me, than *Dei*,
which Gautier has. We may compare Augustine : Ut possi-
derent, occiderunt ; et quia occiderunt, perdiderunt.

Sed non deletur penitus
Caïn, in signum positus.

Reprobatus et abjectus
Lapis iste, nunc electus,   45
In tropæum stat erectus,
Et in caput anguli.
Culpam delens non naturam,
Novam creat creaturam,
Tenens in se ligaturam   50
Utriusque populi.

Capiti sit gloria
Membrisque concordia!   Amen.

------

43. *in signum positus*]   The poet with only the Vulgate
before him, in which he found (Gen. iv. 15), Posuitque Dominus Cain signum (Cain being undeclined), understood the passage
thus: "The Lord set Cain for a sign," instead of "The Lord set
a sign upon Cain."   In his application of these words to the
Jewish people, the great collective Cain, the murderer of Him
whose blood spake better things than that of Abel, he had many
forerunners.   They too, it was said, were not destroyed, but,
while other nations were fused and absorbed and lost in the
great Roman world, abode apart, being not slain, despite their
sin, but set for an everlasting sign.   Thus Augustine; who even
in his time found a wonderful significance in this continued and
separate existence of the Jews, and therein a prophetic fulfilment
of these words of Genesis, as also of those of the Psalmist:
"Slay them not, lest my people forget it" (*Con. Faust.* 12, 13;
Enarr. in Ps. lviii. 12).

ADAM OF ST VICTOR.

XXXIII. DE RESURRECTIONE DOMINI.

ZYMA vetus expurgetur,
  Ut sincere celebretur
Nova resurrectio.
Hæc est dies nostræ spei,
Hujus mira vis diei   5
Legis testimonio.

Hæc Ægyptum spoliavit,
Et Hebræos liberavit
De fornace ferreâ:
His in arcto constitutis   10
Opus erat servitutis
Lutum, later, palea.

XXXIII. Clichtoveus, *Elucidat. Eccles.* p. 169; Rambach, *Anthol. Christl. Gesänge*, p. 290; Daniel, *Thes. Hymnol.* vol. ii. p. 69; Gautier, *Adam de S. Victor*, vol. i. p. 88.—Clichtoveus says truly here: Sane hæc prosa admodum divina est, paucis multa complectens, et tota ex sacris literis præclare desumpta, cujus et historias et sententias congruenter copioseque adaptat proposito, ut hoc suo opificio auctor ipsius liquido prodat se in divinis Scripturis apprime exercitatum et promptum fuisse.

1—3. Cf. 1 Cor. v. 7, 8; Exod. xii. 19.

4—6. Cf. Exod. xii. 41, 42.

12. *Lutum, later, palea*] Cf. Exod. i. 14; v. 12. In the "mortar," "brick," and "straw" were often seen, as here, the works of the old man, while still serving sin in the spiritual Egypt. Thus Hugh of St Victor (*Alleg.* iii. 1): Lutum, in quo servierunt filii Israel Pharaoni, eo quod lutum inquinat, luxuriam

Jam divinæ laus virtutis,
Jam triumphi, jam salutis
Vox erumpat libera: 15
Hæc est dies quam fecit Dominus,
Dies nostri doloris terminus,
Dies salutifera.

Lex est umbra futurorum,
Christus finis promissorum,   20
Qui consummat omnia.
Christi sanguis igneam
Hebetavit rhomphæam,
Amotâ custodiâ.

Puer, nostri forma risûs,   25
Pro quo vervex est occisus,
Vitæ signat gaudium.

---

designat. Palea, eo quod levis est, et cito transvolat, vanam gloriam significat. Later quoque, qui de molli terrâ confectus, per decoctionem ignis durescit, humani cordis duritiam, per longam sive concupiscentiæ, sive libidinis, aut avaritiæ consuetudinem decoctam ostendit.

15. Cf. Ps. cxvii. 24 (Vulg.).

25. *risûs*]   Daniel has made this verse unintelligible, printing *visus*, whether by mistake, or intending a correction. The emendation, if such, and no mere error of the press, rests on ignorance of that ever-recurring thought in early and medieval theology, of Christ as our Isaac, in that He made us to laugh, and thus, our *laughter*, with allusion to Gen. xxi. 6 (Vulg.): Risum fecit mihi Deus: quicumque audierit, corridebit mihi. Thus Ambrose (*De Isaac et Animâ*, c. 1): Ipso nomine gratiam signat, Isaac etenim *risus* Latine significatur, risus autem insigne lætitiæ est. Quis autem ignorat quod is universorum lætitia sit, qui mortis formidolosæ vel pavore compresso, factus omnibus est

Joseph exit de cisternâ,
Christus redit ad superna
Post mortis supplicium. 30

Hic dracones Pharaonis
Draco vorat, a draconis
Immunis malitiâ,
Quos ignitus vulnerat,
Hos serpentis liberat 35
Ænei præsentia.

Anguem forat in maxillâ
Christus, hamus et armilla;

---

remissio peccatorum?   That the thought was a familiar one with
our poet we have proof in another poem of his, in which he expresses himself thus:

> Prole serâ tandem fœta,
> Anus Sara ridet læta,
> Nostrum lactans Gaudium.

The use of *forma* here as=*figura*, τύπος, is frequent ; thus Hugh
of St Victor: Melchisedek, qui est *forma* Christi.

31—33. Cf. Exod. vii. 10—12.

38. *hamus et armilla*]   Cf. Job xl. 20, 21 (Vulg.); xli. 1, 2,
(E. V.), where the Lord asks Job, An extrahere poteris Leviathan
hamo, et fune ligabis linguam ejus?   Numquid pones circulum
in naribus ejus, aut armillâ perforabis maxillam ejus?   This
question, by the help of Isai. xxvii. 1 ("Leviathan, that crooked
serpent") was mystically interpreted, Wilt thou dare to contend
with Satan and the powers of spiritual wickedness? (cf. Jerome
on Isai. xxvii. 1).   But this, which a mortal man like Job could
not do, Christ did.   He did "draw out Leviathan with a hook."
It is a favourite thought with the old Fathers, that Christ's humanity was as the bait which Satan seized, not perceiving the
hook for his jaws, which lay beneath, in Christ's latent Divinity.
Thus Gregory the Great (*Mor.* xxxiii. 7): In hamo ergo ejus in-

In cavernam reguli
Manum mittit ablactatus,   40
Et sic fugit exturbatus
Vetus hospes sæculi.

Irrisores Helisæi,
Dum conscendit domum Dei,
Zelum calvi sentiunt.   .   45
David arreptitius,

---

carnationis captus est, quia dum in illo appetit escam corporis, transfixus est aculeo divinitatis. Ibi quippe inerat humanitas, quæ ad se devoratorem duceret: ibi divinitas quæ perforaret: ibi aperta infirmitas quæ provocaret: ibi occulta virtus, quæ raptoris faucem transfigeret. In hamo igitur captus est, quia inde interiit unde devoravit.

39. *reguli*] *Regulus*, the diminutive of *rex*, exactly answers to βασιλίσκος, and to *basilisk*, a name we give to a serpent with crownlike, and so *kingly*, marks upon its head; Pliny (*H. N.* viii. 33): Candidâ in capite maculâ, ut quodam diademate insignis; cf. Gregory the Great (*Mor.* xv. 15): Regulus namque serpentum rex dicitur. These lines must be explained by Isai. xi. 8 (Vulg.): Et in cavernam reguli qui ablactatus est, manum suam mittet. Christ, according to a favourite interpretation, was "the weaned child;" this evil world the cockatrice's hole into which He thrust in his hand, dragging out Satan from his lurking-place and den. Thus Jerome (*in loc.*), and Gregory the Great (*Mor.* xxvi. 32).

43—45. Cf. 2 Kin. ii. 23—25. Hugh of St Victor: Eliseus interpretatur salus Dei. Huic, id est, Christo, illuserunt Judæi exaltato in cruce...Sed postquam Christus ascendit in Bethel, id est, in domum Dei, in quadragesimo anno immisit duos ursos de filiis gentium, Vespasianum et Titum, qui crudeli strage eos dejecerunt. Cf. Augustine, *Enarr. in Ps.* xliv. in init.

46. *arreptitius*] = arreptus furore. The word occurs in Augustine, *De Civ. Dei*, ii. 4. The allusion is to 1 Sam. xxi. 14, where instead of the Vidistis hominem *insanum?* of the Vulgate, the older Latin version must have had *arreptitium*; as is plain

Hircus emissarius,
Et passer effugiunt.

In maxillâ mille sternit,
Et de tribu suâ spernit   50
Samson matrimonium:
Samson Gazæ seras pandit,
Et asportans portas scandit
Montis supercilium.

Sic de Judâ Leo fortis,   55
Fractis portis diræ mortis,
Die surgit tertiâ.
Rugiente voce Patris,
Ad supernæ sinum matris
Tot revexit spolia.   60

---

from Augustine, *Enarr.* 1ᵃ *in Ps.* xxxiii., where he expounds at
length the mystery of David's supposed madness, and of the
prophecy which was herein of Christ, of whom the people said,
"He is mad, and hath a devil." David's escape from the presence of Achish represents to him Christ's escape at his resurrection from the Jews.

48. *Et passer*] The allusion is not to Ps. xi. 1: Transmigra
in montem sicut passer (Daniel); but to Lev. xiv. 49—53.

52. *Gazæ seras*] Thus Hugh of St Victor: Samson apportans
portas Gazæ ascendit montis supercilium, et Christus, fractis
portis inferni, ascendit in cœlum. The typical character of Samson's feat is brought out at length and with admirable skill by
Gregory the Great (*Hom.* 21 *in Evang.*), and by Augustine
(*Serm.* 364).

58. *Rugiente*] I have touched already, p. 68, on the medieval
legend of the lion's whelps born dead, but roused on the third
day by the roar of their sire. Thus Hugh of St Victor (*De Best.*
ii. 1): Cum leæna parit, suos catulos mortuos parit, et ita custo-
dit tribus diebus, donec veniens pater eorum in faciem eorum

Cetus Jonam fugitivum,
Veri Jonæ signativum,
Post tres dies reddit vivum
De ventris angustiâ.
Botrus Cypri reflorescit,   65
Dilatatur et excrescit:
Synagogæ flos marcescit,
Et floret Ecclesia.

Mors et vita conflixere,
Resurrexit Christus vere,   70
Et cum Christo surrexere
Multi testes gloriæ.
Mane novum, mane lætum,
Vespertinum tergat fletum;

---

exhalet, ut vivificentur.   Sic omnipotens Pater Filium suum tertiâ die suscitavit a mortuis.   And Hildebert (*De Leone*);

> Natus non vigilat dum sol se tertio gyrat,
> Sed dans rugitum pater ejus suscitat illum:
> Tunc quasi vivescit, tunc sensus quinque capescit;
> Et quotiens dormit sua nunquam lumina claudit.

This last line expresses another belief, namely that the lion slept with its eyes open: these open eyes being an emblem of that divine life of Christ which ran uninterrupted through the three days' sleep of his body in the grave.   Cf. Cant. v. 2, often quoted in this sense: "I sleep, but my heart waketh."—It need hardly be said that the *mater* (ver. 59) is the New Jerusalem, "the *mother* of us all."

65. *Botrus Cypri*]   Cf. Cant. i. 13 (Vulg.), i. 14 (E. V.): Botrus Cypri dilectus mihi, in vineis Engaddi; on which Bernard (*In Cant., Serm.* 44) with allusion to the verse preceding ("A bundle of myrrh is my beloved unto me"): Dominus meus Jesus myrrha mihi in morte, botrus in resurrectione.

72. Cf. Matt. xxvii. 52.

73, 74. The allusion is to Ps. xxix. 6 (Vulg.), xxx. 5 (E. V.):

Quia vita vicit letum,   75
Tempus est lætitiæ.

Jesu victor, Jesu vita,
Jesu, vitæ via trita,
Cujus morte mors sopita,
Ad paschalem nos invita   80
Mensam cum fiduciâ.
Vive panis, vivax unda,
Vera vitis et fœcunda,
Tu nos pasce, tu nos munda,
Ut a morte nos secundâ   85
Tua salvet gratia.

Ad vesperum demorabitur fletus, et ad matutinum lætitia ; words often regarded as a prophecy of Him who turned by his resurrection the night of sorrow into the morning of joy. Thus Jerome: Ad vesperum demorabitur fletus, quia passo et sepulto Domino Apostoli et mulieres in fletu et gemitu demorabantur. Et ad matutinum lætitia, quia mane [cf. Marc. xvi. 9] venientes ad sepulcrum gloriam resurrectionis ab angelis acceperunt. And compare Augustine (*in loc.*), who carries on his thought to yet another morning of joy, after a yet longer night of weeping: Matutinum, quo exsultatio resurrectionis futura est, quæ in matutinâ Domini resurrectione præfloruit.

XXXIV. DE MYSTERIO ASCENSIONIS DOMINI.

PORTAS vestras æternales,
   Triumphales, principales,
Angeli, attollite.
Eja, tollite actutum,
Venit Dominus virtutum,   5
Rex æternæ gloriæ.

Venit totus lætabundus,
Candidus et rubicundus,

XXXIV. Corner, *Promp. Devot.* p. 788.   Nothing is poorer
throughout the whole Christian Church than the hymnology of the
Ascension.   Even the German Protestant hymn-book, so incom-
parably rich in Passion and Resurrection and Pentecost hymns, is
singularly ill-furnished with these.   It is not here the place to enquire into the causes of this poverty, which certainly is not the
effect of chance, but only to observe that the Latin forms no exception ; it does not possess a single first-rate hymn on the Ascension. At the same time the following stanzas are not without a real
merit of their own ; and strangely enough, they have never
found their way into any of the more modern collections of
Latin hymns.

1—6. Cf. Ps. xxiii. 9, 10 (Vulg.): Attollite portas principes
vestras, et elevamini, portæ æternales : et introibit rex gloriæ.
Quis est iste rex gloriæ? Dominus virtutum, ipse est rex gloriæ.

8. Cf. Cant. v. 10 (Vulg.): Dilectus meus candidus et rubicundus.   A few words from Richard of St Victor (*in Cant.*
c. 36) will shew in what sense the epithets were continually
applied to the Lord : Candidus, quia immunis est ab omni
peccato ; et rubicundus, quia in Passione sanguine suo est
perfusus.

Tinctis clarus vestibus.
Novâ gloriosus stolâ, 10
Gradiens virtute solâ,
Multis cinctus millibus.

Solus erat in egressu,
Sed ingentem in regressu
Affert multitudinem. 15
Fructum suæ passionis,
Testem resurrectionis,
Novam cœli segetem.

Eja, jubilate Deo,
Jacent hostes, vicit leo, 20
Vicit semen Abrahæ.
Jam ruinæ replebuntur,
Cœli cives augebuntur,
Salvabuntur animæ.

Regnet Christus triumphator, 25
Hominumque liberator,
Rex misericordiæ:
Princeps pacis, Deus fortis,
Vitæ dator, victor mortis,
Laus cœlestis curiæ. 30

Tu, qui cœlum reserâsti,
Et in illo præparâsti

9—11. Cf. Isai. lxiii. 1 (Vulg.): Quis est iste, qui venit de
Edom, tinctis vestibus de Bosrâ, iste formosus in stolá suâ,
gradiens in multitudine fortitudinis suæ?
32, 33. Cf. John xiv. 3.

> Locum tuis famulis,
> Fac me tibi famulari,
> Et te piis venerari   35
> Hic in terrâ jubilis;
>
> Ut post actum vitæ cursum,
> Ego quoque scandens sursum
> Te videre valeam,
> Juxta Patrem considentem,   40
> Triumphantem et regentem
> Omnia per gloriam.

---

42. I have spoken in no high terms of the hymns on the Ascension. I must not however leave unsaid that one of these, first published by Dr. Neale (*Ecclesiologist*, Feb. 1854), yields the following noble stanzas:

> Intrat tabernaculum
> Moÿses, et populum
> Trahit ad spectaculum
> Tantæ virtus rei:
> Stant suspensis vultibus,
> Intendentes nubibus
> Jesum subducentibus,
> Viri Galilæi.
>
> Dum Elias sublevatur,
> Eliseo duplex datur
> Spiritus et pallium.
> Alta Christus dum conscendit,
> Servis suis mnas appendit
> Gratiarum omnium.
>
> Transit Jacob hunc Jordanem,
> Luctum gerens non inanem,
> Crucis usus baculo.
> Redit turmis cum duabus,
> Angelis et animabus,
> Et thesauri sacculo.

In the last line I have ventured to substitute *sacculo* for *sæculo*.

XXXV. DE SPIRITU SANCTO.

VENI, Creator Spiritus,
   Spiritus recreator,
Tu dans, tu datus cœlitus,
Tu donum, tu donator :
Tu lex, tu digitus,   5
Alens et alitus,
Spirans et spiritus,
Spiratus et spirator.

XXXV. Flacius Illyricus, *Poëmm. de Corrupto Ecclesiæ Statu,*
p. 66.

4. *Tu donum*] Medieval theology made much of the term
donum, as a *nomen proprium* of the third Person of the Holy
Trinity. He was not *a* gift, but *the* gift, of God, in so high and
exclusive a sense, that the term competed only to Him, and thus
became his proper name. See an interesting discussion by
Aquinas (*Summ. Theol., pars* 1ª, *Qu.* 38): Spiritui S. donum est
proprium nomen, et personale. But this application of the
term *donum Dei* is indeed as old as Augustine (*Enchir.* 12).

5. *lex*] *Rex* in the volume of Flacius Illyricus, where only
I have seen this hymn ; yet I cannot doubt that *lex* is the right
reading. In the two preceding and two following lines there is
an evident antithesis, and plainly one intended also here ; but
what such would there be between *rex* and *digitus?* not to say
that *rex* is a title nowhere specially applied to the Holy Spirit.
But the antithesis comes excellently out when we read : *Tu lex,
tu digitus :* "Thou the law, the living law, and the finger which
writes that law,"—with allusion to such promises as that contained Heb. viii. 10.

Tu septiformis gratiæ
Dans septiforme donum,   10
Virtutis septifariæ,
Septem petitionum.
Tu nix non defluens,
Ignis non destruens,
Pugil non metuens,   15
Propinator sermonum.

Ergo accende sensibus,
Tu, te, lumen et flamen,
Tu te inspira cordibus,
Qui es vitæ spiramen.   20
Tu sol, tu radius,
Mittens et nuncius,
Persona tertius,
Salva nos. Amen.

9—12. We find continually in medieval theology the seven-fold grace of the Holy Spirit (Isai. xi. 2) brought as here into connection with the seven beatitudes (the *virtus septifaria*), and with the seven petitions of the Lord's Prayer. Thus Gregory the Great, *Mor.* xxxv. 15; *in Ezek. Hom.* 2. 6, 7; and Anselm, in a sermon on the Beatitudes (*Hom.* 2): Superna Gratia saluti nostræ providens orationem nobis contulit, in quâ septiformi prece Spiritum septiformem possemus impetrare; ut suffragio gratiæ septiformis septem supradictas virtutes assequamur: et per eas ad beatitudinem pertingere mereamur. So too Hugh of St Victor: Septem ergo petitiones in Dominicâ Oratione ponuntur, ut septem dona mereamur Spiritûs Sancti, quibus recipiamus septem virtutes, per quas, a septem vitiis liberati, ad septem perveniamus beatitudines.

16. *Propinator sermonum*] Cf. Luke xxi. 15.

ADAM OF ST VICTOR.

XXXVI. DE SPIRITU SANCTO.

SIMPLEX in essentiâ,
Septiformis gratiâ,
Nos illustret Spiritus:
Cordis lustret tenebras,
Et carnis illecebras,   5
Lux emissa cœlitus.

Lex præcessit in figurâ,
Lex pœnalis, lex obscura,

XXXVI. Clichtoveus, *Elucidat. Eccles.* p. 178; Gautier, *Adam de S. Victor*, vol. i. p. 124.

7—28. These stanzas are in the true spirit of St Paul and St Augustine, and hardly to be fully understood without reference to the writings of the latter, above all to his Anti-pelagian tracts; wherein he continually contrasts, as Adam does here, the killing letter of the Old, and the quickening spirit of the New, Covenant. A few chapters of his treatise *De Spiritu et Litterâ*, c. 13—17, would furnish the best commentary on these lines which could be found. Their first point is the contrast between the giving of the law *de monte*, and of the Spirit *in cœnaculo*. In other words, *there* was a God far off who uttered His voice, and that which He spake only set men further from Him (Exod. xx. 18), while *here* it was a God coming into the very midst of them, yea, into that upper-chamber itself. Thus Augustine, c. 17: In hâc mirabili congruentiâ illud certe plurimum distat, quod ibi populus accedere ad locum ubi lex dabatur,

Lumen evangelicum.
Spiritalis intellectus,   10
Literali fronde tectus,
Prodeat in publicum.

Lex de monte populo,
Paucis in cœnaculo
Nova datur gratia :   15
Situs docet nos locorum
Præceptorum vel donorum
Quæ sit eminentia.

---

horrendo terrore prohibetur: hic autem in eos supervenit Spiritus Sanctus, qui eum promissum expectantes in unum fuerant congregati. This, the poet adds, still in the spirit of his great teacher, shews whether are better, *precepts* or *gifts* (ver. 17), the precepts of the old law, or the gifts of the new— a God requiring as of old, or a God giving as now—requiring indeed still, but only what He Himself has first given. The fearful accompaniments of the law's promulgation, he goes on to say (ver. 19—24), were but the outward clothing of the eternal truth, "The law worketh wrath." A law of fear, it may restrain acts of sin, the *illicita*, but cannot beget that love which alone is the fulfilling of the commandment (ver. 25—28). That can only be through the Holy Ghost, whose descent we on this day commemorate.

13—28. A few stanzas from one of Abelard's recently dis- covered hymns will shew how entirely Adam of St Victor is here falling in with the typical interpretation of his time:

Tradente legem Domino	Horrendæ sonum buccinæ
Mons tremens metum attulit ;	Pavebat illic populus ;
Spiritus in cœnaculo	Verbum intelligentiæ
Susceptus illum abstulit.	Sonus hic fuit Spiritûs.
Micabant illic fulgura,	Fumus illic caliginem
Mons caligabat fumigans ;	Obscuræ signat literæ :
Hic est flamma multifida,	Splendentis ignis speciem
Non urens, sed illuminans.	Clare signum hic accipe,

Ignis, clangor buccinæ,
Fragor cum caligine,   20
Lampadum discursio,
Terrorem incutiunt;
Nec amorem nutriunt,
Quem effudit unctio.

Sic in Sinâ lex divina   25
Reis est imposita,
Lex timoris, non amoris,
Puniens illicita.

Ecce patres præelecti
Dii recentes sunt effecti,   30
Culpæ solvunt vincula :
Pluunt verbo, tonant minis,
Novis linguis et doctrinis
Consonant miracula.

19, 20. Cf. Exod. xix. 16 (Vulg.).

21. *Lampadum*] Cf. Exod. xx. 18 (Vulg.): Cunctus autem populus videbat voces et lampades. This word, signifying, as it may, the bickering meteoric flames, perhaps better expresses what is meant than the "lightnings," by which the E.V. has rendered the original.

30. *Dii recentes*] Such the Apostles might be said to have been made, when attributes properly divine, such as the forgiveness of sins, were made over to them.

32. *Pluunt—tonant*] Augustine (*Enarr. in Ps.* lxxxviii. 7): Prædicatores nubes esse dictas ex illâ prophetiâ intelligimus, ubi Deus iratus vineæ suæ dicit, Mandabo nubibus meis ne pluant super eam imbrem, Isai. v. 6: which words Augustine found fulfilled when the Apostles said, "Lo, we turn to the Gentiles" (Acts xiii. 46); cf. Gregory the Great, *Mor.* xxvii.

Exhibentes ægris curam,   35
Morbum damnant, non naturam ;
Persequentes scelera,
Reos premunt et castigant ;
Modo solvunt, modo ligant,
Potestate liberâ.   40

Typum gerit jubilæi
Dies iste, si dici
Requiris mysteria,
In quo tribus millibus
Ad fidem currentibus   45
Pullulat Ecclesia.

---

24.   And thus in another hymn on St Peter and St Paul, Adam
of St Victor has these noble stanzas:

Hi sunt nubes coruscantes,	Ipsi montes appellantur,
Terram cordis irrigantes	Ipsi prius illustrantur
Nunc rore, nunc pluviâ :	Veri Solis lumine.
Ili præcones novæ legis,	Mira virtus est eorum,
Et ductores novi gregis	Firmamenti vel cœlorum
Ad Christi præsepia.	Designantur nomine.

We may compare Damiani :

Paule, doctor egregie,	Nobis potenter intona,
Tuba clangens Ecclesiæ,	Ruraque cordis irriga ;
Nubes volans ac tonitrum	Cœlestis imbre gratiæ
Per amplum mundi circulum :	Mentes virescant aridæ.

41. *jubilæi*]   The poet has a true insight into the typical
significance of the year of jubilee, the great Pentecostal year,
the year of restitution and restoration, in which every man
came to his own, all yokes were broken, and all which any
Israelite had forfeited and alienated, was given back to him
once more (Lev. xxv.).   He sees in it rightly a type and a prophecy
of that great epoch of recreation and restoration which at Pentecost
began.   Durandus (*Rational.* vi. 107): Similiter in diebus
Pentecostes hunc numerum post Domini resurrectionem obser-

Jubilæus est vocatus
Vel *dimittens* vel *mutatus,*
Ad priores vocans status
Res distractas libere.   50
Nos distractos sub peccatis
Liberet lex caritatis,
Et perfectæ libertatis
Dignos reddat munere.

---

vamus, suscipientes advenientem in nos Spiritûs Sancti gratiam, per quem efficimur filii Dei, et virtutum possessio nobis restituitur, et remissa culpa, et totius debiti chirographo evacuato, ab omni servitutis nexu liberi efficimur.

47, 48. *Vel dimittens vel mutatus*] These etymologies of "jubilee," that it is so called either as the year of *remission* (*dimittens*) or the year when all things are *changed* for the better (*mutatus*), have long been given up.

HILDEBERT.

XXXVII. IN LAUDEM SPIRITUS SANCTI.

SPIRITUS Sancte, pie Paraclite,
  Amor Patris et Filii, nexus gignentis et geniti,
Utriusque bonitas et caritas, et amborum essentiæ pu-
  ritas,
Benignitas, suavitas, jocunditas,
Vinculum nectens Deum homini, virtus adunans ho-
  minem Numini;   5
Tibi soli digno coli cum Patre Filioque
Jugis cultus, honor multus sit semper procedenti ab
  utroque.
Tu mitis et hilaris, amabilis, laudabilis,
Vanitatis mundator, munditiæ amator,
Vox suavis exulum mœrentium, melodia civium gau-
  dentium,   10
Istis solamen ne desperent de te,
Istis juvamen ut suspirent ad te;
Consolator piorum, inspirator bonorum, consiliator mœs-
  torum,
Purificator errorum, eruditor ignotorum, declarator
  perplexorum,
Debilem erigens, devium colligens, errantem corrigens,
Sustines labantem, promoves conantem, perficis aman-
  tem;   15

XXXVII. *Hildeberti et Marbodi Opp.* p. 1340.

Perfectum educis de lacu fæcis et miseriæ,
Deducis per semitam pacis et lætitiæ,
Inducis sub nube in aulam sapientiæ.
Fundamentum sanctitatis, alimentum castitatis,   20
Ornamentum lenitatis, lenimentum paupertatis,
Supplementum largitatis, munimentum probitatis,
Miserorum refugium, captivorum suffragium,
Illis aptissimus, istis promptissimus,
Spiritus veritatis, nodus fraternitatis,   25
Ab eodem missus a quo et promissus,
Tu crederis omnium judex qui crederis omnium opi-
     fex;
Honestans bene meritos præmio,
Onustans immeritos supplicio,
Spiras ubi vis et quando vis; doces quos vis et quan-
.   tum vis: 30
Imples et instruis certos in dubiis,
Firmas in subitis, regis in licitis:
Tu ordo decorans omnia, decor ordinans et ornans
     omnia,
Dicta, facta, cogitata,
Dicta veritate, facta honestate, cogitata puritate;   35
Donum bonum, Bonum perfectum,
Dans intellectum, dans et affectum,
Dirigens rectum, formans affectum, firmans provectum,
Et ad portas Paradisi coronans dilectum.

XXXVIII. DE SPIRITU SANCTO.

VENI, Creator Spiritus,
  Mentes tuorum visita,
Imple supernâ gratiâ
Quæ tu creâsti pectora.

Qui Paraclitus diceris,   5
Altissimi donum Dei,
Fons vivus, ignis, caritas,
Et spiritalis unctio.

Tu septiformis munere,
Dextræ Dei tu digitus,   10

XXXVIII. Clichtoveus, *Elucidat. Eccles.* p. 41 : Cassander, *Hymni Ecclesiastici* (*Opp.* Paris, 1616), p. 242 ; Mone, *Hymni Lat. Med. Ævi*, vol. i. p. 241.—This hymn, of which the authorship is popularly ascribed to Charlemagne, but which is certainly older, has had always attributed to it more than an ordinary worth and dignity. Such our Church has recognized and allowed, when, dismissing every other hymn, she has yet retained this in the offices for the ordering of priests, and the consecrating of bishops. It was also in old time habitually used, and the use in great part still survives, on all other occasions of a more than common solemnity, as at the coronation of kings, the celebration of synods, and, in the Romish Church, at the creation of popes, and the translation of the relics of saints.

7, 8. *Fons vivus*, cf. John vii. 38, 39 ; —*ignis*, cf. Luke xii. 49 ; —*caritas*, cf. Rom. v. 5 ;—*unctio*, cf. 1 John ii. 20, 27.

10. *Dei tu digitus*] The title *digitus Dei*, so often given to the Holy Ghost, rests originally on a comparison of Luke xi. 20,

Tu rite promissum Patris,
Sermone ditans guttura.

Accende lumen sensibus,
Infunde amorem cordibus,
Infirma nostri corporis   15
Virtute firmans perpeti.

Hostem repellas longius,
Pacemque dones protinus,
Ductore sic te prævio
Vitemus omne noxium.   20

Da gaudiorum præmia,
Da gratiarum numera,

Si in *digito Dei* ejicio dæmonia, with Matt. xii. 28, Si autem ego
in *Spiritu Dei* ejicio dæmonia, where evidently the *digitus* Dei
of Luke is equivalent to the *Spiritus* Dei of Matthew. Cf.
Augustine, *Enarr.* 2ª *in Ps.* xc. 11; who also elsewhere unfolds
a further fitness in this appellation : Quia per Spiritum S. dona
Dei sanctis dividuntur, ut cum diversa possint, non tamen disce-
dant a concordiâ caritatis, in digitis autem maxime apparet
quædam divisio, nec tamen ab unitate præcisio, propterea Spiritus
S. appellatus est digitus Dei : and again, *Enarr. in Ps.* cxliii.
1: In digitis agnoscimus divisionem operationis, et tamen
radicem unitatis; so also *Quæst. Evang.* ii. 17. Elsewhere he
has another explanation of the name (*De Civ. Dei*, xvi. 43):
Spiritus S. dictus est in Evangelio digitus Dei, ut recordationem
nostram in primi præfigurati facti memoriam revocaret, quia et
legis illæ tabulæ digito Dei scriptæ referuntur. Jerome gathers
from this title an intimation of the ὁμοουσία of the Spirit with
the Father and the Son (*In Matt.* xii.): Si igitur manus et
brachium Dei Filius est, et digitus ejus Spiritus Sanctus, Patris
et Filii et Spiritûs Sancti una substantia est. Gregory of Nazianzum draws the same conclusion.

Dissolve litis vincula,
Adstringe pacis fœdera.

Per te sciamus, da, Patrem,
Noscamus atque Filium,
Te utriusque Spiritum
Credamus omni tempore.

Sit laus Patri cum Filio,
Sancto simul Paraclito,
Nobisque mittat Filius
Charisma Sancti Spiritûs.

ADAM OF ST VICTOR.

XXXIX. DE SPIRITU SANCTO.

QUI procedis ab utroque,
  Genitore, Genitoque,
Pariter, Paraclite,
Redde linguas eloquentes,
Fac ferventes in te mentes   5
Flammâ tuâ divite.

Amor Patris Filiique,
Par amborum, et utrique
Compar et consimilis:
Cuncta reples, cuncta foves,   10
Astra regis, cœlum moves,
Permanens immobilis.

Lumen clarum, lumen carum,
Internarum tenebrarum
Effugas caliginem.   15

XXXIX. Clichtoveus, *Elucidat. Eccles.* p. 179; Daniel, *Thes. Hymnol.* vol. ii. p. 73; Gautier, *Adam de S. Victor*, vol. i. p. 115.— In Horst's *Paradisus Animæ, Sect.* 1, this hymn and the following are huddled together, the two in one, and with grossest departures from the authentic text. Under this tasteless process the whole beauty of both, each complete in itself, and moving in its own sphere of thought and feeling, has quite disappeared.

Per te mundi sunt mundati;
Tu peccatum et peccati
Destruis rubiginem.

Veritatem notam facis,
Et ostendis viam pacis
Et iter justitiæ.
Perversorum corda vitas,
Et bonorum corda ditas
Munere scientiæ.

Te docente nil obscurum,
Te præsente nil impurum;
Sub tuâ præsentiâ
Gloriatur mens jucunda,
Per te læta, per te munda
Gaudet conscientia.

Quando venis, corda lenis,
Quando subis, atræ nubis
Effugit obscuritas.
Sacer ignis, pectus ignis,
Non comburis, sed a curis
Purgas, quando visitas.

Mentes prius imperitas,
Et sopitas et oblitas,
Erudis et excitas.
Foves linguas, formas sonum,
Cor ad bonum facit pronum
A te data caritas.

O juvamen oppressorum,
O solamen miserorum,

Pauperum refugium, 45
Da contemptum terrenorum,
Ad amorem supernorum
Trahe desiderium;

Consolator et fundator,
Habitator et amator 50
Cordium humilium,
Pelle mala, terge sordes,
Et discordes fac concordes,
Et affer præsidium.

Tu qui quondam visitâsti, 55
Docuisti, confirmâsti
Timentes discipulos,
Visitare nos digneris,
Nos, si placet, consoleris,
Et credentes populos. 60

Par majestas personarum,
Par potestas est earum,
Et communis Deitas.
Tu procedens a duobus,
Coæqualis es ambobus, 65
In nullo disparitas.

Quia tantus es et talis
Quantus Pater est et qualis,
Servorum humilitas
Deo Patri, Filioque 70
Redemptori, tibi quoque
Laudes reddat debitas.

ADAM OF ST VICTOR.

XL. DE SPIRITU SANCTO.

LUX jucunda, lux insignis,
  Quâ de throno missus ignis
In Christi discipulos,
Corda replet, linguas ditat,
Ad concordes nos invitat   5
Linguæ, cordis, modulos.

Christus misit quod promisit,
Pignus sponsæ quam revisit

XL. Clichtoveus, *Elucidat. Eccles.* p. 177; Daniel, *Thes.
Hymnol.* vol. ii. p. 71; Gautier, *Adam de S. Victor*, vol. i. p.
107.—If this were not the third of Adam of St Victor's Pentecostal hymns which I have quoted, I should be tempted to make
room for a very grand one, *Veni, summe Consolator*, published by
Gautier (vol. i. p. 135) for the first time.

2. *missus ignis*] Durandus (*Rational.* vi. 107) tells us that it
was customary to scatter fire from on high in the church on the
day of Pentecost; and he gives the explanation of this and other
similar practices, as the letting loose of doves: Tunc enim ex alto
ignis projicitur, quia Spiritus Sanctus descendit in discipulos in
igneis linguis. He omits reference to another passage without
which this custom would scarcely have found place, and which
is necessary to complete the explanation—I mean Rev. viii. 5
(Vulg.): Et accepit angelus thuribulum, et implevit illud de
igne altaris [altare aureum quod est ante thronum Dei, ver. 3],
et misit in terram; et facta sunt tonitrua et voces et fulgura et
terræmotus magnus.

Die quinquagesimâ.
Post dulcorem melleum　　　　　　10
Petra fudit oleum,
Petra jam firmissima.

In tabellis saxeis,
Non in linguis igneis
Lex de monte populo :　　　　　　15
Paucis cordis novitas
Et linguarum unitas
Datur in cœnaculo.

O quam felix, quam festiva
Dies, in quâ primitiva　　　　　　20
Fundatur Ecclesia.
Vivæ sunt primitiæ

10—12. Daniel, who remarks here, Petrus Apostolus, cujus nomen die Pentecostes et omen habebat, confertur cum petrá mellifluâ in deserto; has missed the meaning, doing equal wrong to the poetry and the theology of the stanza. The poet has Deut. xxxii. 13 in his eye, "He made him to suck honey out of the rock. and oil out of the flinty rock." This will be abundantly clear, when the words of the Vulgate are quoted: Suxerunt mel de petrâ, et oleum de *firmâ* petrâ ; with the comment of Gregory the Great (*Hom.* 26 *in Evang.*): Mel de petrâ, suxerunt, qui Redemptoris nostri facta et miracula viderunt. Oleum vero de firmâ petrâ suxerunt; quia [qui?] effusione Sancti Spiritûs post resurrectionem ejus ungi meruerunt. Quasi ergo in firmâ petrâ mel dedit, quando adhuc mortalis Dominus miraculorum suorum dulcedinem discipulis ostendit. Sed firma petra oleum fudit; quia post resurrectionem suam factus jam impassibilis, per afflationem Spiritûs donum sanctæ unctionis emanavit. Cf. Hugh of St Victor, *De Claustro Animæ*, iii. 8. It may be that the poet had also in his eye as a secondary allusion, Ps. lxxx. 17 (Vulg.): Et de petrâ, melle saturavit eos.

Nascentis Ecclesiæ,
Tria primum millia.

Panes legis primitivi,   25
Sub unâ sunt adoptivi
Fide duo populi.
Se duobus interjecit,
Sicque duos unum fecit
Lapis, caput anguli.   30

Utres novi, non vetusti,
Sunt capaces novi musti:

---

25. *Panes legis*] On the day of Pentecost *two* loaves, the *primitiæ* of the completed harvest, were offered to the Lord (Lev. xviii. 16, 17). Why *two*, has often been enquired. The medieval interpreters answered, that by this twofold offering it was indicated that the Church, which was founded and presented in its living firstfruits to the Lord on the day of Pentecost, should consist alike of Gentile and of Jew; to this interpretation we have evident allusion here. See Bähr, *Symb. d. Mos. Cult.* vol. ii. p. 650; and Iken, *De duobus Panibus Pentecostes.*

31. *non vetusti*] The Jews were the old vessels, or old skins, which would not receive the *mustum*, or new wine of the Spirit (Matt. ix. 17); and they signally shewed that they were so on the day of Pentecost, when they so misunderstood the thing which was done, as to say mocking, "These men are full of new wine" (Acts ii. 13). And yet these mocking words had their truth; for the Apostles were as *utres novi*, in which the new wine of the Spirit *was* being poured, and there is, as St Paul teaches, a πληροῦσθαι ἐν Πνεύματι, which is the spiritual counterpart to the carnal μεθύσκεσθαι οἴνῳ (Ephes. v. 18). Thus Augustine (*Serm.* 267): Utres novi erant; vinum novum de cœlo expectabatur, et venit; jam enim fuerat magnus ille Botrus calcatus et glorificatus: and again *Serm.* 26: Utres novos utres veteres mirabantur, et calumniando nec innovabantur, nec implebantur.

Vasa parat vidua;
Liquorem dat Elisæus;
Nobis sacrum rorem Deus,   35
Si corda sint congrua.

Non hoc musto vel liquore,
Non hoc sumus digni rore,
Si discordes moribus.
In obscuris vel divisis   40
Non potest hæc paraclisis
Habitare cordibus.

Consolator alme, veni,
Linguas rege, corda leni;
Nihil fellis aut veneni   45
Sub tuâ præsentiâ.
Nil jucundum, nil amœnum,
Nil salubre, nil serenum,
Nihil dulce, nihil plenum,
Nisi tuâ gratiâ.   50

Tu es lumen et unguentum,
Tu cœleste condimentum,
Aquæ ditans elementum,
Virtute mysterii.

------

34. *dat Elisæus*] Cf. 2 Kin. iv. 1—6. The Church is the
widow, in danger of coming, unless helped from above, to utter-
most poverty, of losing her very sons. All that she can do is to
prepare and bring the "vessels" of empty hearts, for Christ, the
true Elisha, to fill them with that oil from above, which is only
stayed when there is no more room in human hearts to receive
it (ver. 6).

53, 54. Not one, but two broodings of the Holy Ghost over the

Nova facti creatura,   55
Te laudamus mente purâ,
Gratiæ nunc, sed naturâ
Prius iræ filii.

Tu qui dator es et donum,
Tu qui condis omne bonum,   60
Cor ad laudem redde pronum,
Nostræ linguæ formans sonum
In tua præconia.
Tu purga nos a peccatis,
Auctor ipse puritatis,   65
Et in Christo renovatis
Da perfectæ novitatis
Plena nobis gaudia.

---

waters, at the first creation (Gen. i. 2), and at the second, are here
referred to; for the Church has ever loved to contemplate them
in their relation one with the other. Thus Tertullian, on our
Lord's Baptism (*De Bapt.* c. 8): Tunc ille Sanctissimus Spiritus
super baptismi aquas, tanquam pristinam sedem recognoscens,
acquiescit. Cf. Ambrose, *De Spir. Sanct.* i. 7, and in a sequence
appointed for chanting at Pentecost, these lines occur :—

Quando machinam per Verbum suum fecit Deus, cœli, terræ, marium,
Tu super aquas foturus eas, numen tuum expandisti, Spiritus :
Tu animabus vivificandis aquas fœcundas.—(Clichtovæus, p. 175.)

ROBERT THE SECOND, KING OF FRANCE.

THE loveliest,—for however not the grandest, such we call it,—of all the hymns in the whole circle of Latin sacred poetry, has a king for its author. Robert the Second, son of Hugh Capet, succeeded his father on the throne of France in the year 997. He was singularly addicted to Church-music, which he enriched, as well as the hymnology, with compositions of his own, such as, I believe, to this day hold their place in the services of the Romish Church.

Even were the story of the writer's life unknown to us, we should guess that the hymn which follows could only have been composed by one who had been acquainted with many sorrows, and also with many consolations. Nor should we err herein: for if the consolations are plain from the poem itself, the history of those times contains the record of the manifold sorrows, within his own family and without it, which were the portion of this meek and greatly afflicted king. Sismondi (*Hist. des Français*, vol. iv. p. 98—111) brings him very vividly before us in all the beauty of his character, and also in all his evident unfitness, a man of gentleness and peace, for contending with the men of iron by whom he was surrounded. He died in 1031.

XLI. AD SPIRITUM SANCTUM.

VENI, Sancte Spiritus,
  Et emitte cœlitus
Lucis tuæ radium.

Veni, pater pauperum,
Veni, dator munerum,   5
Veni, lumen cordium :

Consolator optime,
Dulcis hospes animæ,
Dulce refrigerium :

XLI. Clichtoveus, *Elucidat. Eccles.* p. 176; Daniel, *Thes. Hymnol.* vol. ii. p. 35; Mone, *Hymni Lat. Med. Ævi,* vol. i. p. 244.—Clichtoveus shows a just appreciation of this hymn : Neque satis hæc oratio, meâ quidem sententiâ, commendari potest; nam omni commendatione superior est, tum ob miram ejus suavitatem cum facilitate apertissimâ, tum ob gratam ejus brevitatem cum ubertate et copiâ sententiarum, ut unaquæque fere clausula rhythmica unam complectatur sententiam, tum denique ob concinnam ejus in contextu venustatem, quâ opposita inter se aptissimo nexu compacta cernuntur. Crediderimque facile auctorem ipsum (quisquis is fuerit), cum hanc contexuit orationem, cœlesti quâdam dulcedine fuisse perfusum interius, quâ, Spiritu Sancto auctore, tantam eructavit verbis adeo succinctis suavitatem. Some later writers have attributed this hymn, and, on grounds as slight, the *Stabat Mater,* to Pope Innocent the Third; so the *Biographie Universelle :* but there exists no sufficient reason for calling in question the attribution which has been commonly made of it, to king Robert (Durandus, *Rationale,* iv. 22).

In labore requies,   10
In æstu temperies,
In fletu solatium.

O lux beatissima,
Reple cordis intima
Tuorum fidelium.   15

Sine tuo numine
Nihil est in homine,
Nihil est innoxium.

Lava quod est sordidum,
Riga quod est aridum,   20
Sana quod est saucium:

Flecte quod est rigidum,
Fove quod est languidum,
Rege quod est devium.

Da tuis fidelibus   25
In te confidentibus
Sacrum septenarium;

Da virtutis meritum,
Da salutis exitum,
Da perenne gaudium.   30

---

17. *Nihil*] It is difficult not to suspect that the text is here corrupt, and that this first *nihil* occupies the place of some more appropriate word.

XLII. LIGNUM VITÆ.

EST locus ex omni medium quem credimus orbe,
   Golgotha Judæi patrio cognomine dicunt :
Hic ego de sterili succisum robore lignum
Plantatum memini fructus genuisse salubres ;

XLII. Fabricius, *Poëtt. Vet. Christ. Opp.* p. 302.—This graceful allegory of course is not Cyprian's, though in time past sometimes attributed to him, and not unfrequently printed with his works. Whosoever it may be, the allegory is managed with singular skill, nor could one beforehand have supposed that, keeping so close to the one image with which he starts, and introducing no new element not perfectly consistent with it, the poet could have set out so admirably Christ's cross (1—10), his death and burial (11), his resurrection (12—14), his ascension (15—17), his constitution in the Twelve of a Church (18—21), the gifts of Pentecost (22—25), and the whole course of the Christian life from its initiation in baptism and repentance (27, 37—39), to its final consummation in glory (68).

3. *sterili robore*] Does this mean the tree of life? Early and medieval legends innumerable connect in one way or other the cross of Christ with the tree of life; the aim of all being to shew how the cross, as the true *lignum vitæ*, was fashioned from the wood of that tree which stood in the Paradise of God. The legend appears oftenest in this shape, namely, That Seth was sent by his dying father to obtain a slip of that tree; which having by the grace of the angel at the gate obtained, he set it upon his father's grave, that is, on Golgotha, the "place of the skull," or spot where Adam was buried. It grew there from generation to generation—each significant implement for the kingdom of God, Moses' staff, Aaron's rod, the pole on which the brazen serpent was exalted, having been taken from it; till

Non tamen hos illis, qui se posuere, colonis   5
Præbuit; externi fructus habuere beatos.
Arboris hæc species; uno de stipite surgit,
Et mox in geminos extendit brachia ramos:
Sicut plena graves antennæ carbasa tendunt,
Vel cum disjunctis juga stant ad aratra juvencis.   10
Quod tulit hoc primo, maturo semine lapsum
Concepit tellus: mox hinc (mirabile dictu)
Tertia lux iterum terris superisque tremendum
Extulerat ramum, vitali fruge beatum.
Sed bis vicenis firmatus et ille diebus   15
Crevit in immensum; cælumque cacumine summo
Contigit, et tandem sanctum caput abdidit alto;
Dum tamen ingenti bissenos pondere ramos
Edidit, et totum spargens porrexit in orbem:
Gentibus ut cunctis victum vitamque perennem   20
Præberent, mortemque mori qui posse docerent.
Expletis etiam mox quinquaginta diebus,
Vertice de summo divini nectaris haustum
Detulit in ramos cœlestis spiritus auræ:
Dulci rore graves manabant undique frondes.   25

---

at last, in its extreme old age, the wellnigh dead stock furnished the wood of passion, and thus it again became, and in the
highest sense, the true tree of life, bearing the fruit which is
indeed unto eternal life. This, and other forms of the same
legend, constitute some of the fairest portions of what may without offence be called the Christian mythology. We find allusions
to them in the *Evangelium Nicodemi* (Thilo, *Codex Apocryphus*,
vol. i. p. 686); and Calderon has wrought them up into two
magnificent dramas, *La Sibilla del Oriente*, and *El Arbol del
mejor Fruto.*

20, 21. Cf. Ezek. xlvii. 12; Rev. xxii. 2.

Ecce sub ingenti ramorum tegminis umbrâ
Fons erat : hic nullo casu turbante serenum
Perspicuis illimis aquis, et gramina circum
Fundebant lætos vario de flore colores.
Hunc circum innumeræ gentes populique coibant,   30
Quam varii generis, sexûs, ætatis, honoris,
Innuptæ, nuptæque simul, viduæque, nurusque,
Infantes, puerique, viri, juvenesque, senesque :
Hic ubi multigenis flexos incumbere pomis
Cernebant ramos, avidis attingere dextris   35
Gaudebant madidos cœlesti nectare fructus.
Nec prius hos poterant cupidis decerpere palmis,
Quam lutulenta viæ vestigia fœda prioris
Detererent, corpusque pio de fonte lavarent.
Ergo diu circum spatiantes gramine molli,   40
Suspiciunt altâ pendentes arbore fructus.
Tum si qui ex illis delapsa putamina ramis,
Et dulces, multo rorantes nectare, frondes
Vescuntur, veros exoptant sumere fructus.

Ergo ubi cœlestem ceperunt ora saporem,   45
Permutant animos, et mentes perdere avaras
Incipiunt, dulcique hominem cognoscere sensu.
Insolitum multis stomachum movisse saporem
Vidimus, et fellis commotum melle venenum
Rejecisse bonos turbatâ mente sapores,   50
Aut avide sumptum non dilexisse, diuque
Et male potatum tandem evomuisse saporem.
Sæpe quidem multi, renovatis mentibus, ægros
Restituere animos; et quæ se posse negabant,
Pertulerant, fructumque sui cepere laboris.   55
Multi etiam sanctos ausi contingere fontes,

Discessere iterum subito, retroque relapsi
Sordibus et cœno mixti volvuntur eodem.
Multi vero bono portantes pectore, totis
Accipiunt animis, penitusque in viscera condunt.   60

    Ergo qui sacros possunt accedere fontes,
Septima lux illos optatas sistit ad undas,
Tingit et in liquidis jejunos fontibus artus.
Sic demum illuviem mentis, vitæque prioris
Deponunt labem, purasque a morte reducunt   65
Illustres animas, cœlique ad lumen ituras.
Hinc iter ad ramos et dulcia poma salutis;
Inde iter ad cœlum per ramos arboris altæ;
Hoc lignum vitæ est cunctis credentibus.   Amen.

---

62. *Septima lux*] *Forty* rather than *seven* was the number of days which generally the ancient Church desired to set apart for the immediate preparation for baptism : yet within that forty, the last seven may, and would, have had an intenser solemnity, even as the *traditio symboli* very often did not take place till the seventh day preceding; thus, not till Palm Sunday, for those who should be baptized on Easter Eve.

ADAM OF ST VICTOR.

XLIII. DE S. APOSTOLIS.

STOLA regni laureatus,
Summi Regis est senatus
Cœtus apostolicus;
Cuï psallant mens et ora;
Mentis mundæ vox sonora   5
Hymnus est angelicus.

Hic est ordo mundi decus,
Omnis carnis judex æquus,
Novæ petra gratiæ;
Ab æterno præelectus,   10
Cujus floret architectus
Ad culmen Ecclesiæ.

XLIII. Gautier, *Adam de S. Victor*, vol. ii. p. 407.—This magnificent hymn, a glorious addition to the medieval hymnology, was
published by Gautier for the first time. The unity which pervades
the hymns of Adam of St Victor is very worthy of remark and
admiration. Thus he has, besides this, two others, *In Communi
Apostolorum.* In them he traces the *history* of the Apostles,
their calling, their characters, the spheres of their labour, with
no slightest introduction of symbolism. This on the contrary
deals with the symbolism alone, and does not once touch what
would be to it the alien element of history.

1—3. Cf. Matt. xix. 28 ; Luke xxii. 29, 30 ; 1 Cor. vi. 3.
8. *judex*] Cf. Matt. xix. 28.
11. *architectus*] Elsewhere the Apostles are honoured with the

Ili præclari Nazaræi
Bella crucis et tropæi
Mundo narrant gloriam ;   15
Sic dispensant verbum Dei
Quod nox nocti, lux dici
Indicant scientiam.

Onus leve, jugum mite
Proponentes, semen vitæ   20
Mundi spargunt terminis;
Germen promit terra culta,
Fœneratur fruge multâ
Fides Dei-hominis.

Paranymphi novæ legis   25
Ad amplexum novi Regis
Sponsam ducunt regiam,

---

title of the "architects" of the Church; as in a fine hymn addressed to St Paul (Mone, vol. iii. p. 85), which commences thus:—

Paulus, Syon architectus,
Est a Christo præelectus.

So too St Augustine styles the same Apostle (*Ep.* 185) Ecclesiæ magnus ædificator. Here, however, it is the architect in chief who manifestly is intended.

14. *tropæi*] See note, p. 89.

16—18. It is well known that the words of the nineteenth Psalm (1—4), mainly on the strength of St Paul's adaptation of them (Rom. x. 18), have constantly received a spiritual application. The Church is the firmament which shews the handy-work of God; in which day transmits to day and night to night in unbroken succession to the end of time, and to all the world, the wondrous story of the glory and grace of God.

25. *Paranymphi*] = υἱοὶ νυμφῶνος (Matt. ix. 15 ; cf. John iii. 29 ; 2 Cor. xi. 2).

Sine rugâ, sine nævo,
Permansuram omni ævo
Virginem Ecclesiam.   30

Hæc est virgo gignens fœtus,
Semper nova, tamen vetus,
Sed defectûs nescia ;
Cujus thorus mens sincera,
Cujus partus fides vera,   35
Cujus dos est gratia.

Hi sunt templi fundamentum,
Vivus lapis et cæmentum
Ligans ædificium.
Hi sunt portæ civitatis,   40
Ili compago unitatis
Israël et gentium.

Ili triturant aream,
Ventilantes paleam

---

28. Cf. Ephes. v. 27.

37. Cf. Ephes. ii. 20 ; Rev. xxi. 14.

40. *portæ*] Cf. Rev. xxi. 12 ; Ezek. xlviii. 31—34. Richard of St Victor (*Sup. Apoc.* xxi. 21): Per portas vero S. Apostolos intelligimus, per quorum fidem et doctrinam sanctam Civitatem introimus. Augustine (*Enarr. in Ps.* lxxxvi. 2): Quare sunt portæ [Apostoli]? Quia per ipsos introimus ad regnum Dei. Prædicant enim nobis.

41, 42. Cf. Ephes. ii. 20.

43—48. The treading out the corn on the barn floor, which is the work of oxen, is the link between the first part of this stanza and the last. The Apostles, the treaders out of the corn (St Paul, by his quotation at 1 Tim. v. 18, of Deut. xxv. 4, justifies the image), from which afterwards they winnow away the chaff (cf. Matt. iii. 12), are prefigured by the twelve brazen

Ventilabri justitiâ; 45
Quos designant ærei
Boves maris vitrei
Salomonis industriâ.

Patriarchæ duodeni,
Fontes aquæ gustu leni, 50
Panes tabernaculi,
Gemmæ vestis sacerdotis;
Hæc figuris signant notis
Novi duces populi.

Horum nutu cedat error, 55
Crescat fides, absit terror
Finalis sententiæ,
Ut soluti a delictis,
Sociemur benedictis
Ad tribunal gloriæ. 60

---

oxen round the molten sea, which Solomon made (1 Kin. vii. 23—25; 2 Chron. iv. 2—4).

50. *Fontes*] Cf. Exod. xv. 23, 25, 27.

51. Cf. Lev. xxiv. 5—9. Bede: Duodecim panes in mensâ tabernaculi duodecim sunt Apostoli, qui cum usque ad consummationem seculi populum Dei reficiunt panibus Verbi, duodecim panes propositionis nunquam recedunt de mensâ Domini.

52. *Gemmæ*] Cf. Exod. xxxix. 10—14.

53, 54. Compare Hugh of St Victor (*Alleg. in Gen.* iii. 16): Jacob est Christus: ejus filii, duodecim Apostoli. Hi sunt enim fontes deserti, quæ Israel reperit in Helim (Exod. xv. 27); duodecim panes propositionis; duodecim lapides in veste pontificali; duodecim lapides de Jordane sublevati (Josh. iv. 3—8); duodecim boves sub æreo mari (1 Kin. vii. 25); duodecim stellæ in coronâ sponsæ (Rev. xii. 1); duodecim fundamenta (Rev. xxi. 19—20); duodecim portæ (Rev. xxi. 12); duodecim menses anni; duodecim horæ diei; duodecim fructus ligni vitæ (Rev. xxii. 2).

ABELARD.

ABELARD was born in 1079 at Palais, near Nantes, and died in 1142. His talents, his vanity, his rare dialectic dexterity, his rationalism, his relations to a woman of so far nobler and deeper character than his own, the cloistral retirement in which he spent the later years of his stormy life—all these are matters of too familiar knowledge to need to be repeated. Of his poetry, to which, and to the great popularity which it enjoyed, both he and Heloise more than once refer, it was thought that the greater part had perished. There was indeed an Advent hymn of no high merit, beginning, *Mittit ad Virginem Non quemvis angelum*, which had been sometimes ascribed to Abelard (Clichtoveus, *Elucidat. Eccles.* p. 153), and a few other verses of no great significance were current under his name. Not very long since, however, six poems were discovered in the Vatican, which undoubtedly are of his composing. They are styled *Lamentations* (*planctus*), as of David over Abner, the virgins of Israel over Jephthah's daughter, and are published in Greith's *Spicilegium Vaticanum*, Frauenfeld, 1838, p. 123—131. Their merit is inconsiderable. But this was not all, for about the same time a large body of his hymns, no fewer than ninety-seven, came to light in the Royal Library at Brussels, and are included in the complete edition of Abelard's writings, edited by Cousin, *Abælardi Opp.* Paris, 1849. These too, it must be acknowledged, for

the most part, disappoint expectation. This certainly
would not be the case, if there were many among them
like the following, which is as pregnant as it is brief;
and curious, moreover, as shewing how entirely Abelard conformed to the typical interpretation of his
time.

XLIV. DE S. PAULO APOSTOLO.

TUBA Domini, Paule, maxima,
De cœlestibus dans tonitrua,
Hostes dissipans, cives aggrega.

Doctor gentium es præcipuus,
Vas in poculum factus omnibus,   5
Sapientiæ plenum haustibus.

Mane Benjamin prædam rapuit,
Escas vespere largas dividit,
Vitæ ferculis mundum reficit.

XLIV. *Petri Abælardi Opp.* Paris, 1849, vol. i. p. 320.

1—3. The trumpets of silver under the Old Law were to be used
for the calling of the assembly (Num. x. 2), and for the hearten-
ing of the people when they went forth against their enemies
(x. 9 ; xxxi. 6).   Such a trumpet, and the greatest of such, was
St Paul.

7, 8. *Benjamin*] The immense significance of St Paul's conversion for the Church not unnaturally led the early interpreters
to seek some intimation of it in the Old Testament, or at least
to welcome there anything which seemed like such.   They
believed that they found such in the words of Jacob's prophecy,
Gen. xlix. 27.   Paul, in whom it might be fitly said that the

> Ut rhinoceros est indomitus,   10
> Quem ad aratrum ligans Dominus
> Glebas vallium frangit protinus.
>
> Nunc nequitiæ laudat villicum,
> Quem prudentiâ dicit præditum,   15
> Ac pro filiis lucis providum.

---

glory of the tribe of Benjamin culminated, was the wolf in the morning devouring the prey, and in the evening dividing the spoil. Thus Tertullian, arguing with the Gnostics, would shew how deeply rooted the New Testament was in the Old, the latter containing prophecies not of Christ only, but of his Apostles; and proceeds (*Adv. Marc.* v. 1): Mihi Paulum etiam Genesis olim repromisit. Inter illas enim figuras et propheticas super filios suos benedictiones, Jacob, cum ad Benjamin direxisset, Benjamin, inquit, lupus rapax, ad matutinum comedet adhuc, et ad vesperam dabit escam. Ex tribu enim Benjamin oriturum Paulum providebat, lupum rapacem, ad matutinum comedentem, id est, primâ ætate vastaturum pecora Domini ut persecutorem Ecclesiarum, dehinc ad vesperam escam daturum, id est, devergente jam ætate, oves Christi educaturum, ut doctor nationum. Cf. Hilary, *in Ps.* lxvii. § 28 ; Augustine, *Enarr. in Ps.* lxxviii; *Serm.* 279, 1; and 333.

10. *Ut rhinoceros*] The reference is to Job xxxix. 9, 10: Numquid volet rhinoceros servire tibi, aut morabitur ad præsepe tuum? Numquid alligabis rhinocerota ad arandum loro tuo? aut confringet glebas vallium post te? (Vulg.) It was a favourite and a very grand fancy of the medieval interpreters, that all this (ver. 9—12) found its highest fulfilment, this impossible with man proving possible with God, in the conversion of St Paul: thus see Gregory the Great, *Moral.* xxxi. 16, 30.

13—15. Cf. St Luke xvi. 1—9. St Jerome (*ad Algas.* § 7) records at length the exposition of this parable, deriving it from Theophilus, bishop of Antioch, by aid of which these lines must be explained. Paul is the Unjust Steward, scattering his lord's

Perpes gloria Regi perpeti,
Exercituum Christo Principi,
Patri pariter et Spiritui.

---

goods so long as he is a persecutor of the Church. He was put out of his stewardship, when the Lord met him on the way to Damascus; but afterwards found acceptance with his lord's debtors through lowering their bills—that is, through abating the rigour of the ceremonial law; and not acceptance with them only, but favour and praise from his Lord Himself.

ST AMBROSE.

XLV. DE SS. MARTYRIBUS.

ÆTERNA Christi munera,
   Et martyrum victorias,
Laudes ferentes debitas,
Lætis canamus mentibus.

Ecclesiarum principes,   5
Belli triumphales duces,
Cœlestis aulæ milites,
Et vera mundi lumina;

Terrore victo sæculi,
Spretisque pœnis corporis,   10
Mortis sacræ compendio
Vitam beatam possident.

Traduntur igni martyres
Et bestiarum dentibus;
Armata sævit ungulis   15
Tortoris insani manus.

XLV. *Ambrosii Opera*, Paris, 1836, vol. iv. p. 201; Clichtoveus, *Elucidat. Eccles.* p. 75; Daniel, *Thes. Hymnol.* vol. i. p. 27; Mone, *Hymn. Lat. Med. Ævi*, vol. iii. p. 143.—Whether this hymn be St Ambrose's, to whom the Benedictine editors ascribe it, or not, it is certainly not later than the fifth century.

Nudata pendent viscera,
Sanguis sacratus funditur,
Sed permanent immobiles
Vitæ perennis gratiâ.   20

Devota sanctorum fides,
Invicta spes credentium,
Perfecta Christi caritas,
Mundi triumphat principem.

In his Paterna gloria,   25
In his voluntas Filii,
Exultat in his Spiritus;
Cœlum repletur gaudiis.

Te nunc, Redemtor, quæsumus
Ut ipsorum consortio   30
Jungas precantes servulos
In sempiterna sæcula.

ADAM OF ST VICTOR.

XLVI. DE S. STEPHANO.

HERI mundus exultavit,
  Et exultans celebravit
Christi natalitia :

XLVI. Clichtoveus, *Elucidat. Eccles.* p. 158; Rambach, *Anthol. Christl. Gesänge,* p. 285; Daniel, *Thes. Hymnol.* vol. ii.
p. 64; Gautier, *Adam de S. Victor,* vol. i. p. 212.—There is
another fine hymn by Adam of St Victor on the martyrdom of
St Stephen, *Rosa novum dans odorem*; but fine as it is, it is
very inferior to this sublime composition. Gautier (vol. i. p 223)
has published it for the first time.

1. *Heri*] The Church has always loved to bring out the
significance of the day on which it commemorates the martyrdom
of St Stephen—namely, that it is the day immediately following
the day of Christ's nativity. Thus Durandus (*Rational.* vii. 42);
Augustine, *Serm.* 314 and often; Bernard, vol. i. p. 794, Bened.
ed.; and Fulgentius (*Appendix to Augustine,* vol. v. p. 357):
Hesterno die celebravimus Natalem quo Rex martyrum natus
est in mundo; hodie celebramus natalem quo primicerius martyrum migravit ex mundo. Et ideo natus est Dominus ut moreretur pro servo; ne servus timeret mori pro Domino. Natus est
Christus in terris, ut Stephanus nasceretur in cœlis: altus ad
humilia descendit, ut humiles ad alta adscenderent. Another
hymn on St Stephen (Clichtoveus, p. 20) has these noble lines
expressing the same thought :

Tu per Christum hebetatam primus transis rhomphæam,
Primum granum trituratum Christi ditans aream.

The *rhomphæa* here is the fiery sword of the Cherubim, which
precluded all access to Paradise, but which sword was quenched

Heri chorus angelorum
Prosecutus est cœlorum 5
Regem cum lætitiâ.

Protomartyr et Levita,
Clarus fide, clarus vitâ,
Clarus et miraculis,
Sub hâc luce triumphavit, 10
Et triumphans insultavit
Stephanus incredulis.

Fremunt ergo tanquam feræ,
Quia victi defecere
Lucis adversarii : 15
Falsos testes statuunt,
Et linguas exacuunt
Viperarum filii.

Agonista, nulli cede ;
Certâ certus de mercede, 20
Persevera, Stephane :
Insta falsis testibus,
Confuta sermonibus
Synagogam Satanæ.

---

and blunted in the blood of Christ, so that Stephen could now
pass it by, and enter into life.

7. *Protomartyr*] Called therefore ἀρχὴ μαρτύρων, ἀθλητῶν
προοίμιον, πρώταθλος, ἀθλητῶν ἀκροθίνιον, in the Greek Church.
By a very natural transfer of Jewish terms to Christian things,
Levita in the early Church language was = *diaconus* (Bingham,
Antiqq. xi. 20, 2).

11. *insultavit*] Cf. Acts vii. 51—53.

24. *Synagogam Satanæ*] Cf. Rev. iii. 9.

Testis tuus est in cœlis,   25
Testis verax et fidelis,
Testis innocentiæ.
Nomen habes Coronati,
Te tormenta decet pati
Pro coronâ gloriæ.   30

Pro coronâ non marcenti
Perfer brevis vim tormenti,
Te manet victoria.
Tibi fiet mors, natalis,
Tibi pœna terminalis   35
Dat vitæ primordia.

Plenus Sancto Spiritu
Penetrat intuitu
Stephanus cœlestia.
Videns Dei gloriam   40
Crescit ad victoriam,
Suspirat ad præmia.

---

26. Cf. Rev. iii. 14.

28. *Coronati*] The *nomen et omen* which lay in that name Stephen (στέφανος) for the first winner of the martyr's *crown*, is a favourite one with the early Church writers. Thus Augustine (*Enarr. in Ps.* lviii. 3): Stephanus lapidatus est, et quod vocabatur, accepit. Stephanus enim corona dicitur. Cf. *Serm.* 314, 2. He plays in like manner with the name of the martyr Vincentius, noting that he too was in like manner φερώνυμος (*Serm.* 274): *Vincentium* ubique *vincentem.* So in the legendary life of St Victor, a voice from heaven is heard at the moment of his death, *Vicisti, Victor,* beate, *vicisti;* and all this is embodied in a hymn addressed to the former of these martyrs:

O Vincenti ! qui vicisti,
Et invictus jam cepisti
Præmia vincentium,

Des invictum robur menti
Soli Christus nam vincenti
Manna dat absconditum.

En a dextris Dei stantem
Jesum, pro te dimicantem,
Stephane, considera.   45
Tibi cœlos reserari,
Tibi Christum revelari
Clama voce liberâ.

Se commendat Salvatori,
Pro quo dulce ducit mori   50
Sub ipsis lapidibus.
Saulus servat omnium
Vestes lapidantium,
Lapidans in omnibus.

---

43. *stantem*] The one occasion on which Christ appears in Scripture as *standing* at the right hand of God, is that of Stephen's martyrdom (Acts vii. 55, 56). The reason why in all other places he should be spoken of as *sitting*, and here only as *standing*, Gregory the Great, whom our poet follows, has no doubt rightly given (*Hom.* 19, *in Fest. Ascens.*): *Sedere* judicantis est, *stare* vero pugnantis vel adjuvantis. Stephanus stantem vidit, quem adjutorem habuit. So too Arator, long before:

> Lumina cordis habens cœlos conspexit apertos,
> Ne lateat quid Christus agat : pro martyre surgit,
> Quem tunc *stare* videt, confessio nostra *sedentem*
> Cum soleat celebrare magis. Dux præscius armat
> Quos ad dona vocat.

Our Collect on St Stephen's day has not failed to bring this point out—" O blessed Jesus, who *standest* at the right hand of God *to succour* all those that suffer for Thee." This is but one example out of many, of the rich theological allusion, often unmarked by us, which the Collects of the Church contain.

54. *Lapidans in omnibus*] Augustine (*Serm.* 315): Quantum sæviebat [Saulus] in illâ cæde, vultis audire? Vestimenta lapidantium servabat, ut omnium manibus lapidaret.

Ne peccatum statuatur   55
His, a quibus lapidatur,
Genu ponit et precatur,
Condolens insaniæ :
In Christo sic obdormivit,
Qui Christo sic obedivit,   60
Et cum Christo semper vivit,
Martyrum primitiæ.

55—62. Cf. Acts vii. 59 (Vulg.): Positis autem genibus, clamavit voce magnâ dicens, Domine, ne statuas illis hoc peccatum. Et cum hoc dixisset, obdormivit in Domino.

I cannot forbear quoting two stanzas, the first and fifth, from that other of Adam's hymns on the same martyr, alluded to already. I will observe, for the explanation of the first line, that roses were the floral emblems of martyrs, as lilies of virgins, and violets of confessors.

Rosa, novum dans odorem,
Ad ornatum ampliorem
  Regiæ cœlestis,
Ab Ægypto revocatur ;
Illum sequi gratulatur,
  Cujus erat testis.

Uva, data torculari,
Vult pressuras inculcari,
  Ne sit infecunda :
Martyr optat petrâ teri,
Sciens munus adaugeri
  Sanguinis in undâ.

BEDE.

BORN 672, died 735. The circumstances of his life are in fresher remembrance among English Churchmen, than to need to be repeated here.

XLVII. S. ANDREAS ALLOQUITUR CRUCEM.

SALVE, tropæum gloriæ,
  Salve, sacrum victoriæ
Signum, Deus quo perditum
Mundum redemit mortuus.

O gloriosa fulgidis
Crux emicas virtutibus,
Quam Christus ipse proprii
Membris dicavit corporis.

XLVII. Cassander, *Hymni Ecclesiastici* (*Opera*, Paris, 1616), p. 281.—These stanzas form part of one of the eleven hymns which Cassander attributed to Bede, and published for the first time in his *Hymni Ecclesiastici*, Paris, 1556. The last editor of the works of Bede, Dr. Giles, has not been able to find any MS. containing these hymns, and, though not excluding, expresses (vol. i. p. clxxi.) many doubts in regard of their authenticity. Whether they are Bede's or not, I must dissent from the judgement of his editor in one respect, since, whatever the value or the poems as a whole, these lines have a real worth.

Quondam genus mortalium
Metu premebas pallido,　　　　　　10
At nunc reples fidelium
Amore læto pectora.

En! ludus est credentium
Tuis frui complexibus,
Quæ tanta gignis gaudia,　　　　　　15
Pandis polique januas;

Quæ Conditoris suavia
Post membra, nobis suavior
Es melle facta, et omnibus
Prælata mundi honoribus.　　　　　　20

Te nunc adire gratulor,
Te caritatis brachiis
Complector, ad cœlestia
Conscendo per te gaudia.

Sic tu libens me suscipe,　　　　　　25
Illius, alma, servulum,
Qui me redemit per tuam
Magister altus gloriam.

Sic fatur Andreas, crucis
Erecta cernens cornua,　　　　　　30
Tradensque vestem militi,
Levatur in vitæ arborem.

ADAM OF ST VICTOR.

XLVIII. DE S. LAURENTIO.

SICUT chorda musicorum
Tandem sonum dat sonorum
Plectri ministerio,

XLVIII. Clichtoveus, *Elucidat. Eccles.* p. 208.—These three stanzas are but the fragments of rather a long poem, in which the *manner* of St Lawrence's martyrdom (he is said to have been broiled to death on a gridiron), is brought rather too prominently out; even in these present the *assatus* of ver. 11 we could willingly have missed. They are notwithstanding, well worthy to find a place here, being full of striking images, and singularly characteristic of their author's manner—most of all, perhaps, of his rich prodigality in the multiplication, and of his somewhat ostentatious skill in the arrangement, of his rhymes.—St Lawrence was archdeacon of Rome in the third century, and died in the persecution of Valerian. His festival was held in great honour by the Church of the middle ages, and himself accounted to hold a place only second to St Stephen, in the glorious army of martyrs (Durandus, *Rational.* vii. 23).

1—10]. These and other like images appear in some lines of Hildebert upon a martyrdom (*Opp.* p. 1259):

Sicut chorda solet dare tensa sonum meliorem,
Sic pœnis tensus dat plenum laudis honorem;
Utque probat fornax vas fictile consolidando,
Utque jubes late redolere unguenta liquaudo,
Ut feriendo sapis fervorem vimque sinapis,
Utque per ardorem tus undique fundit odorem,
Sic odor insignis fiunt et vulnus et ignis.
Si caro tundatur, granum paleâ spoliatur,
Si comburatur, tolli robigo putatur.

Sic in chely tormentorum
Melos Christi confessorum   5
Martyris dat tensio.

Parum sapis vim sinapis,
Si non tangis, si non frangis;
Et plus fragrat, quando flagrat,
Tus injectum ignibus :   10
Sic arctatus et assatus,
Sub ardore, sub labore,
Dat odorem pleniorem
Martyr de virtutibus.

Hunc ardorem factum foris   15
Putat rorem vis amoris,
Et zelus justitiæ :
Ignis urens, non comburens,
Vincit prunas, quas adunas,
O minister impie.   20

---

4. *chely*] Χέλυς = testudo, originally the tortoise, out of the
shell of which Hermes is said to have fashioned the first lyre.
The poet would say: "It is with the martyrs of God in their
sufferings as with the strings of the lyre, which are drawn tight
and stricken, that so they may yield their sweetest sounds."

16. *Putat rorem*] An allusion probably to Dan. iii. 50
(Vulg.): Et fecit medium fornacis quasi ventum roris flantem.

HILDEBERT.

XLIX. SOMNIUM DE LAMENTATIONE PICTAVENSIS ECCLESIÆ.

NOCTE quâdam, viâ fessus,
   Torum premens, somno pressus,
In obscuro noctis densæ,
Templum vidi Pictavense,
Sub staturâ personali,   5
Sub personâ matronali :

XLIX. *Hildeberti et Marbodi Opp.* p. 1357.—In the *Gallia Christiana*, vol. ii. p. 1172, the circumstances are detailed which enable us to understand this noble vision. William Adelelm, the rightful bishop of Poitiers, was in 1130 violently expelled from his see, and driven into exile, by the faction of the anti-pope, Anacletus the Second, and of the Count of Poitiers, who sided with him ; and an intrusive and schismatic bishop, Peter of Chasteleraut, usurped his throne, and exercised infinite vexations and oppressions upon the Church. William was at length restored in 1135, mainly owing to the menacing remonstrances of St Bernard. See in his *Life* (*Opp.* vol. ii. p. 1122) a most characteristic account of the manner in which Bernard terrified the Count into this restoration. It was during the period of the usurpation, and when now it had lasted three years (ver. 79—81), that this poem was composed. I cannot be sure how far the reader's impressions will coincide with my own, nor whether I may not somewhat overrate its merits ; but certainly it seems to me to deserve something very different from that utter oblivion into which it has fallen. I know of no nobler piece of versification, nor more skilful management of rhyme, in the whole circle of Latin rhymed poetry.

Situs quidem erat ei
Reverendæ facici;
Sed turbârat froutem ejus
Omni damno damnum pejus;   10
Sic est tamen rebus mersis,
Ut perpendas ex adversis
Quanti esset illis annis,
Quibus erat sine damnis.
Juvenilis ille color,   15
Nullus erat unde dolor,
Nullus erat, sed in ore
Livor erat pro colore.
Hæret crini coronella,
Fracta nimbis et procellâ :   20
Vicem complet hic gemmarum
Grex corrosor tinearum.
Sunt in ventre signa famis,
Quem ostendit rupta chlamys :
Hæc est chlamys, hic est cultus,   25
Quem attrivit annus multus,
Ab extremo quidem limbo
Gelu rigens, madens nimbo.
Est vetustas hujus vestis
Novitatis suæ testis,   30

29—34. I understand Hildebert to mean—The oldness of
this, the Church's robe, and that it had endured so long, and
survived so much, was a witness for its everlasting freshness and
youth, and implied with how great care it had been woven at the
first, even though now it was rent and tangled and torn, and
scarcely hung about her limbs :—but doubtless the *novitatis* is
difficult.

Innuendo quantâ curâ
Facta esset hæc textura:
Nunc se tenet mille nodis,
Implicata centum modis.

Hæc ut stetit fletu madens,   35
Flendi causam mihi tradens,
De se quidem in figurâ
Loquebatur inter plura,
Non desistens accusare
Navem, nautas, ventos, mare,   40
Ut ex verbis nesciretur
Quid vel quare loqueretur.
Mox infigens vultum cœlis,
Ora solvit his querelis:
Deus meus, exclamavit,   45
Quis me turbo suffocavit?
Quæ potestas impotentem?
Quæ vis urget me jacentem?
Unde metus? unde mœror?
Unde veni? vel quo feror?   50
Qui vel quales hi piratæ,
Qui insultant mersâ rate?
Quæ procellæ vel qui venti
Sic insurgunt resurgenti?
Nauta bone, via bonis,   55
Utens remo rationis,
Quam inepte, quam incaute
Sese habent mei nautæ!
Sed nec nautæ dici debent,
Qui fortunæ manus præbent,   60

Nec rectorum more degunt,
Qui reguntur, et non regunt.
His tam cæcis quam ignavis
Est commissus clavus navis,
Quam curtavit parte unâ
Piratæ vis importuna;
Nec a nautis est subventum
Contra ictus ferientum.
Timent viris non timenda
Ili a quibus sunt regenda;
Motum frondis, umbram lunæ
Timet illa gens fortunæ.
Sic me cæcam cæco mari
Patiuntur evagari;
Procul collum a monili,
Procul latus a cubili;
Vilipendor a marito
Cum ad torum hunc invito.
Tribus annis noctem passa,
Vehor mari nave quassâ;
Non exclusit annis tribus
Potus sitim, famem cibus:
Vicem potûs, vicem panis
Spes explebat, sed inanis;
·Nam exspecto tribus annis,
Quasi stultus, fluxum amnis;
Amnis tamen elabetur,
Nec ad horam haurietur.
Malo fracto, scisso velo,
Ad extremum nunc anhelo;
Nondum ventus iram lenit,
Sed a parte portûs venit,

Ad occasum flat ab ortu,
Non ad portum sed a portu.

Dispensator, qui dispensas   95
Cum privatis res immensas,
Bene cuncta, nil inique;
Ita nusquam ut ubique;
Ortum suum cujus curæ
Debent omnes creaturæ,   100
Quas creâsti non creatus,
Factus nunquam, tamen natus;
Tu qui magnus sine parte,
Princeps pacis sine Marte;
Tu qui bonus, immo bonum,   105
Quem amplecti paucis pronum;
Tibi constat id me velle,
Ne me vexent hæ procellæ,
Ne jam credar sorte regi,
Desponsata regum Regi.   110
Me lædentes, Rex, inclina,
Ne exultent de rapinâ;
Facientibus rapinam
Sit rapina in ruinam;
Arce lupos cum piratis,   115
Ne desperet portum ratis.
Audi, Pastor, qui me regis,
Da pastorem doctum gregis,
Se regnantem ratione,
Deviantem a Simone,   120

---

120. *a Simone*] Here, as so often, *Simon* is put for the sin of
simony to which he lent his name. Thus, in some energetic

Qui sic pugnet in virtute
Ne sint opes parum tutæ;
Sic dispenset;—et hoc dicto
Somnus abit, me relicto.

———————

lines first published by Edélestand du Méril (*Poés. popul. Lat.*
1847, p. 178), and by him confidently ascribed to Thomas à
Becket :

> Rosæ fiunt saliunca,
> Domus Dei fit spelunca :
> Simon malos præfert bonis,
> Simon totus est in donis ;
> Simon regnat apud Austrum,
> Simon frangit omne claustrum.
> Cum non datur, Simon stridet ;
> Sed, si detur, Simon ridet.
> Simon aufert, Simon donat,
> Hunc expellit, hunc coronat ;
> Hunc circumdat gravi peste,
> Illum nuptiali veste ;
> Illi donat diadema,
> Qui nunc erat anathema.
> Jam se Simon non abscondit,
> Res permiscet et confundit.
> Simon Petrus hunc elusit,
> Et ab alto jussum trusit :
> Quisquis cum imitatur
> Cum eodem puniatur,
> Et, sepultus in infernum,
> Pœnas luat in æternum !

122. *opes*]   Should we read *oves?*

ADAM OF ST VICTOR.

L. IN DEDICATIONE ECCLESIÆ.

QUAM dilecta tabernacula
Domini virtutum et atria !
Quam electi architecti,
Tuta ædificia,
Quæ non movent, immo fovent,   5
Ventus, flumen, pluvia !

L. Clichtoveus, *Elucidat. Eccles.* p. 186; Gautier, *Adam de S. Victor*, vol. i. p. 155.—This hymn, of which the theme is, the dignities and glories of the Church, as prefigured in the Old Testament, and fulfilled in the New, is the very extravagance of typical application, and, were it only as a study in medieval typology, would be worthy of insertion; but it has other and higher merits; even though it must be owned that the poet's learned stuff rather masters him, than that he is able effectually to master it. Its title indicates that it was composed for the occasion of a church's dedication, the services of which time were ever laid out for the carrying of men's thoughts from the temple made with hands to that spiritual temple, on earth or in heaven, " whose builder and maker is God."

1—6. The first two lines are a manifest allusion to Ps. lxxxiii. 2, 3 (Vulg.): Quam dilecta tabernacula tua, Domine virtutum ! Concupiscit, et deficit anima mea in atria Domini. The last four lines adapt the Lord's words, Matt. vii. 24, 25, to that house built indeed upon a Rock, upon Christ Himself. The poet writes *architecti*, including among these such as, under the great master-builder, carried up the walls—Apostles and prophets (Ephes. ii. 20 ; Rev. xxi. 14).

Quam decora fundamenta,
Per concinna sacramenta
Umbræ præcurrentia.
Latus Adæ dormientis   10
Evam fudit, in manentis
Copulæ primordia.

Arca ligno fabricata
Noë servat, gubernata
Per mundi diluvium.   15
Prole serâ tandem fœta,
Anus Sara ridet læta,
Nostrum lactans Gaudium.

Servus bibit qui legatur,
Et camelus adaquatur   20

10—12. *Latus Adæ*] Augustine (*Enarr. in Ps.* lvi. 5), shewing the mystery of the sleep which God sent on Adam, when
about to fashion the woman from his side, asks, Quare voluit
costam dormiente auferre? and replies, Quia dormiente Christo
in cruce facta est conjux de latere. Percussum est enim latus
pendentis de lanceâ, et profluxerunt Ecclesiæ sacramenta. Hugh
of St Victor: Adam obdormivit, ut de costâ illius fieret Eva;
Christus morte sopitus est, ut de sanguine ejus redimeretur
Ecclesia.

18. *Gaudium*] Hugh of St Victor: Isaac, qui interpretatur
risus, designat Christum, qui est gaudium nostrum. See note,
p. 166.

19. *Servus bibit*] Eliezer, the servant of Abraham, represents,
in the allegorical language of that day, the apostles or legates of
Christ, who were themselves refreshed by the faith of that Gentile world which they brought as a bride to Christ—who, so to
speak, drank of the streams which that world ministered to
them, as Eliezer drank from the pitcher of Rebecca. The whole

Ex Rebeccæ hydriâ;
Hæc inaures et armillas
Aptat sibi, ut per illas ·
Viro fiat congrua.

Synagoga supplantatur 25
A Jacob, dum divagatur,
Nimis freta literæ.
Lippam Liam latent multa,
Quibus videns Rachel fulta
Pari nubit fœdere. 30

In bivio tegens nuda,
Geminos parit ex Judâ

---

allegory of Gen. xxiv. is set out at length in a sermon of Hildebert's, *Opp.* p. 741.

23. *Aptat sibi*] As Rebecca puts on the bracelets and earrings which Isaac sent her (Gen. xxiv. 22), so the Gentile Church adorns herself for her future Lord; but with ornaments of his giving.

25—27. *divagatur*] Hugh of St Victor (*Alleg.* ii. 11): Esau foris venationi deserviens, benedictionem amittens, populum Israel significat, qui foris in literâ justitiam quærit, et benedictionem cœlestis hæreditatis dimittit.

28, 29. *Liam—Rachel*] Leah and Rachel signify, as is well known, the active and contemplative life; they are, so to speak, the Martha and Mary of the Old Testament; but they also signify the Synagogue and the Church—Leah the Synagogue, *lippa*, unable to see Christ, the true end of the law; but Rachel, or the Church, *videns*, seeing the things that belong to her peace.

31. *tegens nuda*] Cf. Gen. xxxviii. 14. For a general defence of such ugly types as this, and that which presently follows, 49—51, and of the seeking a prophetic element even in the sins of God's saints, see Augustine, *Con. Faust.* xxii. 83;

Thamar diu vidua.
Hic Moÿses a puellâ,
Dum se lavat, in fiscellâ   35
Reperitur scirpeâ.

Hic mas agnus immolatur,
Quo Israel satiatur,
Tinctus ejus sanguine.
Hic transitur rubens unda,   40
Ægyptios sub profundâ
Obruens voragine.

---

and again 87: Oderimus ergo peccatum, sed prophetiam non
extinguamus; cf. Gregory the Great, *Mor.* iii. 28. St Bernard
somewhere speaks of the New Testament sacraments (using that
word in its largest sense), as fair both within and without, while
in the Old, some are fair only within, and ill-favoured without.
It is not my part here to discuss the fituess or unfitness of the
use of such types, but merely to indicate what is needful for
their full understanding. These words of Augustine will explain
the present; who cares to see the matter brought out in greater
detail may follow up the reference (*Con. Faust.* xxii. 86):
Habitus meretricius confessio peccatorum est. Typum quippe
jam Ecclesiæ ex gentibus crocatæ gerit Thamar. A non agno-
scente fœtatur, quia de illâ prædictum est, Populus quem non
cognovi, servivit mihi.

34—36. *Moÿses*] Hugh of St Victor (*Alleg.* iii. 1): Moÿses
juxta flumen significat quemlibet hominem juxta fluvium præ-
sentis sæculi positum; filia regis Gratiam designat, quæ quemlibet ad vitam prædestinatum de fluxu sæculi liberat, et in filium
adoptat, ut qui prius fuerat filius iræ, deiuceps existat filius
gratiæ. The words *fiscella scirpea* occur in the Vulgate, Exod.
ii. 3.

37—39. Cf. Exod. xii. 5; 1 Cor. v. 7.

40—42. Hugh of St Victor: In Mari Rubro submersus est
Pharao, et principes ejus; et in baptismo liberamur a potestate
diaboli et principum ejus.

Hic est urna mannâ plena,
Hic mandata legis dena,
Sed in arcâ fœderis;   45
Hic sunt ædis ornamenta,
Hic Aäron indumenta,
Quæ præcedit poderis.

Hic Varias viduatur,
Barsabeë sublimatur,   50
Sedis consors regiæ:
Hæc Regi varietate
Vestis astat deauratæ,
Sicut regum filiæ.

---

46. *ædis ornamenta*] The candlestick, altar of incense, table of shewbread, and the like. He would say, Here, in the tabernacle which the Lord has pitched, are these in their truth, and not, as in that old, the mere figures of the true (Heb. ix.). See Gregory the Great, *in Ezech. Hom.* vii. § 2.

48. *poderis*] = ποδήρης, vestis talaris. The word was quite naturalized in ecclesiastical Latin; thus Hugh of St Victor: Tunica illa quæ Græce *poderis*, hoc est, *talaris* dicitur; being for once right in his etymology of a Greek word. The *poderis* is the "robe" of Exod. xxviii. 3 (ποδήρης, LXX. and Josephus: tunica, Vulg.). The poet would say, Here, in the Church, are the realities which the *garments* of the High Priest (*indumenta*), and the *robe* (*poderis*), the chief among them, did but foreshew. A mystical meaning has always been found in these garments; see Braun, *De Vest. Sacerd. Hebr.* p. 701—752.

49. *Varias viduatur*] See note on ver. 31. I could hardly quote, without offence, the lines of Hildebert (*Opp.* p. 1217), in which he traces the mystery of Rom. vii. 1—6 as foreshewn at 2 Sam. xi. 26, 27.

52—54. Cf. Ps. xliv. 10 (Vulg.): Astitit regina a dextris tuis in vestitu deaurato, circumdata varietate.

Huc venit Austri regina,   55
Salomonis quam divina
Condit sapientia;
Hæc est nigra, sed formosa;
Myrrhæ et turis fumosa
Virga pigmentaria.   60

Hæc futura, quæ figura
Obumbravit, reseravit
Nobis dies gratiæ;
Jam in lecto cum dilecto
Quiescamus, et psallamus,   65
Adsunt enim nuptiæ:

---

55. *Austri regina*] The coming of the queen of the South
(Matt. xii. 24) to hear the wisdom of Solomon (1 Kin. x.), was
a favourite type of the coming of the Gentile world to hear the
wisdom of a greater than Solomon. Hugh of St Victor (*Alleg.*
vii. 2): Venit ad Salomonem regina Austri ut audiret sapientiam ejus, et venit ad Christum Gentilitas ut audiret sapientiam
ejus.

58. *nigra, sed formosa*] In these words, drawn from Cant. i.
5 (nigra sum, sed formosa, Vulg.), the middle age expositors
found, not the Church's confession of sin as still cleaving to her;
but rather made them parallel to such words as the Apostle's:
"We have this treasure in earthen vessels" (2 Cor. iv. 7), or the
Psalmist's, "The king's daughter is all glorious within" (Ps.
xlv. 12), *within* and not without; having no form nor comeliness,
no glory in the eyes of the world—"black" therefore to it, but
beautiful to her Lord (Bernard, *In Cant. Serm.* 25).

60. *Virga pigmentaria*] Cf. Cant. iii. 6 (Vulg.): Quæ est
ista, quæ ascendit per desertum, sicut virgula fumi ex aromatibus
myrrhæ, et turis, et universi pulveris pigmentarii? The Bride,
or Church, is likened to the "pillar of smoke perfumed with
myrrh and frankincense."

Quarum tonat initium
In tubis epulantium,
Et finis per psalterium.
Sponsum millena milia   70
Unâ laudant melodiâ,
Sine fine dicentia,
Alleluia.   Amen.

67—69. The marriage of Christ with his Church, which began under the Old Covenant, was completed in the New. The *trumpets* belong to the feasts of the Old (Num. x. 10; cf. Ps. xli. 5, Vulg., sonus *epulantis*); the *psaltery* or decachordon (modulationem edens longe suaviorem et gratiorem auditu quam sit tubarum sonitus obstreperus: Clichtoveus) to the New; it is on it that the *new song* is sung, even as David says (Ps. cxliii. 9, Vulg.): Deus, *canticum novum* cantabo tibi: *in psalterio* decachordo psallam tibi. Cf. Augustine, *Serm.* 9; *De decem Chordis,* 5.

Walter Mapes' clever irony on this so favourite school of Scripture interpretation, his complaint that, although he had cultivated it so diligently, it had brought no worldly preferment to him, as it had brought to many, all this may be found at length in Leyser's *Hist. Poëtt. et Poëmm. Med. Ævi,* pp. 779—784. These are some stanzas:

Opulenti solent esse,
Qui aptabant virgam Jessæ
Partui virgineo,
Sive rubum visionis,
Sive vellus Gideonis
Sparsum rore vitreo.

Solet Christus appellari
Lapis sumptus de altari
Non manu sed forcipe.
Hoc est notum sapienti,
Sed præbendam requirenti
Nemo dicet, Accipe.

Duo ligna Sareptenæ,
Spiritalis escam cœnæ
Coquunt in Ecclesiâ;
Abrahamque tulit ligna,
Per quæ digne Deo digna
Cremaretur hostia.

Hæc scrutari quidam solent,
Post afflicti fame dolent
Se vacâsse studio.
Unde multi perierunt,
Et in ipso defecerunt
Scrutantes scrutinio.

LI. DE VITA MUNDANA.

EHEU! eheu! mundi vita,
    Quare me delectas ita?
Cum non possis mecum stare,
Quid me cogis te amare?

Eheu! vita fugitiva,   5
Omni ferâ plus nociva,
Cum tenere te non queam,
Cur seducis mentem meam?

Eheu! vita, mors vocanda,
Odienda non amanda,   10
Cum in te sint nulla bona,
Cur exspecto tua dona?

LI. Edélestand du Méril, *Poésies Populaires Latines du Moyen Age*, Paris, 1847, p. 108; Mone, *Hymn. Lat. Med. Ævi*, vol i. p. 411.—The poem from which these stanzas are drawn consists of nearly four hundred lines. It was first completely published by Du Méril, as indicated above, from a MS. in the Imperial Library at Paris. The MS. is of the twelfth century, and the poem itself can scarcely be of an earlier date. Three or four stanzas of it had already got abroad. Thus two are quoted by Gerhard, *Loci Theoll.* xxix. 11, and see Leyser, *Hist. Poem. Med. Ævi*, p. 423. The attribution of these fragments of the poem, and thus implicitly of the whole, to St Bernard, rests on no authority whatever; it is merely a part of that general ascription to him of any poems of merit belonging to that period, whereof the authorship was uncertain.

Vita mundi, res morbosa,
Magis fragilis quam rosa,
Cum sis tota lacrymosa, 15
Cur es mihi gratiosa?

Vita mundi, res laboris,
Anxia, plena timoris,
Cum sis semper in languore,
Cur pro te sum in dolore? 20

Vita mundi, mors futura,
Incessanter ruitura,
Cum in brevi sis mansura,
Cur est mihi de te cura?

Vita mundi, res maligna, 25
Ut ameris nunquam digna,
Quid putas tibi prodesse,
Si me ducas ad non esse?

Vita mundi, res immunda,
Solis impiis jucunda, 30
Nutrimentum vitiorum,
Quid habes in te decorum?

Desine mihi placere,
Noli mihi congaudere,
Desine me conturbare, 35
Noli, quæso, me amare.

Execro tuum amorem,
Renuo tuum favorem;
Desero tuum decorem,
Non amo tuum odorem. 40

Per te ipsam tibi juro,
Donis tuis nihil curo,
Quare nil potes donare
Nisi pœnas et plorare.

Pellam te de corde meo, 45
Adjuvante Christo Deo,
Nec permittam te redire,
Si debeas interire.

Nec mireris, pestis dira,
Si te persequor cum irâ, 50
Quare tu mihi fecisti
Quicquid mali potuisti.

Idcirco, vita inepta,
Solis fatuis accepta,
Cum sis tota plena sorde, 55
Te refuto toto corde.

Toto corde te refuto,
Nec sententiam commuto,
Mortem plus volo subire,
Tibi, vita, quam servire. 60

LII.

UT jucundas cervus undas
  Æstuans desiderat,
Sic ad rivum Dei vivum
Mens fidelis properat.

Sicut rivi fontis vivi
Præbent refrigerium,
Ita menti sitienti
Deus est remedium.

Quantis bonis superponis
Sanctos tuos, Domine:
Sese lædit, qui recedit
Ab æterno lumine.

Vitam lætam et quietam,
Qui te quærit, reperit;
Nam laborem et dolorem
Metit, qui te deserit.

Pacem donas, et coronas,
His qui tibi militant;
Cuncta læta sine metâ
His qui tecum habitant.

LII. Mommey, *Supplementum Patrum*, Paris, 1686, p. 165.
He attributes the poem from which these lines are drawn, but
on grounds entirely insufficient, to St Bernard.

Heu quam vanâ mens humana
Visione falleris!
Dum te curis nocituris
Imprudenter inseris.

Cur non caves lapsus graves, 25
Quos suädet proditor,
Nec affectas vias rectas,
Quas ostendit Conditor?

Resipisce, atque disce
Cujus sis originis; 30
Ubi degis, cujus legis,
Cujus sis et ordinis.

Ne te spernas, sed discernas,
Homo, gemma regia:
Te perpende, et attende 35
Quâ sis factus gratiâ.

Recordare quis et quare
Sis a Deo conditus;
Hujus hæres nunc maneres,
Si fuisses subditus. 40

O mortalis, quantis malis
Meruisti affici,
Dum rectori et auctori
Noluisti subjici.

-----

34. *gemma regia*] Thus a later hymn, on the recovery of the
lost sinner:

> Amissa drachma regio
> Recondita est ærario:
> Et gemma, deterso luto,
> Nitore vincit sidera.

Sed majores sunt dolores 45
Infernalis carceris;
Quo mittendus et torquendus
Es, si male vixeris.

Cuï mundus est jucundus,
Suam perdit animam: 50
Pro re levi atque brevi
Vitam perdit optimam.

Si sunt plagæ, curam age
Ut curentur citius:
Ne, si crescant et putrescant, 55
Pergas in deterius.

Ne desperes, jam cohæres
Christi esse poteris,
Si carnales, quantum vales,
Affectus excluseris; 60

Si vivorum et functorum
Christum times judicem:
Debes scire, quod perire
Suum non vult supplicem.

Preces funde, pectus tunde, 65
Flendo cor humilia:
Pœnitenti et gementi
Non negatur venia.

ALARD.

WILLIAM ALARD, born 1572, and descended from a noble family in Belgium, was the son of Francis Alard, a confessor of the Reformed Faith during the persecutions of the Duke of Alva. The father, hardly escaping from the Low Countries with his life, settled in Holstein, at the invitation of Christian the Fourth, king of Denmark. For three or four generations the family, which appears to have established itself there, or in the neighbouring parts of Germany, was distinguished in the walks of theology and classical learning; so much so that one of its later members published a *Decas Alardorum Scriptis Clarorum*, Hamburg, 1721, from which my information is derived. Besides other works which William composed, he was the author of two small volumes of Latin hymns, which, however forgotten now, appear to have found much favour at the time of their publication: *Excubiarum piarum Centuria*, Lipsiæ, 1623; and *Excubiarum piarum Centuria Secunda*, 1628; I believe that there was also a third *Century*, though it has never come under my eye. Of the first *Century* four editions were published in the author's lifetime. He died Pastor of Krempe in Holstein in 1645.

LIII. DE ANGELO CUSTODE.

CUM me tenent fallacia
   Mundi fugacis gaudia,
Cœlo vigil mihi datus
Flet atque plorat Angelus.

Sed quando lacrimis mea
Deploro tristis crimina,
Lætatur Angelus Dei,
Qui tangitur curâ mei.

Proinde abeste, gaudia
Mundi fugacis omnia;
Adeste lacrimæ, mea
Plorem quibus tot crimina:

Ne, lætus in malo, Angelis
Sim causa fletûs cœlicis,
Sed his, nefas lugens meum,
Creem perenne gaudium.

———

LIII. *Excubiarum Piarum Centuria* 2da, Lips. 1628, p. 304.

LIV. ACCESSURI AD SACRAM COMMUNIO-
NEM ORATIO AD JESUM SERVATOREM.

SIT ignis atque lux mihi
  Reo tui perceptio,
Jesu beate, corporis,
Sacerrimique sanguinis ;

Ut ignis hic cremet mei
  Cordis nefas, et omnia
Delicta, noxios simul
Affectuum rubos cremet ;

Ut ista lux suâ face
  Tenebricosa pectoris
Illuminet mei, prece
Te semper ut piâ colat.

LIV. *Excub. Piar. Cent.* Lips. 1623, p. 336.—The reader
acquainted with the Greek *Euchologion* will recognize this as
little more than the versification of a prayer therein.

ST AMBROSE.

LV. HYMNUS AD GALLICANTUM.

ÆTERNE rerum Conditor,
Noctem diemque qui regis,
Et temporum das tempora,
Ut alleves fastidium;

Præco diei jam sonat,   5
Noctis profundæ pervigil,

LV. *S. Ambrosii Opp.* Paris. 1836, p. 200.—There can be
no doubt that many so called Ambrosian hymns are not by St
Ambrose; out of which it has come to pass, that some, in an
opposite extreme, have affirmed that we possess none which
can certainly be affirmed to be his.   Yet, to speak not of others,
this is lifted above all doubt, Augustine, the cotemporary of
Ambrose, and himself for some time a resident at Milan, distinctly ascribing it to him, *Retract.* i. 21; cf. his *Confess.* ix. 12,
in proof of his familiarity with the hymns of St Ambrose.
Moreover, the hymn is but the metrical arrangement of thoughts
which he has elsewhere (*Hexaëm.* xxiv. 88) expressed in prose:
Galli cantus...et dormientem excitat, et sollicitum admonet, et
viantem solatur, processum noctis canorâ significatione protest-
ans.   Hoc canente latro suas relinquit insidias; hoc ipse lucifer
excitatus oritur, cœlumque illuminat; hoc canente mœstitiam
trepidus nauta deponit; omnisque crebro vespertinis flatibus
excitata tempestas et procella mitescit;...hoc postremo canente
ipsa Ecclesiæ Petra culpam suam diluit—with much more, in
which the very turns of expression used in the hymn recur.

Nocturna lux viantibus,
A nocte noctem segregans.

Hoc excitatus lucifer
Solvit polum caligine ;   10
Hoc omnis erronum cohors
Viam nocendi deserit.

Hoc nauta vires colligit,
Pontique mitescunt freta ;
Hoc, ipsa petra Ecclesiæ,   15
Canente, culpam diluit.

Surgamus ergo strenue,
Gallus jacentes excitat,

7, 8. Clichtoveus: *Nocturna lux* est *viantibus* quantum ad
munus et officium, quod noctu iter agentibus nocturnas significat
horas, perinde atque interdiu viam carpentibus lux solis eas in-
sinuat conspicantibus solem .. *A nocte noctem segregare* memoratur, quoniam priorem noctis partem a posteriore suo cantu dirimit
ac disseparat, quasi noctis discretor.

11. *erronum*] A preferable reading to *errorum*, which might
so easily have supplanted it, but which it, the rarer word, would
scarcely have supplanted. In the hymn of Prudentius we read:

Ferunt *vagantes dæmones*,	Invisa nam vicinitas
Lætos tenebris noctium,	Lucis, salutis, numinis,
Gallo canente exterritos	Rupto tenebrarum situ,
Sparsim timere et cedere.	Noctis fugat satellites.

15. *petra Ecclesiæ*] That St Ambrose was very far from
believing in a Church built upon a man, that therefore here he
can mean no such thing, is plain from other words of his (*De
Incarn. Dom.* 5): Fides ergo est Ecclesiæ fundamentum: non
enim de carne Petri, sed de fide dictum est, quia portæ mortis ei
non prævalebunt.

17. *Surgamus ergo*] The cock-crowing had for the early

Et somnolentos increpat;
Gallus negantes arguit. 20

Gallo canente, spes redit,
Ægris salus refunditur,
Mucro latronis conditur,
Lapsis fides revertitur.

Jesu, labantes respice, 25
Et nos videndo corrige:
Si respicis, lapsus cadunt,
Fletuque culpa solvitur.

Tu lux refulge sensibus,
Mentisque somnum discute: 30
Te nostra vox primum sonet,
Et vota solvamus tibi.

Christians a mystical significance. It said, "The night is far
spent, the day is at hand." And thus the cock became, in the
middle ages, the standing emblem of the preachers of God's
Word. The old heathen notion, that the lion could not bear the
sight of the cock (Ambrose, *Hexaëm.* vi. 4: Leo gallum et
maxime album veretur; cf. Lucretius, iv. 716; Pliny, *H. N.*
viii. 19) easily adapted itself to this new symbolism. Satan, the
roaring lion, fled away terrified, at the faithful preaching of God's
Word. Nor did it pass unnoted, that this bird, clapping its
wings upon its sides, first rouses itself, before it seeks to rouse
others. Thus Gregory the Great (*Reg. Pastor.* iii. 40): Gallus,
cum jam edere cantus parat, prius alas excutit, et semetipsum
feriens vigilantiorem reddit: quia nimirum necesse est, ut hi,
qui verba sanctæ prædicationis movent, prius studio bonæ actionis evigileut, ne in semetipsis torpentes opere, alios excitent
voce.

25—28. A beautiful allusion to Luke xxii. 60—62.

ST BERNARD.

LVI. DE NOMINE JESU.

JESU dulcis memoria,
  Dans vera cordi gaudia,
Sed super mel et omnia
Ejus dulcis præsentia.

Nil canitur suavius,   5
Nil auditur jucundius,
Nil cogitatur dulcius,
Quam Jesus Dei Filius.

Jesu, spes pœnitentibus,
Quam pius es petentibus,   10
Quam bonus te quærentibus,
Sed quid invenientibus?

LVI. *Bernardi Opp.* ed Bened. 1719, vol. ii. p. 914.—This poem, among those of St Bernard perhaps the most eminently characteristic of its author, consists, in its original form, of nearly fifty quatrains, and, unabridged, would have been too long for insertion here; not to say that, with all the beauty of the stanzas in particular, the composition, as a whole, lies under the defect of a certain monotony and want of progress. Where all was beautiful, the task of selection was certainly a hard one; but only in this way could the poem have found place in this volume; nor, for the reasons just stated, did I feel that it would be altogether a loss to it to present it in this briefer form.

Jesu, dulcedo cordium,
Fons vivus, lumen mentium,
Excedens omne gaudium,   15
Et omne desiderium.

Nec lingua valet dicere,
Nec littera exprimere,
Expertus potest credere
Quid sit Jesum diligere.   20

Quando cor nostrum visitas,
Tunc lucet ei veritas,
Mundi vilescit vanitas,
Et intus fervet caritas.

Qui te gustant, esuriunt;   25
Qui bibunt, adhuc sitiunt;
Desiderare nesciunt
Nisi Jesum quem diligunt.

Quem tuus amor ebriat,
Novit quid Jesus sapiat;   30
Quam felix est quem satiat!
Non est ultra quod cupiat.

Jesu, decus angelicum,
In aure dulce canticum,
In ore mel mirificum,   35
In corde nectar cœlicum:

Desidero te millies,
Mi Jesu, quando venies?
Me lætum quando facies?
Me de te quando saties?   40

O Jesu mi dulcissime,
Spes suspirantis animæ,
Te quærunt piæ lacrimæ,
Te clamor mentis intimæ.

Tu fons misericordiæ,
Tu veræ lumen patriæ:
Pelle nubem tristitiæ,
Dans nobis lucem gloriæ.

Te cœli chorus prædicat,
Et tuas laudes replicat:
Jesus orbem lætificat,
Et nos Deo pacificat.

Jesus ad Patrem rediit,
Cœleste regnum subiit:
Cor meum a me transiit,
Post Jesum simul abiit:

Quem prosequamur laudibus,
Votis, hymnis, et precibus;
Ut nos donet cœlestibus
Secum perfrui sedibus.

LVII. PHŒNIX INTER FLAMMAS EXSPIRANS.

TANDEM audite me,
  Sionis filiæ!
Ægram respicite,
Dilecto dicite:
Amore vulneror,   5
Amore funeror.

Fulcite floribus
Fessam languoribus;
Stipate citreis
Et malis aureis;   10
Nimis edacibus
Liquesco facibus.

Huc odoriferos,
Huc soporiferos
Ramos depromite,   15
Rogos componite;
Ut phœnix moriar!
In flammis oriar!

LVII. [Walraff,] *Corolla Hymnorum*, p. 57.—The poet has
drawn his inspiration throughout from the Canticles. The
whole of this beautiful composition is but the further unfolding
of the words of the Bride, "I am sick of love" (ii. 5).

An amor dolor sit,
An dolor amor sit,   20
Utrumque nescio;
Hoc unum sentio,
Jucundus dolor est,
Si dolor amor est.

Quid, amor, crucias?   25
Aufer inducias,
Lentus tyrannus es;
Momentum annus est;
Tam tarda funera
Tua sunt vulnera.   30

Jam vitæ stamina
Rumpe, O anima!
Ignis ascendere
Gestit, et tendere
Ad cœli atria;   35
Hæc mea patria!

ABELARD.

LVIII. DIXIT AUTEM DEUS: FIANT LUMI-NARIA IN FIRMAMENTO CŒLI.

Gen. i. 14.

ORNARUNT terram germina,
  Nunc cœlum luminaria;
Sole, lunâ, stellis depingitur,
Quorum multus usus cognoscitur.

Hæc quâque parte condita   5
Sursum, Homo, considera;
Esse tuam et cœli regio
Se fatetur horum servitio.

Sole calet in hieme,
Qui caret ignis munere;   10
Pro nocturnæ lucernæ gratiâ
Pauper habet lunam et sidera.

Stratis dives eburneis,
Pauper jacet gramineis;

LVIII. Edélestand du Méril, *Poésies Popul. Lat.* 1847, p. 444.
—I have already spoken unfavourably of Abelard's poetry; but
this poem, one of a series on the successive days' work of Creation, of a sort of *Hexaëmeron* in verse, despite its prosaic com-
mencement and unmelodious rhythm, must be acknowledged to
rest on a true poetical foundation.

Hinc avium oblectant cantica,   15
Inde florum spirat fragantia.

Impensis, Dives, nimiis
Domum casuram construis;
Falso sole pingis testudinem,
Falsis stellis in cœli speciem.   20

In verâ cœli camerâ
Pauper jacet pulcherrimâ;
Vero sole, veris sideribus
Istam illi depinxit Dominus.

Opus magis eximium   25
Est naturæ quam hominum;
Quod nec labor nec sumptus præparat,
Nec vetustas solvendo dissipat.

Ministrat homo diviti,
Angelus autem pauperi,   30
Ut hinc quoque constet cœlestia
Quam sint nobis a Deo subdita.

17—24. Augustine: Plus est pauperi videre cœlum stellatum quam diviti tectum inauratum.

31, 32. There are some good lines in the poem, *De Contemptu Mundi*, found in St Anselm's *Works*, pp. 195—201, on the same theme.

Cur dominus rerum, quare Deitatis imago
  Parva cupis? cupias maxima, magnus homo.
Luna tibi fulget, tibi volvitur orbita solis,
  Et tibi sunt toto sidera sparsa polo.
Nempe dies tuus est, tua nox, tuus igneus æther,
  Et tibi commutant tempora quæque vices.

BUTTMANN.

Born 1764, died 1829.

LIX.   ARX FIRMA DEUS NOSTER EST.

A RX firma Deus noster est,
  Is telum, quo nitamur;
Is explicat ex omnibus
Queis malis implicamur.
Nam cui semper mos,   5
Jam ter terret nos;
Per astum, per vim,
Sævam levat sitim;
Nil par in terris illi.

LIX. Mohnike, *Hymnol. Forschungen*, Stralsund, 1832, vol. ii.
p. 250.—This is a good translation, perhaps as good as could
be made, of Luther's " Heldenlied," as it well has been called,—

Ein feste Burg ist unser Gott :

the hymn, among all with which he has enriched the Church,
most characteristic of the man, the truest utterance of his great
heart.   Much of the heroic strength of the original has vanished
in the translation; yet, beside its merits, which are real, it is
interesting as shewing the eminent philologist whose work it is,
in somewhat a novel aspect.   It was first published in 1830,
shortly after Buttman's death, on occasion of the third jubilee to
celebrate the publication of the Confession of Augsburg.   The
original hymn was probably composed in 1530, during the time
when the Diet was sitting there.

In nobis nihil situm est, 10
Quo minus pereamus:
Quem Deus ducem posuit,
Is facit ut vivamus.
Scin quis hoc potest?
Jesus Christus est, 15
Qui, dux cœlitum,
Non habet æmulum;
Is vicerit profecto.

Sit mundus plenus dæmonum,
Nos cupiant vorare; 20
Non timor est; victoriâ
Nil potest nos frustrare.
Hem dux sæculi!
Invitus abi!
In nos nil potes, 25
Jam judicatus es;
Vel vocula te sternat.

Hoc verbum non pessumdabunt,
Nec gratiam merebunt;
In nobis Christi Spiritus 30
Et munera vigebunt:
Tollant corpus, rem,
Mundique omnem spem:
Tollant! jubilent!
Non lucrum hinc ferent; 35
Manebit regnum nobis.

ST BERNARD.

LX. DE CONTEMPTU MUNDI.

CUM sit omnis homo fœnum,
  Et post fœnum fiat cœnum,
Ut quid, homo, extolleris?
Cerne quid es, et quid eris;
Modo flos es, et verteris   5
In favillam cineris.

Per ætatum incrementa,
Immo magis detrimenta,
Ad non-esse traheris.
Velut umbra, cum declinat,   10
Vita surgit et festinat,
Claudit meta funeris.

Homo dictus es ab humo;
Cito transis, quia fumo
Similis efficeris.   15
Nunquam in eodem statu
Permanes, dum sub rotatu
Hujus vitæ volveris.

LX. *Bernardi Opp.* ed. Bened. 1719, vol. ii. p. 915; Rambach, *Anthol. Christl. Gesänge,* p. 281.

13. *ab humo*] Quintilian (*Inst.* i. 6, 34) throws scorn on this derivation—quasi vero non omnibus animalibus eadem origo, aut illi primi mortales ante nomen imposuerint terræ quam sibi; but see Freund, *Wörterbuch d. Lat. Sprache,* s. v. Homo.

O sors gravis ! o sors dura !
O lex dira, quam natura
Promulgavit miseris !
Homo, nascens cum mœrore,
Vitam ducis cum labore,
Et cum metu moreris.

Ergo si scis qualitatem
Tuæ sortis, voluptatem
Carnis quare sequeris?
Memento te moriturum,
Et post mortem id messurum,
Quod hic seminaveris.

Terram teris, terram geris,
Et in terram reverteris,
Qui de terrâ sumeris.
Cerne quid es, et quid eris,
Modo flos es, et verteris
In favillam cineris.

ALANUS.

LXI. RHYTHMUS DE NATURA HOMINIS FLUXA ET CADUCA.

OMNIS mundi creatura
Quasi liber et pictura
Nobis est, et speculum ;
Nostræ vitæ, nostræ mortis,
Nostri status, nostræ sortis   5
Fidele signaculum.

Nostrum statum pingit rosa,
Nostri status decens glosa,
Nostræ vitæ lectio :
Quæ dum primo mane floret,   10
Defloratus flos effloret
Vespertino senio.

LXI. *Alani Opp.* ed. C. de Visch, Antwerp, 1654, p. 419.—
This fine poem has found its way into very few collections of
sacred Latin verse.   Indeed the only one in which I have met
it is that of Rambach, and there two stanzas, the seventh,
perhaps the finest in the whole poem, being one of them, are
omitted.

8. *glosa*] *Glosa*, or *glossa*, is thus explained by Du Cange :
Interpretatio, imago, exemplum rei; it is our English *gloss* or
glose ; which yet is used generally in a bad sense, the tongue
(for the word is of course derived from $\gamma\lambda\tilde{\omega}\sigma\sigma\alpha$) being so often
the setter forth of deceit, interpretation being so frequently
misinterpretation.   The German *glcissen*, to make a fair shew,
belongs probably to the same family of words.

Ergo ,spirans flos exspirat,
In pallorem dum delirat,
Oriendo moriens.
Simul vetus et novella,
Simul senex et puella,
Rosa marcet oriens.

Sic ætatis ver humanæ
Juventutis primo mane
Reflorescit paululum.
Mane tamen hoc excludit
Vitæ vesper, dum concludit
Vitale crepusculum :

Cujus decor dum perorat,
Ejus decus mox deflorat
Ætas, in quâ defluit.
Fit flos fœnum, gemma lutum,
Homo cinis, dum tributum
Homo morti tribuit.

Cujus vita, cujus esse
Pœna, labor, et necesse
Vitam morte claudere.
Sic mors vitam, risum luctus,
Umbra diem, portum fluctus,
Mane claudit vespere.

In nos primum dat insultum
Pœna, mortis gerens vultum,
Labor, mortis histrio :

Nos proponit in laborem,　　　　40
Nos assumit in dolorem,
Mortis est conclusio.

Ergo clausum sub hâc lege
Statum tuum, homo, lege,
Tuum esse respice :　　　　45
Quid fuisti nasciturus,
Quid sis præsens, quid futurus,
Diligenter inspice.

Luge pœnam, culpam plange,
Motus fræna, fastum frange,　　　　50
Pone supercilia.
Mentis Rector et Auriga,
Mentem rege, fluxus riga,
Ne fluant in devia.

HILDEBERT.

LXII. DE EXILIO SUO.

NUPER eram locuples, multisque beatus amicis,
  Et risere diu fata secunda mihi :
Jurares Superos intra mea vota teneri,
  Et res occasum dedidicisse pati.
Sæpe mihi dixi : Quorsum tam prospera rerum ? 5
  Quid sibi vult tantus, tam citus agger opum ?
Hei mihi ! nulla fides, nulla est constantia rebus,
  Res ipsæ quid sint mobilitate docent.
Res hominum atque homines levis alea versat in horas,
  Et venit a summo summa ruina gradu. 10
Quicquid habes hodie, cras te fortasse relinquet,
  Aut modo, dum loqueris, desinit esse tuum.
Has ludit fortuna vices, regesque superbos
  Aut servos humiles non sinit esse diu.
Ecce quid est hominis, quid jure vocare paterno, 15
  Quâ miser ille sibi plaudere dote potest.
Hoc est, hoc hominis, semper cum tempore labi,
  Et semper quâdam conditione mori.
Est hominis nudum nasci, nudumque reverti
  Ad matrem, nec opes tollere posse suas. 20
Est hominis putrere solo, saniemque fateri,
  Et miseris gradibus in cinerem redigi.

LXII. *Hildeberti et Marbodi Opp.* p. 1344. Hommey, *Supplementum Patrum,* p. 453.

Istius est hæres homo prosperitatis, et illum
  Certius his dominum prædia nulla manent.
Res et opes præstantur ei, famulantur ad horam, 25
  Et locuples mane, vespere pauper erit.
Nemo potest rebus jus assignare manendi,
  Quæ nutus hominum non didicere pati.
Jus illis Deus ascribit, statuitque teneri
  Legibus, et nutu stare vel ire suo.   30
Ille simul semel et solus prævidit et egit
  Cuncta, nec illa aliter vidit, agitque aliter.
Ut vidit facienda facit, regit absque labore,
  Distinguit formis, tempore, fine, loco.
Crescendi studium rebus metitur, et illas   35
  Secretis versat legibus, ipse manens.
Ipse manens, dum cuncta movet, mortalibus ægris
  Consulit, et quâ sit spes statuenda docet.
Si fas est credi te quicquam posse vel esse,
  O fortuna, quod es, quod potes ipse dedit.   40
Pace tuâ, fortuna, loquar, blandire, minare,
  Nil tamen unde querar, aut bene læter ages.
Ille potens, mitis tenor et concordia rerum,
  Quidquid vult in me digerat, ejus ero.

JACOBUS DE BENEDICTIS.

JACOBUS de Benedictis, or familiarly Jacopone, to whom the following poem in all probability appertains, was in every regard a memorable man and of a remarkable history. There are two very careful sketches of his life and writings, drawn entirely from the original sources, and far richer than any to be found in ordinary biographies, given, one by Mohnike (*Studien*, Stralsund 1825, vol. i. pp. 335–406), another by Ozanam (*Les Poëtes Franciscains en Italie au troisième Siècle*, Paris, pp. 164–272); though indeed that in the *Biographie Universelle* is far from being slightly or inaccurately done. The year of his birth is not known, but, as he died in 1306 at a great age, it must have fallen early in the preceding century. He was born at Todi in Umbria, of a noble family, and lived a secular life, until some remarkable circumstances attending the violent death of his wife made so deep an impression upon him, that he withdrew himself to that which was then counted exclusively the religious life, and entered the Order of St Francis, just then at its highest reputation for sanctity; though he was never willing to be more than a lay brother therein.

Of his Latin poems I said in my former edition that only this and the far more celebrated *Stabat Mater* had been preserved; though of Italian spiritual songs and satires a very large amount; but Ozanam has since that time published, though apparently from an imperfect

MS., a beautiful pendant to that poem. It is the *Stabat Mater* of the Blessed Virgin by the cradle of Bethlehem, and not by the cross of Calvary. The great freedom of speech with which, in his vernacular poems, he handled the abuses of his time, and especially those of the hierarchy, drew on him long imprisonments, and he only went out of prison when his persecutor, Boniface the Eighth, whom to have had for an adversary was itself an honour, went in. An earnest humorist, he seems to have desired to carry the being a fool for Christ into every-day familiar life. The things which with this intent he did, some of them morally striking enough, others mere extravagances and pieces of gross spiritual buffoonery — wisdom and folly, such as we often find, side by side, in the saints of the Romish Calendar — are largely given by Wadding, the historian of the Franciscan Order, and by Lisco, in a separate treatise which he has published on the *Stabat Mater*, Berlin, 1843, p. 23. Not a few of these leave one in doubt whether he was indeed perfectly sound in his mind, or whether he was only a Christian Brutus, feigning folly, that he might impress his wisdom the more deeply, and utter it with a greater freedom.

Balde, the Bavarian Jesuit, of whom there will presently be occasion to say something more, has recorded in a graceful little poem (*Silv.* vii. 2) what his feelings were, on first making acquaintance with the life and writings of Jacopone:

> Tristis nænia funerum,
> Vanæ cum gemitu cedite lacrimæ.
> Me virtutis iter docent
> Intermista jocis gaudia mutuis;

Me cœlo lepor inserit;
Me plus quam rigidi vita Pachomii,
Jacopone, trahit tua,
Florens lætitiis mille decentibus.
Sancto diceris omnia
Risu perdomuisse; egregiâ quidem
Dementis specie viri.
Chaldæosque magos, et Salomoniam
Transgressus sapientiam,
Curarum vacuus, plenior ætheris,
Non urbis, neque dolii,
Sed mundi fueras publicus incola.

The key-note to this beautiful composition is supplied
by the epitaph which graces a monument raised to him,
in 1596, at his native Todi :

Ossa B. Jacoponi de Benedictis, Tudertini, qui, stultus propter
Christum, novâ mundum arte delusit, et cœlum rapuit.

LXIII. DE CONTEMPTU MUNDI.

CUR mundus militat sub vanâ gloriâ,
  Cujus prosperitas est transitoria ?
Tam cito labitur ejus potentia,
Quam vasa figuli, quæ sunt fragilia.

Plus fide litteris scriptis in glacie,   5
Quam mundi fragilis vanæ fallaciæ;
Fallax in præmiis, virtutis specie,
Qui nunquam habuit tempus fiduciæ.

LXIII. *Bernardi Opp.* ed Bened. vol. ii. p. 913; Mohnike.
Hymnol. Forschungen, vol. ii. p. 173.—Tusser has translated this
hymn.

Credendum magis est viris fallacibus,
Quam mundi miseris prosperitatibus,   10
Falsis insaniis et vanitatibus,
Falsisque studiis et voluptatibus.

Quam breve festum est hæc mundi gloria !
Ut umbra hominis, sic ejus gaudia,
Quæ semper subtrahunt æterna præmia,   15
Et ducunt hominem ad dura devia.

O esca vermium ! o massa pulveris !
O ros, o vanitas, cur sic extolleris?

---

9. *viris*] Manifestly there is something here amiss. The *viri fallaces* themselves constituting the world, there cannot be a comparison between them. Mohnike (i. 377) proposes to read *ventis*; yet better still is a later suggestion which he makes (ii. 177), *vitris* fallacibus. Opitz, as he observes, in his grand old German translation of the hymn, must have so read, for he writes :

> Lieber will ich Glauben fassen
> *Auf ein Glas*, das bäld zerfüllt,
> Als mich trösten mit den Schätzen,
> Und dem Glücke dieser Welt.

18. *O ros, o vanitas*] Some editions read, *O roris vanitas;* others, *O nox, o vanitas;* Mohnike suggests *O flos, o vanitas,* with allusion to such passages as Job xiv. 2; Ps. ciii. 15; Isai. xxviii. 1, 4; 1 Pet. i. 24. Yet this image the poet seems to have reserved for the second line of the next stanza; while the early drying up of the morning dew is also a scriptural image for that which quickly passes away and disappears (Hos. vi. 4; xiii. 3); and one appearing in medieval, as indeed in all, poetry. Thus the author of the *Carmen Parœneticum,* sometimes ascribed to St Bernard (*Opp.* vol. ii. p. 910, Bened. ed.):

> Quam male fraudantur, qui stulte ludificantur ;
> Qui propter florem mundi vanumque decorem,
> Qui prius apparet quasi ros, et protinus aret,
> Vadit in infernum, perdens diadema supernum.

Ignorans penitus, utrum cras vixeris,
Fac bonum omnibus, quamdiu poteris.   20

Hæc carnis gloria, quæ tanti penditur,
Sacris in litteris flos fœni dicitur;
Ut leve folium, quod vento rapitur,
Sic vita hominis luci subtrahitur.

Nil tuum dixeris quod potes perdere,   25
Quod mundus tribuit, intendit rapere:
Superna cogita, cor sit in æthere,
Felix, qui potuit mundum contemnere!

Dic, ubi Salomon, olim tam nobilis,
Vel ubi Sampson est, dux invincibilis,   30
Vel pulcher Absalon, vultu mirabilis,
Vel dulcis Jonathas, multum amabilis?

Quo Cæsar abiit, celsus imperio,
Vel Dives splendidus, totus in prandio?
Dic, ubi Tullius, clarus eloquio,   35
Vel Aristoteles, summus ingenio?

Tot clari proceres, tot rerum spatia,
Tot ora præsulum, tot regna fortia,
Tot mundi principes, tanta potentia,
In ictu oculi clauduntur omnia.   40

BALDE.

JACOB BALDE, born at Ensisheim in Alsace, in 1603, entered the Order of the Jesuits in 1624, and died in 1668. The greater part of his life was spent in Bavaria; where he could watch only too well the unspeakable miseries of the Thirty Years' War. Filling up, as that war did, exactly the central period of his life, he was spectator of these from first to last: and many pages of his poetry bear witness with what a bleeding heart he beheld the wounds of his native land. This sympathy of his, so true and so profound, with the sufferings of Germany, gives a reality to his verse which modern Latin poetry so often wants. Yet with all this, and with a free recognition, not of his talents merely, but of his genius, I cannot think but that there is some exaggeration in the language in which it has become the fashion to speak of him among his fellow-countrymen. They exalt him as the first of modern Latin poets—not, of course, as having reached the highest perfection of classical style, for no one would be so absurd as to attribute this praise to him, which every page of his writings would abundantly refute—but for the grandeur of his thoughts, the originality and boldness of his imagery; so that they regard him, not so much as an accomplished Latin versifier, but rather as a great German poet in the disguise of a foreign tongue. It was not one of his co-religionists, but Herder, who first began to speak this language about him, and who indeed re-

vived his forgotten memory in the minds of his fellow-
countrymen, publishing in his *Terpsichore* a translation
of a large number of his odes. A. W. Schlegel followed
in the same track, with yet more enthusiastic praise:*
and since his time several editions of Balde's works,
entire or selected, have been published, thus two by
Orelli, Zurich, 1805, 1818; and in like manner translations of the whole, or a portion of them, have
appeared.

Nor is his poetry, which has thus been brought to
light a second time, inconsiderable in bulk. It fills
four closely-printed volumes. Next to his odes his
Solatium Podagricorum (Munich, 1661) has perhaps
been the most widely read. It must be owned that the
gout is a somewhat ghastly subject for merriment, especially when the jest is continued through some thousands
of lines. The poem, of which the tone is mock-heroic,
is intended no doubt to set forth the praises of abste-
miousness. Thus one of the most frequent topics of
consolation which he offers to the martyrs to this dis-
ease, is the dignity of their complaint (" *lordly* gout," as
Swift calls it, μισόπτωχος θέα, as Lucian)—that it is

---

* These are Schlegel's words : Ein tiefes, regsames, oft schwär-
merisch ungestümes Gefühl, ein Einbildungskraft, woraus starke
und wunderbare Bilder sich zahllos hervordrängen, ein erfinder-
ischer, immer an entfernten Vergleichungen, an überraschenden
Einkleidungen geschäftiger Witz, ein scharfer Verstand. grosse
sittliche Schnellkraft und Selbständigkeit, kühne Sicherheit des
Geistes, welche sich immer eigene Wege wählt, und auch die
ungebahntesten nicht scheut : alle diese Eigenschaften erscheinen
in Balde's Werken allzu hervorstechend, als dass man ihn nicht
für einen ungewöhnlich reich begabten Dichter erkennen müsste.

only the rich and the luxurious whom it honours with its visits; as in these lines :

> Morbus hic induitur gemmis et torquibus aureis,
> Armillasque gerit manibus colloque smaragdos:
> Non est communis lixis vulgoque frequenti.
> Cerdones refugit, nec de lodice paratur;
> Mæcenas te laute petens, multumque supine :
> Seligit aulaï thalamos in turribus altis,
> Auratumque habitat, vel eburno ex dente lacunar;
> Fulcitur plumis et pulvinaribus albis.
> Vive diu, infelix, morbo indignissimus isto.

Now and then, however, the religious earnestness, which is the ground-tone of all which Balde writes, openly appears, as when he reminds the fretful and impatient sufferer, of One who had no such solaces and alleviations of pain, as are largely granted to him :

>   ···non dormiit ostro,
> Mollibus effultus cygnis, foliisque rosarum :
> Affixus fuit ILLE cruci, clavisque quaternis
> Ex ferro fossus terram inter et astra pependit;
> Felle sitim relevans, pertusus vocibus aures
> Sacrilegis; toto laniatum corpore funus.
> Te capit infusum lectica simillima Ledæ,
> Invitum quæ vel queat invitare soporem ;
> Accinit Amphion, et fundit dulcia Rhenus;
> Demulcet conjux ; lepidi solantur amici ;
> Et potes, heu ! lecto trux indignarier isti,
> Duraque fata queri, quæ sunt mollissima fatu.

These brief extracts may suffice to give a slight conception of what the character of this poem is. But it is, undoubtedly, as a lyric poet that Balde is greatest; and in that aspect the grand poem which follows will shew him.

LXIV. CHOREA MORTUALIS SIVE LESSUS

DE SORTIS ET MORTIS IN HUMANAS RES IMPERIO:

Argumentum
Inter funebres tædas, ad modulatos Umbrarum
passus decantandum.

EHEU, quid homines sumus?
Vanescimus, sicuti fumus;
Vana, vana terrigenûm sors,
Cuncta dissipat improba mors.

Exstincta est Leopoldina,   5
Frustra clamatâ Lucinâ;
Lacrymosa puerperæ mors!
Miseranda mulierum sors!

Cum falcibus ageret æstas,
Est et hæc succisa majestas: 10
Ah, aristæ purpureæ sors!
Sicne dira te messuit mors?

LXIV. Balde, *Poëmata*, Coloniæ, 1660, vol. iv. p. 424.—The empress Leopoldina, wife of Ferdinand the Third, died in childbirth at Vienna after one year's marriage, in the year 1649. The great commonplaces of death, which, if always old, are yet always new, have seldom clothed themselves in grander form, or found a more solemn utterance, than they do in this sublime poem. How noble the third, the fourth, and the sixth stanzas, and how much to be regretted that Balde so seldom exchanged his alcaic and other classical metres for these Christian rhythms.

9. *æstas*] The empress died on the 7th of August.

Quo more vulgaris urtica,
Jacet hæc quoque regia spica;
   Suo condidit horreo mors,   15
   Brevi posuit angulo sors.

Ut bulla defluxit aquosa,
Subsedit, ut vespere rosa;
   Brevis omnis est flosculi sors,
   Rapit ungue celerrima mors.   20

Quam manibus osseis tangit,
Crystallinam phialam frangit;
   O inepta et rustica mors!
   O caduca juvenculæ sors!

Ubi nunc decor ille genarum,   25
Ubi formæ miraculum rarum?
   Bina lumina subruit mors,
   Cœca tenebras intulit sors.

----

17. *Ut bulla*] Crashaw's Latin poem, entitled *Bulla (De-
lights of the Muses*, 1648, p. 54) can find no place here. I wish
it might, for it is one of the most gorgeous pieces of painting in
verse which anywhere I know—far more poetical than any of
his English poetry, of which it shares the conceits and other
faults. These are a few of the lines in which the bubble gives
an account of itself:

   Sum venti ingenium breve,
   Flos sum, scilicet, aëris,
   Sidus scilicet æquoris,
   Naturæ jocus aureus,
   Naturæ vaga fabula,
   Naturæ breve somnium,
   Auræ filia perfidæ,
   Et risûs facilis parens;
   Tantum gutta superbior,
   Fortunatius et lutum.

Ubi corporis bella figura !
Ubi lactis ostrique mixtura !　　　　　　30
　　Lac effudit in cespitem sors,
　　Texit ostrum sandapila mors.

Ubi rubra coralla sunt oris !
Ubi retia, crines amoris !
　　Parcæ rapuit forficem sors,　　　　35
　　Scidit istâ cæsariem mors.

Ubi cervix et manus eburna !
Heu funebri jacent in urnâ !
　　Atra nives imminuit sors,
　　Colla pressit tam candida mors.　　40

Quæ pulcrior fuit Aurorâ,
Hanc, Cæsaris aula, deplora ;
　　Vana species, lubrica sors,
　　Tetra facies, pallida mors.

Quæ vides has cunque choreas,　　　45
Augebis et ipsa mox eas ;
　　Subitam movet aleam sors,
　　Certa rotat hastilia mors.

Huc prompta volensque ducetur,
Capillis invita trahetur ;　　　　　　50
　　Ducet inevitabilis sors,
　　Trahet inexorabilis mors.

Quod es, fuimus : sumus, quod eris ;
Præcessimus, tuque sequeris ;
　　Volat ante levissima sors,　　　　55
　　Premit arcu vestigia mors.

Nihil interest pauper an dives,
Non amplius utique vives;
   Simul impulit clepsydram sors,
   Vitæ stamina lacerat mors.   60

Habere nil juvat argentum,
Nil regna prætendere centum;
   Sceptra sarculis abigit sors,
   Ridet albis hæc dentibus mors.

Nihil interest, turpis an pulcra,   65
Exspectant utramque sepulcra;
   Legit lappas et lilia sors,
   Violasque cum carduis mors.

Nec interest, vilis an culta,
Trilustris, an major adultâ;   70
   Vere namque novissimo sors,
   Populatur et hyeme mors.

Linquenda est aula cum casâ,
Colligite singuli vasa;
   Jubet ire promiscua sors,   75
   Ire cogit indomita mors.

Ex mille non remanet unus,
Mox omnes habebitis funus;
   Ite, ite, quo convocat sors,
   Imus, imus, hoc imperat mors.   80

Ergo vale, o Leopoldina,
Nunc umbra, sed olim regina;
   Vale, tibi nil nocuit sors,
   Vale, vale, nam profuit mors.

T

Bella super et Suecica castra, 85
Nubesque levaris, et astra;
   Penetrare quo nequeat sors,
   Multo minus attonita mors.

Inde mundi despiciens molem,
Lunam pede calcas et solem; 90
   Dulce sonat ex æthere vox,
   Hyems transiit, occidit nox.

Surge, veni; quid, sponsa, moraris?
Veni, digna cœlestibus aris;
   Imber abiit, mœstaque crux, 95
   Lucet, io, perpetua Lux.

---

85. *Suecica castra*] A fine allusion to the recent desolations of Germany. It was only four years before that the smoke of the Swedish watch-fires had been visible from the ramparts of Vienna. It is true that when the empress died, peace had been restored for nearly a year, the Treaty of Westphalia having been signed in October, 1648. But the wounds of Germany had scarcely begun to heal.

MARBOD.

MARBOD, born in 1035, of an illustrious family in Anjou, was chosen bishop of Rennes in 1095 or in the year following, and having governed with admirable prudence his diocese for thirty years, died in 1125. He has left a large amount of Latin poetry, in great part the versified legends of saints. His poem *De Gemmis* was a great favourite in the Middle Ages, and has been often reprinted. It is perhaps worth reading, not as poetry, for as such it is of very subordinate value, but as containing the whole rich mythology of the period in regard of precious stones and the virtues popularly attributed to them. His poems are for the most part written in leonine verse, but he has shewn in more than one no contemptible skill in the management of the classical hexameter.

LXV. ORATIO AD DOMINUM.

DEUS-HOMO, Rex cœlorum,
   Miserere miserorum;
Ad peccandum proni sumus,
Et ad humum redit humus;

LXV. *Hildeberti et Marbodi Opp.* p. 1557.

Tu ruinam nostram fulci   5
Pietate tuâ dulci.
Quid est homo, proles Adæ?
Germen necis dignum clade.
Quid est homo nisi vermis,
Res infirma, res inermis.   10
Ne digneris huic irasci,
Qui non potest mundus nasci:
Noli, Deus, hunc damnare,
Qui non potest non peccare;
Judicare non est æquum   15
Creaturam, non est tecum:
Non est miser homo tanti,
Ut respondeat Tonanti.
Sicut umbra, sicut fumus,
Sicut fœnum facti sumus: 20
Miserere, Rex cœlorum,
Miserere miserorum.

DAMIANI.

PETER DAMIANI, cardinal-bishop of Ostia, was born at Ravenna in 1002, and died in 1072. Profoundly impressed with the horrible corruption of his age, and the need of a great reformation which should begin with the clergy themselves, he was the enthusiastic friend and helper of Hildebrand, his *Sanctus Satanas*, as fondly and with a marvellous insight into the heights and depths of his character, he calls him, in all the good and in all the evil which he wrought for the Church. He has left a considerable body of Latin verse; but, not to say that much of it is deeply tinged with superstitions of which he was only too zealous a promoter, there is little of it, which, even were this otherwise, one would much be tempted to extract save this, and the far grander poem *De Gaudiis Paradisi*, which will be found a little later in this volume. Yet doubtless his epitaph, written by himself, possesses a solemn and a stately grandeur. It is as follows:

Quod nunc es, fuimus: es, quod sumus, ipse futurus;
   Illis sit nulla fides, quæ peritura vides.
Frivola sinceris præcurrunt somnia veris,
   Succedunt brevibus sæcula temporibus.
Vive memor mortis, quo semper vivere possis;
   Quidquid adest, transit; quod manet, ecce venit.
Quam bene providit, qui te, male munde, reliquit,
   Mente prius carni, quam tibi carne mori.
Cœlica terrenis, præfer mansura caducis,
   Mens repetat proprium libera principium:

> Spiritus alta petat, quo prodit fonte recurrat,
>   Sub se despiciat quicquid in ima gravat.
> Sis memor, oro, mei:—cineres pius aspice Petri;
>   Cum prece, cum gemitu dic: Sibi parce, Deus.

Surely it is nothing wonderful that he who had so realized what life and death are, did not wait till the latter had stripped him of his worldly honours, but himself anticipated that hour; having some time previously laid down his cardinal's hat, that what remained of his life he might spend in retirement and in prayer. It is probable that he had already so done, when this epitaph was composed. He died as abbot of Sta Croce d'Avellano in the States of the Church.

LXVI.   DE DIE MORTIS.

GRAVI me terrore pulsas, vitæ dies ultima;
  Mœret cor, solvuntur renes, læsa tremunt viscera,
Tuam speciem dum sibi mens depingit anxia.

Quis enim pavendum illud explicet spectaculum,
Quum, dimenso vitæ cursu, carnis ægra nexibus   5
Anima luctatur solvi, propinquans ad exitum?

Perit sensus, lingua riget, resolvuntur oculi,
Pectus palpitat, anhelat raucum guttur hominis,
Stupent membra, pallent ora, decor abit corporis.

LXVI. Corner, *Prompt. Devot.* p. 701; Rambach, *Anthol. Christl. Gesänge*, p. 238; Daniel, *Thes. Hymnol.* vol. i. p. 224; vol. iv. p. 291.

Præsto sunt et cogitatus, verba, cursus, opera,   10
Et præ oculis nolentis glomerantur omnia:
Illuc tendat, huc se vertat, coram videt posita.

Torquet ipsa reum sinum mordax conscientia,
Plorat apta corrigendi defluxisse tempora;
Plena luctu caret fructu sera pœnitentia.   15

Falsa tunc dulcedo carnis in amarum vertitur,
Quando brevem voluptatem perpes pœna sequitur;
Jam quod magnum credebatur nil fuisse cernitur.

Quæso, Christe, rex invicte, tu succurre misero,
Sub extremâ mortis horâ cum jussus abiero,   20
Nullum in me jus tyranno præbeatur impio.

Cadat princeps tenebrarum, cadat pars tartarea;
Pastor, ovem jam redemptam tunc reduc ad patriam,
Ubi te videndi causâ perfruar in sæcula.

---

24. I know no fitter place to append a poem, which can claim
no room in the body of this volume, being almost without any
distinctly Christian element whatever, and little more than a
mere worldling's lamentation at leaving a world which he knows
he has abused, yet would willingly, if he might, continue still
longer to abuse. But even from that something may be learned;
and there is a force and originality about the composition, which
make me willing to insert it here, especially as it is very far
from common. I would indeed gladly know something more
about it. I find it in a *Psalteriolum Cantionum Catholicarum*,
Coloniæ, 1813, p. 283, with the title *De Morte*, but with the
fifth, sixth, and seventh stanzas omitted; and in its fuller form
in Königsfeld's *Latein. Hymnen und Gesänge*, Bonn, 1847.
This is a small and rather indifferent collection of mediæval
Latin poetry, with German translations annexed—so carelessly

edited as to inspire no confidence in the text.　Daniel also has
it (*Thes. Hymnol.* vol. iv. p. 351), but avowedly copied from
Königsfeld.　The thoughts have a more modern air about them,
than that I can suppose the poem rightly included in a collection
of *medieval* verse at all.　It bears the not very appropriate title
of *Cygnus Exspirans,* and is as follows :

Parendum est, cedendum est,
　Claudenda vitæ scena ;
Est jacta sors, me vocat mors,
　Hæc hora est postrema :
Valete res, valete spes ;
　Sic finit cantilena.

O magna lux, sol, mundi dux,
　Est concedendum fatis ;
Duc lineam eclipticam,
　Mihi luxisti satis :
Nox incubat ; fax occidit ;
　Jam portum subit ratis.

Tu, Cynthia argentea,
　Vos, aurei planetæ,
Cum stellulis, ocellulis,
　Nepotibus lucete ;
Fatalia, letalia
　Mi nunciant cometæ.

Ter centies, ter millies
　Vale, immunde munde !
Instabilis et labilis,
　Vale, orbis rotunde !
Mendaciis, fallaciis
　Lusisti me abunde.

Lucentia, fulgentia
　Gemmis valete tecta,
Seu marmore, seu ebore
　Supra nubes erecta.
Ad parvulum me loculum
　Mors urget equis vecta.

Lucretiæ, quæ specie
　Gypsatâ me cepistis,
Imagines, voragines !
　Quæ mentem sorbuistis,
En oculos, heu ! scopulos,
　Extinguit umbra tristis.

Tripudia, diludia,
　Et fescennini chori,
Quiescite, rancescite ;
　Præco divini fori,
Mors, intonat et insonat
　Hunc lessum ; Debes mori.

Deliciæ, lautitiæ
　Mensarum cum culinâ ;
Cellaria, bellaria,
　Et coronata vina,
Vos nauseo, dum haurio
　Quem scyphum mors propinat.

Facessite, putrescite,
　Odores, vestimenta ;
Rigescite, deliciæ,
　Libidinum fomenta !
Deformium me vermium
　Manent operimenta.

O culmina, heu ! fulmina,
　Horum fugax honorum,
Tam subito dum subeo
　Æternitatis domum.
Ridiculi sunt tituli ;
　Foris et agunt momum.

Lectissimi, carissimi
　Amici et sodales,
Heu ! insolens et impudens
　Mors interturbat sales.
Sat lusibus indulsimus :
　Extremum dico vale !

Tu denique, corpus, vale,
　Te, te citabit totum [? forum] ;
Te conscium, te socium
　Dolorum et gaudiorum !
Æqualis nos exspectat sors—
　Bonorum vel malorum.

PRUDENTIUS.

LXVII. IN EXEQUIIS DEFUNCTORUM.

JAM mœsta quiesce querela,
  Lacrimas suspendite, matres,
Nullus sua pignora plangat,
Mors hæc reparatio vitæ est.

Sic semina sicca virescunt,   5
Jam mortua jamque sepulta.
Quæ reddita cæspite ab imo
Veteres meditantur aristas.

Nunc suscipe, terra, fovendum.
Gremioque hunc concipe molli :   10
Hominis tibi membra sequestro,
Generosa et fragmina credo.

Animæ fuit hæc domus olim,
Factoris ab ore creatæ,

LXVII. *Prudentii Opp.* ed. Obbarius, 1845, p. 41.—These
lines, the crowning glory of the poetry of Prudentius, form only
a part (the concluding part) of his tenth *Cathemerinōn.* But it
has long been the custom to contemplate them apart from their
context, and as an independent poem.   This continued till a late
day as the favourite funeral-hymn in the Evangelical Church in
Germany, being used either in the original, or in the fine old
translation, Hört auf mit Trauern und Klagen.

Fervens habitavit in istis 15
Sapientia principe Christo.

Tu depositum tege corpus,
Non immemor ille requiret
Sua munera fictor et auctor,
Propriique ænigmata vultûs. 20

Veniant modo tempora justa,
Cum spem Deus impleat omnem,
Reddas patefacta necesse est,
Qualem tibi trado figuram.

Non, si cariosa vetustas 25
Dissolverit ossa favillis,
Fueritque cinisculus arens
Minimi mensura pugilli:

Nec, si vaga flamina et auræ,
Vacuum per inane volantes, 30
Tulerint cum pulvere nervos,
Hominem periisse licebit.

Sed dum resolubile corpus
Revocas, Deus, atque reformas,
Quânam regione jubebis 35
Animam requiescere puram?

Gremio senis addita sancti
Recubabit, ut est Eleazar,

17—32. We may compare with these stanzas the latter chapters of Tertullian's treatise, *De Resurr. Carnis.*

38. *Eleazar*] The question whether the scriptural names,

Quem floribus undique septum
Dives procul aspicit ardens.   40

Sequimur tua dicta, Redemptor,
Quibus atrâ morte triumphans,
Tua per vestigia mandas
Socium crucis ire latronem.

Patet ecce fidelibus ampli   45
Via lucida jam Paradisi,
Licet et nemus illud adire,
Homini quod ademerat anguis.

Nos tecta fovebimus ossa
Violis et fronde frequente,   50
Titulumque et frigida saxa
Liquido spargemus odore.

Lazarus and Eleazar, are only forms of the same, has been often
debated; and it is now generally agreed that they are. Tertullian calls once the Lazarus of Luke xvi Eleazar, in the same
manner as Prudentius does here.

MARBOD.

LXVIII. DE RESURRECTIONE MORTUORUM.

CREDERE quid dubitem fieri quod posse probatur,
  Cujus et ipse typum naturæ munere gesto?
Quâque die somno, ceu mortis imagine pressus,
Rursus et evigilans veluti de morte resurgo;
Ipsa mihi sine voce loquens natura susurrat: 5
Post somnum vigilas, post mortis tempora vives.
Clamat idem mundus, naturaque provida rerum,

LXVIII. *Hildeberti et Marbodi Opp.* p. 1615.—These lines attest the very respectable mastery of the classical hexameter, possessed in the eleventh and twelfth century. The arguments for a resurrection drawn from the analogies of the natural world had of course continually been handled before, by none perhaps so memorably as by Tertullian, *De Res. Carnis,* 12; *De Animâ,* 43, in whose footsteps Marbod here very closely treads. Compare the *Panegyricus* of Paulinus of Nola.

3. *mortis imagine*] Compare the fine address to Sleep in the *Hercules Furens* of Seneca:

> Pavidum leti genus humanum
> Cogis longam discere mortem;

and the same is very often beautifully brought out by Calderon; thus in his sublime Auto *La Cena de Baltasar:*

Descanso del sueño hace	Cada dia, pues rendida
El hombre, ay Dios, sin que advierta	La vida à un breve homicida,
Que quando duerme, y despierta,	Que es su descanso no advierte
Cada dia muere y nace:	Una leccion que la muerte
Que vivo cadaver yaze	Le và estudiando à la vida.

Quas Deus humanis sic condidit usibus aptas,
Ut possint homini quædam signare futura.
Mutat luna vices, defunctaque lumine rursum   10
Nascitur, augmentum per menstrua tempora sumens;
Sol quoque, per noctem quasi sub tellure sepultus,
Surgens mane novus reditum de morte figurat:
Signat idem gyros agitando volubile cœlum,
Aëra distinguens tenebris et luce sequente.   15
Ipsa parens tellus quæ corpora nostra receptat,
Servat in arboribus vitæ mortisque figuram,
Et similem formam redivivis servat in herbis.
Nudatos foliis brumali tempore ramos,
Et velut arentes mortis sub imagine truncos   20
In propriam speciem frondosa resuscitat æstas;
Quæque peremit hyems nova gramina vere resurgunt.
Ut suus incipiat labor arridere colonis.
Nos quoque spes eadem manet et reparatio vitæ,
Quâ revirescat idem, sed non resolubile corpus.   25
An mihi subjectis data sit renovatio rebus,
Totus et hanc speciem referens mihi serviat orbis,
Me solum interea premat irreparabile damnum?
Et quid erit causæ modico cur tempore vivens,
Optima pars mundi, vitæque Datoris imago,   30
Post modicum percam, sublatâ spe redeundi,
At pro me factus duret per sæcula mundus?
Nonne putas dignum magis inferiora perire
Irreparabiliter, quam quæ potiora probantur?
Sed tamen illa manent, ergo magis ista manebunt. 35

LXIX. DE DIE JUDICII.

CUM revolvo toto corde
  In quâ mundus manet sorde,
Totus mundus cordi sordet,
Et cor totum se remordet.

Cum revolvo purâ mente,　　　　　5
Cadit mundus quam repente,
Ne mens cadat cum cadente,
Mundum fugit mens attente.

Cum revolvo mente sanâ
Quam sit stulta spes humana,　　　10
A spe mentem ad spem verto,
Et spem mundi spe subverto.

Cum revolvo mundi laudem,
Et mundanæ laudis fraudem,
Laus et fraus in cordis ore　　　　15
Idem sonant uno more.

Cum revolvo mundi florem,
Et quem habet flos dolorem,
Tantus dolor est in flore,
Ut non sit flos in dolore.　　　　20

LXIX. Edélestand du Méril, *Poés. Popul. Latines*, 1847, p.
114 ; Mone, *Hymn. Lat. Med. Ævi*, vol. i. p. 415.—These are
some of the concluding stanzas of a poem, an earlier portion of
which is given p. 234.

Cum revolvo dies breves,
Et recordor dies leves,
Grave fit, quod fuit leve,
Et fit longum quod est breve.

Cum revolvo moriturus,   25
Quid post mortem sim futurus,
Terret me terror futurus,
Quem exspecto non securus.

Terret me dies terroris,
Iræ dies et furoris,   30
Dies luctûs et mœroris,
Dies ultrix peccatoris.

Expavesco miser multum
Judicis severi vultum,
Cui latebit nil occultum,   35
Et manebit nil inultum.

Et quis, quæso, non timebit,
Quando Judex apparebit,
Ante quem ignis ardebit,
Peccatores qui delebit?   40

Judicabit omnes gentes,
Et salvabit innocentes;
Arguet vero potentes,
Et deliciis fruentes.

Tunc et omnes delicati   45
Valedicent voluptati,
Et vacantes vanitati
Evanescent condemnati.

Oh quam grave, quam immite
A sinistris erit : ' Ite '
Cum a dextris ' Vos venite'
Dicet Rex, largitor vitæ.

Appropinquat enim dies,
In quâ justis erit quies,
Quâ cessabunt persequentes,
Et regnabunt patientes ;

Dies illa, dies vitæ,
Dies lucis inauditæ,
Quâ nox omnis destruetur,
Et mors ipsa morietur !

Ecce Rex desideratus,
Et a justis exspectatus,
Jam festinat exoratus,
Ad salvandum præparatus.

Oh quam pium et quam gratum,
Quam suâve, quam beatum
Erit tunc Jesum videre,
His qui eum dilexere.

Oh quam dulce, quam jucundum
Erit tunc odisse mundum,
Et quam triste, quam amarum
Habuisse mundum carum !

Oh beati tunc lugentes,
Et pro Christo patientes,
Quibus sæculi pressura
Regna dat semper mansura.

Ibi jam non erit metus,
Neque luctus, neque fletus,
Non egestas, non senectus,
Nullus denique defectus.   80

Ibi pax erit perennis,
Et lætitia solennis,
Flos et decus juventutis,
Et perfectio salutis.

Nemo potest cogitare   85
Quantum erit exultare,
Tunc in cœlis habitare,
Et cum angelis regnare.

Ad hoc regnum me vocare,
Juste Judex, tu dignare,   90
Quem exspecto, quem requiro,
Ad quem avidus suspiro.

LXX. DE DIE JUDICII.

APPAREBIT repentina dies magna Domini,
  Fur obscurâ velut nocte improvisos occupans.
Brevis totus tunc parebit prisci luxus sæculi,
  Totum simul cum clarebit præterîsse sæculum.

LXX. Thomasius, *Hymnarium, Opp.* vol. ii. p. 433; Rambach, *Anthol. Christl. Gesänge*, p. 126; Daniel, *Thes. Hymnol.* vol. i. p. 194.—This hymn, as will at once be observed, is alphabetic. Latin hymns which have submitted themselves to this constraint are not very numerous; and, though I suppose there is not, there appears something artificial in an arrangement, which, while it is a restraint and difficulty, confers few compensating benefits, and, when all is done, is rather for the eye than for the ear. In the sacred Hebrew poetry the chief examples in the kind are the *Lamentations* of Jeremiah, and some Psalms which are among the latest in the whole collection. The hymn before us is certainly as old as, if not a good deal older than, the seventh century; for Bede, who belongs to the end of this and the beginning of the eighth, refers to it in his work *De Metris.* It was then almost or altogether lost sight of, till Cassander published it in his *Hymni Ecclesiastici.* Although too exclusively a working up of Scripture passages which relate to the last judgment, indeed we may say of one Scripture passage (Mt. xxv. 31—46), in a narrative form, and wanting the high lyrical passion of the *Dies Iræ*, yet it is of a very noble simplicity, Daniel saying of it well: Juvat carmen fere totum e Scripturâ sacrâ depromptum comparare cum celebratissimo illo extremi judicii præconio, *Dies iræ, dies illa*, quo majestate et terroribus, non sanctâ simplicitate et fide, superatur.

Clangor tubæ per quaternas terræ plagas concinens, 5
  Vivos una mortuosque Christo ciet obviam.
De cœlesti Judex arce, majestate fulgidus,
  Claris angelorum choris comitatus aderit.
Erubescet orbis lunæ, sol vel obscurabitur,
  Stellæ cadent pallescentes, mundi tremet ambitus:
Flamma ignis anteibit justi vultum Judicis, 11
  Cœlum, terras, et profundi fluctus ponti devorans.
Gloriosus in sublimi Rex sedebit solio,
  Angelorum tremebunda circumstabunt agmina.
Hujus omnes ad electi colligentur dexteram, 15
  Pravi pavent a sinistris, hædi velut fœtidi:
Ite, dicet Rex ad dextros, regnum cœli sumite,
  Pater vobis quod paravit ante omne sæculum.
Karitate qui fraternâ me juvistis pauperem,
  Caritatis nunc mercedem reportate divites. 20
Læti dicent: Quando, Christe, pauperem te vidimus,
  Te, Rex magne, vel egentem miserati juvimus?
Magnus illis dicet Judex: Cum juvistis pauperem,
  Panem, domum, vestem dantes, me juvistis humiles.
Nec tardabit et sinistris loqui justus Arbiter: 25
  In gehennæ, maledicti, flammas hinc discedite:
Obsecrantem me audire despexistis mendicum,
  Nudo vestem non dedistis, neglexistis languidum.
Peccatores dicent: Christe, quando te vel pauperem,
  Te, Rex magne, vel infirmum contemplantes spre-
    vimus? 30
Quibus contra Judex altus: Mendicanti quamdiu
  Opem ferre despexistis, me sprevistis improbi.

---

12. *devorans*] So Cassander, Thomasius, and Rambach.
Daniel has *decorans*, but probably as a misprint.

Retro ruent tum injusti ignes in perpetuos,
    Vermis quorum non morietur, flamma nec restin-
        guitur;
Satan atro cum ministris quo tenetur carcere,   35
    Fletus ubi mugitusque, strident omnes dentibus.
Tunc fideles ad coelestem sustollentur patriam,
    Choros inter angelorum regni petent gaudia:
Urbis summæ Hierusalem introibunt gloriam,
    Vera lucis atque pacis in quâ fulget visio,   40
Xristum Regem, jam paternâ claritate splendidum,
    Ubi celsa beatorum contemplantur agmina.
Ydri fraudes ergo cave, infirmantes subleva,
    Aurum temne, fuge luxus, si vis astra petere:
Zonâ clarâ castitatis lumbos nunc accingere,   45
    In occursum magni Regis fer ardentes lampadas.

---

43. *Ydri*] for *Hydri.* The Latin language possessing originally no *y*, and every Greek word beginning with υ which had
been naturalized in the language, being necessarily aspirated, it
was only by such an irregularity as this that the alphabetic
arraugement of the poem could have been preserved throughout.
Hydrus = ὕδρος, properly a *sea-serpent*; but here the ὄφις ἀρχαῖος
of Gen. iii.; Rev. xii. 9.

THOMAS OF CELANO.

THOMAS, named of Celano, from a small town near the lake Fucino in the further Abruzzo, and so called to distinguish him from another of the same name and Order, was a friend and scholar of St Francis of Assisi—one indeed of the earliest members of the new Order of Minorites, which in 1208 was founded by him. He appears to have lived in near familiarity with his master, and, from the great matters in which he was trusted by him to have enjoyed his highest confidence. After the death of St Francis, which took place in 1226, he was the first who composed a brief account of his life, which he afterwards greatly enlarged, and which even now is the most authentic record of the life of the saint which we possess. The year of his own death is not known. His connexion with the founder of that influential Order might have just preserved his name from utter forgetfulness; but it is the *Dies Iræ* which has given him a much wider fame.

It is with no absolute certainty that the authorship of this grand hymn is ascribed to Thomas of Celano. Seeming to lie, as it has done, like a waif and stray, and yet at the same time so precious a one, that who would might make it his own, it is not very wonderful that claims of ownership have been put in on behalf of many. Several of these, however, may be set aside at once. Thus we are quite sure that Gregory the Great could not have been the author; seeing that rhyme, although not unknown or unused in his day, was very far from having reached the perfection which in this poem it displays; add to which, that the poem would then have remained unknown for the first six hundred years of its existence. Again, St Bernard has been sometimes named as the author. But, not to say that its character is austerer and texture more masculine, than any of those, beautiful as in their kind they are, which rightly belong to him, he also lived at too early a day. The hymn was not known till the thirteenth century; while he died in the middle of the twelfth, and enjoyed too high a reputation in life and after death to have rendered it possible that such a composition of his could have remained unnoticed for a hundred years. It would be long, and alien to the purposes of this volume, to consider all the names which have been suggested, or to give more than the results of the enquiry. The question has been thoroughly discussed by Mohnike, *Hymnologische Forschungen*, vol. i. pp. 1—24. He and others who have gone the fullest into the matter, are agreed that the preponderance of evidence is very much in favour of the friend and follower of St Francis, a notice of whose life I have in consequence given. The fact that two other hymns which are certainly of his composition are of very inferior merit cannot be urged as seriously affecting his claims. How many a poet has risen for once very much beyond the level which at any other time he attained. Moreover, these two hymns, which are both in honour of St Francis, are not at all so poor in poetical merits as some would imply. Indeed the first, *Fregit victor virtualis*, has to my mind very considerable merit, and displays a true poetical handling of its theme; though it does not come within the range of this volume. It and its fellow, *Sanctitatis nova signa*, are to be found in Daniel, *Thes. Hymnol.* vol. v. pp. 314, 317. In my former edition, I too lightly took Wadding's word, the Irish Franciscan, and the learned and laborious historiographer of his Order (b. 1580, d. 1657), that one or both of these hymns had perished, and expressed my regret at their loss. This is not, however, the case; the first is printed in some of the earlier Paris Missals, and the second, which ought not to have escaped me, in the *Acta Sanctorum*, Oct. 2, p. 801. Knowing as we do the bitter rivalry which reigned between the two mendicant Orders, it somewhat confirms the view that the hymn is the work of a Franciscan, that the Dominican, Sixtus Senensis, should speak slightingly of it, terming it, as he does, an uncouth poem (rhythmus inconditus); this he would scarcely have done, had there not been that in the authorship of the poem, which caused him to look at it with a jaundiced eye.

LXXI. DE NOVISSIMO JUDICIO.

D IES iræ, dies illa
     Solvet sæclum in favillâ,

LXXI. Mohnike, *Hymnol. Forschungen*, pp. 33, 39, 45: Lisco, *Dies Iræ, Hymnus auf das Weltgericht*, Berlin, 1840; Daniel, *Thes. Hymnol.* vol. ii. p. 103.—Of all the Latin hymns of the Church this has the widest fame; for as Daniel has truly remarked: Etiam illi quibus Latini Ecclesiæ hymni prorsus ignoti sunt, hunc certe norunt, et si qui inveniuntur ab humanitate tam alieni ut carminum sacrorum suavitatem nihil omnino sentiant, ad hunc certe hymnum, cujus quot sunt verba tot tonitrua, animum advertunt. The grand use which Goethe has made of it in his *Faust* may have helped to bring it to the knowledge of some who would not otherwise have known it; or, if they had, would not have believed its worth, if the sage and seer of this world, "a prophet of their own," had not thus set his seal of recognition upon it. To another illustrious man this hymn was eminently dear. How affecting is that incident recorded of Sir Walter Scott by his biographer,—how in those last days of his life when all of his great mind had failed or was failing, he was yet heard to murmur to himself some lines of this hymn, an especial favourite with him in other days. Nor is it hard to account for its wide and general popularity. The metre so grandly devised, of which I remember no other example, fitted though it has here shewn itself for bringing out some of the noblest powers of the Latin language—the solemn effect of the triple rhyme, which has been likened to blow following blow of the hammer on the anvil—the confidence of the poet in the universal interest of his theme, a confidence which has made him set out his matter with so majestic and unadorned a plainness as at once to be intelligible to all,—these merits, with many more, have given the *Dies Iræ* a foremost place among the masterpieces of sacred song.

1. *Dies iræ, dies illa*] The opening of this poem acquires

Teste David cum Sibyllâ.

additional grandeur when it is kept in mind that this line, striking the key note to the whole, was already familiar to the minds of men, being drawn, exactly as it stands, from the Vulgate, namely from Zeph. i. 15. The day of judgement continually appears under this title of *dies iræ* in the Latin medieval verse : thus in a poem of considerable merit by Peter of Blois :

Cessa, caro, lascivire,	Fraus Spiritûs immundi.
Quia dies instat iræ :	Nos hæc vita deserit,
Non te mundus rapiat,	Et ut umbra præterit
Non te circumveniat	Hujus figura mundi.

3. *cum Sibyllâ*] An unwillingness to allow a Sibyl to appear as bearing witness to Christian truth, has caused that we sometimes find this third line omitted, and in its stead *Crucis expandens vexilla*, as the second of this triplet. It rests on Matt. xxiv. 30, and on the expectation that the apparition of a cross in the sky would be " the sign of the Son of man in heaven" there spoken of. It is, however, a late alteration of the text ; and the line as above is quite in the spirit of the early and medieval theology. In those uncritical ages the Sibylline verses were not seen to be that transparent forgery which indeed they are ; but were continually appealed to as only second to the sacred Scriptures in prophetic authority ; thus on this very matter of the destruction of the world, by Lactantius, *Inst. Div.* vii. 16—24 ; cf. Piper, *Mythol. d. Christl. Kunst*, p. 472—507. It is not too much to say that these Sibylline oracles, with other heathen testimonies of the same kind, were not so much subordinated to more legitimate prophecy, as co-ordinated with it, the two being regarded as parallel lines of prophecy, the Church's and the world's, bearing consenting witness to the same truths. Thus is it in a curious medieval mystery on the Nativity, published in the *Journal des Savans*, 1846, p. 88. It is of simplest construction. One after another patriarchs and prophets and kings of the Old Covenant advance and repeat their most remarkable word about Him that should come : but side by side with them a series of heathen witnesses, Virgil, on the ground of his fourth Eclogue, Nebuchadnezzar (Dan. iii. 25), and the Sibyl : and that

Quantus tremor est futurus,
Quando Judex est venturus,   5
Cuncta stricte discussurus.

Tuba, mirum spargens sonum
Per sepulchra regionum,
Coget omnes ante thronum.

Mors stupebit et natura,   10
Quum resurget creatura,
Judicanti responsura.

Liber scriptus proferetur,
In quo totum continetur,
De quo mundus judicetur.   15

---

it was the writer's intention to parallelize the two series, and to
shew that Christ had the testimony of both, is plain from
some opening lines of the prologue:

O Judæi, Verbum Dei
Qui negatis, hominem
Vestræ legis, testem Regis
Audite per ordinem.

Et vos, gentes, non credentes
Peperisse virginem,
Vestræ gentis documentis
Pellite caliginem.

And such is the meaning here—"That such a day shall be
has the witness of inspiration, of David,—and of mere natural
religion, of the Sibyl—Jew and Gentile alike bear testimony to
the truths which we Christians believe." To look at the matter
from this point of view, makes certain that we ought to read
Teste David, and not *Teste Petro*. It is true that 2 Pet. iii.
7—11 is a more obvious prophecy of the destruction of the world
by fire than any in the Psalms; but there are passages enough
in these (as Ps. xcvi. 13; xcvii. 3; xi. 6), to which the poet
may allude; and the very obviousness of that in St Peter, makes
the reading, which introduces his name, suspicious.

Judex ergo quum sedebit,
Quidquid latet, apparebit,
Nil inultum remanebit.

Quid sum miser tum dicturus,
Quem patronum rogaturus, 20
Quum vix justus sit securus?

Rex tremendæ majestatis,
Qui salvandos salvas gratis,
Salva me, fons pietatis.

Recordare, Jesu pie, 25
Quod sum causa tuæ viæ;
Ne me perdas illâ die!

Quærens me sedisti lassus,
Redemisti crucem passus:
Tantus labor non sit cassus. 30

Juste Judex ultionis,
Donum fac remissionis
Ante diem rationis.

Ingemisco tanquam reus,
Culpâ rubet vultus meus: 35
Supplicanti parce, Deus!

Qui Mariam absolvisti,
Et latronem exaudisti,
Mihi quoque spem dedisti.

---

28. *sedisti lassus*] Cf. John iv. 6.

Preces meæ non sunt dignæ, 40
Sed tu bonus fac benigne
Ne perenni cremer igne !

Inter oves locum præsta,
Et ab hædis me sequestra,
Statuens in parte dextrâ. 45

Confutatis maledictis,
Flammis acribus addictis,
Voca me cum benedictis.

Oro supplex et acclinis,
Cor contritum quasi cinis : 50
Gere curam mei finis.

---

51. It is not wonderful that a poem such as this should have continually allured, and continually defied, translators. Jeremy Taylor in a letter to John Evelyn suggests to him that he should make a version of it : "I was thinking to have begged of you a translation of that well-known hymn, *Dies iræ, dies illa*, which, if it were a little changed, would make an excellent divine song." Evelyn did not comply, but we have several versions in English, of which the earliest that I know is one by Sylvester, *Works*, 1621, p. 1214 ; also a very noble one by Crashaw (*Steps to the Temple*, London, 1648, p. 105) ; it is in quatrains, and rather a reproduction than a translation. These are the first and last stanzas :

Hear'st thou, my soul, what serious things
Both the Psalm and Sibyl sings,
Of a sure Judge, from whose sharp ray
The world in flames shall fly away.
*   *   *   *   *
Oh hear a suppliant heart all crusht,
And crumbled into contrite dust ;
My Hope, my Fear, my Judge, my Friend,
Take charge of me, and of my end.

The list of English translations will include one by Roscommon,

and one by Walter Scott; while among the still more recent
translations are two in the *Irish Ecclesiastical Journal,* May and
June, 1849.   In German they are yet more numerous, including
highest names, such as Herder, Fichte, and Augustus Schlegel.
A volume before me by Lisco, is exclusively dedicated to these.
It was published in 1840, and contains forty-three versions;
while in an *Appendix,* which followed three years after, seven-
teen more are given, which either had before escaped the editor's
notice, or had been published since the publication of his book.
Among these, it is true, there is one French and one Romaic :
but all the rest are German.

LXXII. DE CRUCE DOMINI.

CRUX ave benedicta!
  Per te mors est devicta,
In te pependit Deus,
Rex et Salvator meus.

LXXII. [Walraff,] *Corolla Hymnorum*, p. 23 ; Daniel, *Thes.
Hymnol.* vol. ii. p. 349.—This little poem, so perfect in its kind,
might fitly have had its place among the earlier hymns upon the
Passion, pp. 130-151, and may seem as out of due order here.
But the sublime and awful judgement-hymns which have just
gone before, seem to want one of this nature—one which should
set forth Him in whom and through whose cross alone there
shall be no condemnation there—as a transitional hymn to those
which presently follow, and of which the theme is everlasting
life. I cannot refuse to set beside these lines, some of Calderon's,
of no inferior grace, and on the same theme :

> Arbol, donde el cielo quiso
> Dar el fruto verdadero
> Contra el bocado primero,
> Flor del nuevo paraiso,
> Arco de luz, cuyo aviso
> En piélago mas profundo
> La paz publicó del mundo,
> Planta hermosa, fértil vid,
> Harpa del nuevo David,
> Tabla del Moises segundo ;
> Pecador soy, tus favores
> Pido por justicia yo;
> Pues Dios en tí padeció,
> Solo por los pecadores.

Which lines may thus be translated :

> Tree, which heaven has willed to dower
> With that true fruit whence we live,

Tu arborum regina,   5
Salutis medicina,
Pressorum es levamen,
Et tristium solamen.

O sacrosanctum lignum,
Tu vitæ nostræ signum,   10
Tulisti fructum Jesum,
Humani cordis esum.

Dum crucis inimicos,
Vocabis, et amicos,
O Jesu, Fili Dei,   15
Sis, oro, memor mei.

As that other, death did give ;
Of new Eden loveliest flower ;
Bow of light, that in worst hour
Of the worst flood signal true
O'er the world, of mercy threw :
Fair plant, yielding sweetest wine ;
Of our David harp divine ;
Of our Moses tables new ;
Sinner am I, therefore I
Claim upon thy mercies make,
Since alone for sinners' sake
God on thee endured to die.

BERNARD OF CLUGNY.

BERNARD, a monk of Clugny, born at Morlaix, in Brittany, but of English parents, flourished in the twelfth century, the cotemporary and fellow-country-man of his own more illustrious namesake of Clairvaux.

LXXIII. LAUS PATRIÆ CŒLESTIS.

HIC breve vivitur, hic breve plangitur, hic breve fletur :
Non breve vivere, non breve plangere retribuetur;

LXXIII. Flacius Illyricus, *Poëmm. de Corrupto Ecclesiæ Statu,* p. 247.—The author, in an interesting preface, dedicates the poem *De Contemptu Mundi,* of which these lines form a part, to Peter the Venerable, General of the Order to which he belonged. The poem, which contains nearly three thousand lines, was first published by Flacius Illyricus, in the curious, and now rather scarce, collection of poems, intended by him as a verse-pendant and complement to his *Catalogus Testium Veritatis,* or, Catalogue of Witnesses against the Papacy who were to be found in all ages of the Church. This poem has been several times reprinted; Mohnike (*Hymnol. Forschungen,* vol. i. p. 458) knows of and indicates four editions, to which I could add a fifth. This is not wonderful; for no one with a sense for the true passion of poetry, even when it manifests itself in forms the least to his liking, will deny the breath of a real inspiration to the author of these dactylic hexameters. It must be confessed that uniting, as they do, the leonine and tailed rhyme, with every line broken up of

O retributio! stat brevis actio, vita perennis;
O retributio! cœlica mansio stat luc plenis;
Quid datur et quibus? æther egentibus et cruce dig-
    nis,   5
Sidera vermibus, optima sontibus, astra malignis.
Sunt modo prælia, postmodo præmia; qualia? plena;
Plena refectio, nullaque passio, nullaque pœna.
Spe modo vivitur, et Syon angitur a Babylone;
Nunc tribulatio; tunc recreatio, sceptra, coronæ; 10
Tunc nova gloria pectora sobria clarificabit,
Solvet enigmata, veraque sabbata continuabit.
Liber et hostibus, et dominantibus ibit Hebræus;
Liber habebitur et celebrabitur hinc jubilæus.
Patria luminis, inscia turbinis, inscia litis,   15
Cive replebitur, amplificabitur Israëlitis:

------

necessity into exactly three equal parts, they present as unat-
tractive a garb for poetry to wear as can well be imagined—to
say nothing of the extravagantly difficult laws which the poet
has imposed upon himself. He, it is true, in that dedicatory
epistle, glories in the difficulties of the metre he has chosen,
which he is convinced nothing but an especial grace and inspiration could have enabled him to overcome. Besides the
awkwardness and repulsiveness of the metre, which indeed is
felt much more strongly at first than after a little familiarity
with it, a chief defect in the poem, one which in my quotation
from it has been mitigated by some prudent omissions, is its
want of progress. The poet, instead of advancing, eddies round
and round his subject, recurring again and again to that which
he seemed to have thoroughly treated and dismissed. But even
with these serious drawbacks, high merits remain to it still. I
may mention that the often quoted lines, beginning

        Hora novissima, tempora pessima,

are the opening lines of this poem.

X

Patria splendida, terraque florida, libera spinis,
Danda fidelibus est ibi civibus, hic peregrinis.
Tunc erit omnibus inspicientibus ora Tonantis
Summa potentia, plena scientia, pax pia sanctis ;   20
Pax sine crimine, pax sine turbine, pax sine rixà,
Meta laboribus, atque tumultibus anchora fixa.
Pars mea Rex meus, in proprio Deus ipse decore
Visus amabitur, atque videbitur Auctor in ore.
Tunc Jacob Israël, et Lia tunc Rachel efficietur,   25
Tunc Syon atria pulcraque patria perficietur.

25. *Tunc Jacob Israël*] The earthly shall be transformed
into the heavenly, as Jacob became Israel, and in sign of the new
nature received the new name (Gen. xxxii. 28). According to
Augustine (*Serm.* 122), Israel=Videns Deum, which gives an
additional fitness to these words.—*et Lia tunc Rachel*] Leah and
Rachel represent, respectively, the active and the contemplative
Christian life, see p 229. Leah becoming Rachel is the swal-
lowing up of the laborious active in the more delightful contemplative, in that vision of God wherein all blessedness is included.
Cf. Augustine, *Con. Faust.* xxii. 52—54; and Hugh of St Victor
(*Miscell.* i. 79): Duæ sorores duas vitas significant. Lia, quæ
interpretatur *laboriosa*, significat vitam activam, quæ est fœcunda in fructu boni operis, sed parum videt in luce contemplationis. Rachel, quæ interpretatur *visum principium*, designat
vitam contemplativam, quæ est sterilis foris in opere, sed perspi-
cax in contemplatione. In his duabus vitis quasi quædam
contentio est animæ sanctæ alternatim nitentis ad amplexum
Sponsi sui, id est, Christi, sapientiæ videlicet Dei. Contendunt
ergo contemplatio et actio pro amplexu sapientiæ (cf. Gen.
xxx. 14—16). Qui in contemplatione est, suspirat pro ste-
rilitate operis; qui in opere est, suspirat pro jubilo contemplationis. In a sublime passage with which Augustine
concludes his Commentary upon St John, he makes the two
Apostles, Peter and John, to represent these two lives. It begins
thus: Duas itaque vitas sibi divinitus prædicatas et commen-
datas novit Ecclesia, quarum est una in fide, una in specie; una

O bona patria, lumina sobria te speculantur,
Ad tua nomina sobria lumina collacrimantur :
Est tua mentio pectoris unctio, cura doloris,
Concipientibus æthera mentibus ignis amoris.   30
Tu locus unicus, illeque cœlicus es paridisus,
Non ibi lacrima, sed placidissima gaudia, risus.
Est ibi consita laurus, et insita cedrus hysopo ;
Sunt radiantia jaspide mœnia, clara pyropo :
Hinc tibi sardius, inde topazius, hinc amethystus; 35
Est tua fabrica concio cœlica, gemmaque Christus.
Tu sine littore, tu sine tempore, fons, modo rivus,
Dulce bonis sapis, estque tibi lapis undique vivus.
Est tibi laurea, dos datur aurea, Sponsa decora,
Primaque Principis oscula suscipis, inspicis ora :   40
Candida lilia, viva monilia sunt tibi, Sponsa,
Agnus adest tibi, Sponsus adest tibi, lux speciosa :
Tota negotia, cantica dulcia dulce tonare,
Tam mala debita, quam bona præbita conjubilare.

Urbs Syon aurea, patria lactea, cive decora,   45

---

in tempore peregrinationis, altera in æternitate mansionis; una
in labore, altera in requie ; una in viâ, altera in patriâ ; una in
opere actionis, altera in mercede contemplationis.

45—58. In these lines the reader will recognize the original
of that lovely hymn, which within the last few years has been
added to those already possessed by the Church. A new hymn
which has won such a place in the affections of Christian people
as has *Jerusalem the Golden* is so priceless an acquisition that
I must needs rejoice to have been the first to recall from oblivion
the poem which yielded it. Dr. Neale, as is known, no doubt.
to many of my readers, in his *Rhythm of Bernard de Morlaix on
the Heavenly Country,* London, 1859, has translated a large
portion of the poem.

Omne cor obruis, omnibus obstruis et cor et ora.
Nescio, nescio, quæ jubilatio, lux tibi qualis,
Quam socialia gaudia, gloria quam specialis :
Laude studens ea tollere, mens mea victa fatiscit :
O bona gloria, vincor; in omnia laus tua vicit.   50
Sunt Syon atria conjubilantia, martyre plena,
Cive micantia, Principe stantia, luce serena :
Est ibi pascua, mitibus afflua, præstita sanctis,
Regis ibi thronus, agminis et sonus est epulantis.
Gens duce splendida, concio candida vestibus albis 55
Sunt sine fletibus in Syon ædibus, ædibus almis ;
Sunt sine crimine, sunt sine turbine, sunt sine lite
In Syon ædibus editioribus Israëlitæ.
Urbs Syon inclyta, gloria debita glorificandis,
Tu bona visibus interioribus intima pandis :   60

59—72. I quote, for comparison and contrast, a few lines from
Casimir, the great Latin poet of Poland. They turn upon the
same theme, the heavenly home-sickness; but with all their
classical beauty, and it is great, who does not feel that the
poor Clugnian monk's is the more real and deeper utterance,—
that, despite the strange form which he has chosen, he is the
greater poet ?

> Urit me patriæ decor,
> Urit conspicuis pervigil ignibus
> Stellati tholus ætheris,
> Et lunæ tenerum lumen, et aureis
> Fixæ lampades atriis.
> O noctis choreas, et teretem sequi
> Juratæ thiasum faces !
> O pulcher patriæ vultus, et ignei
> Dulces excubiæ poli !
> Cur me stelliferi luminis hospitem,
> Cur heu ! cur nimium diu
> Cœlo sepositum cernitis exulem ?

The Spanish scholar will remember and compare the noble
ode of Luis de Leon, entitled *Noche Serena.*

Intima lumina, mentis acumina te speculantur,
Pectora flammea spe modo, postea sorte lucrantur.
Urbs Syon unica, mansio mystica, condita cœlo,
Nunc tibi gaudeo, nunc mihi lugeo, tristor, anhelo:
Te quia corpore non queo, pectore sæpe penetro,   65
Sed caro terrea, terraque carnea, mox cado retro.
Nemo retexere, nemoque promere sustinet ore,
Quo tua mœnia, quo capitalia plena decore;
Opprimit omne cor ille tuus decor, o Syon, o pax,
Urbs sine tempore, nulla potest fore laus tibi mendax; 70
O sine luxibus, o sine luctibus, o sine lite
Splendida curia, florida patria, patria vitæ!

Urbs Syon inclyta, turris et edita littore tuto,
Te peto, te colo, te flagro, te volo, canto, saluto;
Nec meritis peto, nam meritis meto morte perire, 75
Nec reticens tego, quod meritis ego filius iræ:
Vita quidem mea, vita nimis rea, mortua vita,
Quippe reatibus exitialibus obruta, trita.
Spe tamen ambulo, præmia postulo speque fideque,
Illa perennia postulo præmia nocte dieque.   80
Me Pater optimus atque piissimus ille creavit;
In lue pertulit, ex lue sustulit, a lue lavit.
Gratia cœlica sustinet unica totius orbis
Parcere sordibus, interioribus unctio morbis;
Diluit omnia cœlica gratia, fons David undans   85
Omnia diluit, omnibus affluit, omnia mundans:
O pia gratia, celsa palatia cernere præsta,
Ut videam bona, festaque consona, cœlica festa.
O mea, spes mea, tu Syon aurea, clarior auro,
Agmine splendida, stans duce, florida perpete lauro,

O bona patria, num tua gaudia teque videbo?   91
O bona patria, num tua præmia plena tenebo?
Dic mihi, flagito, verbaque reddito, dicque, Videbis:
Spem solidam gero ; remne tenens ero? dic, Retinebis.
O sacer, o pius, o ter et amplius ille beatus,   95
Cui sua pars Deus: o miser, o reus, hâc viduatus.

LXXIV. IN DEDICATIONE ECCLESIÆ,

URBS beata Hirusalem, dicta pacis visio,
   Quæ construitur in cœlis vivis ex lapidibus,
Et ab angelis ornata, velut sponsa nobilis :

LXXIV. Clichtoveus, *Elucidat. Eccles.* p. 46; Thomasius, *Hymnarium, Opp.* vol. ii. p. 378; Rambach, *Anthol. Christl. Gesänge,* p. 179; Mohnike, *Hymnol. Forschungen,* vol. ii. p. 187.— This rugged but fine old hymn, of which the author is not known, is probably of date as early as the eighth or ninth century; such at least is Mohnike's conclusion. I have observed already upon the manner in which these grand old compositions were recast in the Romish Church, at the revival of learning, which was, in Italy at least, to so great an extent a revival of heathenism. This is one of the few which have not utterly perished in the process; while yet if we compare the first two rugged and somewhat uncouth stanzas, but withal so sweet, with the smooth iambics which in the Roman Breviary have taken their place, we shall feel how large a part of their beauty has disappeared. They are read there in the following form :

Cœlestis urbs Jerusalem,
Beata pacis visio,
Quæ celsa de viventibus
Saxis ad astra tolleris,
Sponsæque ritu cingeris
Mille angelorum millibus :

O sorte nupta prosperâ,
Dotata Patris gloriâ,
Respersa Sponsi gratiâ,
Regina formosissima,
Christo jugata Principi,
Cœlo coruscas civitas.

A little further on, we are amidst the heathen associations of Olympus. But the most illustrious example of what I mean, is yielded by a comparison of the grand old Paschal hymn (how old, it is impossible to say), *Ad cœnam Agni providi,* with the same as burnished and brightened up in the Roman Breviary. It is easy to compare them, Daniel (*Thes. Hymnol.* vol. i. p. 88) giving the old and the new in parallel columns.

Nova veniens e cœlo, nuptiali thalamo
Præparata, ut sponsata copuletur Domino; 5
Plateæ et muri ejus ex auro purissimo.

Portæ nitent margaritis, adytis patentibus;
Et virtute meritorum illuc introducitur
Omnis qui ob Christi nomen hoc in mundo pre-
  mitur.

Tunsionibus, pressuris expoliti lapides 10
Suis coaptantur locis; per manus artificis
Disponuntur permansuri sacris ædificiis.

Angulare fundamentum lapis Christus missus est,
Qui compage parietum in utroque nectitur,
Quem Syon sancta suscepit, in quo credens per-
  manet. 15

Omnis illa Deo sacra et dilecta civitas,
Plena modulis et laude et canoro jubilo,
Trinum Deum unicumque cum favore prædicat.

---

7. *margaritis*] Cf. Rev. xxi. 21. What were tears here shall reappear as pearls there. Der verklärte Schmerz bildet die Eingänge zu der Residenz der ewigen Wonne (Lange).

15. *Syon*] It is not an accident that the poet uses *Syon* here speaking of the Church militant, and *Hirusalem*, ver. 1, where addressing the Church triumphant. Durandus (*Rational.* i. 1), explains the distinction: Dicitur enim præsens Ecclesia Syon, eo quod ab hâc peregrinatione longe posita promissionem rerum cœlestium speculatur; et ideo Syon, id est, *speculatio*, nomen accepit. Pro futurâ vero patriâ et pace, Hierusalem vocatur: nam Hierusalem *pacis visio* interpretatur. The necessities of metre caused this distinction to be often neglected.

Hoc in templum, summe Deus, exoratus adveni,
Et clementi bonitate precum vota suscipe,   20
Largam benedictionem hic infunde jugiter.

Hic promereantur omnes petita acquirere,
Et adepta possidere cum sanctis perenniter,
Paradisum introire, translati in requiem.

19—24. These two last stanzas, Daniel (vol. i. p. 240), conceives not to have belonged to the hymn, as first composed, but to have been added to it, to adapt it to a Feast of Dedication. Yet this is certainly a mistake. The hymn coheres intimately in all its parts, and in ceasing to be a hymn *In Dedicatione Ecclesiæ*, it would lose its chiefest beauty. It is most truly a hymn "of degrees," ascending from things earthly to things heavenly, and making the first to be interpreters of the last. The prevailing intention in the building and the dedication of a church, with the rites thereto appertaining, was to carry up men's thoughts from that temple built with hands, which they saw, to that other built of living stones in heaven, of which this was but a weak shadow (Durandus, *Rational.* i. 1). Compare two beautiful sermons by Hildebert, pp. 641, 648. A sequence, *De Dedicatione Ecclesiæ*, which Daniel himself gives (vol. ii. p. 23), should have preserved him from this error. These are the first lines:

> Psallat Ecclesia, mater illibata et virgo
> Sine rugâ, honorem hujus ecclesiæ ;
> Hæc domus aulæ cælestis probatur particeps,
> In laude Regis cælorum et ceremoniis,
> Et lumine continuo æmulans civitatem sine tenebris.

24. This poem witnesses for its own true inspiration, in the fact that it has proved the source of manifold inspiration in circles beyond its own. To this we owe our own

> "Jerusalem, my happy home!"

or the same, in a less common but still more beautiful form (it is published with excellent notes under the title, *The New Jerusalem*, Edinburgh, 1852),

> "O mother dear, Jerusalem!"

The rich hymnology of Protestant Germany possesses two noble
hymns at the least, which had their first motive here, while
the subject is handled with a freedom which leaves them original
compositions, notwithstanding. The older of these is Meyfart's
(1590—1642), Jerusalem, du hochgebaute Stadt (No. 495, in
Bunsen's *Gesangbuch*), a lovely hymn, yet perhaps inferior to
Kosegarten's (1758—1818); from this, as I do not find it in
Bunsen's collection, I quote three glorious stanzas:

> Stadt Gottes, deren diamantnen Ring
> Kein Feind zu stürmen wagt:
> Drin kein Tyrann haust, drin kein Herrscherling
> Die freien Bürger plagt;
> > Recht nur und Licht und Wahrheit
> > Stützt deines Königs Thron,
> > Und Klarheit über Klarheit
> > Umglänzt den Königssohn.
>
> Stadt, deren Gassen sind durchlauchtig Gold,
> Die Mauern Marmelstein;
> Der Glanzstrom, der durch deine Strassen rollt,
> Wälzt Wellen silberrein.
> > Krystallne Fluthen baden
> > Der Königsgärten Saum,
> > Und längs den Lustgestaden
> > Schattet der Lebensbaum.
>
> Dir scheint, o Stadt, der Sonne Antlitz nicht,
> Und nicht ihr bleiches Bild;
> Es leuchtet dir ein himmlisch Angesicht,
> Das wunderlich und mild.
> > Gott Selbst ist deine Sonne,
> > Dein leuchtend Licht das Lamm,
> > Das—aller Heilkraft Bronne—
> > Gebüsst am Marterstamm.

DAMIANI.

LXXV. DE GLORIA ET GAUDIIS PARADISI.

A D perennis vitæ fontem mens sitivit arida,
Claustra carnis præsto frangi clausa quærit anima;
Gliscit, ambit, eluctatur exul frui patriâ.

Dum pressuris ac ærumnis se gemit obnoxiam,
Quam amisit, dum deliquit, contemplatur gloriam ; 5
Præsens malum auget boni perditi memoriam.

Nam quis promat summæ pacis quanta sit lætitia,
Ubi vivis margaritis surgunt ædificia,
Auro celsa micant tecta, radiant triclinia?

LXXV. *Augustini Opp.* Bened. ed. vol. vi. p. 117 (*Appendix*);
Rambach, *Anthol. Christl. Gesänge*, p. 241; Daniel, *Thes.
Hymnol.* vol. i. p. 116; Mone, *Hymni Lat. Med. Ævi.* vol. i. p.
422.—This poem has been often attributed to Augustine, finding place as it does in the *Meditationes*, long ascribed to him.
These *Meditationes*, however, are plainly a cento from Anselm,
Gregory the Great, and many others besides Augustine ; from
whom they are rightly adjudged away in the Benedictine
edition, as indeed in earlier as well. The hymn is Damiani's,
and quite the noblest he has left us. There is a very fine translation by Sylvester, *Works*, 1621, p. 1114.

Solis gemmis pretiosis hæc structura nectitur,   10
Auro mundo tanquam vitro urbis via sternitur;
Abest limus, deest fimus, lues nulla cernitur.

Hiems horrens, æstas torrens illic nunquam sæviunt;
Flos perpetuus rosarum ver agit perpetuum,
Candent lilia, rubescit crocus, sudat balsamum.   15

-----

11. *Auro mundo*] Cf. Rev. xxi. 21; and the commentary of
Gregory the Great (*Moral.* xviii.): Appellatione auri in sacro eloquio aliquando splendor supernæ civitatis accipitur. Aurum namque, ex quo civitas illa constat, simile vitro dicitur, ut per aurum
clara, et per vitrum perspicua, designetur. Auri quippe metallum
novimus potiori metallis omnibus claritate fulgere, vitri vero
natura est, ut extrinsecus visu pura, intrinsecus perspicuitate per-
luceat. In alio metallo quicquid intrinsecus continetur, abscon-
ditur: in vitro vero quilibet liquor qualis continetur interius, talis
exterius demonstratur, et, ut ita dixerim, omnis liquor in vitreo
vasculo clausus patet. Quid igitur aliud in auro vel vitro accipi-
mus, nisi illam beatorum civium societatem, quorum corda sibi
invicem et claritate fulgent, et puritate translucent? Quia enim
omnes sancti in æternâ beatitudine summâ claritate fulgebunt,
instructa auro dicitur. Et quoniam ipsa eorum claritas sibi
invicem in alternis cordibus patet, et cum uniuscujusque vultus
ostenditur, simul et conscientia penetratur, hoc ipsum aurum
simile vitro mundo esse memoratur. Cf. ver. 38, 39 of this
hymn.

12. *lues*] This must have here that meaning which once it
obtains in Petronius (*Sat.* 123), namely, of snow in act of melt-
ing, and now fouled by contact with the impurities of earth.
As nothing is purer than the new fallen snow, so nothing impurer
than the snow in process of dissolution. Here is the band of
connexion between the several meanings of *lues*; for, as Döder-
lein says truly, tracing the modifications of its meaning (*Lat.
Syn.* vol. ii. p. 58): Die Begriffe von Unreinigheit und Krank-
heit liegen ziemlich nahe neben einander.

Virent prata, vernant sata, rivi mellis influunt;
Pigmentorum spirat odor, liquor et aromatum ;
Pendent poma floridorum non lapsura nemorum.

Non alternat luna vices, sol, vel cursus siderum ;
Agnus est felicis urbis lumen inocciduum,   20
Nox et tempus desunt ei, diem fert continuum.

Nam et sancti quique velut sol præclarus rutilant,
Post triumphum coronati mutue conjubilant,
Et prostrati pugnas hostis jam securi numerant.

Omni labe defæcati carnis bella nesciunt,   25
Caro facta spiritalis et mens unum sentiunt,
Pace multâ perfruentes scandalum non perferunt.

Mutabilibus exuti repetunt originem,
Et præsentem veritatis contemplantur speciem,
Hinc vitalem vivi fontis hauriunt dulcedinem.   30

Inde statum semper idem existendi capiunt,
Clari, vividi, jucundi, nullis patent casibus:
Absunt morbi semper sanis, senectus juvenibus.

Hinc perenne tenent esse, nam transire transiit;
Inde virent, vigent, florent ; corruptela corruit,   35
Immortalis vigor auræ mortis jus absorbuit.

19—21. Augusti (*Beitr. zur Christl. Kunst-Gesch.* vol. i. p. 72, sq.) has an interesting essay on the *artistic* element in the Apocalypse, adducing this poem as an example of the ample use made of it by the chief Latin hymnologists.

22. *velut sol*] Cf. Matt. xiii. 43.

Qui scientem cuncta sciunt, quid nescire nequeunt :
Nam et pectoris arcana penetrant alterutrum,
Unum volunt, unum nolunt, unitas est mentium.

Licet cuique sit diversum pro labore meritum,   40
Caritas hoc facit suum quod amat in altero :
Proprium sic singulorum fit commune omnium.

Ubi corpus, illic jure congregantur aquilæ,
Quo cum angelis et sanctæ recreantur animæ ;
Uno pane vivunt cives utriusque patriæ.   45

Avidi et semper pleni, quod habent desiderant,
Non satietas fastidit, neque fames cruciat :
Inhiantes semper edunt, et edentes inhiant.

---

43. *Ubi corpus*] From the connexion in which these words
(drawn from Matt. xxiv. 28), appear, Damiani evidently understands them thus: "Where Christ is, there his saints and
servants will be gathered to Him, by the same unerring instinct
which assembles the eagles to their prey ;" and this was the
accepted explanation of the passage in the early Church. Whether it be the right one, or whether the sense is not rather,
"Wherever there is a Church or nation abandoned by the spirit
of life, and which has become a dead carcase, to this the eagles,
the ministers and messengers of the divine judgements, are
quickly gathered together, to remove it out of the way"—is an
interesting question, but not for discussion here.

46—48. *Avidi...pleni*] Prosper has two fine lines on the same
theme :

> Semper erunt quod sunt, æternæ gaudia vitæ,
> Gaudenti quoniam causa sit ipse Deus.

Hildebert (*Serm.* 25) expresses himself nearly in the same
way concerning the angels. Of Christ he says, Ipse est enim
in quem angeli desiderant prospicere [1 Pet. i. 12]. Prospiciunt quidem in eum, et cum desiderio, quia quæ habent

Novas semper melodias vox meloda concrepat,
Et in jubilum prolata mulcent aures organa,   50
Digna per quem sunt victores, Regi dant præconia.

Felix cœli quæ præsentem Regem cernit anima,
Et sub sede spectat altâ orbis volvi machinam,
Solem, lunam, et globosa cum planetis sidera.

Christe, palma bellatorum, hoc in municipium   55
Introduc me post solutum militare cingulum,
Fac consortem donativi beatorum civium :

Præbe vires inexhausto laboranti prælio,
Nec quietem post procinctum deneges emerito,
Teque merear potiri sine fine præmio.   60

---

desiderant, et quæ desiderant habent. Si enim desiderarent, et
illud non obtinerent, esset in desiderio anxietas, et ita pœna. Si
autem haberent et non cuperent, videretur fastidium sequi satie-
tatem. Ne autem sit in desiderio anxietas, vel in satietate
fastidium, desiderantes satiantur, et satiati desiderant.

60. Some lines of Adam of St Victor have much sweetness in
them, and may fitly be appended here :

Confusa sunt hic omnia,
Spes, metus, mœror, gaudium ;
Vix hora vel dimidia
Fit in cœlo silentium.

Sed una vox lætantium,
Et unus ardor cordium.

Illic cives angelici,
Sub hierarchiâ triplici,
Trinæ gaudent et simplici
Se monarchiæ subjici.

Quam felix illa civitas,
In quâ jugis solemnitas,
Et quam jucunda curia,
Quæ curæ prorsus nescia !

Mirantur nec deficiunt
In illum, quem prospiciunt ;
Fruuntur nec fastidiunt
Quo frui magis sitiunt.

Nec languor hic, nec senium,
Nec fraus, nec terror hostium,

Having quoted these lines, I must quote from Hugh of St
Victor (*De Claust. Animæ,* c. 36) what alone will make intel-

ligible the third and fourth lines : De hoc secreto cordis dictum
est : Factum est silentium in cœlo quasi media hora (Rev.
viii. 1). Cœlum quippe est anima justi. Sed quia hoc silentium
contemplationis et hæc quies mentis in hâc vitâ non potest esse
perfecta, nequaquam hora integra factum in cœlo dicitur silentium, sed quasi media ; ut nec media plene sentiatur, cum præ-
mittitur quasi : quia mox ut se animus sublevare cœperit, et
quietis intimæ lumine perfundi, redeunte motu cogitationum
confunditur et confusus cæcatur.

Nor are these lines of Alanus without merit :

> Hic risus sine tristitiâ, sine nube serenum,
> Deliciæ sine defectu, sine fine voluptas,
> Pax expers odii, requies ignara laboris,
> Lux semper rutilans, sol veri luminis, ortus
> Nescius occasûs, gratum sine vespere mane :
> Hic splendor noctem, saties fastidia nescit,
> Gaudia plena vigent, nullo respersa dolore.
> Non hic ambiguo graditur Fortuna meatu,
> Non risum lacrimis, adversis prospera, læta
> Tristibus infirmat, non mel corrumpit aceto,
> Aspera commiscens blandis, tenebrosa serenis,
> Connectens luci tenebras, funesta jocosis :
> Sed requies tranquilla manet, quam fine carentem
> Fortunæ casus in nubila vertere nescit.

THOMAS OF KEMPEN.

THOMAS Hamerken, of Kempen or Kampen in Over-Yssel, to whom generally, and, I believe, with justice, the *Imitation of Christ* is attributed, was born in 1380, and died in 1471. His works, apart from that disputed one, are numerous. Among them are various ascetic and devotional treatises, possessing the same kind of merit, though in an inferior degree, which has caused the *Imitation of Christ* to be, next to the Bible, the most widely diffused and oftenest reprinted book in the world. They include also a not unimportant life of Gerhard, the founder of the Fratres Communis Vitæ, to which Order, if such it may be called, Thomas himself belonged. His poems are not many, nor would they yield a second extract at all to be compared in beauty with the very beautiful fragment which follows.

LXXVI. CANTICUM DE GAUDIIS CŒLESTIBUS.

ASTANT angelorum chori,
Laudes cantant Creatori;
Regem cernunt in decore,
Amant corde, laudant ore,

LXXVI. *Thomæ à Campis Opp.* Antverpiæ, 1634, p. 364; Corner, *Prompt. Devot.* p. 760.

Tympanizant, citharizant,   5
Volant alis, stant in scalis,
Sonant nolis, fulgent stolis
Coram summâ Trinitate.
Clamant: Sanctus, Sanctus, Sanctus;
Fugit dolor, cessat planctus   10
In supernâ civitate.
Concors vox est omnium,
Deum collaudantium:
Fervet amor mentium,
Clare contuentium   15
Beatam Trinitatem in unâ Deitate;
Quam adorant Seraphim
Ferventi in amore,
Venerantur Cherubim
Ingenti sub honore;   20
Mirantur nimis Throni de tantâ majestate.

   O quam præclara regio,
Et quam decora legio
Ex angelis et hominibus!
O gloriosa civitas,   25
In quâ summa tranquillitas,
Lux et pax in cunctis finibus!
Cives hujus civitatis
Veste nitent castitatis,
Legem tenent caritatis.   30
Firmum pactum unitatis.
Non laborant, nil ignorant;
Non tentantur, nec vexantur;
Semper sani, semper læti,
Cunctis bonis sunt repleti.   35

HILDEBERT.

LXXVII. ORATIO DEVOTISSIMA AD TRES PERSONAS SS. TRINITATIS.

§ AD PATREM.

ALPHA et Ω, magne Deus,
Heli, Heli, Deus meus,
Cujus virtus totum posse,
Cujus sensus totum nosse,

LXXVII. *Hildeberti et Marbodi Opp.* p. 1337 ; Hommey, *Sup-plementum Patrum*, p. 446 ; Mone, *Hymni Lat. Med. Ævi*, vol. i. p. 14.—I am pleased that the natural arrangement of this volume has enabled me to reserve to the last a poem which will supply to it so grand a close — a poem which, so soon as it has escaped the straits and embarrassments of doctrinal definition,—although even there it has a most real value, from the writer's theological accuracy and distinctness, and his complete possession of his theme,—gradually rises in poetical animation, until towards the end it equals the very best productions which Latin Christian poetry anywhere can boast. And this, its excellence, makes not a little strange that almost entire oblivion, even among lovers of the Latin hymnology, into which it has fallen. Hugh of St Victor indeed, a cotemporary of Hildebert's, quotes six of its concluding lines with a well-deserved admiration, but as one unacquainted with the name of its author (*Serm.* 83): Qualis autem sit exsultatio sanctorum in cœlesti gloriâ, et lætitia in cubilibus istis, exsultationes quoque in gutture eorum, illorum

Cujus esse summum bonum,   5
Cujus opus quicquid bonum;

---

solummodo est cognoscere quibus datum est et habere. Unde *quidam* rhythmico carmine supernam affatus Hierusalem, pulchre dixit:

> Quantum tui gratulentur,
> Quam festive conviventur,
> Quis affectus eos stringat,
> Aut quæ gemma muros pingat,
> Chalcedon an hyacinthus,
> Norunt illi qui sunt intus.

It is true that there was no complete edition of the works of Hildebert until the Benedictine, Paris, 1708. But Ussher, in an appendix to his work *De Symbolis*, first published 1660 (*Works*, vol. vii. p. 335, Elrington's ed.), had already printed these lines, not knowing however the name of their author (*ex veteribus membranis rhythmos istos elegantes descripsimus*). They were subsequently printed by Hommey, as he supposed for the first time, in his *Supplementum Patrum*, but with a text far inferior to Ussher's; indeed so inaccurate as to be often wellnigh unintelligible. Guericke, in his excellent *Christl. Archæologie*, Leipsic, 1847, p. 258, quotes a considerable part of this "magnificent" hymn with a just recognition; while Rambach (*Christl. Anthologie*, vol. i. p. 260), includes in his collection a fragment of it, but with so little sense of its, or its author's, merits, that he so does to the end, "that he may give something of this author's."

1. Ω] This is sometimes printed *Omega*, but the metre plainly requires that it should appear as above: unless indeed we should resolve the Ω into the Oo, of which it was originally composed, and as which it might be here pronounced, and then print the line thus: A *et* Oo, *magne Deus*. It needs not to say what a favourite symbol of Him who is the first and the last (Alpha et Ω cognominatus, *ipse fons et clausula*: Prudentius) the monogram A—Ω or $\alpha'\omega$ supplied to the early Christians, or

Super cuncta, subter cuncta ;
Extra cuncta, intra cuncta ;
Intra cuncta, nec inclusus ;
Extra cuncta, nec exclusus :   10
Super cuncta, nec elatus ;
Subter cuncta, nec substratus ;
Super totus, præsidendo ;
Subter totus, sustinendo ;
Extra totus, complectendo ;   15
Intra totus es, implendo ;
Intra, nunquam coarctaris,
Extra, nunquam dilataris ;
Super, nullo sustentaris ;
Subter, nullo fatigaris.   20
Mundum movens, non moveris,
Locum tenens, non teneris,
Tempus mutans, non mutaris,
Vaga firmans, non vagaris.
Vis externa, vel necesse   25
Non alternat tuum esse :
Heri nostrum, cras, et pridem
Semper tibi nunc et idem :
Tuum, Deus, hodiernum
Indivisum, sempiternum :   30
In hoc totum prævidisti,
Totum simul perfecisti,
Ad exemplar summæ mentis
Formam præstans elementis.

---

how often it is found on lamps, gravestones, gems, and other
relics which they have bequeathed to us (see Muratori, *Anec-
dota*, i. 45)..

§ ORATIO AD FILIUM.

Nate, Patri coæqualis,　　　　35
Patri consubstantialis,
Patris splendor et figura,
Factor factus creatura,
Carnem nostram induisti,
Causam nostram suscepisti :　　40
Sempiternus, temporalis ;
Moriturus, immortalis ;
Verus homo, verus Deus ;
Impermixtus Homo-Deus.
Non conversus hic in carnem ;　45
Nec minutus propter carnem :
Hic assumptus est in Deum,
Nec consumptus propter Deum ;
Patri compar Deitate,
Minor carnis veritate :　　　50
Deus pater tantum Dei,
Virgo mater, sed est Dei :

---

37. *splendor et figura*] These are the Latin equivalents for ἀπαύγασμα and χαρακτήρ, Heb. i. 3 (Vulg.); making plain that to that setting forth of the dignity of the Son Hildebert refers. Ἀπαύγασμα might either mean *ef*fulgence or *re*fulgence ; and *splendor* does not necessarily determine for either meaning. The Church, however, has ever made ἀπαύγασμα = φῶς ἐκ φωτὸς = *ef*fulgence. Thus we have in another hymn : Splendor paternæ gloriæ (a fuller translation of the ἀπαύγασμα τῆς δόξης), Qui lumen es e lumine.

48. *Non consumptus*] Augustine (*Ep.* 170, 9) : Homo assumtus est a Deo ; non in homine consumptus est Deus.

In tam novâ ligaturâ
Sic utraque stat natura,
Ut conservet quicquid erat,   55
Facta quiddam quod non erat.
Noster iste Mediator,
Iste noster legislator,
Circumcisus, baptizatus,
Crucifixus, tumulatus,   60
Obdormivit et descendit,
Resurrexit et ascendit:
Sic ad coelos elevatus
Judicabit judicatus.

§ ORATIO AD SPIRITUM SANCTUM.

Paraclitus increatus,   65
Neque factus, neque natus,
Patri consors, Genitoque,
Sic procedit ab utroque
Ne sit minor potestate,
Vel discretus qualitate.   70
Quanti illi, tantus iste,
Quales illi, talis iste.
Ex quo illi, ex tunc iste;
Quantum illi, tantum iste.
Pater alter, sed gignendo;   75
Natus alter, sed nascendo;
Flamen ab his procedendo;
Tres sunt unum subsistendo.
Quisque trium plenus Deus,
Non tres tamen Dî, sed Deus.   80

In hoc Deo, Deo vero,
Tres et unum assevero,
Dans Usiæ unitatem,
Et personis Trinitatem.
In personis nulla prior,   85
Nulla minor, nulla major:
Unaquæque semper ipsa,
Sic est constans atque fixa,
Ut nec in se varietur,
Nec in ullâ transmutetur.   90

Hæc est fides orthodoxa,
Non hic error sine noxâ;
Sicut dico, sic et credo,
Nec in pravam partem cedo.
Inde venit, bone Deus,   95
Ne desperem quamvis reus:
Reus mortis non despero,
Sed in morte vitam quæro.
Quo te placem nil prætendo,
Nisi fidem quam defendo: 100
Fidem vides, hanc imploro;
Leva fascem quo laboro;

101—137. The four images of deliverance which run through
these lines, will be best understood in their details, by keeping
closely in view the incidents of the evangelical history on which
they rest, and which lend them severally their language and
imagery. In ver. 101—112 the allusion is to Christ's raisings
of the dead, and mainly to that of Lazarus. The *Extra portam
jam delatus* belongs indeed to the history of the widow's son
(Luke vii. 12); but all else is to be explained from John xi.
39—44. The second image seems, in a measure, to depart from

Per hoc sacrum cataplasma
Convalescat ægrum plasma.
Extra portam jam delatum,   105
Jam fœtentem, tumulatum,
Vitta ligat, lapis urget;
Sed si jubes, hic resurget;
Jube, lapis revolvetur,
Jube, vitta dirumpetur: 110
Exiturus nescit moras,
Postquam clamas: Exi foras.
In hoc salo mea ratis
Infestatur a piratis;
Hinc assultus, inde fluctus,   115
Hinc et inde mors et luctus;
Sed tu, bone Nauta, veni,
Preme ventos, mare leni;
Fac abscedant hi piratæ,
Duc ad portum salvâ rate.   120
Infecunda mea ficus,
Cujus ramus ramus siccus,

---

the miracles of the stilling of the storm (Matt. viii. 26; cf.
xiv. 32), and to introduce a new feature in the *piratæ*; but on
closer inspection it will be seen that in these we have only a
bold personification of the winds and waves, as *hi piratæ* of ver.
119 plainly proves. In the third (ver. 121—128) he contemplates himself as the barren fig-tree of Luke xiii. 6—9, and, as
such, in danger of being hewn down. The fourth image (ver.
129—138) rests plainly on the healing of the lunatic child (Matt.
xiv. 21 ; Mark ix. 22).

103. *cataplasma*] Bernard: Ex Deo et homine factum est
cataplasma, quod sanaret omnes infirmitates nostras, Spiritu
Sancto tanquam pistillo hasce species suaviter in utero Mariæ
commiscente.

Incidetur, incendetur,
Si promulgas quod meretur;
Sed hoc anno dimittatur,   125
Stercoretur, fodiatur;
Quod si necdum respondebit,
Flens hoc loquor, tunc ardebit.
Vetus hostis in me furit,
Aquis mersat, flammis urit: 130
Inde languens et afflictus
Tibi soli sum relictus.
Ut infirmus convalescat,
Ut hic hostis evanescat,
Tu virtutem jejunandi   135
Des infirmo, des orandi:
Per hæc duo, Christo teste,
Liberabor ab hâc peste;
Ab hâc peste solve mentem,
Fac devotum, pœnitentem;   140
Da timorem, quo projecto,

---

132. *Tibi soli*] Cf. Matt. xvii. 16: "I spake to thy disciples
that they should cast him out, and they could not." It is as
though he would say, "Man's help is vain; Thou must heal me,
or none."

137, 138. Cf. Matt. xvii. 21.

141. *Da timorem*] This and the following line must be explained by 1 John iv. 18: Perfecta caritas foras mittit timorem.
He asks for the fear which is the *beginning* of wisdom, but this
only as introducing the love, which at last, casting out the fear,
shall give him confidence toward God and assurance of salvation.
Thus Augustine (*In* 1 *Ep. Joh.* iv. 18): Sicut videmus per setam
introduci linum, quando aliquid suitur, seta prius intrat, sed nisi
exeat, non succedit linum: sic timor primo occupat mentem, non
autem ibi remanet timor, quia ideo intravit, ut introduceret
caritatem.

De salute nil conjecto;
Da fidem, spem, caritatem;
Da discretam pietatem;
Da contemptum terrenorum,   145
Appetitum supernorum.
Totum, Deus, in te spero;
Deus, ex te totum quæro.
Tu laus mea, meum bonum,
Mea cuncta, tuum donum: 150
Tu solamen in labore,
Medicamen in languore;
Tu in luctu mea lyra,
Tu lenimen es in irâ;
Tu in arcto liberator,   155
Tu in lapsu relevator;
Motum præstas in provectu,
Spem conservas in defectu;
Si quis lædit, tu rependis;
Si minatur, tu defendis: 160
Quod est anceps tu dissolvis,
Quod tegendum tu involvis.
Tu intrare me non sinas
Infernales officinas;
Ubi mœror, ubi metus,   165
Ubi fœtor, ubi fletus,
Ubi probra deteguntur,
Ubi rei confunduntur,
Ubi tortor semper cædens,
Ubi vermis semper edens;   170
Ubi totum hoc perenne,
Quia perpes mors gehennæ.

Me receptet Syon illa,
Syon, David urbs tranquilla.
Cujus faber Auctor lucis, 175
Cujus portæ lignum crucis.
Cujus muri lapis vivus,
Cujus custos Rex festivus.
In hâc urbe lux solennis,
Ver æternum, pax perennis : 180
In hâc odor implens cœlos,
In hâc semper festum melos:
Non est ibi corruptela,
Non defectus, non querela ;
Non minuti, non deformes, 185
Omnes Christo sunt conformes.
Urbs cœlestis, urbs beata,
Super petram collocata,
Urbs in portu satis tuto.
De longinquo te saluto, 190
Te saluto, te suspiro,
Te affecto, te requiro.
Quantum tui gratulantur,
Quam festive convivantur.
Quis affectus eos stringat. 195
Aut quæ gemma muros pingat.
Quis chalcedon, quis jacinthus,

---

179. Cf. Rev. xxi. 23.

190—192. This is but Augustine (*De Spir. et Anim.*) in verse :
O civitas sancta, civitas speciosa, de longinquo te saluto, ad te
clamo, te requiro.

196, 197. Cf. Rev. xxi. 19, 20.

Norunt illi qui sunt intus.
In plateis hujus urbis, ,
Sociatus piis turbis,   200
Cum Moÿse et Eliâ,
Pium cantem Alleluya.
                    Amen.

ADDENDUM.

Note for p. 73, l. 37—42.

A very fine hymn on the Four Evangelists, published for the first time, as far as I am aware, by Dr. Neale, and since in the *Missale de Arbuthnott*, 1864, p. 405, yields the following noble stanzas, which might have been fitly brought into comparison here:

<table>
<tr><td>

Illos per bis bina
Visio divina
Signat animalia :
A quibusdam visa,
Formis tunc divisa,
Gestu sed æqualia.

Pennis decorata,
Terris elevata,
Cum rotis euntia ;
Facie serenâ,
Oculorum plena,
Verbi Dei nuntia.

In his possunt cerni
Annuli quaterni
Quibus arca vehitur ;

</td><td>

Quorum dogma sanum
Per Samaritanum
Circumquaque seritur.

Tali quasi plaustro
Mulier ab Austro
Salomonem adiit,
In hâc ceu quadrigâ
Agnus est auriga,
Qui pro nobis obiit.

Istis in bis binis
Caput est et finis
Christus complens omnia :
Horum documentis,
Horum instrumentis
Florens stat Ecclesia.

</td></tr>
</table>

INDEX OF POEMS.

INDEX OF BIOGRAPHICAL NOTICES.